P9-DJU-718

CANCELLED

The Book of Luce

By the same author

Farundell
A Hermetic Novel

Fate
A Rosicrucian Tale

The
Book of Luce

A Gnostic Gospel

L. R. FREDERICKS

HODDER &
STOUGHTON

First published in Great Britain in 2017 by Hodder & Stoughton
An Hachette UK company

Copyright © L. R. Fredericks 2017

The right of L. R. Fredericks to be identified as the Author
of the Work has been asserted by L. R. Fredericks in accordance with the
Copyright, Designs and Patents Act 1988.

All rights reserved. No part of this publication may be reproduced,
stored in a retrieval system, or transmitted, in any form or by any means without
the prior written permission of the publisher, nor be otherwise circulated in any
form of binding or cover other than that in which it is published and without a
similar condition being imposed on the subsequent purchaser.

All characters in this publication, other than a few historical figures, are fictitious
and any resemblance to real persons, living or dead is purely coincidental.

A CIP catalogue record for this title is available from the British Library

Hardback ISBN 978 1 848 54334 8
Trade Paperback ISBN 978 1 848 54335 5

Typeset in New Caledonia by Palimpsest Book Production Ltd, Falkirk, Stirlingshire

Printed and bound by Clays Ltd, St Ives plc

Hodder & Stoughton policy is to use papers that are natural,
renewable and recyclable products and made from wood grown in
sustainable forests. The logging and manufacturing processes are expected
to conform to the environmental regulations of the country of origin.

Hodder & Stoughton Ltd
Carmelite House
50 Victoria Embankment
London EC4Y 0DZ

www.hodder.co.uk

for
Phanes Autogeniton

If the doors of perception were cleansed
every thing would appear to man as it is, Infinite.
For man has closed himself up, till he sees all things
thro' narrow chinks of his cavern.

William Blake,
The Marriage of Heaven and Hell

THE
BOOK OF LUCE

Chimera Obscura

HODDER AND STOUGHTON

LONDON SYDNEY AUCKLAND TORONTO

For Luce,
always and only

Table of Contents

Clot on the Brain. Luce's Final Resting Place(s).
Demonology in the British Library.

Some might find it offensive that I, of all people, should write the story of Luce. Others may find it ironic. It may well be both, but it is also the completion of the task I began fifty years ago. It has always been my life's true purpose, though they did their damnedest to convince me that Luce was just a figment of my deranged imagination. And, to survive, I did my damnedest to persuade them that I believed them. I did this so well that I almost forgot. But now I have been called again; I have received Signs.

I won't pretend to be an ordinary biographer. I'm not sure I can be any more objective about my subject - or should that be object? - than about myself. But if Luce's story is tangled with mine it can only be because Luce wanted it that way.

I'll never know why they finally decided to deport me. What I took for yet another chapter in the long-running saga of my persecution by the obtuse officials of the Nevada State Council for Adult Offender Supervision seems to have spirited me back to my old life, my Real life, my life with Luce. The door that I've spent more than half of my life pretending to ignore has opened and, like a rogue joker sneaking out of the pack during the course of a fumbling card trick, I've returned to myself at last.

Maintaining an attitude of utter compliance and mild, baffled disinterest in my circumstances has been an essential part of my strategy for so long that if anyone bothered to tell me exactly where I was to go, I paid no heed. Back to England, back to England, that was all I knew. I didn't let myself think about it. Never betray interest. Play dead. My brother had made arrangements, they said; it was meant to be reassuring.

What with jet lag and shock at so much change in such a short time, not to mention the temazepam I took to get through the flight, I was a bit out of it when I arrived last night. It had all been a blur: car, airport, aeroplane, airport, come with us please, car, roads, a building, sign in please, stairs, this way please. A door, a flat: my flat. Good night.

The first thing I did was open a window. It was raining hard – good, serious English rain. The rain of home. I hadn't realised how much I'd missed it, trapped for all these years in dry and dusty Nevada. I let the dark drops wash my face.

The building looked out over what I, in my muddled state, took for a lake; across the expanse of black water was a house with many windows glowing. I blinked and squinted through the rain. Could it be? My God, of all the places to have ended up. The poignancy of it nearly killed me. It was Farundell, where Luce first initiated me into his mysteries, long before I knew who she was. Over the decades it had apparently been swallowed up in some kind of ghastly suburban sprawl.

Of course I was wrong; it wasn't Farundell. (I'm in

2

Enfield, as it turns out. Enfield! And not just Enfield, but an obscure district on its western edge called, with stupendous aptness, World's End.) The lake, the house - it was a brief trick of the light, or maybe a trick of Luce. Before long the rain slackened, the air cleared, delusion receded. I beheld a wide black slick of tarmac, not a lake. A car park, deserted, and beyond it a smattering of streetlights, not a house. But in that sudden recognition, mistaken though it was, something jolted in me, shook itself, unfurled creaky, neglected wings, rose and lifted itself out into the night to soar and dance among the softly raining stars above Farundell, above a dark island and a chamber darker still. And last night I dreamed the Dream again, the one I'd almost forgotten. The Dream of the Cavern. I woke with the feeling of the thread in my hand. That thread, so long lain lax, is tightening. I know it's a Sign.

The second Sign arrives with my brother. It isn't Neil himself, of course, but what he brings, unasked-for, un-heralded. He's a bit early; I'm not quite prepared and the knock on my door sends a jolt of anxiety through my nerves. I straighten my clothes, smooth my hair and open the door.

'Hey Weirdo,' he says.

'Hey Arsehole.'

He's changed remarkably little: fatter, balder, an extra chin or two. It is the immense blandness of his face (a feature, or should I say a lack of feature, apparent from infancy) that has always bothered me the most, and it's hard to forget that for many years I believed he was a demon-simulacrum, not a real human being at all.

3

'Good to see you,' he says. 'Glad you're back. Yes. Glad you're back. So . . .' His eyes slide this way and that; he doesn't know where to look.

'It's this one.' I point to my right eye. 'This is the glass one.'

'Oh, right. Sorry.' He makes that shrug, that little wince of repugnance I remember so well. It always had the capacity to enrage me with its implication of distaste and disdain that he was too polite (or cowardly) to express openly. Now his attitude has a sound basis in history; when we were children, it was pure instinct. Dear old Arsehole. We just don't get along.

'Thanks for arranging all this.' My gesture endeavours to convey my gratitude for the grandeur of these lino-floored, woodchip-wallpapered three hundred and sixty-six square feet. (I paced it out last night.)

'No problem. Glad I could help. Yes. Glad to be of use. So . . . you all right, then? Good journey? How was the flight? Get a decent meal? How do you like this place? Pretty nice, huh? Everything you need. You always were for the simple life.'

Is this a snide reference to the massive complication I made of my life? Just because I'm criminally insane, I want to say, it doesn't mean I'm stupid. But it does, it does. I play stupid as if my life depends upon it. I make my face smile.

He looks around, rubs his hands. 'It's not bad, is it? Not bad at all. Gets the morning sun. Little kitchen, nice. Cosy bedroom, en-suite. Comfy bed? Good. Nice people, too, don't you think? Oh, by the way, thought you'd like . . . we brought that stuff you left in the attic. Some boxes, remember? Years, long time ago. From before . . . well, you know. We thought it might help you feel at home, to have your old things.'

My teeth have been grinding of their own accord. I have always found Neil's chummy, pseudo-familial familiarity grating in the extreme. I say pseudo because he is not, *Deo gratias*, my real brother. I was adopted shortly before he was conceived; my presence in the 'family' as a second-best and not-really-needed-after-all appendage has always been awkward for him and for the parents. This awkwardness was only exacerbated by the fact that he, the younger, was very soon much the bigger - physically if not morally. While maintaining a fond and patronising demeanour in public, in private he used the crude advantage of size to subject me to innumerable indignities. My superiority in the intellectual sphere, which I could never fully conceal, did not mitigate his hostility. Quite the reverse.

We go downstairs. Something begins to tickle at my mind through the sticky, gritty cloud of my irritation with Neil. I'm getting the first inkling that an event of possible significance may be waiting, concealed in this mild April morning. Stepping outside, bright sunshine stings my eyes. *Luce*, I think, and hear a sort of hum in reply. My heart starts to pound.

Neil's parked in front. He has one of those vast, shiny contraptions that look like they could scale the Himalayas before breakfast, except they'd rather not get their skirts dirty. That must be his wife in the driver's seat, talking on the phone. Rather a lot of make-up for a woman of her age who's not - as far as I know - a professional whore. And she's obviously

5

on the Botox. It's like she's wearing a hypothetical face. No wonder I thought she was a simulacrum, too. Still talking, she waves cheerily to me like we last saw each other day-before-yesterday. What's her name? I never remember her name. Oh yeah, Dot. Ridiculous name for a woman.

'Hi Dot,' I say.

'Jesus, Weirdo. This is Cindy. My. Wife. Cindy.' Neil gives me a look that says he knows - and wants me to know he knows - that I do this sort of thing deliberately. I don't.

'Sorry.'

Neil thinks I'm being sarcastic. 'Back a day and already impossible.'

'I'm glad not to be changed beyond recognition, then,' I say, immediately chastising myself for the slip into acerbity.

He opens the back of the car. His attempt to make a tetchy gesture of it is foiled by the hydraulics, which lift the door ever so gently, emitting a sedate hiss. Boxes, five or six boxes. But could it be? Oh my God. I recognise it. I think I do. That small one at the back. Yes! Would he have brought it if he'd known what it was? Certainly not. Would I have dared ask for it? I assumed he'd destroyed everything long ago. It's what demons do.

Treasure, long-hidden treasure. Going incognito, pretending to be an ordinary box, one of several, nothing special. Scuffed, corners squashed, bound with packing tape, now brittle and peeling, and green sisal twine. The address label has fallen off but I remember that twine, how it left green streaks on my scared, sweaty hands as I tied it up. The box seems

6

to glow from within - I sincerely hope no one else can see that. It's Luce's box. This is the second Sign.

My face never gives anything away. 'Oh, thanks,' I say. 'Wonder what's here. I forgot all about this stuff.'

We carry the boxes to my flat, where they take up most of the space in the sitting room. Neil leaves, what a relief, mercifully declining my offer of a cup of tea. It's just me and the boxes now: me and my past. Dear God, let me not become one of those pathetic, repulsive old people who shuffle about in a narrow space crowded to death by stacks of newspapers and the mouse-infested relics of their long-dead lives.

Two boxes contain miscellaneous stuff, including some wonderful old clothes: my floppy fedora with the peacock feather, a silk scarf with an Aubrey Beardsley print that Charlie gave me, a green velvet jacket from the King's Road, an Indian-print shirt from Haight-Ashbury. Others contain books - I'll deal with them later. They served their purpose: the flock of sheep that smuggled in the goat.

I turn at last to Luce's box. I had never dared to hope it would come back to me; I'd grown accustomed to the idea that my past was non-existent, in any reliable way. And now I have a flash of doubt. Might this be the work of a demon of False Hope? Cunning little buggers, but I thought I'd extinguished them years ago. All I have is my memory of the green twine and the stains it left on my hands. I look at them; obviously they're not green any more. And the glow I saw in the back of Neil's car? I might have imagined that. If I see it now, it's only wishful thinking.

I get impatient with myself. This box either is or isn't what I think it is. My past is either dead or alive; like Schrödinger's cat, it is both and neither until the box is opened. Do I truly want to know? Oh for fuck's sake. Open the damn thing. Cut the twine, peel away the packing tape. Open the box.

I have to sit back and take a deep breath. This is it, this is it, this is it! Tears come to my eyes. I feel like a resurrected corpse. With trembling hands I unpack the treasures, untouched for all these years: my draft manuscript of *The Book of Luce*, plus notebooks and files, interview tapes and transcripts, articles, diaries and journals, newspaper clippings, letters. The records of my search for Luce, the testimonies of the witnesses. Here is René, here is Karen, and here, oh here, is Rachel. I'm half afraid all this will disintegrate like ancient bones in a too-suddenly unsealed tomb. Here's my original *Human* album; here is *L'Age Atomique*, a priceless rarity, perhaps the only one in the world.

Thank you, I say. *Thank you, thank you, thank you.*

At the bottom, an old box of Gitanes, Luce's brand and therefore my own, when I can get them. It must have fallen out of my pocket as I packed. All unsuspecting, I open it.

It's full of rose petals, but they're not dry or faded. They spill onto the table, soft and fresh and sublimely fragrant. They cannot possibly have fallen from the flower more than an hour ago. I put the box down and back away. Owing to the modest dimensions of the room, I cannot back very far. I close my eyes, count to a hundred. I open my eyes. The rose petals are still there, blithely emitting their rapturous

8

impossibility. It's the third Sign. I make myself a strong cup of tea.

These three Signs have convinced me that the time has come to write *The Book of Luce*. Contrary to popular opinion, including my own, it would appear that I am not ashes on the dust-heap of history. My life in the Real world, so long an underground river running deep beneath the polluted realm of mundane Earth and the semi-conscious parasites who inhabit its surface, has emerged.

My mission is now clear: to fulfil my task, to tell the story of Luce. And his mission? Will I ever know? Was she Messiah, Avatar, Bodhisattva? A Superhuman, the long-awaited Nietzschean *Übermensch*? Was he the first of a new type of human, and will we all be like her one day? Or was he a fluke, an accident, a random confluence of powers and perceptions, a freak, a genetic quirk, merely the greatest artist of all time? As I assemble these fragments of her life and work, as I line them up, put them in order, draw arcs of influence and association, cause and effect, as I try to make the dull-minded world understand . . . surely I will find the real Luce at last.

So wake up, Chimera Obscura! I summon you to remember. Here you come, stepping out of the shadows: a ghost in green velvet, a peacock feather in your hat. Go forth, beautiful one! Go forth and remember.

Introduction

Everyone has heard of Luce and the Photons, yet to this day no one knows who they were. The *Human* album is cited as a seminal influence by artists from the Beatles to Philip Glass, John Tavener to David Bowie, John Cage to Brian Eno, and is widely acknowledged as among the most important musical statements of the twentieth century. It is certainly one of the most enigmatic, though nowhere near as enigmatic as its creator. Luce appeared on the cover of every major publication from *Life* to *Oz*, presenting the designers with unique challenges of representation. *Time* got it best, I think (in their edition of 10 March 1967), creating an illustration reminiscent of Magritte's *The Son of Man*: a halo of white hair, a rakishly tilted bowler hat and, where the face should be, a shining question mark. The caption read, simply, 'Human?'

The 'rock star' played by Luce during his Luce and the Photons phase was just one of many faces that she presented to the world. I believe I am the only person to have followed him through all these guises. Confused about Luce's sex? That's understandable. The exigencies of this language, to which I am acolyte and slave, require the sex of the subject to be so continuously marked, remarked, forced, enforced and reinforced that one suspects it masks a deep inner uncertainty. Nevertheless, protracted confusion can become unpleasant, and while there's no doubt that Luce intended to disconcert, I have no wish to alienate my readers by imposing awkward doubts on a sentence-by-sentence basis. Therefore (I flip a coin) I will usually refer to Luce in the feminine unless I am speaking of a specifically male character.

The Book of Luce will be based on the testimonies of many people. Luce was a different person to each, and told each one a different tale. Of course they're all lies, but each in its way reveals the truth even as it conceals it. I believe she left this trail of lies precisely in order to tell the truth: to tell it to me, her Scribe.

Pierre Lumière, Lou Peterson, Petra Lumis, Lukas Steiner, Piers Lightfoot, Hikaru Ishi, Peter Lucian: all these self-chosen names contain variations on 'light' and 'stone'. This unnecessary, indeed risky consistency is one of the factors that convinces me she wanted these lives, these stories, to be linked. She was deliberately leaving a trail even as she lied and evaded and covered her tracks.

Two thousand years on, New Testament scholars continue to argue about which, if any, of the many preacher/magician figures cavorting around Galilee during the reign of Caesar Augustus was the real Jesus Christ. Future scholars of Lucianity, hear this from someone who was there: the ones listed above were all Luce – man and woman, human and god. And, dear scholars, if you are tempted to regard this story as purely metaphorical, hear this: it all really happened.

In his book, *The Reality of Myth: Evolution and the Avatar*,* John Greyling maintains that Luce was the avatar of the aeon. Of course she is not named, but he never denied that it refers to her. An avatar (from Sanskrit *avatāra*, 'descent') is the delib-

* John Greyling, *The Reality of Myth: Evolution and the Avatar* (London: Hutchinson Granger, 1955).

erate embodiment of a deity on the material plane and is usually translated as incarnation, appearance or manifestation. For example, Christians consider Jesus Christ to have been an avatar: 'Incarnation is central Christian doctrine that God became flesh . . . assumed a human nature and became a man in the form of Jesus Christ.'[*]

Every religion has its avatar or avatars, but it's possible that many avatars never become famous or start religions. Luce regarded all organised religions as equally deceptive and imprisoning, though I suspect she had a soft spot for Buddhism. 'Buddha', after all, simply means 'awake'.

According to Karen Cooper (see Chapter 6) Luce wanted to 'turn things inside out, to make people look into their own minds. And maybe see something real. And then maybe *know* for themselves.' Luce *knew*, and she was able to impart that knowledge to others through her art in all its forms and through direct mind-to-mind contact.

This emphasis on inner knowing is characteristic of Gnosticism, and I think I do no disservice to either Lucianity or Gnosticism when I say that they have some things in common.

> 'Gnostics' means 'Knowers', a name they acquired because, like the initiates of the Pagan Mysteries, they believed that their secret teachings had the power to impart Gnosis – direct experiential knowledge of God. Just as the goal of a Pagan initiate was to become a god, so for the Gnostics the goal of the Christian initiate was to become a Christ.[†]

If I simply set out the facts of Luce's life no one would believe me; it would be thought a work of fiction. Therefore I will present

[*] *Encyclopedia Britannica.*
[†] Timothy Freke and Peter Gandy, *The Jesus Mysteries* (London: Thorsons, 2000), p. 10.

13

my research (my quest, if you will) exactly as it happened, my discoveries in the order in which they occurred. It's Luce, after all, who laid out that path for me: it's another of her many and varied works of art.

Everything I learned about Luce is the result of my own experience or the experience of others who knew her, who worked closely with her, lived with her, loved her. But they knew only what she told them; the facts they believed they were telling me were the fictions she devised to fit her purpose. I alone was allowed to see that all these selves were roles, postures, personae: masks that conceal and yet, despite or because of her art, reveal. Although my own direct contacts with Luce were few, they were of unparalleled intensity. I believe I came as close as any human can to knowing her.

1

The Secret Gig

Cryptic Clues. A Trap Street. An Invitation.
The Rose Blotter. The Camden Catacombs.
The Chosen Ones. Frankenstein and the
Cat-girls. Luce's Astral Kiss.

London, April 1967

It begins in the dark. From somewhere ahead of me, a small whimper. Excitement? Fear? Many people are afraid of the dark, but I have always found it soothing. Off to the left, a shriek of nervous laughter, quickly hushed. The echoes suggest I'm in a vast, cavernous space of some kind, though I could have sworn that a few minutes ago I was in Camden. My fingers follow the thread they gave me and I shuffle on. There's a soft roaring sound and a warm wind blows in my face, carrying the scent of roses. Colours waft through the air, fragrant aurora borealis. The acid is coming on.

Thus began my account (in my weekly 'Night Eye' column in *NME*) of Luce and the Photons' legendary last secret gig . . . and thus begins my Dream of the Cavern. Images start wheeling

15

by, rising and falling in waves. Always, at a certain point in the dream, I realise that these images are not random: they're part of a story, my story, which is Luce's story. *The thread will lead me to you. I feel it even now, alive in my hand.*

On the night of 23 April, in the Real world and in this one, the thread led me to a secret gig by the most famous unknown band in the world. Luce and the Photons were famous because everyone was listening to and talking about the *Human* album (released December 1966); they were unknown because no one knew who they were. No photographs, no names, no interviews. Two masked and unannounced appearances as 'special mystery guests' at other bands' concerts: 31 March 1967 at the Astoria with the Walker Brothers and Cat Stevens (this was the same show at which Jimi Hendrix first set fire to his guitar. He burned his hands and had to be taken to hospital); 8 April 1967 with the Who at the Saville Theatre. At each of these they performed an extended version of one song from the album. The first was 'The Aetherose', the second 'Immortality'.

These songs also formed the bases of the two enigmatic ten-minute films which appeared fleetingly in nightclubs and cinemas. As far as I know, there are no surviving copies of these. No doubt they were found and destroyed by the demon-simulacra or the police soon after their appearance. Their imagery was almost entirely abstract, though included glimpses of natural things such as trees, flowers and mountains, and the occasional human or animal form among complex, shifting geometries that had mind-altering effects such as time-distortion and synaesthesia. Many people spoke of being overwhelmed with strange emotions for which they could find no words. Some also spoke of a residual sense of awe, beauty, peace or joy that lingered for hours, days or weeks. This imagery and these sorts of effects are typical of Luce's work in a variety of media.

Aside from the two surprise appearances, Luce and the

Photons' only gigs were secret, and you could not buy a ticket for love or money or drugs; they were not for sale. In fact there were no tickets, only invitations. How to get an invitation? You had to be in the right place at the right time. Ah, but what place, what time? Clues would appear in personal advertisements, classifieds, lonely hearts, help wanted columns. In conversations with others who'd been to a gig, I learned that people had been led by these clues to the furthest and most obscure parts of London, to wharves, tower blocks, public lavatories, museums, a chip shop in Hackney, a tailor's in Bermondsey, trees on Hampstead Heath, the crypts of Highgate Cemetery, the stacks of the London Library, the lions in Trafalgar Square, Cleopatra's Needle on the Embankment.

'All secret orders develop initiatory mechanisms of varying degrees of complexity; most aim for a balance between earned and serendipitous choosing.'* This is precisely what Luce did with these secret gigs. She wanted to be found, but not by everyone, and not easily. You had to have desire, perseverance and intelligence; you had to be willing to take risks and you had to be lucky.

On that April night, heart full of hope and feeling rather clever, I'd followed my clues to an ordinary road of flat-faced twenties pebbledash in a grim corner of Kensal Rise. The rusty cylinders of the gas works loomed in the distance; streetlamps glowed in the mild, dense night air. I walked back and forth, scrutinising the page I'd torn from the A–Z, which indicated that right around here was a small square called Cigam Square – but there was no square, just a solid terrace of identical houses. I stopped and laughed aloud. Could it be? Cigam . . . Magic backwards. A magic square. This must be one of the A–Z's secret trap streets,

---

* Simon Rosenfeld, *A History of Secret Orders*, (Oxford: Oxford University Press, 1962), p. 140.

fictitious places inserted into the map by the publishers to catch out copyright thieves. I was hunting for an imaginary place.

There was no square, unless it was very tiny indeed, but between two houses I spotted a narrow gap concealed by leylandii. I pushed through a creaking iron gate, which bore a freshly painted sign, 'Beware the Dog', stepped in something squishy, nearly upset a row of rubbish bins and tiptoed along an alley between walls topped with broken glass. At the end was a tall fence in which was set a high wooden door with a brass knocker. I knocked.

The door opened at once and a torch glared into my eyes. 'Who are you?'

'Well, who are you?'

'Are you looking for the light?'

'Absolutely.'

'Go away.' He slammed the door in my face; footsteps receded. Was this someone who'd decoded the same clues and beaten me to it? I hadn't come all this way to let it go at that. At first the door wouldn't budge, but I gave it a good shove. How different my life would have been if I was the sort of person who went away when told.

I stood at the edge of a wide waste ground. The streetlamps didn't penetrate this far and the only illumination came from the reddish, clouded sky. The terrain was rubbly and uneven, with clumps of straggling shrubs. There was no one in sight. An owl hooted, but I never believed it was a real owl. It had to be a signal of some sort, or so I thought until I saw the long silent swoop and heard the sharp squeal of a mouse or rat.

My halloos received no response. The chap with the torch must have made for the far side; obviously we'd both misread the clues. Defeated, I sat on a lump of concrete and lit a cigarette. I liked it here, cushioned from the encircling city by darkness and the sweet scent of some flower I couldn't identify.

I smoked my cigarette slowly and when I returned to the door I saw, pinned to the inside and unnoticed as I'd entered, a blank white envelope. An invitation? Had the fellow at the door missed it – or was he the one who'd put it there for whoever persevered?

I took it out to the street and opened it under a lamp. It contained a card: 'Admit One', followed by an address in Camden. Paper clipped to the corner was a square of blotting paper with a rose printed on it. Full of glee, I tucked the acid under my tongue, the invitation into my pocket and set off briskly towards Harrow Road, where I hailed a cab.

The Camden street, ill lit and part cobbled, was lined with the high brick walls of warehouses; sandwiched between them lay a row of dingy two-up two-downs with boarded windows. Number six was at the end. I knocked and the door opened at once.

'Invitation, please.'

A pencil beam flicked over the card and I was given a gentle push along the passage. It was so dark I couldn't see my hand in front of my face; all I could hear was my own breathing and the scrape of my cautious feet.

A voice at my elbow made me jump. 'Two flights down.'

I edged forward and my foot encountered the first step. I descended, then groped along the banister to descend another flight. This was evidently not your usual two-up two-down. At the bottom of the stairs, a voice said, 'Follow this,' and a thread was put in my hand.

'To the Minotaur?' I asked, and received a brief, knowing laugh and a whiff of patchouli. As I wrote in my column that week:

We follow our threads through the dark, echoing caverns, approaching from every direction. Someone starts singing 'Immortality', others join in. The air is shivering with anticipation. A single flickering candle seems terribly bright and draws us like moths. Faces appear, eyes starry-wide; we're all tripping, smiling, greeting each other as long-lost friends, touching hands, kissing. We're the chosen ones, the beautiful ones. We climb a spiralling iron stair and emerge into a room like a womb, tented and draped, walls, ceiling and floor awash with swirling colours and images, subtle fragrances suffusing the air and the music, the music, the music coming from everywhere.

At the time, the first thing that struck me was a memory: the image of a pixie-faced girl jumping out of a tree. As I struggled to place it the soundtrack shifted to splashing water, the scent of hay meadow drifted by and I remembered – the island, the lake. That party. For reasons then entirely obscure, though now perfectly obvious, I was remembering my first acid trip nine years before, one summer afternoon when, with some Oxford friends, I'd crashed a party on an island in a lake. I'd been strolling through the woods following the sound of a flute when a pixie-faced girl dropped out of a tree holding, between thumb and index finger in the gesture that means 'perfect', a white sugar cube. I knew right away what it was. She asked if I was ready. When I replied, 'Of course,' she told me to close my eyes and open my mouth; she put it on my tongue and I was off. It was the most extraordinary experience of my life.

For weeks afterwards I'd wandered around in a haze of radiant euphoria (fortunately it was the Long Vac), but the heart of the trip had been so strange and powerful, so beyond my everyday mentality, that I was unable to retain the memory of what had really happened – for something definitely had. Often in the following months, as the ecstasy faded, I'd probed for it in the recesses of my mind, trying to resurrect it, to get another dose, to return to that state of inexpressible bliss . . . but it was lost.

The image of the pixie-faced girl remained, and certain details of the trip – the amazing pink-leafed singing trees, the forest grove with ancient marble columns and star-flowers glowing beneath the earth, the luminous night-flying bird – but the core of it had dropped so deep into my consciousness that it remained hidden for years. Only after many other pieces of the puzzle had fallen into place did I understand that it had been the real beginning of my life.

There at Luce's secret gig I had the sense, for the briefest moment, that it was in my power to seize that memory. I felt it quickening in me like an ember. Time paused as I strained for it, I could almost touch it . . . but I'd tried too hard, it was gone and I was soon swirled away in a heavenly storm of sound and image, emotion and sensation.

Splashing water and hay meadow blended into soaring flutes and wailing sitar, a sunflower exploded in a burst of arpeggios, the leafy ceiling wavered, rose and parted to reveal a perfect sapphire-blue sky, filled with cascades of rose petals like rain. The floor, impressed, rolled and twitched and offered cool, springy, green-scented moss. A flock of birds trailed ribbons; one drifted down into my hand. It bore a message – three words: 'Elucidate! Love, Luce.'

I'm trying, Luce, I'm trying.

On the floor, damned near sensory overload. I climbed up into a network of scaffolding and found the control booth on a platform overlooking the room. Slide projectors clicked round their trays, movie projectors ran films, liquid light projectors, with coloured blobs of oil and water in shallow glass dishes, were being rhythmically manipulated by a pair of dancing girls with ink-stained fingers and cat-masks. Like a spider in the centre of hundreds of twisting cables, a man in a Frankenstein mask played an array of electric key pads, dials, knobs and sliders. Lights twirled, changed colour, strobed.

My colleagues who were music critics always complained about the difficulty of describing their subject on the printed page in ways that others could understand. The terminology was either too abstruse, as with classical and jazz, or toe-curlingly banal, if one tried to describe pop or rock. Luce and the Photons' music defied all genres then and still does, so I won't even try. Anyone can listen to it but very few experienced a performance. At the gig I attended, no more than a hundred of us, though at times we felt like all the world's billions, at other times like one alone.

The band was on a small raised stage at the far end of the room. There were three of them. The one I immediately took to be Luce was wearing a loose, high-necked suit of some black, glimmery material and a black Japanese Noh-theatre mask. He was lit by a bank of black lights, a sort of non-light that slid off without illuminating. I'll use the masculine pronoun for the moment, because my first impression that night – my mind in those days still needing to parse things into one or t'other – was that Luce was a young man. This impression was created not only by the clothes, which were but slightly on the masculine side of androgynous, and the height of the figure, which I guessed was five ten or eleven but also by its air of relaxed, consummate mastery, which in those sexist times suggested masculinity if not actual maleness.

'Despite wearing a mask,' I wrote in my column, 'the figure of Luce was so deeply compelling because one felt that he was being himself with utter abandon and utter perfection; there was no gap, as there always is with people, between who he was and who he seemed to be.' This is one of Luce's paradoxes, because there can have been few times in her life when she was not pretending to be somebody else in a simple effort to stay alive.

Upon rereading the clipping, I see that I concluded the column with a declaration that I would find out who Luce really was;

that remarkably arrogant assertion may have been what brought me to the attention of the demon-simulacra in the first place.

Luce played a modified nine-string Stratocaster,* standing behind an arc of about a dozen foot pedals and three mikes. The vocals were put through such varied filters and effects that, as on the *Human* album, one couldn't tell whether the singer was male or female. In that dark pool of light, it was his hands that drew the eye as they caressed the guitar, sometimes too rapidly to see: pale, long-fingered, strong and dextrous hands. They were the only bit of skin that showed, and more than one witness spoke of Luce's hands as being overwhelmingly erotic to watch.

As I looked at him a peculiar feeling ran through me. Although his body didn't move, I felt him turn towards me. It was like he kissed me from across the room, a deep astral kiss. He kissed my mind, though I certainly felt it in my body as well. It was, and is even in memory, the most remarkably sensual experience, yet involving no physical senses. I was being tasted, savoured, known – and I was tasting, savouring, knowing something, someone so painfully beautiful it was almost too much to bear. The thing is, it felt to me like a kiss of recognition, and I swear I heard him say, *Ah, it's you, it's you,* as though we already knew each other. And then, *Time to wake up, beloved.* And he gave me, like a sip of elixir, a wave of the most delicious laughter I have ever experienced. It flew through me, activating circuits, flicking switches. It woke me up; it turned me on.

Beside Luce on the stage was a slender though unmistakably feminine figure in a white mask and a white suit. She played violin, cello and theremin, and also sang. I saw no drummer or percussionist, and assumed that the rhythm tracks were provided

* 'The most singular instrument in the history of the electric guitar. No one has ever been able to replicate the tuning Luce used for his live shows.' Patrick M. Henderson, 'Luce and the Photons in Perspective', *Journal of Musicology*, 46 (July, 1986), 74-117 (pp. 89–90).

by the array of reel-to-reel tape decks stacked at the back of the stage and controlled by Luce's foot pedals, or perhaps by the tall man who was half hidden behind a piano, an electric organ, a Moog synthesiser and other pieces of equipment that I didn't recognise. I got an impression of long auburn hair, scarlet frock coat and maniac grin. He wore a plain red domino mask.

The tented ceiling and walls served as screens onto which images were projected, some sourced from live camera feeds showing the guests as they danced or strolled about or laughed or cried or stood very still staring at the ever-changing ceiling. I caught a glimpse of myself, wide-eyed and raptured, smiling like I was in love.

It is an odd, retroactive dilemma: in some ways, I wish I'd paid closer, more exact attention, made notes, planned to remember every detail . . . but then I wouldn't have experienced it, and I can't wish that. A description of what occurred in the linear sense is in any case useless, even demeaning. Some hours chugged by in the outer world; in the infinite inner world, at that moment paradoxically, telepathically, psychedelically shared with those others, something real was touched, felt, known, made: 'a single flower formed from the petals of all possibles,' as Luce sings in 'The Aetherose'.

The journey finally over, we were washed up on the shore of day, given sweet cool orange juice to drink and shooed gently on our way by a silent person in a Green Man mask. Arrows chalked onto the walls of the caverns, now greyly lit by occasional shafts from above, led off in every direction. I wandered around in a daze for a bit, then found a door; it opened onto the south-bound platform of the Northern Line at Mornington Crescent.

Never feeling more like an alien, I joined the workaday throng jolting into town, wedged against a pretty shop girl in microscopic Quant and too much Shalimar, and a dandruff-crusted City gent who was surreptitiously prodding the dolly bird's thigh with his

24

rolled umbrella. The girl shifted her weight so as to lean against him, gave a little wriggle, then placed her kitten heel over his wing-tipped foot and stomped hard. He went red, then white with pain, but made no sound or movement.

Home, bed, slept till afternoon, then out in search of coffee. Bar Italia was jammed. I had two double espressos in rapid succession and squeezed back onto the pavement. I listened to the conversations ricocheting around me but heard only football, politics, scandals. All the same rubbish as yesterday, but I had such a strong feeling that something had changed, really changed, in the world as a whole. Was I the only one who noticed? Were the rest of these humans just animals going about their day-to-day cud-munching, oblivious to . . . to what? I couldn't put my finger on it, but I knew things were not the same, and Luce was the cause.

More than anything, I wanted to be back where I'd been the night before. There had been moments that stretched into infinities; exquisite eternities had blossomed around me with all the profligacy of never-ending springtime . . . where had they all gone? Why couldn't I slip back into one of those? Why was I stuck in this thick-headed, hard-edged, gravity-bound, mechanical robot of a life?

The double espressos on an empty stomach perhaps a mistake, I hailed a cab and returned to Camden. The street was as I remembered: boarded up and deserted. No one answered the door at number six, at the other houses or the warehouses. At the newsagent's on the corner I learned that the whole street was due for demolition to make way for a council estate. Down in Mornington Crescent, the door on the platform was locked.*

* Although at the time I was quite prepared to believe I had left the sphere of mundane Earth altogether and entered a cavern of myth, I was in a real place. Forgotten for decades, the Camden Catacombs were a vast network of underground tunnels, stables and warehouses built in the nineteenth century between Euston Road and Primrose Hill.

Now.

A fly is buzzing at the window; I let it out. Not for
the first time, I ask myself if it's wrong to mislead
insects into believing in divine intervention, the
miraculous overturning of seemingly immutable laws of
nature, the sudden release from ignorance and suffering
into light and freedom. What if he should find himself
once again trapped, but this time with no one to come
to his aid? Will he remember the time he achieved
release, and will the memory lessen or increase his
anguish as he dies? I wonder about this every time I
help one poor idiot to escape a fate of futile battering
at an invisible and incomprehensible barrier. Am I
really doing him a favour?

But I can't do otherwise. Luce could never let an
animal suffer. And I feel her with me, looking over
my shoulder, whispering in my ear - *yes, I can hear
you* - guiding me - *as you always did* - from within.
This book I'm writing is a living thing, fed by my
thoughts, my memories, my feelings . . . but most of
all by the clear, inextinguishable light of Luce.

I know this will be the last thing I do. I'm at World's End, and that's all right. I'm playing myself backwards like a spiral galaxy reversing its centrifugal fugue and rewinding, withdrawing space and time, starry tendrils receding from the void.

Luce is alpha and omega, beginning and end: the big bang and the black hole at the centre of it all.

2

Looking for Luce

❧

*The Other Secret Gigs. Bobby Fisk and the Sheet of
Blotter. The* Human *Album. Pymander Productions
and Monad Management. Golden Square. The
Painted Room. The Demon-simulacra. A Bad Trip.
Mr Greyling and the Amaretto Biscuits.*

London, May 1967

My contact with Luce at the secret gig left me both exalted
and confused. I no longer seemed to fit my life, or it no
longer fitted me. I'd taken off a glove, and when I tried to put
it on again its shape, or mine, had changed, and short of breaking
my hand, there was no way to resume it. I had seen that the
world was not the opaque, impermeable and self-evidently solid
thing, or collection of things I'd thought it was. Yes, it was all
still here around me in the usual way, but invisibly resonant
with . . . something else. The part of it that I had taken for the
whole was revealed to be the flimsiest cardboard cut-out of a
reality; the cardboard ground had dropped from beneath my feet
and I discovered myself to be treading a far wilder realm than
I'd ever suspected.

When I encountered others who had been to the Camden gig, or an earlier one, many reported having a similar experience of maladjustment to their old, ordinary lives. There can be no doubt that engendering these feelings was Luce's purpose, or one of them, when she created the secret gigs and lured us, her chosen ones, into her web. 'The function of a Gnostic teacher is to break open assumptions about the nature of reality, to instigate cracks in the smug, unquestioning self-belief of the unawakened mind. The effects are often mistaken for insanity, whereas to the Gnostic, they represent the first dawning of long-sought sanity.'[*]

There had been three other secret gigs: in Nine Elms (20 January 1967), Brompton (17 February) and North Kensington (29 March). I refer readers to Felicity Neville's 1968 collection of eyewitness accounts: *101 True Stories of Luce*, though I advise you to bring your own salt. She seems to have believed absolutely everything she was told. One of my sources recounted to me with great relish how he'd spun her a wild tale merely to hear her increasing murmurs of amazement, which he'd manipulated to a satisfying crescendo. His story is there in the book, verbatim. I won't say which one.

At each of the gigs the guests were required to traverse a space of complete darkness before gaining access to the light and music. Luce knew how to manipulate the mind. She knew, too, what all true magicians know: one must act on the material plane in order for all the gears of consciousness to be fully engaged. 'The motions of the physical body in . . . ritual function as root, anchor and lightning-rod to the intention of the mind.'[†] It was necessary that we walked in the darkness, that we had the faith to put one foot in front of the other and dare to enter

[*] Jean Dellida, 'The Eternal Present: Gnosis Then and Now', *Trends in Consciousness* 7 (2000), 87-168 (p. 102).
[†] Bernard de Gaussère, *The Meaning of Action* (Chicago: Reiland Jacobson, 1949), p. 185.

the unknown. I encountered a few people who'd been too scared to set foot into that preliminary darkness. Some reported visions of terrifying figures barring their way and ordering them to turn back. They had unhesitatingly complied.

Why were there no bootleg recordings? Four secret gigs, perhaps four or five hundred altogether in attendance, all of whom had truly wanted to be there, had worked for it, taken risks for it. Surely one of them had brought recording equipment? Apparently several had, yet all, when they returned to the surface world, realised that they'd forgotten to turn it on.

And why, amid the frenzy to discover Luce's identity that obsessed the media and fired the imagination of the whole world, did no one, at any time during the gigs, go up to him and try to remove the mask? I'd have thought someone would have been unable to resist the temptation. Why didn't I? I asked myself that, of course, and the answer is that it would have been rude and disrespectful. I was just surprised that everyone else had been as polite.

But no, it shouldn't be a surprise. We were all encompassed in the charism of Luce. I believe that all of us who attended a secret gig felt, and wanted to feel, deeply complicit in whatever Luce was doing. We were the chosen ones: out of all the great seething sea of London, we were the fishes who found his net. Like another before him, Luce was a fisher of men. We were participating in something beautiful and important; there was no desire to rend the veil.

After Camden, I was among the thousands who scoured the papers in vain for clues to the next gig. In the past, these had begun appearing soon after the previous gig and were, by this time, recognised at once. But there were no more clues. Stories circulated that Luce had been kidnapped or arrested, deported or sectioned, imprisoned or assassinated, killed in a plane or motorcycle crash in Paris, in California, in Tangiers. And still no one knew who Luce was, or even if Luce was a man or a woman. I was convinced that I would be the one to find out. Luce had told me to wake up; he'd given me the task of elucidating. I would dedicate my life to that task.

Under my pen name Chimera Obscura (Chimera: 'An unreal creature of the imagination'; also a play on *camera obscura*: 'dark chamber') I'd been commissioned to write a book (large, glossy, lavishly illustrated, 'Not too intelligent, please,' said the editor) about some of the wilder currents in the pop culture maelstrom: the influence of drugs, of Eastern mysticism, Western occultism, paganism, etc. As with my earlier, improbably successful little guide books to esoteric forms of urban nightlife in various cities (the *Night Eye* series, which begat my weekly column, which begat this commission), I exerted no great effort and just wrote more or less truthfully about what happened to me. I seemed to have a knack for finding myself in interesting situations, and considered myself fortunate to make a living from it. Now, for the first time, I would be a proper journalist: doing research, interviewing witnesses, tracking down sources. Finding the truth. Finding Luce. On the way I'd check out the mysticism, occultism, paganism, drugs (in any case impossible to avoid) and so justify my expenses.

I reckoned that at least ten people, probably more, had to have been involved in setting clues, distributing invitations and staging Luce and the Photons' secret gigs, but everyone had been either masked or in darkness. I started with the light show and sound system. There were only a couple of outfits with that sort of skill and equipment; both denied having been the one. Of course they'd heard of the shows. Had I really been to one? What was it like? How did they do it? I told them I was tripping too hard to pick up much technical detail.*

---

* 'Despite painstaking analyses of the *Human* album and the accounts of eye-witnesses to their performances, we are unable fully to determine how [Luce and the Photons] achieved the effects they undeniably did.' Arthur

I did run into one of the girls with ink-stained fingers who'd operated a liquid light projector, but she'd just tagged along with a school friend whose brother was the set builder who'd put up the tent-like walls and ceiling. I bribed her with a chunk of hash to tell me his name – Bobby Fisk – and tracked him down to the wilds of Notting Hill only to be told that he knew nothing about his employer. Payment in cash had arrived by courier. He'd been sent the drawings – good technical drawings, he said – and built the set as directed in each location, having been told the address only on the morning of the gig. It was all parachute silk and scaff-poles, designed so that one man could put it up and take it down in a few hours. He had done this four times, after which he'd received a bonus. What was the bonus? I asked, and he showed me with great reverence what remained of a sheet of the rose-printed blotter acid, originally six by six.

I turned to the single known artefact of Luce and the Photons, the *Human* album. It had to have been recorded somewhere, produced, pressed, the jacket designed, printed, the product sold and delivered – and yet reliable information proved elusive.

The iconic cover photograph of the lone figure in the desert, with his back to us and his arms outstretched like Christ on the cross, was surely an image of Luce himself. There was something in the intensity of the gesture, the slim height of the figure and its air of splendid isolation that was unmistakably Lucian. As for the location, opinions varied according to the imagination and erudition of the respondent and their degree of stonedness: Mexico, Morocco, Australia, Texas, Sinai, the Rift Valley, the moon, Mars, Krypton, Middle Earth, a parallel universe, the chronosynclastic infundibulum.

The motif of the desert runs through much of Luce's life and

Abercrombie, 'The Uncanny Arts of Luce and the Photons: Still Inscrutable After All These Years', *NME, Luce and the Photons 30th Anniversary Special Edition*, December 1996, 74.

work. When, on the cover of the album, Luce chose to present himself as a solitary human figure in the midst of a barren landscape, he was saying something not just about the state of the human spirit in the desert of matter, but also about his personal sense of exile. Was he lonely, out there by himself? What was he looking at? What was he feeling? The answers are to be found in the *Human* album itself: the story of the god who came to Earth.

The inside sleeve is covered with a dense scribble of imagery – foliage, stars, spirals, strange creatures, trees, birds and complex geometries – interspersed with fragments of song lyrics in many languages. T. K. Quelling, whose 1970 book *The Light of Many Tongues* remains the definitive study of the *Human* album's lyrics, identifies eight: English, German, French, Latin, Greek, Japanese, Russian and Arabic. A ninth language which he failed to identify is, I have come to believe, Enochian.

I examined the sleeve with a magnifying glass, but found that after a couple of minutes I became dizzy and had to stop. It was as though the lines squirmed away from scrutiny, and it was only by returning to it over and over again at half-hour intervals that I finally saw something that gave a clue.

Hidden in a drawing of the convoluted, thorny stem of a rose, in tiny letters, four words: 'Pymander Productions Monad Management'. No address. Could this be the mysterious record company behind the band? I looked them up in the telephone directory: no listing. I talked to my extremely well-connected friend Charlie, who was trying to make it in the music business, managing a couple of bands, running a record label, organising concerts, doing promotion. He'd never heard of Pymander Productions or Monad Management, who did not seem to have any connection with anyone else in the music business – no other records, no other bands. Did they actually exist, or were they a joke that I wasn't getting?

I spoke to the chap called Malcolm who ran the record shop on my corner, where I'd bought the album on the strength of his recommendation. He told me it had not arrived in the usual way from a distributor, but a box of them had simply appeared in the shop one afternoon. He had no idea how to contact whoever supplied them, 'but if you find them please tell them I'd like some more. It sold out inside of two days and there's hundreds on the waiting list. You want a bootleg tape? Two quid. If you want to sell yours, I can get you fifty quid for it, easy.'

The *Human* album, it emerged, was sent or delivered anonymously to record shops and radio stations all around the world. It's believed that just ten thousand LPs were pressed; by far the greatest distribution of the album occurred via bootleg tapes.

I declined Malcolm's offer – both of them – and returned to my study of the artefact. The terms 'Pymander' and 'Monad' were unusual, yet vaguely familiar. A quick trawl through reference books at the library revealed that *The Divine Pymander* was the seventeenth-century English translation of a set of Egyptian–Greek texts (second and third century CE) dealing with spiritual philosophy, metaphysics, alchemy and magic, attributed to the semi-mythic author Hermes Trismegistus. The word 'Pymander' was of obscure etymology, meaning either 'Shepherd' or 'Mind of God'.

The hieroglyph Monad (☿) is a symbol designed by Dr John Dee, Elizabethan mage, to represent the cosmos. Dr Dee, originator/recorder of the Enochian or 'Angelic' language, was clearly a figure of some significance to Luce: 'Dear Doctor Dee in his angelic tree/Tongue-tied, humble pride/Alphabetising his enchanted memory,' as she sings in 'Ed Kelley's Monkey'. (Edward Kelley was the psychic medium, usually considered to have been a fraud and a scoundrel, employed by Dee to communicate with the angels.)

A glyph that looked somewhat like the Monad appeared here

and there among the drawings on the liner. But not quite Dee's Monad: where he had a circle above a cross, here was a spiral within a square. In a sudden revelation, I saw that the whole design of the inner sleeve was laid out as a spiral within a square. It was the kind of thing you'd notice only if you were gazing at it with your eyes unfocused, when it would emerge in three dimensions. As soon as you looked for it, it disappeared. I'm not the only person to have noted this strange effect. According to L. J. Kranstein's *History of Optical Art*, the inner sleeve of the *Human* album is the first example of an autostereogram, now known as 'magic eye' art.*

Nor was it just any spiral: I recognised the precise proportions of the Golden Section. Very profound, no doubt, but could it also hold a clue? I did not for one instant believe that these oh-so-clever, game-playing, head-fucking pranksters had not left a trail, if only to torment people like me.

Why had they altered the Monad's circle to the Golden Section, its cross to a square? Philosophical, even mathematical reasons suggested themselves, then something clicked. It was a bit more literal than that. I tipped the LP out of the sleeve. The paper label stuck on the disc was square, not the usual round, it was golden in colour and had no words, song titles or anything at all on it except for a spiral of exact Golden proportion. Golden + square . . . Golden Square? The heart of Soho, Dickens's 'region of song and smoke' from *Nicholas Nickleby*. How very apt, and only a few streets away. This had to be a clue, and I was the only one to have deciphered it. I walked there in five minutes.

Golden Square is not large, and it didn't take me long to establish that the names I sought appeared on no door, doorbell, shop front or sign. And I thought I'd been so clever. Deflated, I

* L. J. Kranstein, *The History of Optical Art* (London: Routledge & Kegan Paul, 2003) p. 56.

sat on a bench under a plane tree and lit a joint. Before long I was joined by Tim, the Golden Square busker. When I told him I was looking for Luce and the Photons he took up his guitar and went into a scrappy rendition of 'Shoot the Buddha on the Road to Emmaus'. (The title refers to the Buddhist edict that if you happen to meet the Buddha you should kill him, because if you see him as a discrete individual, he can only be yet another deceiving manifestation of your own ego and must therefore be exterminated forthwith, as well as the episode in the Gospel of Luke in which Jesus appears on the road to Emmaus the day after he died.)

I applauded politely. Had he heard of Pymander Productions, Monad Management? He shook his long, rank locks. I showed him the glyph, which I'd copied into my notebook; had he seen anything like it? To my surprise, he nodded.

He'd seen it, he said, on a scrap of paper in a house on the other side of Golden Square where he goes sometimes for a cup of tea. 'Good people. But they left a few days ago, except for the old man in the bookshop, and he's going, too. I gave him a hand with some boxes this morning.'

He led me across the square and, squinting into the sun, pointed out number eleven, a nondescript Georgian town house with a shop at street level and three floors above. I shook him loose with a few bob and approached the building. A sign indicated that the ground floor housed an antiquarian bookseller. The front door was ajar; I pushed it open and stepped into a dim hallway. On the right, the door to the shop, part glazed, revealed half-empty shelves and a few boxes. A sign said 'Out to Lunch'.

Further on, the passage ended in another door, which led to a flight of stairs. I could tell at once that the place was unoccupied; there was no bustle of activity, no sound of movement or voices. I made my way upstairs on bare, creaking boards, past rooms containing only the odd chair, a desk or two. I looked in the drawers of the desks, but they'd been cleared out.

Here and there I came upon a few items of detritus: a champagne cork, an empty cigarette box (Gitanes), paperclips, a pencil stub. In a room on the first floor a slanting beam of sunlight drew my eye to a corner of something slipped down between the floorboards. It turned out to be a strip of 35mm negatives. I prised it out, blew off the dust and held it to the light. There were six frames, most showing a landscape, but a division into earth and sky was all I could distinguish. Absurdly triumphant for someone whose days of journalistic diligence had been rewarded with a tiny scrap of rubbish, I tucked the film into my gas bill, which I'd stuffed into my pocket as I left my flat.

On the second floor, the front room held nothing but a large electric clock, though the walls, ceiling and floor were covered with paintings: trees, animals and birds, strange figures, fanciful geometries. They were like the drawings on the album liner, but vividly coloured and vibrating with intensity, uncannily alive, shifting and changing as I looked, and looked again. The more closely I examined them, the more they expanded to draw me in. To this day I'm not sure what I saw – even the next morning I found it hard to remember the images with any clarity. I had no doubt, however, that this was the work of Luce. The sensibility, the aesthetic, the whole gestalt of that room was unquestionably the same as the *Human* album.

I emerged blinking, with a peculiar and rather pleasant tingling in my head, as though my brain cells had been rinsed in soda water. It felt like I'd spent half an hour in there. Thinking I'd better get a move on, I glanced at the clock on the wall and was astonished to see that only two minutes had passed. I stepped back into the room, this time trying to keep an eye on the clock – now I understood why it was there – but every time I looked at the paintings, time misbehaved and instants expanded into eternities. The effect was reminiscent of what I'd experienced at the secret gig: a sea of infinities bubbling all around me, each of which, when entered, went on for ever. At the gig, I'd attributed the effect to the acid I'd taken, combined with the intense sensory reality of Lucian sound and vision, but here the effect was induced by imagery alone. I tore myself away and paused in the doorway to take some pictures.

I looked around the rest of that floor, and the top floor, but found nothing. As I was about to leave I heard some people coming up the stairs and stepped out to the landing to meet them. In the lead was a man of exceptional ordinariness: colourless hair, colourless dead-fish eyes and a banal, flabby face, wearing a grey suit and a striped tie. His two companions, a young man and woman, were similarly bland, plumpish, with pale round faces, wearing similar grey suits – brother and sister, perhaps. I named them at once: Tweedledum and Tweedledee.

It was then that I noticed the gun in the girl's hand, and the friendly greeting I'd prepared stuttered to a stop. Were they police? Gangsters? Debt collectors? The thought crossed my mind that PP/MM might have neglected to pay their bills before they left.

I backed into the room from which I'd emerged and, as if following a well-known script, put my hands in the air, even though no one told me to. Under the watchful gaze of T-dee and her gun – which, alarmingly, seemed to have a silencer attached – T-dum searched me, turning out my shoulder bag onto the floor. My protests were ignored. He passed my things one by one to the first man, clearly the leader, whom I'd begun in my mind to call Mr Big. That is because I had decided I was tripping, which explained a lot. Furthermore, I deduced that this had become a Bad Trip. I had heard of them, had occasionally been with a friend having one, but in all my years of quite regular ingestion of the biochemical miracle that is LSD, I had never had one myself. I couldn't recall having taken any acid that day, but perhaps inability to remember taking the acid was one of the features of a Bad Trip. The hallucinations were of unsurpassed sensory power, detail, consistency and persistence. I was awestruck.

I studied Mr Big and his companions closely – usually, that causes things to transform into other things, but these guys didn't change at all. Their eyes never blinked, their hair never moved and there was a nebulous, blancmange quality to their faces and bodies. These and other hard-to-pin-down anomalies in their appearance and behaviour gave them an unnatural look, as though they were simulacra made of exceptionally life-like plastic, expertly moulded and adorned. I expected them to disappear at any moment, melt, fade away or pop, like soap bubbles. They didn't.

With unwilling fascination I watched Mr Big paw through my things, scrutinising my ID as though he suspected it was forged. He missed the negatives, which were hidden in my gas bill, though my notebook received close attention. He lingered over the latest entries, where I'd recorded the progress, or lack of progress, of my quest for Luce. He handled my camera with great care, as though it might be booby-trapped, then opened the back and pulled out the film. Everything was tossed into a heap on the floor when he was done with it.

My state of wary perplexity was giving way to an awful sensation that I realised must be extreme fear. This trip had gone very bad indeed, but the more I tried to make it stop, the more I felt myself helplessly sucked in.

Some people, I remembered, had reported that their Bad Trips involved confrontations with demons. That struck me as a highly plausible, even an obvious explanation of the situation. In my view at the time, demons were imaginary, mere representations of our own fears. Somehow, I concluded, the acid (where had I got it? When had I taken it? How long would this last?) had enabled my inner demons to take on these externalised forms and let them loose to torment me in this peculiar way. I was not surprised that my demons presented themselves as ultra-normal, quasi-human simulacra in suits and ties; I have always had a horror of the ordinary. The very banality of today's demons turns out to be far more terrifying than horns and forked tails, which I would have found impossible to take seriously.

Though recognising the absurdity of invoking divine aid in warding off what I believed to be merely the chemically enhanced products of my own psychopathology, I nevertheless tried to recall a prayer. Having been raised an atheist (except for Christmas and Easter, when we went to church in much the same way as we went to the dentist, with a similar mixture of duty and dread), I couldn't, but what came to mind were some words from the Twenty-third Psalm – something about the Lord being my shepherd, and walking through the valley of the shadow of death, fearing no evil. No doubt it sprang to mind because of my recent ponderings on the etymology of 'Pymander', with its possible meaning of 'Shepherd'.

The psalm did not seem to be working. Trip or reality – it made no difference any more. Terror was making me dizzy and nauseous, flooding my bloodstream with a paralysing toxin. I tried to back away but couldn't make my legs move; I tried to speak but no words came out. Events seemed to move infinitely slowly, freeze-frame fragments broken into milliseconds, sharp edged and icy clear. Tiny noises, hugely magnified, echoed in the vast, panic-filled void that my mind had become.

And then there came the sound of footsteps on the stairs and a voice called, 'Hullo, hullo, hullo! Who's there?'

An elderly gentleman appeared and close on his heels, Tim the busker. T-dee's gun had disappeared.

'Can I help you?' The old man's tone was affable, but his eyes were alert. 'Are you looking for someone? I'm afraid everyone's moved out.' When he held out his hand to Mr Big, offering a genial handshake, Mr Big recoiled and, with the other two, shuffled off and away down the stairs without a word.

I was experiencing the most almighty rush of relief, but it was short-lived. If other people had seen Mr Big, T-dee and T-dum it meant they'd been real, which was even more troubling than a Bad Trip.

The elderly gent turned out to be the bookshop owner, introduced by Tim as Mr Greyling. Tall and spare, he had sharp blue eyes, a crisp white moustache and a vaguely military demeanour. Tim helped me to gather my things from the floor – I was a bit shaky – and we followed Mr Greyling downstairs to his shop. He unlocked the door and invited us in for a cup of tea.

'Don't you think we should call the police?' I said.

'The police? Whatever for?' asked Mr Greyling.

'That girl had a gun!'

'A gun? Really? Are you quite sure?'

'Maybe you didn't see it. She must have put it away when you came in.'

'I suppose so,' Mr Greyling said.

I had a moment of doubt. Had I really seen a gun? But surely I wouldn't have felt that awful, sick terror if there hadn't been a gun involved. Without the gun, the behaviour of Mr Big and the other two was obnoxious, but not frightening. Maybe the terror and the gun were both delusions. Was I tripping after all? I gazed around the bookshop. Nothing changed colour or shape; everything looked perfectly ordinary. If I backed down now, it would be to admit that I'd suffered some sort of spontaneous psychosis. 'There was definitely a gun,' I said.

'Then of course you must do as you see fit.' Mr Greyling shifted a pile of books to reveal an old black Bakelite telephone. His manner was resigned, as though he was being compelled to undertake a tedious and distasteful task imposed upon him by a person of unparalleled stupidity. Me, for instance. And indeed, one wouldn't have thought that I'd be the sort of person who wished to involve themselves with the police in any way whatsoever. All I can say in excuse is that I was at the time (but not for long thereafter) still naive enough (due to my moderately privileged upbringing) to have a residual notion of the police as good people who were there to protect me from bad people. I made the call, finding some difficulty in describing the incident and perhaps rambling a bit about debt collectors and guns and gangsters.

Mr Greyling had disappeared into the back of the shop. I heard the sounds of a kettle filling and a gas ring being lit – the most lovely, comforting sounds imaginable. Tim was sitting on the floor, picking his guitar. I asked what he thought of those three people.

He hadn't liked the look of them. 'They gave me the creeps, they did. It's the hair, you know? And the eyes. Oh, creepy, creepy creeps,' he sang, 'plastic hair and plastic eyes, plastic looks and plastic smiles, oh yeah, those creepy plastic guy-uy-uys.'

Soon after I'd entered number eleven, he told me, the three creeps got out of a big green van and followed me into the building. 'Big greeeeen van, big green va-a-an.' A few minutes later he'd spotted Mr Greyling on his way back from lunch, told him about me and the three others and tagged along in the hope of a cup of tea. 'Cuppa tea, oh yeah, cuppa cuppa cuppa tee-ee-ee.'

Had he seen a gun?

'A gun? Bang bang, oh my, no gun, no see no gun oh yeah,' strum, strum, 'no gun, oh yeah, bang bang, oh my.' He really was quite good, but never knew when to stop.

Mr Greyling reappeared with three mugs and a tin of my favourite kind of biscuits, amaretti, at the time not easy to obtain outside Italy. The unlikeliness of the biscuits gave me another flash of doubt. Was I tripping after all? Had that episode with the demon-simulacra and the gun been a weird, scary segment of a strange trip that was still going on, albeit in an immensely nicer way? When you're tripping, things can change suddenly, in ways that seem random but perhaps aren't. The thought crossed my mind that the demons and the gun had simply turned into Tim and Mr Greyling and the amaretti biscuits through some magic formula I hadn't realised I'd uttered.

I have always considered a flexible attitude about reality to be one of my strengths. If I was tripping, the bad part was apparently over, so I settled down to enjoy the next phase. I knew from extensive experience that forcing things to make sense in a trip never works; it just adds a layer of misaligned complexity. Resenting the attempt, the things you're trying to pin down will recede from your grasp, spraying a mist of obfuscation behind them that kaleidoscopes their image and covers their escape. Reality, in its essence, is no more graspable than water; the best one can hope for is to feel a bit wet now and then.

Mr Greyling asked me what books I liked; when I replied – can't imagine why – *Alice's Adventures in Wonderland*, he was delighted and, rummaging in a half-packed box, brought out a rare 1865 first edition. We discussed Carroll, rabbit holes, black holes, the nature of time, the Uncertainty Principle, Occam's razor and Schrödinger's cat. We discovered a shared enthusiasm for J. W. Dunne and Dornford Yates.

The episode upstairs – the demons, the gun, the fear – was sealing itself off like a cyst. Had it even happened? By the time the constable appeared at the shop door I was feeling very silly for having summoned him.

I gathered my wits and tried to present a coherent account of what had happened, although by then I was far from certain that it had. The constable's manner of taking notes with one eyebrow raised suggested scepticism about the accuracy of my powers of observation and recall. Noting that nothing had been stolen, he politely enquired what I thought these persons' motive might have been. I offered my debt-collector theory, and speculated that Pymander Productions and Monad Management had got themselves into some sort of money trouble. Mr Greyling professed to know nothing whatsoever about the tenants of the upper floors.

With an authoritative air, the constable informed us that whether the perpetrators were debt collectors or persons of other parties, the episode had been intended as a prank. The gun (*if there was a gun*, the eyebrow said) was a toy. Toy guns looked very real these days. He was sorry that my roll of film had been ruined, but it wasn't exactly a crime, just clumsiness. If he had to arrest people for that he'd spend all day arresting his own left foot, ha ha.

After the constable took his leave, I drank another cup of tea and gave Mr Greyling a hand carrying the last of the boxes of books out to his car, which was parked in the alley behind the building. By the time I left it was early evening. I was trying to accept the prevailing opinion that the whole episode had been some sort of a joke, intended to bully, perhaps to warn, but never to cause real harm. There was much to support that view, yet a sense of unease lingered like a metallic taste in the mouth. I considered myself pretty good at reading people's attitudes and intentions; surely if those three had been joking, I'd have picked up on it. And that gun had looked extremely real. Even in memory a shiver of fear ran through me and I had to lean against some railings until it passed. But maybe I was deluded, still projecting my own fears onto the world. Maybe the fear was within me and I'd never seen it before. Maybe it was within everyone. I gave myself a mental shake. If that sort of thing got out of hand, I could easily see how one might go about in a cloud of fear, seeing demons everywhere and failing to get the world's little jokes. I stopped at the Star and Stone and had a quick shot of vodka, which helped quite a lot.

I went to my photo lab and dropped off the negatives I'd found in the floorboards for overnight printing. It was only then that I realised I'd forgotten to take more pictures of the painted room to replace the ruined roll. I'd go back the next day, I decided.

The more I pondered the events in Golden Square, the more improbable they seemed. The really weird bits, such as my perception that Mr Big and his sidekicks were some kind of demonic simulacra, I dismissed as pure fancy. They were just ordinary goons, debt collectors probably, with a gun, toy or otherwise, to scare people. All that business about their unnatural hair, their dead eyes, was just my aesthetic snobbery. But Tim saw it too, a small part of my mind pointed out. I brushed it aside. Tim was so chronically spaced out that his perceptions could not be taken as an objective guide to reality.

I was inclining towards the view that whatever had gone on there, it had nothing to do with me, and there was no reason to assume it had anything to do with Luce and the Photons. Their management company and record producer, evidently a fly-by-night outfit, had got into trouble, that was all. Fine, leave them to it. There was no point in trying to figure it out. I'd accidentally got caught up in something, had managed to extricate myself, and now could carry on as though it had never happened. How the mundane mind craves convenience! I attempted to ignore all the truly interesting aspects of the situation. As one does.

Now.

There's a knock at the door. It must be another neighbour; one was pestering me an hour ago. Certain of my
fellow inmates, or should I say residents, are as
chummy as they are boring. I long for some serious
nutters to liven things up, but this lot only want me
to join their book club, or ceramics club, or Zumba
class. I call out, 'Bugger off.'

'Hi Weirdo, it's me,' comes Neil's voice, filling
me with scarcely less dread than Zumba. I hastily
close my computer, chuck all my Luce-related material
into its box, push the box under the desk, assume my
mild, dotty face and let him in.

He seems to be alone. When he notices me peering
anxiously behind him he says, 'I know you don't like
Cindy, so I came by myself.'

Such candour, never mind consideration, astonishes
me.

'Tell you the truth,' he says, 'sometimes I don't
like her either. But you know, marriages, well, you
don't know, but let me tell you, liking, not liking,

46

it all evens out in the end. One puts up, you know. Puts up because . . . well, it's what one does. But you never went for all that, did you?'

Do I detect a note of envy in his voice? He potters around the room to cover the awkward moment. 'I see you're making use of your old things,' he says, indicating the half-open boxes stacked here and there. I still haven't got round to sorting through them.

'Yes, thanks again for keeping my stuff. I didn't think you would.'

'Of *course* I did. Of *course* I would. I always kept it. Cindy was for throwing it all out, she nearly did, pretending to do a big clear-out of the whole house, but I knew what she was after and I rescued your boxes from the skip. She worried about bad influences, you see, the effect on the children, but I always over-ruled her. Your stuff, well, it meant a lot to me. It was all I had of you, you know. I'd like to say I always knew you'd come back, but I didn't. You were just . . . gone. I didn't know where you'd gone. Oh, I knew where your body was, all those years in hospital, and prison, and whatnot. But you? Where had you gone? I tried to see you, I tried many times. They kept telling me I couldn't because I was part of the problem, I don't know what that meant, but maybe it was their way of saying you refused to see me?'

He doesn't wait for me to confirm or deny, but hurtles on. 'And it wasn't what you'd *done*, it was who you *were*, or I should say, who you weren't. You weren't you. I missed you, Weirdo. I'm sure you won't believe that.'

He's right, I don't. He must be getting senile. I suggest a cup of tea. The making of it keeps me in

47

the kitchen for a couple of minutes, and when I come
back his smooth, pleasant face is back in place and
he's Arsehole again.

3

Synchronicity City

᠊ᢒ᠊

*The Demons Return. Mr Greyling Is Not What He
Seems. Hellfire and Destruction in Golden Square.
Refuge with Charlie. Ambrose, Magician-about-town,
Explains the Astral.*

London, May 1967

All that evening I felt unsettled. I wandered around, going
here for a drink, there for a bite to eat. I stopped into UFO
and the Marquee, ran into people I knew, got buttonholed by a
record producer with an imitation Hendrix he wanted to flog.
Around twelve thirty I found myself passing through Golden
Square again. It was a mild night, lots of people hanging out.
Tim was busking in his usual spot. Some friends invited me to
join them; we smoked a joint and passed a bottle of wine around
while Tim sang Luce and the Beatles, Dylan, Donovan and the
Stones. An hour or so passed in this convivial way.

Tim had just begun Luce's 'Synchronicity City' when I glimpsed
a large green van driving slowly around the square. Could it be
the same one that had disgorged Mr Big and the other two that
afternoon?

"'That is this and this is that,'" Tim sang. "'There's no such thing as coincidence in Synchronicity City.'"

I slipped away from my friends and crossed the square to keep the van in sight as it turned into the passage that led to the alley behind number eleven. I followed stealthily and positioned myself in a shadowed doorway. The van stopped; Tweedledee and Tweedledum got out and went into the small brick-walled yard at the back of number eleven. The van drove off.

I tiptoed after them. The closer I got, the more I felt a return of the debilitating fear that had paralysed me before. I shook my head to clear it, but an intense, irrational dread was over-whelming my mind. Surely this couldn't be purely subjective, a product of personal derangement, however extreme. It was as though they'd left a noxious cloud in the air as they passed. I had the strongest urge to turn and flee but I forced myself forward, gripping the solid brick corner of the wall, and peered around in time to see them crowbar the back door open. They went in, pushing it closed behind them.

Why had they come back? What were they looking for? I was about to run for the cops when Mr Greyling stepped from the shadows by the bins. He saw me, smiled and brought his finger to his lips, enjoining silence as he crossed to the door. With his back to me, he made an odd gesture in the air before the doorway and murmured some words I couldn't make out. Then he turned and came away. I was still frozen in place by the wall.

'You're really quite nosy, aren't you?' he said. 'Do yourself a favour and don't call the police this time. In fact, I'd make myself quite scarce if I were you.'

From the square came the sound of Tim singing, "'Synchronicity City, isn't it a pity not to meet from time to time to time to time.'"

Greyling listened, and laughed. 'I'll be interested to see

whether we do meet again.' He walked briskly away, got into his car and drove off before I could think of a suitable response.

The miasma of fear still hung in the night air. On the whole, I thought that it would indeed be best to make myself scarce, but I seem to have a chronic inability to go away when told.

I returned to the shadowed doorway where I'd lurked before and from which I could see the corner of number eleven's back wall while also keeping an eye on Golden Square. Within a few minutes I noticed people gathering in front of a building on the square – it had to be number eleven. I went to have a look. To my horror, I saw a glimmer of red in the windows, spreading and brightening. Had T-dee and T-dum returned in order to set a fire? Someone ran past me to the corner box to phone for the fire brigade. Soon the building was well and truly ablaze, the flames most intense on the second floor, in the room with the astounding, time-twisting murals. With a pang of fury I realised I had no photographs, and now never would.

'Is anyone in there?' a girl asked. 'I thought I saw somebody in the shop window.'

'Why don't they come out?' said a man. He ran to the front door and tried it, but found it locked and retreated hastily.

I slipped back to the alley. An ominous glow filled the rear windows of number eleven. As I watched, the door opened and I glimpsed two figures silhouetted against the flickering red light. I ducked out of sight lest they spot me as they passed . . . but they didn't pass. I risked a quick look – they were still inside. Why weren't they leaving? The door stood open, but they seemed unable to cross the threshold. They flung themselves at the opening, only to bounce back. I watched, transfixed, as the flames crept along the floor and caught at their clothes. In an instant they had vanished amid billowing sheets of fire.

Then I remembered the gesture Greyling had made in the doorway, the words he'd spoken. He was not the innocuous old gent I'd taken him for, and things were far stranger than I'd imagined.

Fire engines arrived in the square, the crowd was pushed back and the scene turned into a chaos of shouting and smoke and water, accompanied by the raucous whine of diesel pumps and the sound of breaking glass. I lingered in the shadows, unable to tear myself away until I saw the constable who'd come to the bookshop. I left before he could spot me. Given all that had happened, it would be, as Greyling had reminded me, unwise to be seen in the vicinity now.

Greyling! What was he up to? Of course, like everyone, I'd read some popular books on magic (Eliphas Levi, Aleister Crowley, Dion Fortune, etc.) and had met people who were quite into it. I'd attended occasional Qabalistic rituals, druid ceremonies and witches' covens, so I knew enough about the subject to hazard a guess as to what he'd done. Somehow, he'd sealed T-dee and T-dum into the building. He'd known they would return; he'd been waiting for them. He had lied to me and to the police; without question he knew more than he'd said.

I had to accept that those goons had been real, and the fire was surely proof that they hadn't been joking. But who were they and what did they want? Although a certain amount of uncertainty, even bewilderment, can be enjoyable, I was unaccustomed to feeling so completely baffled. The more I thought, the more tangled my thoughts became. I wanted to tell somebody about what had happened, if only to help me get it straight in my mind. Also, I have to admit that I had a strong disinclination to be alone, so I went to Charlie's house.

Charlie Frith-Haddon was the scion of one of England's oldest families and stinking rich, though he was obsessed with the idea of making it on his own – hence his rather hectic array of enterprises peppered across the music industry. We'd been best friends and comrades in crime since we were twelve or thirteen, distant cousins and kindred rebel spirits united at a huge, dreadful family gathering (his grandfather's funeral) by a shared fondness for smoking behind the tennis courts. We were each the black sheep of our respective families – or proudly believed ourselves to be, though his attempts at non-conformity were played out on a stage immeasurably grander than my own. During our under-graduate days at Oxford his escapades regularly garnered the attention of the tabloids, but I always maintained a certain edge by virtue of being adopted and thus able to project an aura of mystery and disreputable provenance.

Charlie's house in Belgrave Square was a perfect symbol of what he was and what he wanted to be, an often uneasy pairing. A handsome, stately house (Robert Adam, 1764) with a ballroom, four drawing rooms, a library with Chippendale bookcases, a dining room to seat sixty, God knows how many bedrooms and extensive wine cellars through which we were assiduously working our way. The drawing rooms had home-made murals in Day-Glo paint (persons of a sensitive disposition had been known to flee screaming into the street when the black lights were turned on); the ballroom had bearskin rugs, lava lamps and hookahs and was given over to orgies; the library was a recording studio, with the books turfed out and custom-built speakers fitted into the Chippendale; the attics in which legions of domestics once shiv-ered had been gutted and turned into a photo studio where the latest models came to be screwed on the seamless paper and pop sensations pouted and posed.

There was, as usual, a party going on, but Clement, Charlie's seigneurial Rastafarian butler and factotum, said Charlie himself was out. He brought me a joint and a vodka and tonic. Eventually I fell asleep on a sofa.

The next day I woke around noon. Since Charlie had never returned, I headed for home, stopping for coffee at my favourite Egyptian café in Goodge Street. Someone had left a newspaper on the table and I picked it up idly. The headline 'Fire in Golden Square' came as a tremendous shock. The events of the previous night had slipped into the waters of Lethe while I slept; any fragments floating around my still sleep-numbed mind as I stumbled to the café had been categorised as fragments of a weird dream and consigned to oblivion. With the deepest reluctance I dredged them up from memory.

I read the newspaper account carefully, then again. There was no mention of any victims, no bodies, no charred remains. Had T-dum and T-dee managed to get out after all? Or had they been real in the first place? My notions of what was real and what it might mean had lately undergone so many convulsions and inversions that I no longer believed in the reliability of my own internal means of investigation: reason, logic, recollected sense data, time-perception, that sort of thing. Unwilling to assign definite reality to something so outré without further proof, I made my way to Golden Square with a certain amount of trepidation.

Number eleven was less fire-damaged than I'd feared, given the intensity of the blaze. The windows were smashed and I could see into the burned-out shell that had been the wonderful painted room. The front door was cordoned off and a constable stood guard. It was not the fellow from yesterday, but a young, undernourished chap whose ill-fitting uniform had chafed an angry red ring around his scrawny neck. I explained that I knew the old bookseller and was worried about him, but he told me that no one had been hurt in the fire; the building had been empty. Thinking maybe I was being fobbed off with a placatory lie, I said I'd heard that two figures had been seen in the window as it burned.

He shook his head. 'I heard that too. People see things. Shadows and suchlike. Then they want it to be exciting, so they make things up. Convince themselves. Sound important. People don't care what they say, so long as they sound important. If they saw someone, that makes them important, see? There wasn't anyone in there, we've checked. Very thoroughly. Forensics and all that. No one was in that building last night.'

With a resoluteness that belied his meagre, downtrodden appearance, he refused to be drawn into revealing anything more. Either he was lying or I hadn't seen T-dee and T-dum trapped inside as I'd thought. And that might also mean that I hadn't seen Greyling do whatever he did at the back door. On the whole, I decided that I preferred the hallucination explanation, even though it wasn't an explanation at all.

There was no sign of Tim or anyone else I recognised from the previous night, so I continued on my way home, with every step more determined to leave Golden Square behind me mentally as well as physically. Whatever had happened there, I decided to write it off as irrelevant and continue my quest for Luce. The PP/MM clue had led to a dead end, but I had other leads to pursue. I needed a shower and a change of clothes, then I'd collect the photographs from the printers. I was well on my way to a breezy mood when, turning into my road, I saw a large green van parked in front of my flat. A doughy-faced young man with neat brown hair and a beige shirt was standing on the pavement. It needed only a single glance to tell me that he was another like Mr Big, T-dee and T-dum. Plastic hair and plastic eyes: that bland malignity was unmistakable. I stopped so abruptly that a portly woman towing two children ran into me, which caused such a commotion that the young man glanced our way.

I spun around and walked away fast, but didn't run. Don't be conspicuous, I repeated to myself, as if it was a protective mantra. My heart was pounding so hard I couldn't think straight. Mr Big had looked through my things; he knew my name, my real name, and my address. Why hadn't that occurred to me before? If I hadn't crashed at Charlie's last night . . .

I quickened my pace, not daring to glance behind, expecting

at any moment to feel a hand on my shoulder, a knife in my ribs, a gun with a silencer – I knew the damn thing was real – pressed to my spine. In spy novels there is always a convenient shop with a back door through which one can escape. But I knew no such shops. Glancing at my watch as though late, I put on a sudden burst of speed, crossed against the lights at Piccadilly Circus and pelted down the stairs into the tube. I jumped onto the first train that came along, got out at the next stop, then hopped back on as the doors were closing. I kept seeing beige shirts, brown hair. I repeated this at the next station, and the next. All this hopping in and out earned me some queer looks from the other occupants of the carriage, and after the second time, they moved to seats further away from me. At Waterloo I left the train as the doors were closing, crossed to the other side, returned to Charing Cross, changed to the District Line and went to Victoria station. At Victoria I bought a ticket to Brighton but got out at Clapham Junction, where I had a plate of egg and chips in a café on the high street and only then, sure at last that I'd shaken off any possible pursuit, hailed a taxi to take me back to town.

I began to doubt myself. Had there really been a green van in front of my flat? It could have been a blue van, or a black one, or a large green vehicle of another sort. I wished I'd thought to get the licence number. As we drove through south London I saw three green vans; none was following me.

I had myself dropped at the bottom of Regent Street and phoned Charlie from a box. He was home at last and I asked him to go by my flat to see if anybody was lurking outside in a van. He started ragging me about spurned lovers and jealous rivals. I told him that, *au contraire*, I was being pursued by demons. He asked if he should wear a disguise; since my plan was to do exactly that myself, I had to concede it was a good idea. We agreed to meet an hour later by the boat-hire place on the Serpentine in Hyde Park.

In the meantime I made my way to Carnaby Street where I bought new clothes and changed into them, adding a blonde wig, large sunglasses and a sky-blue, wide-brimmed fedora. An hour and a half later, as I strolled for the fifth time past the boat dock, I began to wonder if Charlie and I had, perhaps, outsmarted ourselves with the excellence of our disguises. I examined everyone closely, ruling out children. I would not have put it past Charlie to get himself up in drag, but he did have quite large feet. I ruled out the women.

And then I saw him, puffing in haste, crossing the bridge over the Serpentine. His grandfather's old deer-stalker cap, flaps flapping, a black frock coat of similar vintage, a false moustache and an immense meerschaum pipe clenched in his teeth. I got it right away: he was disguised as Sherlock Holmes.

'The game, regrettably, is not afoot,' he said. 'There are no sinister persons whatsoever lurking in the vicinity of your flat, though I was offered a number of intriguing services by a couple of lovely ladies. You do live in *such* a romantic neighbourhood.'

Although I was relieved, Charlie's report left my confusion intact. If there was no green van now, perhaps there had never been one. Perhaps my mad flight across London had been entirely pointless. Then again, there was no reason to suppose that a single green van was the only vehicle at Mr Big's disposal.

Befuddlement was setting in. We went to Charlie's house and, skirting the parties getting under way in various rooms, retired to his private study on the third floor. Clement brought us a plate of sandwiches and a bottle of the Château Lafite '47. Charlie poured the wine, rolled a joint, settled back in his chair and crossed his bony, velvet-clad legs with the air of a man who has every reason to anticipate a jolly good story. 'Demons, you say? I am intrigued. Start at the beginning, please.'

I explained how I'd traced Pymander Productions and Monad Management to number eleven Golden Square, and recounted, as straightforwardly as I could, the things that had happened there: the painted room and its strange powers, Mr Big, T-dee and T-dum, Mr Greyling, Tim and even, with some embarrassment, my summoning of the constable and his pronouncement that it had been intended as a joke.

'And you found no trace of these Pie-Monad chappies?'

'Just a strip of negatives stuck in the floorboards. It's probably nothing, could have been there for years.'

'Let's see it. Maybe it holds a clue.'

I explained that I'd already dropped it off at the lab.

'What do you think your Mr Big wanted, if it wasn't a joke?' Charlie asked. 'And how do you know they were looking for Pie-Monad, anyway? Did they say so?'

I shook my head. 'No. They didn't say anything at all.'

'Maybe they got the wrong address. Why would such heavy-duty Scaries be going after a harmless record company?'

'Debts? Extortion? One hears about criminal gangs infiltrating the music industry. Or maybe the band reneged on their pact with the devil, so this lot was sent to sort them out.'

'And you're absolutely sure you weren't tripping?'

'Absolutely? Sure? Sure I'm not. When was the last time you were absolutely sure of anything? I don't think I took any acid yesterday, but I might have and forgotten. It didn't feel like a trip – except when it felt like the weirdest trip ever.'

'Could you have dreamed it? I have the most amazing dreams sometimes, can't believe they're not real when I wake up. Hours, days later, I remember a bit of one or another and I swear I can't tell if it was a dream or not.'

'All I can say is, it didn't feel like a dream. Except when it felt like the worst nightmare ever.'

The further I delved into my memory, the less certain I became of what had really happened and what I might only have imagined or maybe even – who could tell? – dreamed while sleeping that night on Charlie's sofa. And then cleverly, unwittingly knitted into an already fading recollection. The more one scrutinises any given scrap of one's own mental substance, the more difficult it becomes to be certain of its source.

Charlie poured us each another glass of wine and relit the joint, which had gone out. 'I hate to say this, but I think I may agree with a policeman. It was intended as a prank.'

'That's what I'd decided, too. But wait till you hear what happened later.'

As Charlie listened in increasing fascination, I related the night's subsequent events – 'Synchronicity City', the reappearance of the green van, T-dee and T-dum breaking into the building – coming at last to the enigmatic behaviour of Mr Greyling. Of all the weird scenes in the surreal drama of the last day and night, that one, played out among the shadows of the brick-walled yard, possessed an uncanny clarity. I described what I'd seen him do at the back door of number eleven: the arcane gesture, the unintelligible words. And then the apparent effect, as the arsonists found themselves unable to escape their own fire.

'This,' said Charlie, 'is right up Ambrose's street. You remember Ambrose Cutler, don't you? He was at Balliol. The old marquess croaked last year and he's Winthrop now.'

He picked up the house telephone and, when Clement answered, asked if Lord Winthrop's seance had ended, and if so, could he please be asked to join us in the study.

While we waited, Charlie explained that Ambrose had begun making a name for himself as a magician-about-town. With the assistance of a Van Dyck portrait, a silver snuff box and whoever happened to be around and feeling psychic, he'd been attempting to contact Charlie's ancestor, the 6th earl, who was reputed to have buried a vast treasure somewhere during the Civil War, then inconsiderately died of an infected toenail without retrieving

59

it or revealing its location. Charlie had abandoned the seance to come to my aid.

Ambrose appeared a few minutes later, accompanied by a faint odour of frankincense. He looked much the same as in our university days, though his wispy blond hair now fell over his shoulders and small round specs perched on his thin nose. He'd always worn those frumpy suits with that air of an oldish man stuck in a body too young for him.

'Ho, Ambrose, any luck?' Charlie offered joint, glass of wine and chair in a single sweeping gesture.

Ambrose dropped into the chair and greeted me warmly. 'We got someone who claimed to be your great-great-great-aunt Hilda,' he told Charlie, 'but she had nothing interesting to say.'

'Ah, well,' said Charlie, 'perhaps the moon isn't in the right house, or whatever. Never mind that for now. We have something that you may find more interesting than Auntie Hilda.'

I told it all again, and Ambrose perked up right away.

'Greyling? I know him, of course, from the bookshop. Got a nice edition of Thomas Vaughan from him one time, but I had no idea he was into the practical stuff, no idea at all. Downy old bird, isn't he? I thought I knew all the magicians in London. Well, just goes to show, you can never tell. Mustn't judge the book by the cover, very apropos, what?'

'But Ambrose, what did he do?' I asked. 'Could he really have shut those two into the building while it burned?'

'Looks that way, doesn't it? Putting up an astral barrier is quite basic, although keeping people in a burning building that they have a strong desire to leave suggests considerable power. It depends a lot on the sensitivity of the subject, of course. Mr Greyling's victims must have been of an uncommonly susceptible disposition. I don't mind admitting that I couldn't do it, not by a long way, but the principle is not difficult to grasp.'

'I've not grasped it,' I said.

'Nor me,' said Charlie.

'I'll demonstrate, how's that? I'll put something across this door, then you summon Clement, and see what happens. I'm not saying I could keep him out, and certainly not if he had an urgent and important reason to come in, but I'll bet I can make him . . . feel somewhat disinclined to enter.'

'Excellent,' said Charlie. 'Please proceed. Should we turn out the lights?'

'No, whatever for?'

'Help you cast your spell, or whatever you do?'

'Don't be ridiculous,' Ambrose said. 'I'm not some back-street spiritualist or hocus-pocus shyster. This is a science. There are techniques. I need to concentrate for a moment, so if you'll kindly shut up I'll get on with it.' He went to stand in front of the door, checking to see that it wasn't locked.

'Should we close our eyes?' Charlie asked.

'I don't care what you do,' said Ambrose over his shoulder, 'as long as you do it without talking. If I were really good, of course, I could do it in the middle of Trafalgar Square while ten thousand Charlies chattered in my ear, but I'm a mere novice so I need a tiny bit of quiet. If you please. Thank you.'

Charlie and I glanced at each other, grinned, then assumed serious expressions. I watched Ambrose closely. He stood a couple of yards from the door, breathing deeply and slowly with his eyes shut, then his body seemed simultaneously to relax and tauten. He opened his eyes, raised his right arm and drew a large pentagram in the air with such intensity that I could almost see the lines traced by his stiffened, pointing finger. He intoned some words that sounded like Hebrew, and appeared to sketch a brief sigil in the centre of the star.

When he returned to his chair, I noticed that beads of sweat stood out on his brow, though the room was not overly warm. 'Call Clement,' he said. 'Ask him to come.'

Charlie obliged, and in a couple of minutes there came a knock at the door. At Ambrose's nod, Charlie called out, 'Enter.'

The door knob twisted, but the door didn't open. 'The door's locked,' came Clement's voice.

Ambrose smiled and shook his head.

'No, it's not locked,' called Charlie. 'Please come in, Clement, we need you in here.'

This time the door opened, but Clement remained on the threshold, frowning. 'I'm sorry, I thought it was locked.'

'Come in, Clement,' said Ambrose.

Clement, about to step forward, stopped.

'Why do you hesitate?' Ambrose asked.

'Well, hard to say. It feels wrong somehow, like I *shouldn't* come in . . . but if you need me . . .' He made a face and seemed to push himself over the threshold with difficulty. Once in, he looked back at the doorway in bewilderment.

'What did you feel, Clement?' said Ambrose.

With a sheepish smile, Clement passed his hand over his face and shook his dreadlocks. 'I think I must be crazy. It felt like I walked through a spider's web, and I thought, Who's not cleaned this?'

'I apologise, Clement,' Ambrose said. 'My fault.' He got up and, with his back to us, made another gesture across the open space of the door, suggestive of pulling aside a curtain. He whispered a few words, then sat down again.

Ascertaining that we didn't actually want him for anything, Clement took his leave with dignity, closing the door carefully behind him.

'How did you do that?' I asked Ambrose.

'Quite simple, really. I made a barrier on the astral plane. Clement sensed it unconsciously – that is, with his astral senses – and it affected him.'

'What *is* this astral plane that everybody talks about all the time?' said Charlie in a complaining tone. 'You know, I've never really understood.'

'Nor me,' I said.

Ambrose, becoming ever more the benign elderly don, steepled his fingers and smiled. 'Elementary metaphysics, my dear Charlie, in a nutshell, just for you. Everything, including us, has an astral body and an astral existence as well as a physical one. There are various other planes, ever more rarefied and all-inclusive, but it's these two that matter here because they're what everyone is experiencing all the time, whether they're aware of it or not. The astral's not somewhere else, it's right here, *inside* the physical. On the physical plane we make things with our hands. On the astral we make them with our minds. It's a matter of switching channels, becoming conscious of what's unconscious for most. The trick is learning how to concentrate. I used the power of my will, and certain symbols that help me to focus. On the physical plane, everybody assumes they're sealed in their private little skulls, but on the astral all our minds are linked, so I can affect others – if I've got enough focus and power.'

'But you didn't have enough focus and power to keep Clement out,' I said.

'No, I told you I wouldn't be able to, if in his own mind he had a strong intention to come in.'

'And if someone had a very strong intention, such as escaping from a burning building . . .'

'That's the extraordinary bit. I can't imagine anyone with the power to stop them, unless . . .'

'Unless?'

'You said the two people were trapped in the building, but the police told you no bodies were found.'

'I reckon they were lying to protect the sensibilities of the public.'

'If they'd found bodies, why conceal it? The public adores that sort of thing. But maybe there weren't any bodies. Any *physical* bodies.'

'You mean they were ghosts or spirits or something like that?' Charlie said. 'Like Auntie Hilda.'

'Not all that much like your Auntie Hilda, apparently. She's a dear. There are far stranger entities on the astral than your garden-variety domestic ghost or ancestral spirit. These chaps seem to be distinctly unfriendly.'

'I thought it was whimsy, my calling them demons,' I said. 'At the time, I believed I was tripping and they were projections of my subconscious, but right from the start I had the feeling that they were some kind of horrid simulacra, not human at all. Their hair was too perfect, and they didn't blink. And they made me so afraid, it was like they were poisoning the air, so maybe I wasn't that far off.'

'But demons don't really exist, do they?' Charlie asked. 'I mean, *really*?'

'Of course they do,' said Ambrose. 'They take many forms, and go by many names.'

A shudder of dread ran through me, a shadow of the paralysing terror that their presence had evoked. The first time, I could blame it on having a gun pointed at me, but the second time, in the alley behind number eleven, I'd not been in grave danger. They didn't even know I was watching, yet the fear crept into me, numbing mind and body. If Mr Greyling had indeed brought about their demise in a hellfire of their own raising, that was fine by me.

'But if they were astral,' Charlie said, 'how come everyone saw them? Most people don't see ghosts or spirits or demons. They don't see entities. Thank God, I might add.'

'If a ghost or a spirit or a demon is defined as something people generally can't see,' said Ambrose, 'obviously if you and others can see it, you'll decide on the spot that it's not one of those. How do you know half the people you see aren't some sort of astral entity?'

'I never thought of that,' said Charlie. 'That's bloody unnerving, that is.'

'Just being realistic,' said Ambrose. 'What do you know? Only what your senses tell you. In dreams, you see, taste, touch and it seems perfectly real at the time. You have no basis in reason for assuming that what your senses are telling you right now is any more – or less – real than a dream. It's a construct. It's *your* construct, maintained by your ideas and beliefs and assumptions. And one mind can influence another's sense perceptions and emotions, as I've demonstrated in my feeble way. I made Clement believe the door was locked, I made him reluctant to cross the threshold, I made him feel something that his mind interpreted as a cobweb. It's only reasonable to think that with more skill and power I could . . . do more.'

Ambrose had taken himself off soon after, pleased to have left us with the nature of the astral plane to ponder, but I was incapable of further pondering. Charlie suggested a restaurant, a nightclub, but all I wanted was to go home, go to bed, go to sleep, in the hope that I would awaken tomorrow in my comfy old universe, the one without an astral plane – at least not one that impinged so violently upon the everyday fabric of my existence. The one without demons.

4

Curiouser and Curiouser

❧

A Mysterious Package. Rubicon, Erstwhile
and Foghorn. A Strange Tea Party. Mrs Big
and the NOHRM. An Offer I Couldn't Refuse. What
the Negatives Revealed. Binoculars Man.
Mr Big Delivers an Envelope. Escape
to America.

Despite Charlie's assurances that he'd seen no dodgy characters near my flat, I was anxious about returning. He
reminded me that, sooner or later, I'd have to. I could either
abandon the place or go back to it, and if the latter, why wait?
'Like riding,' he said. 'Fall off, get right back on.'

Fall off again and this time break your neck, I thought.

'Get it over with,' he said. 'Prove to yourself there's nothing
to fear.'

You didn't see the gun in that girl's hand, I thought. But then
again, I was no longer sure that I really had. Perhaps I'd imagined
it, as Clement had imagined the cobweb.

Charlie walked me home. When we got to my street we strolled
twice past without stopping, then made a quick dash in. I closed

the door behind us, locked it, stepped into the sitting room and flipped on the lights.

At first I thought the place was as I'd left it, then I noticed that the carved rosewood box on the coffee-table was open, exposing my modest stash of drugs (some black hash, some Moroccan hash and a few tabs of acid). Next to it was an unfamiliar object, about the size of a shoebox, wrapped in black plastic.

I had just picked it up to examine it when two men emerged from my bedroom. Not demon-simulacra, these were ordinary, middle-aged men in cheap suits and sturdy shoes, with untidy hair and bleary eyes.

'Welcome home, luv,' said one.

'You're busted, sweetheart,' said the other.

Charlie was sent away, calling over his shoulder that he was getting me the best lawyer in London. I was handcuffed and taken to the police station, where I was questioned and urged to confess. I kept repeating that I wanted to see my lawyer.

After a couple of hours a Mr Inch (or perhaps it was Pinch) appeared, from the venerable firm of Rubicon, Erstwhile and Foghorn (or something like that). He arranged for us to have a private conference, but as it was in a room with a large mirror, I concluded that 'private' was a relative term.

He didn't waste any time. 'Your situation is very grave. If convicted for drug-dealing you face at least fifteen years in prison.'

'But I'm innocent,' I said, thus demonstrating what an innocent I was.

He gave me a patient look. 'There is evidence against you.'

'What evidence?'

'A package found in your flat contains a kilo of white powder. They've sent it off to be tested.'

'I don't know what it is, but it doesn't belong to me.'

'They believe it's heroin.'

'That's ridiculous. I don't even like heroin.'

'So you admit having used it.'

'Once. I didn't particularly care for it, so I never took it again.' It was my turn to put on a patient expression.

'Believe it or not,' he said, 'I am on your side.'

Could have fooled me, I thought, but bit my tongue.

He glanced at his notepad. 'Your fingerprints are on the package.'

'I picked it up to see what it was.'

'And you maintain that you'd never seen it before.'

'Yes, I maintain that because it is true.'

'But the other substances are yours?'

'Well, yes. Only some hash and some acid.'

He tsked and shook his head. 'Juries, I'm afraid, are frequently incapable of making fine distinctions. Drugs are drugs in most people's eyes.'

'But I'm no dealer. The idea is absurd. They'll never find anyone who's bought drugs from me.'

'Are you prepared, then, to say from whom you buy drugs?'

'I don't buy drugs. I'm a critic. People give me presents.'

He sniffed in a way that suggested he didn't believe me, but thought it was a good answer all the same.

'You were sent down from Oxford for . . .' he looked again at his notes, '. . . running an opium den in your rooms.'

'Well, not a den, exactly. And not only opium. I was conducting experiments into the nature of consciousness.'

'For which you charged your fellow students five shillings a go.'

'Which barely covered expenses. And how do you know about that, anyway?'

He ignored the question. 'I have to tell you that it will be difficult to defend you on this charge. The police and the courts feel quite strongly these days that they need to make an example of people like you. This case is precisely the sort of thing they've been looking for.'

'It has to be a set-up. There's no other explanation possible.' At the time, I saw no link between Golden Square and my bust, but could two such extreme events in the space of thirty-six hours be unconnected?

'Why would anybody "set you up" in this way?' His enunciation of the quotation marks carried a considerable weight of disbelief.

I told him about the incidents in Golden Square, the green van, the three visitors and the fire. I suggested he get hold of the complaint I'd made to the police constable yesterday. Only this morning, I told him, I'd seen the van outside my flat and hadn't dared return. Plenty of opportunity for someone to break in and plant that package, then tip off the police.

Mr Inch took notes as I spoke, which I found encouraging. Perhaps with his help I'd finally be able to figure out what was going on. I can, however, read upside down, and I saw that he'd underlined 'LSD', then moved on to scribble *Delusional. Paranoid. Get psych. eval. Poss. defence insanity/incapacity*.

A policeman entered with a note for Mr Inch. He read it (unfortunately I couldn't see it), stood up and left without a word. I was escorted back to my cell.

I had a brief, forlorn hope that I might still be tripping and this was just another chapter, a Bad one, in the very strange trip that had begun in Golden Square. But no, this event had the unambiguous, brutal kick of reality. Fifteen years! It might as well have been a life sentence; it felt like a death sentence. It was the end of everything. Even if I survived, by the time I got out I'd be over forty, too old to enjoy life. Images and memories piled into my mind – all the things I loved, all the things I'd never do again. I was on the beach at St Ives, dancing barefoot at sunset; I was wandering the flower market in Covent Garden at dawn, buying armfuls of lilies, hollyhocks, carnations, giddy with the fragrance . . . I sat shivering on the hard bench, numb with shock and despair.

About an hour later I was taken from my cell to another interview room, this one with no mirrors. Mr Inch came and sat beside me. He said nothing and did not return my questioning glances. His compressed lips suggested he might have had something to say but could or would not speak. The thought crossed my mind that, under some new judicial procedure I'd not heard of, I'd already been tried, convicted and sentenced, and was about to be locked away without further ado.

The door opened and a policewoman came in with a tray, which she placed on the table. On the tray was a china teapot in a lilac floral pattern with gilt trim, matching cups, saucers, milk jug and sugar bowl, silver cake forks and spoons, tea strainer and sugar tongs, diminutive linen napkins in silver napkin rings and a plate of pink-iced seed-cake slices laid out in a circle. There was something very disquieting about this array, despite – or because of – its absolute, one might even say aggressive ordinariness.

The WPC stepped back to the wall as an older woman entered and sat opposite. Well-coiffed grey hair, smart tweed suit, specs on a sparkly chain riding a generous bosom. She had a file, which she opened on the table before her. I saw that it contained not only the record of my arrest, but also the complaint I'd made, with its mention of guns and debt collectors and – the constable had misspelled it – Pymander Productions and Monad Management.

'Thank you,' she said to the WPC. 'You may go.' The woman left. 'And you too,' she said to Mr Inch, who made a small noise that might have wished to be a protest but never got that far. He left.

'I'll be Mother, shall I?' she said, just as I was thinking that she reminded me of my mother, but in some sort of theoretical form – Mum as she imagined that others wanted her to be.

'I suppose no one's even offered you a cup of tea. You poor dear, you must be dying of thirst. Sugar? One lump or two?'

Her manner of speaking, too, was exactly my mother's, though I used to get the feeling, with Mum, that a trace of irony lurked behind the tone. Maybe that was wishful thinking on my part. Here, there was not the slightest suggestion of irony, or perhaps there was so much that we'd gone past the saturation point into some kind of sincerity.

'A little slice of seed cake?'

'Yes, please. Thank you.'

She had not been introduced and never gave me a name. Too dazed to be inventive, I started thinking of her as Mrs Big. Whatever this was, I had no choice but to go along with it. Mrs Big watched as I ate the seed cake and sipped my tea. She didn't say it, but I could hear her thinking, There now, that's better, isn't it? and felt myself nodding in reply.

Things had suddenly taken a turn for the very strange. If this was reality, it was trippier than a lot of trips. Had I perhaps entered a previously unknown state of constant trip? I used to think that would be wonderful, but now I wasn't so sure.

The policewoman came in with a box, which she left on the table next to the tea tray. It contained my possessions – the contents of my shoulder bag and pockets – which I'd been obliged to relinquish when I was brought in. Mrs Big examined my notebook with close attention.

'You are a journalist, is that right?' she said.

I nodded.

'And you specialise in contemporary culture. What a fascinating life you must lead.' Her tone was friendly, conveying to my frightened mind a reassuring sense of calm authority: everything would now be all right. She explained that her department, the National Office of Human Research Management, took an interest in 'current thought'. The noble servants of the NOHRM

71

laboured unceasingly on behalf of the British People, small but deeply worthy cogs in the vast, benevolent and ever-expanding apparatus of Our Government, which has the best interests of All of Us at heart. Perhaps she didn't put it quite like that, but that was the gist. She was the good guys.

Her voice droned on, comforting and soothing. No, actually, it was more than soothing, it was positively hypnotic. Her words seemed to be floating in my head and I wasn't sure if she'd spoken aloud. I answered . . . but had I spoken or only thought my replies?

'And then there is the small matter of the white powder found in your flat.' She gave me an understanding smile: these minor details were so tedious, but they must be addressed. 'Until it is tested in the laboratory, we don't know what it is. It might be heroin, or it might be some harmless substance, such as flour.'

The image that arose was of Schrödinger's cat, which exists in the dual state of alive/dead until you open the box to see. I pictured a little white cat made of heroin and a little white cat made of flour. I remembered that my conversation with Greyling had touched on the Uncertainty Principle. This could be the dominant *leitmotif* of the trip. If this was a trip.

'What would you like it to be?' Mrs Big asked.

'I prefer the flour cat,' I said, before I could stop myself.

'A wise choice.' Had she read my mind? It seemed she understood my reference. There was a deep, purring complacency in her manner that suggested an enormously powerful, well-oiled machine running with perfect efficiency. I had the impression that she really could, by an act of will, make the cat what she wanted it to be before the box was opened.

All this friendliness, I sensed, was a pretext, a blind, a cover for something else. She was trying to get at me. Instinctively, I concealed my wariness, allowing myself to appear vulnerable and afraid, which I certainly was, and deeply compliant, which I have never been.

A part of me was separating from the scene before me, with its tea set and polite conversation, like a life capsule detaching from the besieged mother ship. I began to withdraw, to tiptoe off into the darkness behind my face, leaving a hollow actor, a mask of me, to continue the charade.

Had I been drugged? Was there something in the tea? The cake? That hideous pink icing? I noticed that Mrs Big was not eating or drinking. The shell of ordinary reality cracked and I got a glimpse of her as she really was: deadly, rapacious and icy, icy cold. Later, psychiatrists would make much of this, inducing me to pretend that it had been a reaction to a Mother-figure, but I knew this was no ordinary human being. I'd fallen again into the hands of a demon-simulacrum, like the others horrifyingly banal in form, but subtler and more powerful.

She was leafing through my notebook; she was advancing into my mind. I left the outer part of me conversing with her and started building inner walls. It was my first lesson in dissembling on such a scale and for such stakes, and I was learning fast. The only way to win was to pretend to lose. If I showed that I knew what she was, I was certain she'd kill me.

Mrs Big arrived at the pages in my notebook that covered my investigation of Luce and the Photons, Pymander Productions, Monad Management. I felt her attention quicken: this was what she was after. Certain that she had neutralised my defences, she coiled a tentacle around the events of Golden Square and began to squeeze.

Ignorance, I told myself. Ignorance and stupidity, stupidity and indifference, indifference and apathy, apathy and ignorance. I piled these up like a wall of marshmallows, spongy and insipid. Oh yes, of course I liked Luce and the Photons, everyone did. I let myself babble on the subject for some minutes. I really had no idea what had happened at number eleven Golden Square, but was certain it had been a silly prank.

And what did I know about Pymander Productions and Monad Management? Nothing, absolutely nothing, I was able to say truthfully.

Her next tentacle probed for Greyling. Who? No, I don't think I ever caught the bookseller's name. He seemed a nice old fellow, I said, as I sent him hastily down a rabbit hole in the back cellar of my memory and covered it over with marshmallows.

Did my stupid act take her in? Did I succeed in deceiving her? Or did she decide that it served her just as well to allow me to believe that I had deceived her into believing that my compliance was genuine? Who was deceiving whom?

Gradually I felt her tentacles withdraw. She poured me a fresh cup of tea. Lifting her handbag (black, capacious, steel-clasped) onto her lap, she rummaged within and brought out an envelope, which she placed on the table and pushed across to me. 'Go on, open it,' she said.

I opened it. It contained a bundle of five-pound notes, wrapped in a band stamped '£100'.*

'We would like you to work for us.'

In these perilous times, Mrs Big explained, the interests of The Nation, indeed of All Humanity, were subject to threats from every quarter; thus a constant and subtle counter-war has to be waged. The insatiable machinery of this war must be fed, and information was the soup it craved. One of the tasks of the NOHRM was to supply this rare brew. Like the magical soup in a fairy tale, it required a bit of everything. The irregular corners of society that were my native habitat contained, she told me, certain important ingredients difficult for the average civil servant to acquire.

All I had to do was what I did anyway: gadding about, partic
ipating, observing. I was to make regular reports and occasionally

---

* At the time a substantial though not staggeringly large amount.

investigate particular subjects. If I accepted the offer, the record of my arrest would vanish and a regular cash stipend would be provided – the £100 was just a retainer.

Of course I accepted. Fear and greed are the two great tools of the Oppressors; fear has always been far more effective with me. That well-dressed, grey-haired, smooth-talking creature scared the shit out of me; the idea of fifteen years in prison did not exactly cheer me either. I chose to appear to be thoroughly bought.

It was getting on for four a.m. when I was released. Charlie was waiting outside the police station and took me straight to his house. I broke down in sobs of relief as soon as we were inside the door; the numbness washed away and I looked deeply into the chasm on whose edge I'd been teetering. A few hours in a police station had reduced me to jelly; fifteen years in prison . . . I had to run to the loo to be sick.

Charlie sent for a bottle of the '55 Bollinger – 'Perfect for an unsettled tummy' – then for some scrambled eggs and toast when I realised I was starving. He was bubbling over with questions that I couldn't answer. It was nothing so crude as being sworn to silence, or forced to sign the Official Secrets Act. But it had been made quite clear that I was not to tell anyone.

'Naturally,' Mrs Big had said, 'it is best for all concerned if you remember that this is a private arrangement. Just between us.' If my relationship to the NOHRM was known, I understood that I would at once become useless. A box of white powder could be made to appear anywhere at any time.

So, feebly improvising, I told Charlie it had all been a mistake: they'd wanted the people in the flat upstairs. Pleading exhaustion, I wiped the last of the scrambled eggs from my plate with the final bit of toast, washed it down with champagne, stretched out on the sofa, pulled a cushion over my head and went to sleep.

When I awoke Charlie had gone out. I discovered to my regret that the events of the last couple of days were still firmly lodged in my memory, tangled as ever, not having sorted themselves out at all while I slept, let alone disappeared as I'd hoped. If anything, my confusion had multiplied.

What had happened at that strange tea party in the police station? Apparently I'd been recruited to work for the government in exchange for some money and the expunging of the record of my arrest – which, it was pretty clear, they'd engineered in the first place. I'd figure out how to deal with my new role as a secret agent in due course. But the manner of that recruitment, my perception of Mrs Big as another demon-simulacrum – had that been real, or the delusion of an exhausted, confused person in a terrifying situation, well primed, after Ambrose's comments, to see demons everywhere? A mind-altering drug in the pink icing? It was, I had to admit, exactly the sort of thing I'd relish as a fictional scenario.

At first I'd assumed that Mr Big and the Golden Square arsonists (whatever they might be) were among the Enemies of the State with whom Mrs Big and the noble NOHRM were locked in battle, but I had to wonder. Maybe giving them the same name had been not a failure of imagination but the recognition of affinity. Both seemed to be very interested in Luce and Pymander Productions/Monad Management. What had Mr Big been after in Golden Square? What had Mrs Big been after when she probed my mind and memory? Did they think I was part of PP/MM and/or Luce and the Photons?

Some sort of a deadly game was going on, though I had no idea what its objectives might be. I thought again of Alice, who stepped through the looking glass one day and found herself a pawn in a bizarre chess game. If that's what this was, I suspected that I too was the merest pawn, and I didn't even know if I was black or white.

It was with no little regret that I decided I must finally rule out my two preferred explanations: that it had been a prank or an acid trip of ambiguous origin, duration and scope. 'Real', of course, is a relative term, and depends on so many parameters that are themselves of debatable reality, but I thought it prudent to accept, at least as a working hypothesis, that these events had been and continued to be real in a way that was not only relevant but possibly crucial to me and the particular congruence of spacetime that I called my life. I was unsure of what I'd taken on as an agent of the NOHRM, but had a suspicion there might be more to it than Mrs Big had said. I was in her power no matter what; the question remained of whether I could manoeuvre on this chess board in such a way as to keep her off my back while pursuing my own objective: Luce.

It was midday by the time I left Charlie's, a cool, drizzly day. I went to my Egyptian café, took a seat in the comfortable back room and ordered my usual coffee. Had I been here only yesterday? I felt like I'd crossed the abyss and returned since that time. I gazed fondly at the grimy upholstery of the wall benches, the scarred tables, the deft, silent motions of Ahmet – waiter, chef and proprietor – as he moved among the tables. The patrons, almost all elderly Arab men, chatted quietly to each other, sucked their shishas, exhaled clouds of fragrant smoke. The walls displayed posters of the Pyramids and the Sphinx, eternal mysteries beguilingly laid out under eternally sunny skies. Part of me wanted to go straight to the airport and get the next flight out of town, I cared not where. It was a strategy that had served me well in the past. Nothing like arriving in a strange city with only the clothes one stood in (and one's American Express card, of course) to shake off stale obligations and give a fresh perspective.

But no. I was still determined to find Luce, though the task had grown a bit more complicated. Mr and Mrs Big were both interested in Luce, either directly, for himself, or in relation to the still enigmatic Pymander Productions and Monad Management; therefore it might be wise to give up my own quest for him. But I never seriously considered that. Luce had lit a flame in me that was later to be diagnosed as an obsession of which I needed to be cured. And although I have for many years pretended to be cured of it, I have never once considered allowing myself to be even slightly cured of it: to be cured would be to die, though I don't think even that would effect a cure in me. I would go to death in the hope of meeting Luce again; I would go happily.

My dilemma was how to pursue my goal without leading the Bigs to it, all the while pretending not to know that I knew what they were after. My mission was, as it still is, to elucidate Luce. If I had to deceive the whole world in order to achieve it, that's what I would do.

On the counter as I paid my bill was a box collecting donations for Palestinian refugees. Not without a tiny twinge of regret, I stuffed Mrs Big's hundred pounds into it. Greed, as I said, is not my weakest point. Ahmet saw what I did, and his eyebrows shot up to his turban. I pressed my finger to my lips and smiled. He didn't say a word.

At the photo lab I collected the prints I'd ordered from the Golden Square negatives and took some stick for requesting an overnight express job, then not turning up for two days. I headed to the park, where I hired a boat and rowed out onto the Serpentine. In the middle of the water I felt reasonably safe and blissfully alone. I lit a joint and examined the photographs at last.

There were six. The first showed a barren desert landscape with a pile of old car tyres in the foreground. The next, a crossroads in a similar landscape with a road sign rendered all but illegible by a profusion of bullet holes. What could be read of the two place names seemed to be in English, but this was certainly not England. America? Australia?

The next, I was thrilled to see, was surely the one that had been used as the cover of the *Human* album: the empty landscape, the single figure standing in the distance, arms outstretched. Then came two frames that showed the same figure in motion, dancing or leaping with arms raised in a wild gesture, blurring through the air against a clear sky. The last showed a person sitting on the porch of a house. A wide-brimmed hat was pulled low, the face was in deep shadow and partly turned away but one could discern the line of a strong nose, the set of a firm jaw, a long, slightly smiling mouth. If this was Luce, it was the only image in existence that showed even a glimpse of his features. The background of paint-peeling clapboard and sagging screen door did not help to narrow down the location.

Glancing over my shoulder, I noticed a man on the bridge with binoculars. A bird-watcher? Could he have seen the pictures over my shoulder? I put them away; when I looked again he'd gone. Christ, was I becoming paranoid? The anti-drug propaganda was always screaming warnings about psychosis, schizophrenia, paranoia. Don't be ridiculous, I told myself firmly. Weird shit really has been going on. I rowed slowly back to shore.

A man in a checked suit with binoculars around his neck was sitting on a bench overlooking the lake. Could it be the same fellow? I studied him covertly as I pulled up to the dock. He seemed bland and smooth like Mr Big, but there was also something of the government man about him. Then again, perhaps he was just an office worker doing a spot of bird-watching on his lunch break – a Thermos flask and a half-eaten sandwich sat beside him on the bench. He raised the binoculars to his eyes and scanned the lake. I turned hastily away and didn't dare look back, but I felt his gaze linger on me.

As I clambered out of the boat, Binoculars Man was recorking his flask and tidying the sandwich wrappings as though preparing to make a move. I went straight up to him.

'Seen any interesting birds?' I pointed to the binoculars.

His smile revealed a row of small, yellow teeth; he licked his lips delicately with a small, pink tongue. 'One or two.'

It occurred to me, belatedly, that some sort of sexual signalling might be involved here, the large binoculars a proclamation of his peccadillo – voyeurism, perhaps. And now had he taken me for a willing exhibitionist?

'Good luck,' I said, and walked briskly away, disentangling myself from the sticky web of innuendo into which I'd fallen. When I glanced back he was staring after me, the smile altogether gone from his face.

He might not have been anything other than he seemed, but the encounter increased my unease. I was feeling jumpy, constantly looking over my shoulder, expecting at every corner to see Mr or Mrs Big, or a platoon of bland-faced demon-simulacra, or a large green van. The very normality of the London day was jarring. Beneath its skin I sensed unknown forces contending in a conflict whose rules and reasons no one had bothered to explain to me.

I went to the British Library where I spent an hour poring over atlases and road maps of America and Australia, looking for towns whose names coincided with the few legible letters on the road sign in the photograph: a W and a possible GS from one, and a G or an O and, near the end, an I or L from the other. I was nearly ready to give up when I came across a tiny dot on a map of Nevada labelled Warm Springs, which was a scant hundred and fifty miles from another dot, called Gold Field. I recalled Luce and the Photons' song 'Shoot the Buddha on the Road to Emmaus', and remembered that Emmaus means 'warm springs'. Would Luce know that? He was obviously well read – all the cryptic clues to the secret gigs, the hidden meanings, the Classical and Renaissance references in the lyrics. I felt sure he'd had an education much like my own. Perhaps I'd known him at university. Maybe he'd even been one of the fearless questers who'd come to my 'opium den' to explore the nature of consciousness. Could that be why he'd seemed familiar, why I felt I knew him?

I studied the photographs. Yes, that had to be Luce in the desert, somewhere – I was now certain – near Warm Springs, Nevada. Was that where he'd written those amazing songs? And had he returned there, to that clapboard house, having accomplished whatever he'd set out to do? I had, at last, a destination and an excuse to get out of London.

From the nearest phone box I called my travel agent and booked an evening flight to Los Angeles via New York, then checked in with my service. They read me a message from Charlie: "'Where the . . .'" I'm sorry, but I won't say that word, "are you. Have those demons carried you off. Do you need rescuing again. Call me at once.'"

I rang Charlie and told him what the photographs showed, and that I was heading for Warm Springs, Nevada. He volunteered to come with me because, he said, I required looking after, but I told him I needed him to stay in town to keep an eye open for a possible reappearance of Luce. In any case I prefer travelling alone. I went home for a shower and change of clothes.

Half an hour later I left my flat, only to find a big green van parked in front. Thank God the street was busy, thronged with people on their way home from work or heading out for the evening. There was a constable at the corner, chatting with the greengrocer. I was unlikely to be murdered on the spot – though of course I'd have described most of the events of the last couple of days as unlikely. These thoughts whizzed through my mind in a second or two while I remained frozen on my doorstep.

The simulacrum with the perfect brown hair and the beige shirt got out, opened the side door of the van and gestured for me to get in.

'You must be joking,' I said.

In the shadows at the back of the van I glimpsed the bland face of Mr Big and such a wave of fear passed through me that I thought I was going to be sick on the pavement, but I pushed it down and made myself look at him. He gave me his dead-fish stare, rotating his head as though performing a mechanical scan. I glared right back. It was like those staring contests I used to have with Neil when we were children: the immense and silent hostility of implacable foes.

Was Mr Big trying to hypnotise me with his baleful gaze, bend me to his will, force me like some zombie to get into the van? The hell he would. I stared furiously back. Then the absurdity of the situation struck me like a puff of fresh air and I stuck out my tongue.

I wouldn't say he melted on the spot like the Wicked Witch of the West, but something definitely wavered. He withdrew his gaze, turned away and passed a blank white envelope to the young man, who handed it to me. They drove off.

Shaking with the aftermath of fear, I remained rooted to the spot, staring at the thing in my hand. The last time I'd held a blank white envelope, I recalled, it had been an invitation to the secret gig. Somehow, I knew this did not contain anything so delectable. It was another of those items like the lilac and gilt tea set whose glaring ordinariness was, in context, bizarre and deeply threatening.

I felt it cautiously. It had little thickness and I guessed it contained no more than a sheet or two of paper. I opened it. One sheet of paper and two five-pound notes. The paper bore a single typed sentence: 'Submit fortnightly reports to P.O. Box 4655, London WC.' One question, then, was settled: Mr and Mrs Big were indeed related. But were they mere human civil servants or malign astral entities?

The van had disappeared, though they might have left someone to watch me, perhaps follow me. Peering up and down the road, I saw no lurking simulacra, although the more I studied the passers-by, the more artificial they all appeared.

I set off towards Oxford Street. I never travel with luggage, so was carrying only my usual shoulder bag, having added a few essentials. I strolled into a few shops, meandering towards Selfridges with its labyrinthine back stairs, changing rooms, toilets and multiple entrances. Someone was collecting for the Palestinian refugees; I gave him Mrs Big's money. I spent twenty minutes in Selfridges, up, down and around, and when I left I was fairly sure no one was following me. I went into the tube, got on and off at a few stops, then dashed up to the street, hailed a cab and told the driver to take me to Heathrow via Brondesbury Park, on the western fringe of London, a road that is long, wide, featureless and deserted at all times of day or night. I asked him to drop me off, drive around the neighbouring streets and pick me up in five minutes. During that time not a single car or pedestrian passed by. A few doors down, one woman put her rubbish out. A man near the far end of the street was watering his front garden. Neither paid me any attention. My taxi reappeared, I got in and we drove off. For the first few miles I kept watch out of the back, but no one seemed to be following us, though when we got into the heavier traffic on the A4, I had to give up. I arrived at Heathrow with a scant hour to spare before my flight.

On the way to the gate I bought a box of chocolates and arranged to have it sent to Charlie. I also wrote and posted a brief note to Mr Greyling, saying I needed most urgently to speak to him and asking him to leave a telephone number with my service. I addressed it to the bookshop at number eleven Golden Square, in the hope that it would be redirected.

Now.

Golden Square is smaller than I remember, and much
cleaner. Nearly posh, where it used to be pleasantly
seedy. I step forward, uncertain. I shouldn't have
come; I hadn't meant to. I've been coming down to the
British Library (oh, how I miss the old one) from time
to time for research, but not venturing further into
town. I've avoided my old haunts, determined to eschew
cheap nostalgia. What do I want here? What do I expect?

Everything has changed, the past has been erased
and the space rewritten many times since I last set
foot here, but I do sense a welcome, a familiarity,
a signal of recognition passing back and forth between
place and self.

I make my way around the square. It's lunchtime,
the first really warm day of the year, and the fizz
of ebullient energy that comes over London and
Londoners on this sort of day is irresistible. Someone
smiles at me for no reason as we pass on the crowded
pavement; people never used to do that. I find myself
smiling back. London is nowhere near as English as it

was fifty years ago; I haven't yet decided whether that's a good thing.

Number eleven Golden Square is externally unchanged. A sign in the ground-floor window, where Greyling's bookshop used to be, indicates that this is now the Golden Square Gallery. Their logo - and it gives me a shiver of recognition - is a golden square with a spiral inscribed, just like on the *Human* album. Not too odd, I tell myself; anyone could make that association with the Golden Section. Graphically, it's excellent. But I'm getting that tickle at the back of my mind again, the one that tells me something to do with Luce is happening. *Are you here*? I ask, and I'm sure I hear her laughter.

I go in.

They're showing video art by an American called Robert Cello. There's a bit of a queue to enter the room which contains the main piece, and visitors are passing the time watching a taped interview with the artist, shown on a continuous loop in a side room. I stand in precisely the spot where I sat and drank tea and ate amaretti biscuits and discussed the Uncertainty Principle and Alice in Wonderland and J. W. Dunne with Greyling. I wonder if I will ever have that sort of conversation again. Am I succumbing to cheap nostalgia? I push my memories aside and concentrate on the present.

On the TV, the artist is talking. Rather an old man, I think, then realise with an inward laugh that he's probably in his early sixties, a decade younger than I. I don't feel as old as I used to; it must be my re-immersion in Luce that's making me think I'm in my twenties again. Robert Cello is being asked about his influences. I hear him say 'New York' and '1972' and

85

then 'eleven Broome Street'. My heart makes such a leap that I have to sit down. I slide into the nearest chair. Did I really hear that? Yes, he's speaking of the short-lived gallery on Broome Street in Lower Manhattan where Peter Lucian had a mind-blowing multi-media exhibit . . . before the demons torched it.

I watch the interview through a second time. Could he be that bewildered chap who'd complained, when he came out, about the time-distortion? Was he the fellow who couldn't stop weeping, or the one who couldn't stop laughing? He's speaking of it as an event far beyond a merely aesthetic experience. It was, he says, a huge jolt to his entire being - and here he gestures with both hands, making an exploding cloud around his head - that completely and permanently altered his sense of who and what he was. He's talking about an understanding that came to him of the relation of truth and beauty, of what it is to be human, and what art is or could be. The interviewer asks him who the artist was. He replies that he doesn't know; the exhibit was presented anony-mously, the gallery burned down and although he tried for years to find out the artist's name, he never could. Tears come to my eyes as I listen. This man was touched by Luce and it changed his life, too.

I go into his art. The room is about twenty foot square; every surface - walls, ceiling and floor - is high-definition screen. Technology has come some way since Luce made do with a TV and a pair of headphones. But then Luce was a god and Robert Cello is merely a human artist, though I think he is a great one. Some spark of divinity was awakened in him; it's made him more human than most.

Ten people at a time are let into the room; we can

86

sit on a chair or the floor or stand, though we're advised to pick one position and remain there. If you suffer from vertigo, we're warned, you should certainly sit. I choose a chair near a corner.

Of course the technology is astounding; it simulates the complete immersion in the experience that Luce achieved by other means. Sound and image move together, twisting and accelerating. It's like being inside a living kaleidoscope. A rush of upward-falling rain, accompanied by an ascending cascade of tinkling, chiming sound . . . I see why they warned of vertigo; I'm very glad I'm seated. The rain becomes a river, circling the room; a funnel spins beneath the floor. People gasp. Someone who had chosen to stand makes the abrupt decision to sit. The river is slowly becoming fire, the floor a glowing caldera. I don't precisely feel that I'm burning, as Luce would have been able to make me, but I feel what it would feel like to be burning. The sound is a roaring screaming howl and there must be some massive woofers set into the floor, because I sense a subsonic vibration in my bones. I'm perspiring a little. Faces appear in the flames that surround us: people and animals, angels and monsters. The fire becomes solid ropes coiling, tightening. I'm feeling truly squeezed, it's getting claustrophobic. Darkness falls suddenly with a whoosh, leaving after-images of flittering, floating things that coalesce into a bird with wings of pleated flame, circling a sky that turns from black to lilac, green, blue. The bird shatters the sky, which flutters and falls as rose petals.

The piece ends; we file out past others waiting to go in. People are blown away, but it didn't have the Lucian power to reach in and manipulate one's fundamental

87

perception of reality. I could observe it and observe myself observing it. I knew at all times that I was sitting in a gallery in Golden Square. It doesn't penetrate as far or as deep as Luce did. But it's fabulous art.

'The installation must have cost a fortune,' I say to one of the gallery girls. It did, I'm told, but they've already taken orders for eighteen 'personal' pieces, to be custom installed in a room of your choice, starting at £3 million. Blimey.

I take a page from my notebook and scribble a brief message of appreciation to Robert Cello, then I tell him that the artist at eleven Broome Street was Peter Lucian, who was also known as Luce of Luce and the Photons. The gallery girl promises to send it on to him.

As I leave the building I see a green van parked at the kerb. A hard hand of terror seizes my heart, my knees go weak and I stumble. As though in a nightmare, the door opens and Mr Big steps out. He hasn't aged a day since I killed him. I'm frozen on the steps of the gallery, washed through with fear, anger, dread. I reach into my pocket, but my gun's not there. Someone jostles me from behind, apologises profusely when I jump as though shot. I look back at the street. It's changed. It's Now, not Then – that's why I have no gun. It's not Mr Big; it's a short, chubby man in a grey suit. Just to be sure I look closely at his eyes and his hair. The hair is not especially neat; the eyes blink and move about in a recognisably human way. He's probably not a demon, unless they've got a lot better at simulating humans. The green van is actually blue. My fear fades, leaving me drained. I make my way back to Enfield in a daze.

5

The Revival of Warm Springs

✿

*The Miracles. The Voice of the Waters. The
Transmitter. Jay Cooper's Story. She Chopped Wood.
Another Painted Room. Red Fred's Vision. Police
Again. Arson Again. Rescue by Guardian Angel.
Another Roll of Film Destroyed. Escape by
Eighteen-wheeler.*

Nevada, May 1967

I drank Bloody Marys and slept fitfully and paced the aisles
from London to New York, New York to Los Angeles, rivers
and plains, cities and mountains passing underneath, unseen. At
LAX I hired a car – Ford Mustang, pale blue with a black soft
top and black seats (big mistake in hot, sunny places. I nicked
a towel from the first place I stopped) and set off for the unnerv-
ingly blank area near the centre of the map of the state of Nevada.

Hot, sweaty and way beyond tired, it was mid-afternoon when
I stopped at a Traveler's Lodge ('If You Want the Very Best' or
indeed the only place to lay your head for a hundred miles in
any direction), at Main Street and Route 6, which, although
identified by different styles of sign, were in fact the same road,

here temporarily existing, like Schrödinger's cat, in both states simultaneously and thus managing to intersect itself.

I fell asleep on the brown nylon bed and when I woke the setting sun was slanting in the window. My throat was parched. The room fridge, buzzing like a deranged hornet until I kicked it, offered a chilled Budweiser. I munched a packet of peanuts and watched TV: a country-music show. Tammy Wynette and George Jones sang 'My Elusive Dreams'. I went back to sleep and woke at one a.m. to a screen of scratchy static.

I turned off the TV and stepped outside. It was clear and cold; I dragged the bedspread from the bed and wrapped it around me. Across the road a bare flagpole made a hollow metallic clang as its taut cord snapped rhythmically in the wind. No other sound. A tumbleweed rolled by. A few steps beyond the parking lot and I was in the desert. No moon, but a sky full of coruscating stars. It seemed to me that I could 'wander on and on, between the black land and the icy stars, for ever in this bright night of Amenti,' as Luce sings in 'The Dream of Osiris'. I knew, I just knew that song had been written near here.

In the star-studded night, the Gnostic knows that not all contact with the higher circles is irredeemably lost, and that perhaps he can conquer his fate, break the ancient curse, which made the world a cheat and a sham, and cast us down, far from the sparkle and the blazing illumination of the hyper-world, down to the gloomy circle in which we live.[*]

When the diner opened at six I ate eggs and hash browns and drank vile American coffee. I had to wait until eight for the

[*] Jacques Lacarrière, *The Gnostics* (San Francisco: City Lights Books, 1989), p. 20.

general store to open so that I could buy more appropriate attire, my striped bell-bottoms and pink brocade jacket having drawn doubtful, amused or downright hostile glances. Unless I have a reason to stand out, I always prefer to adopt (like the ancient Rosicrucians) the habits and appearance of the people among whom I must live. (And now? I give, I sincerely hope, every indication of being as meek, insignificant and inconspicuous a creature as ever crawled the earth.) In Nevada I bought jeans, a lightweight chambray shirt for the hot days and a thick woollen sweater for the cold nights.

I drove east into the sun, stoked by the joy of adventure that comes over me whenever I find myself heading into the unknown. The road was a wavering, heat-shimmered line bordered by low cliffs and borne down upon by the turquoise stone-blue sky. The radio played dippy, twangy songs about men and women and the neurotic ties that bind them, interspersed with and virtually indistinguishable from dippy, twangy ads for Pridee's Chevrolet Dealership, Wrigley's chewing gum, the ubiquitous Coca-Cola. News, delivered every fifteen minutes in serious yet folksy tones, consisted of tornado warnings, car crashes, oil prices, baseball scores, UFO sightings and casualty figures from the war *du jour*.

Warm Springs was larger and livelier than I'd expected. There was a motel and a saloon bar, a grocery store, a drugstore with soda fountain, a post office and a garage, a gift-shop-cum-general-store, and three churches (the Church of the Shining Virgin, the Church of the Blessed Holy Ghost and the Chapel of the Divine Visitation). I pulled into the motel; it was nearly full, but a single room had just become available.

I asked the pink-cheeked proprietress if there was a rodeo or some such big show in town; she told me it was always like this nowadays because of the springs. Wasn't that why I'd come? Since the springs started flowing again, everyone came for the springs. 'The lame and the halt, the blind and the dumb and the

91

not-quite-right-in-the-head,' she said with a cheery smile. 'We get 'em all, we bless 'em all and if the good Lord wills, they shall be healed.'

I had a shower, then went for a walk. It was baking hot and few people were about. At the tourist-information shack I collected a bunch of pamphlets and took them to the drugstore where I perused them over a tuna-fish sandwich and a sickly sweet iced tea at the soda fountain, perched on a chrome-banded stool beneath a slowly revolving fan.

The revival of Warm Springs had begun three years earlier, in 1964. The mineral springs, long dead and dry, had suddenly started flowing again, wondrous red chalybeate waters rising, washing away decades of detritus, filling the old pools. Right away, strange things started happening to people who bathed in the springs. There were healings – Barbie Miller's glaucoma, little Betty Cherskie's epilepsy, Henry Feinstein's emphysema, Gloria Simms's leukaemia – and visions: three of them, vouch-safed to a child of ten, an elderly widow and a well-respected local builder. All claimed that they saw a glowing figure hovering over the spring, who conveyed to them somehow – here the versions differed – an extraordinary sense of peace and well-being. Ever since then, miraculous healings had occurred regularly although not, it was freely admitted, to everyone.

After lunch I wandered over to the springs. There were sun beds, umbrellas, snack-sellers; there was a queue for the loos. I purchased a bathing costume and rented a towel from a brightly painted kiosk. As I changed in the bleach-scented locker room I tried to think of an ailment whose alleviation I could attempt, but all I came up with was a general psychological malaise, compounded of equal parts boredom, anxiety and impatience which, I suspected, had begun to afflict most of my generation for any number of good reasons.

I waded into the tepid water, paddled about for a bit, then

floated on my back. The voices of the other bathers receded to a blur and I gazed up at a sky of bluest blue, infinitely far above yet comforting as a blanket. I listened to the small noises of the waters. It seemed I could discern, at the very edge of hearing . . . not words, but perhaps the murmurings of an unworded tongue, a liquid language trickling subtly into my mind. An image came to me of an iridescent bird that flew through solid earth as though it was air. I thought of Luce and how he'd kissed me with his mind and I knew it was his voice I was hearing.

When I climbed from the pool, wrinkled at fingers and toes, my nerve fibres had been soothed, my uneasy inner bramble replaced with filaments of silk. I think some part of me realised even then that Luce had got inside me and was guiding me from within. I've never had a problem with that, other than the necessity of concealing it from others.

Late afternoon brought a cool breeze and in the freshening air I strolled around the town. I showed everyone I met the photos I'd found in Golden Square. Of course they recognised the cover of the famous *Human* album, and agreed that the terrain certainly looked a lot like it did around here, but their 'here' covered hundreds of square miles. No one recognised the person on the porch or the porch itself.

The busiest place in town turned out to be the Chapel of the Divine Visitation, headquarters of the extraterrestrial fanciers.* They claimed the figure seen in the three visions was a star-god from Antares, whose name, Kihala-Imsu, they translated as 'Light-bringer'.

They offered a free Antarean Scripture, transcribed from the trance-speech of their resident seer, who was also available for private consultations. Intrigued, I made a 'suggested donation' of

---

* Warm Springs is adjacent to the notorious top-secret Area 51, part of Andrews Air Force Base and suspected site of extraterrestrial activity.

fifty cents, sat down to wait my turn and leafed through the Scripture. It told how Kihala-Imsu, arriving from Antares with a mission to bring peace and enlightenment to the people of Earth, had been captured and imprisoned by The Government – here seen as a force of abstract but immensely powerful malevolence, whose sole purpose is to control and delude the gullible with the baubles of materialism, and crush anyone who dares to resist. Because of Kihala-Imsu's unwillingness to cause harm, it took him a long time to escape, but now he is free and wanders the earth incognito, doing good in whatever way he can and opening people's minds to the truth hidden behind the veils of earthly existence. His names and appearances are legion; he is known only by the blessings that spring up, flower-like, in his wake.

It now seems obvious that Kihala-Imsu was Luce herself, the story a mythically if not factually accurate précis of her life that trickled into the consciousness of these well-meaning people. That didn't occur to me at the time, of course; Luce was just a rock star. I merely thought it a charming scripture, and not too badly written as these things go. I noted its similarity to the Gnostic mythos, in which the soul, though by nature seeking the highest, is ensnared by the intrinsically evil terrestrial realm which traps us all in delusion. The Gnostic's task is to break free and regain his or her true, god-like nature. The Gnostic teacher, like Kihala-Imsu and, indeed, like Luce, is seen as an emissary from a higher plane of existence.

My turn came and I was shown to a curtained booth at the back. The Transmitter, as she liked to be called, was a middle-aged woman in a sprigged calico frock that left bare her rounded, freckled arms. She had dishwater-blonde hair, a placid, flabby face and eyes of milky blue, which gazed intently at me for a minute, then closed. She sighed once, and spoke.

'You have come from afar, and have further yet to go, further than you can imagine.'

I was unimpressed; I've been told virtually the same thing by every fortune-teller I've ever met.

'You are one of the chosen. Follow your thread and you will not go wrong.'

Again, all too typical, though the reference to the 'thread' certainly struck a chord. Naturally one is flattered to be 'chosen', though my effort to be cynical about it was undermined by the fact that I had myself decided back in London that Luce had indeed chosen me and placed that thread in my hand.

The Transmitter's eyes opened suddenly; she stared past me at something behind my left shoulder. Her gaze was so intense that I instinctively turned to see what she was looking at, but there was nothing. 'You are meddling with dangerous forces,' she hissed. 'Or they are meddling with you. You will not escape unscathed.'

A shiver passed through me, slicing my cynicism with an icy blade of fear. The little booth seemed to close in on me like a prison and I'm afraid I left rather precipitously, without thanking the Transmitter.

It was a relief to get outside, where the mundane sun was setting behind the long dry hills. Children skipped and scooted, women in frilled aprons smoked cigarettes and chatted across their garden fences, a sprinkler waved its water veils indolently back and forth. Whatever dreads the Transmitter had evoked faded in the ordinary air. I strolled to the end of the houses and beyond, into the desert. An eighteen-wheeler thundered by, spinning miniature dust devils in its wake. From the town came a gust of country music as the saloon doors opened and shut. The sky deepened to velvet-blue, stars began to glitter, lights came on here and there in the hills. The headlamps of occasional cars could be seen crossing the slopes that had appeared, in daylight, as uninhabited as the moon. Who lived up there? Ranchers, hermits . . . rock stars?

I stopped into the saloon for a beer and a cheeseburger; during a lull in the jukebox, I showed my photos around. More shaking heads, but one fellow named Red Fred sat up and jabbed a beefy finger at the photo of the figure dancing away into the distance.

'I seen him,' he said. 'Or someone just like him. Out in the desert coupla miles north of here. I seen him runnin' and leapin' along the ridge, wavin' his arms about, just like in your picture.'

'When was this? Recently?'

'Nah, year or two. Mebbe three-four. Heeah, time flies.'

'It sure does,' I said, and bought a round of beers for Red Fred and his mates. By then it was four in the morning, according to my jet-lagged inner clock, and I was yawning uncontrollably. I soon headed off to bed.

I awoke in the pre-dawn darkness, pulled on my clothes and went outside. It was so silent I could hear the faint crystalline chiming of the stars. I ran and danced into the desert. A coyote (I think) howled in the distance. I leapt and spun and whirled, 'The Dream of Osiris' playing in my head, and at last fell panting to the ground as the first red wisp of dawn appeared and extended to a glowing line across the eastern horizon. The sun rose hot and white into the wide, empty sky. I reminded myself to buy a pair of sunglasses. When the diner opened I had coffee and Danish, and they made me some sandwiches to take away.

I drove north out of town and up into the hills. From a distance they'd looked uniformly barren, but proximity revealed surprising variation. Shallow valleys opened out on either side, with irrigated orchards and pastureland. I went down every side road and followed it into the scrub, here and there finding tumbledown houses or mean shacks. The folks up here were a hardscrabble lot, suspicious of strangers and accessorised with shotguns and snarling dogs. I spent most of the time calling out my enquiries from the safety of the car. Anyone who bothered to look at my photos had nothing useful to say. One fellow strung me along for nearly half an hour, inviting me into his hovel, pretending to remember someone like that. But all he wanted was to sell me some moonshine. I bought a jug just to get away from him but never dared to try it. The fumes alone were combustible.

By mid-afternoon I'd covered most of the hills within several miles of Warm Springs, and it was hard not to feel discouraged. I pulled over in the shade of some trees of the sort I believe they call cottonwood, rousting out a brace of partridge from an adjacent shrub. I ate the last of my sandwiches. A buzzard circled the hillside above, diving down and out of sight. Near where it disappeared I glimpsed the chimney of a house. Intrigued, I turned the car and eased it down a narrow and very rutted track, bounced across a dry stream bed and ascended the further slope.

The track ended and I parked next to an ancient pickup truck. The buzzard screamed, high in the pale sky. There were no other signs of life. A little valley appeared below me and, screened by scrub oak, a house. My heart leapt. This had to be the one; I recognised the porch. Merrily whistling 'Shoot the Buddha' I made my way down the path.

The house was in a state of considerable dilapidation and seemed long-deserted, but from the opposite side came the sound of someone chopping wood, which stopped as I approached. I rounded the corner of the building and beheld a burly, brown-bearded man in the midst of a pile of split logs. His face bore a happy, expectant look which faded into disappointment when he saw me.

I introduced myself politely, mindful of the axe, which looked like a toy in his hands but could have dispatched me with a flick of his wrist.

He put it down and we shook hands. His name was Jay Cooper, and his handshake might have broken bones if he'd not had the tenderest manners imaginable. 'When I heard you whistling,' he said, 'I thought you were Lou. Lou used to whistle like that.'

I explained that I was looking for someone called Luce. Could his Lou be my Luce? I showed him the photos and the smile returned to his face. Yes, that was Lou. I got the impression that Jay was, if not exactly simple, definitely not overly complicated. I had photos of his friend; I whistled like his friend; I must be a friend, too.

I was elated. This was the first trace that I'd found – that anyone had ever found – of the person behind the mask of Luce. Here was someone who had known him, someone who had no doubt touched him, if only to shake hands. Here where I was standing, Luce must have stood. This view of the desert and distant mountains Luce had seen, too.

Jay invited me in with bashful courtesy; he didn't often get visitors, he said. He led me to the kitchen, where he evidently slept as well. Against one wall was a narrow bed, neatly made, with a grimy patchwork coverlet and a pillow from which I had to avert my eyes.

I sat on the one whole kitchen chair while he hurriedly wiped the table. I could tell that he had been house-trained at some point, and wished to do his best, but the rag with which he dabbed at the oilcloth was rank with grease and God knows what. This was one of those places where one gathers one's clothes about one and attempts to avoid all physical contact. I declined his offer of refreshment.

Jay was a sweet-natured, lonely man; once he started talking, I got the entire story of his life which, fortunately, had been largely uneventful. He and his sister Karen had grown up here, their parents long 'passed on'. Jay hadn't cared much for school though he'd been good at football, a solid defensive lineman until somebody trod on his ankle and he proved to have unusually fragile bones. He showed me the team picture, holding pride of place on the dresser between a twelve-volt battery and a jar of rusty nails.

Karen had liked 'reading and all that,' finished high school and gone on to secretarial college, acquiring a diploma which she took away with her to California. Jay breathed the name with awe; to him it was Shangri-La. He wasn't clear on when this had happened, but at some point she'd come back with two friends, Frankie and Lou. He was happy Karen had come back, and Frankie and Lou were nice, and made 'nice music'. He missed them.

I was fascinated to hear his impressions of Luce, or Lou. His friend Lou was a tall, skinny girl who dressed like a boy. Though I had thought of Luce as a man, a significant minority of people thought Luce was female, and I felt a touch of regret that they'd turned out to be right.

What colour were her eyes, her hair? This strained Jay's powers of description almost to breaking point. Eyes were grey-blue-green. Hair was 'different colours'. With a great deal of patience and persistence I gathered he meant that it was one colour, brown; then it was two colours, brown on the bottom, blonde on top; then it was blonde all over. I concluded: pale hair, dyed brown, growing out.

I asked what Lou was like. This was a tough question; his understanding did not extend into character or thought. To Jay, people were what they did in his presence. Things that happened outside his field of view, things that happened inside people's heads or hearts, did not register. What Lou did was: walk off into the desert, come back from the desert, sit looking at the desert. Sing, dance, whistle. Drink water. Eat hardly at all. Sleep hardly at all. Look at the stars all night. He added, in seriously impressed tones, that she was very good at chopping wood, could do it for hours and never tire. It was on this point that he was most voluble and articulate, describing in detail the power and elegance of her technique. Even the knottiest pieces yielded to a single blow, yet her judgement was so delicate, her control so absolute that she never struck too hard, embedding the axe awkwardly in the block.

Here was Jay, the sweetest, simplest guy you could imagine, and he'd lived with Luce. I gazed at him in a kind of wonder, touched, amused, affectionate and just a bit jealous. He had seen Luce close up, talked with her, sat with her, listened while she sang. It should have been me, I thought. I'd have been such a wonderful companion to her. Already I saw myself as someone who was in Luce's life, not merely an observer, a fan or a reporter. Every titbit of information I picked up about her, every story, every fragment, I collected with magnetic fervour. I drew these filings of her life to me with the inherent, inevitable attraction of like for like. I knew even then that our destinies were linked.

Frankie was described as Lou's brother, a tall man (Jay, about six feet, gestured above his own head) with reddish hair. He did not chop wood. Instead, he played the piano all day and half the night. I speculated – correctly as it turned out – that Frankie was the keyboard player I'd seen at the Camden gig. Could Karen be the third member of the band? I asked Jay, but he said Karen wasn't musical. She was a good cook, and 'awfully tidy, and really nice'. She baked pies and cleaned.

How long had they stayed? Time wasn't his strong suit. Less than a year, more than a week. His comments about Lou's dyed hair growing out suggested a few months at least.

'Where are they now?'

He frowned; this was another perplexing issue. Karen, he thought, might be back in California; from a drawer he dug out a scrap of paper with a scribbled address: 228 Waller Street, San Francisco.

'And what happened to Lou and Frankie?'

He rubbed his head with his big, blunt hands. They'd all gone away one day but only Karen had returned, and then she went away too and didn't come back. She'd been really upset and scared, but wouldn't tell him why. He 'hated it, hated it, *hated it*' when he couldn't fix things that were wrong.

To Jay, Lou and Frankie had appeared out of nowhere for no reason, then left for no reason. The world was like that, things being here, then gone. None of it had ever made much sense to him; he didn't mind that Lou and Frankie, also, had made no sense.

He led me, with shy pride, into the sitting room, whose walls were covered with paintings. I saw at once that they were by the same hand as the murals at Golden Square. This room did not seem to have quite the same time-distorting power, although perhaps its effects were mitigated by the fact that I was with Jay, who chatted happily and unceasingly about the minutiae of his life, locking me into the ordinary track of time.

As in Golden Square, the imagery danced along the border between abstraction and representation, with a distinctly hypnotic effect. Things seemed to shift beneath one's gaze, much as they do when one's tripping. There were trees and vines, clouds and stars, birds and strange part-human, part-animal forms. This was undoubtedly the work of Luce.

One scene was not abstract. It showed a child of perhaps five or six strapped into a chair with wires leading to its head, tubes and needles inserted in its arms. Its eyes were wide open, filled with fear and pain, but also rage. An evil-faced figure in a white coat and a surgical mask loomed over the child. A caption read 'Cold, fear, pain/the needle to the brain.' Lyrics similar to this appear on the *Human* album in the song 'Mad Matter Mind': 'When they pierce the vein/and stab your mind/and leave you blind/with fear and pain/the needle in your brain.'

As I gazed at the painting an echo of familiarity arose in my mind: it could have been taken directly from a persistent nightmare that had troubled my childhood. It had involved being tied down and tortured by doctors. How old had I been? I couldn't recall. The dream had eventually faded.

101

I now wonder whether Luce and I had been linked even then, when we were five or six. Had my nightmare been a reflection of her actual experience? There in Warm Springs, confronting the image on the wall, I had yet to learn of its significance in Luce's life but its emotive power was considerable. I couldn't bear to look at it for more than a few seconds: my body tensed all over as if in anticipation of horrendous agony. It made me want to scream, but it also made me want to kill that evil 'doctor'.

Jay was leaning against the wall by a figure part angel, part multi-pointed star, part green-leafed tree. He stroked it and smiled a smile of utter bliss. 'Lou made this for me. From the one in my head. The nice one.'

I took some pictures of the room to study later, but the Kodachrome I'd loaded was too slow for the poor light and I knew I wasn't getting any detail. I asked if I could come back the next day with faster film, and Jay agreed. He showed me around the rest of the house, but I saw no other signs of Luce. The sun had set by the time I left, promising over and over that I really would return.

My car wouldn't start. The battery was fine, I couldn't be out of petrol, a peek under the bonnet revealed no loose wires. I trudged back to the house, where Jay was pleased to see me again so soon. He was sure he'd be able to fix whatever was wrong – he got on well with cars. It didn't take him long to spot the puddle of oil on the ground beneath the engine; closer examination confirmed that I'd cracked the sump on the rutted track. Nothing for it – the car couldn't be driven. There was no phone; he'd drive me down to the Warm Springs garage. They'd send a tow truck.

In town, the garage owner said if it was all right with me, he'd get the car in the morning, since his truck was out on another call. I wasn't going anywhere tonight, was I?

Though I invited Jay to join me for a burger and a beer, he

declined. He didn't like so much noise and so many people, he said, climbing back into his pickup. Anyway he'd see me tomorrow, wouldn't he? I assured him that he would.

From the pay phone in the saloon I called the car-hire company; they said they'd deliver a new car to my motel first thing in the morning. I put in a request for a pale interior.

At the bar I met up with Red Fred and his mates, who treated me as some sort of quaint pet and mocked my accent, more or less good-naturedly. Red Fred turned out to be Alfred Burkett, the builder who'd had one of the visions at the springs.

Without difficulty I persuaded him to tell me the story. The account had been so often repeated that the words had acquired a liturgical rhythm. His friends rolled their eyes and shook their heads, grinning. They'd heard it all before. Red Fred only raised his voice louder and prodded the air more insistently with his finger. *This* is what happened, and this, and this and *this*.

The bright light had been 'like a thousand neon signs all flashin' at once', the shining figure 'like an angel with wings as wide as a house'. Then came the glowing aura, 'a cloud of fire', and the uncanny peace that had reached out and enveloped him. 'It was like . . . it was like . . . I wasn't so bad after all.' Tears welled in his eyes. His mates patted him roughly on the back and ordered him another beer. He soon recovered, drank and joked, but whenever my eyes met his I saw a spark of something shy and rather beautiful. Deep down in that thick chunk of solid American flesh burned a light.

Alfred Burkett went on to achieve some national and indeed international prominence. In 1965 (soon after his vision at the spring and two years before I met him, though he hadn't mentioned it), he had started a charity in aid of war orphans. It's now an international foundation, helping thousands all over the world. Wikipedia has a photo of Red Fred in 1996, shaking hands with President Clinton. He died in 2011 at the age of

eighty-eight, but his foundation lives on. In thanks for his contri-
bution to this book, I send a donation.

It was sing-along night at the saloon, and after a couple of
margaritas, I accepted an invitation to lead a rendition of 'God
Save the Queen'. They had different words, but we muddled
through.

I reeled back to the motel around one and instantly fell asleep,
only to be awakened at dawn by loud knocking. Thinking it was
my new hire car, and cursing the zeal of the Avis company ('We
try harder'), I stumbled out of bed, pulled on my clothes and
opened the door to the alarming sight of two over-sized American
policemen, all jutting beer-bellies and lethal ironmongery. Once
it was established that I was who they wanted, they asked me
to accompany them to the sheriff's office in Tonopah, the nearest
large town. They wouldn't tell me what it was about, though they
assured me I was not being arrested. The 'yet' remained
unspoken.

Mystified and still half asleep, my suggestion that we stop for
coffee having been ignored, I climbed into the back of the patrol
car with one chap while the other drove. Mile after mile of
featureless country passed by. The day was already hot and sweat
made my shirt stick unpleasantly to the black plastic seat. The
car had no air-conditioning, just a fan that blew a stream of warm
air into my face, revoltingly scented by the green cardboard pine
tree dangling from the rear-view mirror. Conversation was out
of the question. The two policemen began a new chapter in what
was evidently a long-running and not altogether amicable dispute
about their respective sons, one of whom had hit the other with
a baseball bat at a local Little League match. The drive seemed
to take for ever.

At the station I was shown into an untidy office. A man in
shirtsleeves introduced himself as Sergeant Powalski and offered
me a coffee. Fear of poisoning à la Mrs Big's pink icing warred

with sheer craving; craving won. Two cups of coffee appeared, Sergeant Powalski drinking his with relief not dissimilar to mine. 'Up all night,' he said. I got the distinct impression that this was a real human being, not a simulacrum, and although being hauled into a police station at the crack of dawn is never my favourite experience, my anxiety retreated a bit. Ordinary human trouble I could deal with. It wouldn't be the first time I'd had to talk my way out of a sticky situation.

Sergeant Powalski wanted to know where I'd been between eleven and midnight last night. That was easy: I mentioned Red Fred and one or two others at the saloon as witnesses to my presence there, if they hadn't been too drunk to remember. Red was a well-known local figure; his name seemed to testify in my favour. Someone went off to telephone him to confirm my alibi, and the interview shifted in focus to my time with Jay Cooper the previous afternoon. Why was my rental car there? I explained about the sump and cited the garage proprietor as witness. He, too, was telephoned. And why had I gone there? I explained that I was a journalist, and sketched out the story that had led me to Warm Springs. I'd grabbed my shoulder bag when I left my room and was able to show the sergeant my notebook and the photos of Luce as proof.

'What is this all about?' I asked for the umpteenth time, and finally received an answer.

Jay's house had burned down. He had been found – thank God, because I'd grown very fond of the guy – some distance away, dazed but unhurt except for a mild case of smoke inhalation.

I covered my shock by lighting a cigarette. Once again, a place where Luce had lived and worked had burned down almost immediately after my visit. Once again, I realised with a stab of rage, Luce's paintings had been destroyed before I'd had a chance to make a proper record. Could this have been the work of the same lot who torched Golden Square? At least there were the photos I'd taken yesterday. Maybe not as clear or sharp as I'd like, but I felt that I was, in some small way, one step ahead of them. If, indeed, it had been them. But it was too much of a coincidence to doubt.

Had I been followed after all? I would not have thought they'd consider me worth the trouble, but perhaps I was underrating my own value. Had I led them straight to Jay's house? Here and there on my journey, in airports or car parks or petrol stations, I'd thought I caught a glimpse of someone following me, but had always concluded that paranoia was causing delusions. Nevertheless, there had been something about the people I'd spotted that reminded me of Mr Big, T-dee and T-dum, a particular sort of unblinking blandness that seemed just that little bit too plastic-perfect. I'd dismissed it as aesthetic snobbism again; Americans have a tendency to be over-groomed.

I asked Sergeant Powalski what made him suspect that the fire wasn't an accident. Now that my alibi had been accepted and my presence accounted for, he was not unfriendly. The remains of a kerosene can had been found on the porch; this, in combination with the reports from several people of a stranger (me) prowling the neighbourhood, suggested that the possibility of arson should be considered. He told me, apologetically, that 'those rough hill folk' were always burning down each other's houses in long-standing family feuds, and if not an accident, that's what it was likely to be. I was fairly sure that this was not the case, but wisely refrained from trying to explain about demons from London and their association with arson – which was, as well, my own association with arson.

I went to see Jay in hospital, next door to the police station. He had no idea how the fire had started; all he remembered was that 'she' had wakened him and led him out of the house.

'Who?'

He glanced at the wall and raised his hand in a gesture as though to stroke it, and I knew he meant the angel/star/tree figure that Lou had painted for him. He spoke about going back to the house when they let him out tomorrow, and I hadn't the heart to tell him it had burned down. If I'd got a decent image of his apparently very efficient guardian angel I'd get a print made for him.

As I left Jay's room I encountered his aunt and uncle, who lived in Tonopah and had been contacted by the hospital. They'd told him that his house was gone and he'd be living with them now, but he hadn't taken it in. They had no idea why anyone would have wished to burn down the house. It seemed far more likely that he'd caused it himself, perhaps leaving a lamp burning. Then again, they'd been saying for years that the electrical wiring, home-made to begin with, had been like the rest of the house 'held together only by a wish and a prayer'. It was a wonder the place hadn't blown up or fallen down ages ago.

The kerosene can on the porch? A snort of derision; everybody left kerosene cans on their porch sometimes. They'd been trying to persuade Jay to come and live with them for years. 'He needs a bit of looking after.'

I asked if Karen was still in San Francisco. They exchanged a disapproving glance. 'We don't keep in touch with Karen.'

I got a taxi back to Warm Springs. My plan was to grab a quick shower and some breakfast, drive up to Jay's house to survey what remained, then see if I could get my film processed locally. At the motel, the chambermaid had done up the room, so it took me a little while to realise that someone else had been in there too. My camera, which I'd put in the room safe, was not quite as I'd left it. I don't bother with a case, but I wrap the strap neatly around the lens when I set the camera down. By habit, I always go in the same direction. The instant I picked up the camera I knew something was amiss. The strap was wound the wrong way.

The exposure counter was not showing what it ought. I tried to advance the film, then to rewind it; when I gingerly opened the back I saw that it was empty. The roll of film on which I'd attempted to record the painted room had vanished. There was no longer any doubt in my mind: the demons had been here. Thank God my notebook and the precious photos of Luce had accompanied me to the police station.

I dropped the camera into my shoulder bag and, abandoning everything else, left the room. I stopped at the motel office, informed them loudly that I was staying for another few days and collected the keys to my new Mustang (white inside and out). I drove away as fast as I could.

About a hundred miles on, I pulled into a diner and watched to see if anyone was following. To my frustration, two cars, a pickup truck and an eighteen-wheeler immediately drove in. I went inside and ate an omelette, unable to tell if anyone was paying me particular attention. Several people seemed to have that too-perfect hair, those blank, dead eyes, but maybe they were just vain and vacuous people, of which there has never been a shortage.

It was lunchtime; the place grew quite busy. It was a favourite with the long-haul truckers, which gave me an idea. I left my car keys on the table, tucked a dollar under my plate and went to the toilet. For once, things in real life resembled what spy thrillers lead one to expect. The room had a window that was large enough (just) to permit my ungainly egress. I dropped down between the bins at the back, where the big lorries parked. Having singled out one fellow with a kind, fatherly demeanour, I approached him when he emerged from the diner and asked for a lift in whichever direction he was headed.

'Sure, kid, I'll give y'a ride. Hop in.' His cousin had married someone from Liverpool, he said, and he loved the accent. I never told him that my accent bore absolutely no resemblance to a Scouser's.

I clambered up into the high, hot space of the cab, rolled down the window and surveyed the parking lot. If anyone observed me, I failed to observe them.

My chosen charioteer was a grizzled sixty-something named Eddie O'Brian. He was from Kenosha, Wisconsin and had been driving for forty years; he owned his own rig and another that his son-in-law drove. Boy oh boy, he'd seen some changes. He pulled out of the parking lot in a practised series of gear shifts, brawny arms and booted feet moving in a smooth dance. To my surprise he lit up a joint – I didn't think old geezers liked pot. He allowed as how it helped him drive. 'It smooths out the road,' he said, and I understood exactly what he meant. He'd been introduced to it by his granddaughter, who was at the State University in Madison. 'First one in the family, so proud. So-she-ology, that's what she's learnin'. Whatever that is.'

He was *en route* from Fresno to Chicago, and had stopped at Warm Springs to have a quick soak for his arthritis.

Did it help? He thought it had, but felt he could do without 'the God stuff, if you'll pardon my saying'.

'You don't believe in the miracles, then?'

He didn't dismiss them outright, though he was in no doubt about either the chicanery or the gullibility of his fellow men. He'd seen it all, he said, with a sigh and a laugh.

We were going exactly opposite to the way I wanted to go, which was west to San Francisco to look for Karen Cooper, so it was ideal. If anyone was following me I was leading them away from my true destination.

I left Eddie at a truck stop near Denver and blagged a lift with a mate of his who was heading south. I changed lorries again in Albuquerque and got a ride to Los Angeles. From LA it was easy to hitchhike up the coast highway to San Francisco. I was sure that no one could have followed me through all these manoeuvres. With great relief, I checked into a good hotel,

109

though to be on the safe side I put on an American accent, paid in cash and used a false name. I had a hot bath, a vodka and tonic with ice and lime, a fillet steak with sauce Béarnaise, then a lovely long sleep in the crisp-sheeted bed.

Looking back on it, I note my own naivety. Even within the world of matter, I could be traced easily enough, if not literally followed. Yes, I could stay a few nights in a hotel under a false name, but sooner or later I had to use my American Express, buy aeroplane tickets, show my passport. Now, I believe most people take it for granted that the government can find out where they are, what they're doing and with whom in a few clicks. Back then, long before the internet and with only the most primitive of computers in use, I could not have imagined that the NOHRM, which (if it existed at all) I assumed to be a minor and highly localised sub-department of the not notoriously efficient British government, possessed either the desire or the resources to keep tabs on me as I flitted about. When I boarded my flight out of London, convinced that I hadn't been followed to the airport, I'd really thought that was it, I was out of their net, out of sight, free. I assumed that they regarded me as the smallest of small fish in the small pond of the so-called counter-culture, a mere instrument of information-gathering, one of many in their employ; they'd hooked me in merely because I'd stumbled across their path at Golden Square. It never crossed my mind that it might have been me they'd followed to Golden Square in the first place, since I'd so obligingly declared, in my *NME* column, that I would be the one to find Luce.

I completely failed to grasp how important Luce was to them, or that I, as a possible means to her, was worthy of their close and continuous attention. Why they were interested in Luce remained a mystery. Who was she, that her work had to be hunted down and destroyed? This question was only beginning to form in my mind, but I'd already taken sides in this conflict

I didn't understand, and if the Bigs were against Luce, then I was against them. I supposed that made me some sort of a double agent.

I would learn to get a lot better at evading them, at least on the material plane. Later, I came to wonder whether it was necessary to track me in the physical sense – though it was easily within their capabilities. The niggling suspicion grew in me that Mrs Big had, during her trawl through my mind, done more than observe; had, perhaps, left behind some marker, like a tracking device, programmed to tell them where I was at all times and whether I'd found a trace of Luce.

Now.

Neil has invited me to dinner. Sunday dinner. He says that as though it's a big deal, *Sunday* dinner. He offers to come and pick me up - does he think I'm too gaga to get around town on my own? I tell him No thanks, I'll be in town anyway, an exhibition at the Tate, and can make my own way to Hampstead.

He's still in our parents' old house, that rambling Edwardian in Redington Road. Oddly, the house seems even bigger than I remember; usually, things are disappointingly smaller. Perhaps it's because I've spent the last few decades in rather small rooms.

Inside, the place is almost unrecognisable, and I note Cindy's touch in the anodyne immaculateness of what used to be an engagingly untidy front hall. Everything looks brand new; everything looks John Lewis.

Dinner reaches new heights, or depths, of restrained awkwardness. It's obvious that Neil wanted me and Cindy did not.

'Have some more runner beans,' she says.

I take some. 'Thank you, Dot,' I say. 'Could you please pass the salt?'

Neil covers a smile. I could almost – I say almost, because the weight of history is considerable – begin to like him.

'This is a delicious pot roast,' I say.

'It's leg of lamb,' Cindy says. 'Organic.'

After dinner Neil offers me coffee in his 'snug', while Cindy attends to domestic matters with that air of martyrdom so often deployed by people who, while doing precisely what they want, must have as well the cherry-on-top of laying guilt on others for *making* them do it. It never works with me. I have plenty of real stuff to feel guilty about.

The shelves in the 'snug' hold a complete set of my *Night Eye* books, arranged in order of publication and looking, from the state of their spines, to have been well read. I cannot conceal my astonishment. Neil confesses, with a wistful air, to having read and reread them. 'You seemed to be living an enchanted life,' he says. 'All those places, those adventures. Is it true? I mean the things you describe – did they really happen?'

'Oh yes,' I say. 'All true, I promise.'

I can only take so much of newly nice Neil; I make my excuses and leave, declining his offer to drive me home to Enfield but agreeing to let him call a minicab. It's a relief to get back to my ugly little flat, in which the entire infinity of the past is gently and urgently blossoming.

6

Awarehouse

&.

*The Children of Light. Karen Cooper's Story. Acid
Has No Effect on Her. A Calling Card from Another
Dimension. Alchemy of Sound and Vision. Otis's
Lament. Men in Suits. The Creepy Guy. Escape by
VW Van.*

San Francisco, May 1967

In the pallid Frisco morning I called my service and picked up messages from Charlie ('Thanks for the chocolates. Prefer butterscotch as you well know. What have you found. No sign of Luce here. Auntie Hilda came back and said I was very naughty. Watch out for demons'), my mother ('Don't forget Neil and Cindy's wedding rehearsal tomorrow at six') and the usual sort of stuff from agent, editors, friends. But nothing from Greyling, who was the only person I really wanted to hear from.

The day was bright and cool, the buildings, traffic and crowds of the city reassuring after the wild emptiness of the desert. I bought some blithe new clothes, hippie regalia: a flowered shirt, an embroidered jacket, a fringed scarf. The clothes exhaled a

114

scent of sandalwood, as though they'd travelled from India packed in the same crate as a consignment of joss sticks.

I went in search of Karen Cooper. Waller Street was in the Haight-Ashbury district, whose steep streets were lined with big old houses long since divided into bedsits and now taken over by the vagabond tribe that had been colonising this area since the early sixties. The tidal wave of the Summer of Love was about to crest and the Haight was teeming with wide-eyed, barefoot youngsters drunk on their first intoxicating sips of freedom.

The house in Waller Street was painted in sunrise colours and, with the houses on either side, was occupied by a sprawling commune called the Children of Light. Asking for Karen Cooper got me nowhere: did I want Karen Blue-Eyes, Karen-who-used-to-be-called-Laura, Karen from New Jersey, Saint Karen of the Lost or Karen-who-has-that-little-brown-dog-named-Puck? Everyone was stoned; my enquiries were wafting off into some nethersphere. It felt wrong, somehow, to be straight. I bought a tab of acid from a sweet-faced boy with wilted flowers in his hair and set out for a walk around the neighbourhood.

As I made my way towards Ashbury I was caught up in a street-theatre parade: a ragged procession of rainbow-clothed, drum-beating, banner-waving, horn-tooting freaks, hundreds of them, bearing aloft a litter on which sat a naked couple in yab-yum posture, preceded and followed by dancing girls tossing handfuls of rose petals from plastic buckets.

I recognised Karen as soon as I saw her. A tall woman, big-boned like her brother, with the same thick brown hair and spacious, friendly face. A beaten-up Pentax was slung around her neck and she carried a placard with the words 'YOUR BEAUTY WILL KISS THE FLOWERS OF DEATH' – a quotation from Luce's song 'Immortality'. I came up beside her, greeted her by name and introduced myself. Her eyes were shining, pupils wide, wide, tripping-wide. And she was beautiful.

115

The acid was starting to unfold in my mind and I was feeling Luce's presence very strongly. Indicating that I got the reference on her placard, I told her I was looking for Luce and that photographs I'd found in London had led me to Warm Springs, her brother Jay, and the discovery that Luce was Lou. I didn't mention the fire – any fire – at that point; with a lovely day brimming before us, ready to be sipped, it didn't seem necessary or appropriate.

When I showed her the photos tears came to her eyes, but they weren't tears of sadness. She was smiling and it was clear that the sight of them moved her deeply. She said she'd taken the pictures herself; when the *Human* album came out, she'd recognised the cover.

Perhaps it was that we were both tripping, perhaps it was our shared love of Luce and Luce's music, but I felt like I'd known her for ever. This was the first time, though it would not be the last, that I entered into a startlingly immediate intimacy with someone who had known Luce. When one meets another person, the first assessment one usually makes is, Do I know this person or not? It's a strange and wonderful experience to begin an encounter with feelings of loving familiarity already laid down – the ground, as it were, of the entire relationship. It's perhaps akin to what some people ascribe to having known each other in a past life: the inner certainty of recognition that has no ordinary explanation. It was as though I'd somehow absorbed, through my encounters with Luce and with her mind-penetrating art, Luce's own sense of familiarity with Karen. Just as my path and Luce's intertwined across times and places, so also the border between Luce's mind and my own began to blur. I found it easy and natural to express what were initially Luce's feelings, not mine: fondness, friendship, love. I felt what Luce felt – or at least a diluted version, stepped down to my capacity. Did Luce, on the other end of the thread that connected us, sense my reality? Maybe she sensed everyone's.

116

Of course it was only with distance that this dynamic became apparent to me; only after it had happened again and again with people whom Luce had known. At the time, it was just one of those inexplicable delights that life, so kind and generous in those days, so lavish with her favours, strewed in my carefree path.

After the parade and a picnic in the park (hash brownies and acid punch), I went back to the house in Waller Street with Karen and some of her friends. The place was full of rainbow colours and the constant tinkle of prisms and wind chimes made of shells, bamboo and tiny bells. There were Afghan rugs in pink and blue and ochre, Indian bedspreads embroidered with glinting bits of mirror, candles flickering and dripping over Chianti bottles, windows curtained by lush green fronds of ferns and spider plants. Ravi Shankar played on the hi-fi, then Tim Buckley, Coltrane and madrigals, to which someone played along on a recorder, rather well. We ate apples and Chinese noodles and embarked upon one of those long, meandering acid conversations in which you find truths of extraordinary beauty and relevance never before glimpsed and soon forgotten, like flowers that bloom for one moonlit moment, then vanish. As the windows paled with approaching dawn Karen took me up to her room and we dozed together, entering a shared dream in which we were night-shepherds on a remote hillside, keeping watch over a herd of unicorns as the stars swung by and celestial chords streaked the sky.

※

The next day we sat in the front room with its view over the hills of Haight-Ashbury, sipping mint tea in the sunshine and stroking an absurdly malleable Persian cat called Ebenezer Scrooge. I told Karen in more detail about what had happened in Warm Springs, though I decided it was best to let her believe that the fire had been an accident (after all, I had no proof it was anything else), and said nothing about my missing roll of film. As I was soon

117

to learn, she had her own reasons for wondering about the fire's true cause, but at first her only concern was for Jay. She was relieved to learn that he was OK and laughed when I said her aunt and uncle were going to have him live with them in Tonopah. 'So they think. He'll be out of there and back to the old house in no time. He'll rebuild it from scratch if he has to, and love every minute. It's just the sort of project he's wanted all his life.'

Karen had been nineteen when she arrived in San Francisco in 1960 with her diploma from secretarial school, though she had no wish to be a secretary. After waitressing for a year while studying photography, she got a job with the *Chronicle* (the city's largest daily broadsheet) as a junior staff photographer. Much to her annoyance, the job consisted almost entirely of darkroom work for the lead photographers, making coffee for the picture editor and fending off his good-natured advances. (When I met her in 1967 she'd left the *Chronicle* far behind and was a successful freelance photographer; her series on the homeless children of the Haight had just won a National Press Photographers' Association award.)

Throughout the early sixties she'd spent her spare time hanging out in the bookshops and cafés of North Beach, photographing the poets, artists and wild wanderers washed in from other states of America, other states of mind. 'I had some romantic notions. Everybody was a little bit crazy. I suppose I have a weakness for crazy people.' She'd been in love with the idea of the beatniks, with the idea of breaking free from the formidable strictures of the rabidly conventional 1950s, in particular the 'throttlehold on women' and 'the prison of domesticity'. She regarded herself as a person of the future.

Karen's manner seemed at first uncomplicated and nearly innocent, an open-hearted engagement with whatever life chucked her way, but as I got to know her I saw that her attitude was not as simple as all that, and certainly not naive. She possessed a depth of understanding, though she held it very lightly. Occasionally there was a flash of . . . world-weariness is too strong a term. Perhaps just a small, inner sigh at the unceasing parade of humanity's foibles. I'd learned from her friends that it was she who was called Saint Karen of the Lost, because she was the person to whom one turned if one was feeling lost and confused, and she always helped you to find yourself again.

Karen met Owsley Stanley, the great LSD chemist, at a party and they became friends. Not lovers, she was at pains to point out. She didn't like men 'that way', she told me rather proudly. 'Owsley was crazy, but really smart, too, and the craziness was very specific, very focused. You have to be focused to be a chemist. When he set up his lab in Berkeley I used to help out. What he does, yes, of course he makes money, but he'd give it away if it didn't cost money to make. It's a service, so people know what they're getting. Consistent dose, and no cutting with strychnine or speed. He's a kind of persecuted saint, I think. They keep trying to bust him.'*

Lou Peterson and her brother Frankie visited Owsley at his lab in May 1964, having been told of him by Timothy Leary, whom they'd known on the east coast (see Chapter 17). 'Frankie was a chemist too,' Karen said, 'and apparently a good one. He impressed Owsley, which not many people did, at least not in the field of chemistry. They had a long discussion about precursors, neuro-transmitters, isomerisation, retrosynthesis, all this technical stuff. So then Lou says, What's the highest dose anyone's

---

* Owsley Stanley (1935–2011) was the first private individual to manufacture mass quantities of LSD, producing over a million doses of top-quality acid. His first lab was raided in 1965; they tried to frame him for producing illegal methamphetamine, but all they found was LSD, which was not made illegal until the following year. He sued, successfully, for the return of his equipment. But Karen was prophetic; later that year (1967) he was busted again, and this time it stuck. He served two years in prison.

ever taken? and Owsley says, Twenty-five mikes is threshold, Hofmann* took two hundred and fifty, thinking it was a tiny dose, and it blew his mind. The usual dose is a hundred and fifty to a hundred and eighty micrograms.

'Lou picked up a vial containing a gram of pure, crystalline LSD – enough for five thousand doses – and tipped it into her mouth. You've never seen such panic. She just stood there while we squawked and flapped.

'Nothing happened. Her pupils didn't dilate, her heartbeat, breathing, all remained the same. We made up cognitive tests; she submitted to all of them with good grace. Thinking it was some sort of ultimate test, Owsley challenged her to chess, at which he's pretty good. She beat him really fast. He said two out of three; she beat him even faster. The acid had absolutely no effect on her. She offered to take some more; Owsley yelped. She offered to pay for what she'd taken; he refused. I think he believed – maybe still believes – that there was something wrong with that batch, it had been an inert compound instead, or that she had by sleight of hand switched his vial with another she had brought, though how, let alone why, I can't imagine. Owsley, bless him, is a total materialist. It was easier to chalk it up to flimflam than to consider the possibility that there was a human

* Albert Hofmann of Sandoz Laboratories, a Swiss pharmaceutical company. By synthesising the active chemical ingredient in ergot, he derived lysergic acid diethylamide: LSD. On the day whose anniversary is now celebrated around the world as Bicycle Day (19 April 1943), Hoffman tested his product on himself, administering what he believed was a threshold dose: 250 micrograms. Feeling very strange, he headed home on his bicycle, having the world's first acid trip, which, after some initial anxiety, he ended up enjoying. 'It gave me an inner joy, an open mindedness, a gratefulness, open eyes and an internal sensitivity for the miracles of creation. [. . .] I think that in human evolution it has never been as necessary to have this substance LSD. It is just a tool to turn us into what we are supposed to be.' - Albert Hofmann's speech on his 100th birthday.

being on whom such a quantity had no effect.'

I'd never heard of anyone being completely impervious to the drug, though some people handled it better than others. It had taken me a long time to realise that my own ability to stop tripping at will was quite unique. I have always been able to step out of the trip, as it were, by switching my attention to the adjacent set of tracks where straight reality was rolling along as usual. And then, crisis or obstacle negotiated or avoided, step back into the trip. I described this to Karen and asked if, in her wide experience, she'd known anyone else who could do that; she said not. I took it as another strand in the web of my affinity with Luce.

Why, I wondered, had Lou taken all that acid? Was it just to show off an idiosyncrasy of her biochemical metabolism?

'I can see how it might seem that way,' Karen said, 'and for sure Lou could play the showman when she wanted, make the grand gesture. The *Human* album is a grand gesture, don't you think?'

I could only agree. Why did Jesus change the water to wine? Because he could, one supposes. And his friends were thirsty. Perhaps he couldn't resist a bit of showing off, a grand gesture to knock their socks off. I'll bet it was excellent wine, too: a divine vintage. These sorts of frivolous miracles are typical of saints, magi, avatars through the ages. It would not surprise me to learn that they do these things solely in order to annoy their serious and high-minded hagiographers.

'But I don't believe that's all there was to it,' Karen said. 'She demonstrated that she was different from the rest of us, the ones who needed this helpful chemical in order to glimpse reality. It was like a calling card from another dimension.'

During the course of our conversation, I was often struck by how matter-of-factly Karen treated Lou's exceptional nature. She took it for granted that Lou was a radically different sort of being with radically different capabilities and purposes. At that time, I still thought of Luce as a rock star and artist of exceptional, perhaps even magical ability, whose abstruse clues had teased and tempted me into tracking her down. Through Karen I would, for the first time, begin to grapple with the notion that Luce was . . . something else.

'So what happened after Lou took the acid?'

'We ended up back here. I cooked a big bowl of spaghetti. That was the sort of thing I used to do, to feel useful. I was still, in my way, trapped in the domestic image of woman. I thought Lou was fascinating, but also I felt sorry for her, that she couldn't trip. But then I realised. She can. She does. She's already there, she's always there.'

I asked about the Petersons' family background. I still had it in the back of my mind that they were English, and was slightly disappointed to hear that they were American.

They'd been born in Bethlehem, Pennsylvania, Lou had said, where their grandfathers on both sides had worked in the steel mills. Their father was in the air force and had been somehow involved – Karen wasn't sure of the details – in the development and deployment of the atom bomb. Lou was born on the day the bomb was dropped on Hiroshima.

And what was Frankie like? Karen had always found him inscrutable. 'Whenever you asked him about himself, he told – with absolute sincerity – tales so outrageous, so obviously impossible, that you were charmed and deflected at the same time. Like that he was really two hundred and something years old, or that he'd once possessed the Stone of the Philosophers, or had owned twenty thousand acres in England, or had sailed around the world on clipper ships.

'He always seemed to be laughing at some private joke. Always with this sly twinkle in his eye. Amazing piano player, though, really good. Classically trained, you could tell. He was extremely cool – all the girls liked him a lot. Dressed like something out of the memoirs of Casanova. On anybody else it would have been pretentious, but Frankie did it with such an ironic air that he pulled it off. He was very protective of Lou. That, he took seriously. He knew sometimes she had to be left alone. They had a strong connection, maybe the strongest I've ever seen between two people. Even when they were doing different things, you could feel that they were still . . . in touch. But there was a lot I didn't find out about Frankie until later.

'They set up a studio in a warehouse down at Hunter's Point. Lou wouldn't give it a name, but people started calling it Awarehouse. It's hard to describe what they did. There had never been anything like it. Everybody was part of it simply by being there. Lou and Frankie never seemed to sleep – any time of day or night, they're playing around with tape loops, feedback, synthesisers, mixing boards, cameras, microphones, recording everything, mixing and remixing. You'd sing or talk, or play an instrument, or make some noise on a whistle or a drum, or shake a tambourine or hum or snap your fingers. And they'd weave it into the sound-cloud. Cameras picked up movement and turned it into abstract patterns and sound waves. Everything got drawn into the mix, harmonised, transmuted, then played back in sound and light. It was like living inside a big, wonderful mind, or realising that one's own mind was a big, wonderful space that contained everything and everyone.'

According to a brief entry in Wikipedia, Awarehouse was 'a communal multi-media happening' begun in the summer of 1964 and ended abruptly when a fire on 15 September 1964 destroyed the premises. The source is an article in the *Frisco Free Herald* dated 13 September 1964, a couple of days before the fire. I track it down in the paper's online archives. I won't quote it at length – that sort of fulsome, blown-away Wow! journalism is no longer in fashion – but it's laden with terms like mind-blowing, consciousness-expanding, revolutionary, revelatory, transcendental, transformative and, just once, gnostic. It tells readers that, if they go, they 'will never be the same again'. (This sort of terminology, as I later had occasion to observe, is a red flag to the NOHRM and their ilk.) The Wikipedia entry lists a number of people who have cited Awarehouse as an influence, including Gordon Matta-Clark, Ken Kesey, Michael Murphy, Jerry Garcia and Emmet Grogan.

'Being a materialist, Owsley thought Awarehouse was like chemistry,' Karen said. 'That was the highest compliment he could give. Lou said, like *alchemy*. An "elixir of immortality". she called it. A magical world that you entered, and that entered you. And the paintings – Lou covered the walls, the floor, the ceiling with the most amazing murals. I spent hours and hours looking at them. They got right into your head.'

'Did they affect your sense of time?'

'Oh, yeah. And how. The pictures weren't still, if you know what I mean. You'd look at them, and something would catch your eye, and you wouldn't be sure if you'd really seen it, so you'd look more closely and it would come alive, start living in you, taking you places, showing you things. There were stories in there, journeys, adventures. You'd fall into it, and when you came out you'd know you'd changed in some subtle way that you couldn't quite put your finger on, and you'd try to remember exactly where you'd been and what you'd seen, but it would already be fading. And if you went back, later or the next day, it was never the same. Being at Awarehouse was . . . to say the most amazing experience of my life isn't nearly enough. It was like being alive, and knowing that up until then, I'd been ninety-nine per cent dead.'

Awarehouse, I could see, was a prototype of both the mind-bending painted room at number eleven Golden Square and Luce's secret London gigs. She was trying things out, experimenting with ways to get into people's heads, to provide experiences that, while heard and seen by all, delivered exactly the transformative catalyst required by each person's psychological, emotional and ideational state. LSD was certainly a help, opening 'the doors of perception'. It turns out that opening these doors is not so hard; what you do when they're open, that's the tricky thing. 'The drug dose does not produce the transcendent experience. It merely acts as a chemical key – it opens the mind, frees the nervous system of its ordinary patterns and structures. The nature of the experience depends almost entirely on set and setting,' Timothy Leary wrote.* And, I might add, the skill, power and intentions of the guide or artist.

'More and more people started coming,' Karen said. 'At first it was mainly friends of mine or Owsley's, then they brought friends, and so on. It's not as though there were any performances, just people hanging out. And the idea starts to grow that we're changing, becoming something new. The elixir was taking effect. It may take a long time, decades, centuries, millennia. But I know what we're becoming – what humans were always meant to be. Like her. Like Lou.'

At this point we were joined by Otis, another resident of the building, a stocky youth with tight mouse-brown curls and flat Midwestern vowels. When he heard that we were talking about Lou and Frankie he made a face. 'They conned you, Karen baby.' And to me, 'They conned her. Got her to leave everything just to help them escape from—'

'You have no idea, Otis.'

'Oh, I have a very good idea. They had the cops on their ass. Debt collectors, too. They just barged in, no warrant, searched the house. We had a hell of a time convincing those creepy morons in suits that we had nothing to do with your precious

---

* Timothy Leary, *The Psychedelic Experience*, http://www.leary.ru, pdf. p.1.

Lou.' He pulled up a chair and turned to me. 'Lou could do no wrong, according to *her*.' He jerked his thumb at Karen. 'Saint Karen would never tell a lie, but she won't tell you the whole truth either. That Lou of hers was all over the place. She even put the moves on me one time.'

Over his shoulder I saw Karen shake her head and smile.

'What do you mean?' I asked Otis.

'She kissed me, and when I turned her down she laughed at me. Not a very nice person, you see.' He slapped his knees and stood up. 'Just wanted you to know the truth. Got to do my bit for truth, justice and the American Way.' He stomped off.

I couldn't imagine that anyone would have turned Luce down, and suspected that the real situation had been exactly the reverse, and this was a fragile masculine ego protecting itself. 'Did she really kiss him?'

Karen laughed. 'Lou kissed people sometimes, but not the way he likes to think. For her, it was a way of reaching through, touching the real person in there. Otis likes to pretend she was coming on to him, but that's not what she was doing. He was coming on to her, and couldn't get it that his approach wasn't working. She only kissed him on the forehead, and she laughed to show him not to take it all so seriously. But Otis just wasn't ready for Lou.'

'Did Lou do more than kiss people?'

'Are you asking me about her sex life? If there were anything to tell, I'd tell you it was none of your damn business. But the simple truth is, Lou didn't do sex. At least I don't think she did, and I'd have known. Even if she hadn't said, the other person would certainly have, to someone, some time. If she'd slept with anyone, I like to think it would have been me, but no, she just didn't. The connection she sought was so much deeper than that.'

Karen clearly felt the subject was closed, so I returned to what Otis had said. 'What did he mean, you "helped them escape"?'

'Awarehouse had been going for about three months, and was

126

getting to the point where people had to be turned away because there was no room. That night, Lou and Frankie told everybody to leave really early, about ten o'clock. They said they needed to clean the place. I offered to stay and help, but they said no, so I came back here and went to sleep. Next thing I know it's two in the morning and they appear by my bed, saying they want to get out of the city for a while. I figured they came to me because I was one of the few people who had a functioning set of wheels – an old VW bus.

'For some reason, they were dressed like bums, really shabby. Lou had dyed her hair brown. Frankie had shed his usual glad rags and wore an old overcoat that looked like it came from the Salvation Army reject pile. I didn't recognise them at first – it wasn't until Lou spoke that I realised it was them.

'I had no idea where to go, so I drove us home to Warm Springs. I'd told her about the place, and she'd said how lovely it sounded and she'd like to see it one day. We'd been talking about the desert – she loved the desert. At Awarehouse she made a painting of the desert on the four walls of a room at the back. It felt like you were right in it. Strange things used to happen in that room, especially if you spent a night alone in there, people said. I never quite dared. At Warm Springs she started right away, painting the living-room walls. I got paints for her in Tonopah . . . I thought she'd stay longer, do the whole house.' She paused. 'She told me to paint over them, but I didn't. And now it's burned down, too. I wonder . . .'

'Too?' I hadn't yet told her about Golden Square.

'We had no phone, practically no contact with the outer world at all. Later, when I came back here, I learned that Awarehouse had burned down the night we left. But we didn't know about that. At least, I didn't. It seems obvious now that Lou and Frankie knew something about it. And then there were those visits from strange men, like Otis said, searching for them and asking questions he couldn't answer. I didn't tell anyone where we were headed, I didn't even decide until we got going. No one, as far as I know, had seen Lou and Frankie arrive, or leave with me. But apparently someone thought to look for them here, and when they weren't to be found, these . . . people had to be persuaded that they were barking up the wrong tree.'

The Awarehouse fire had to have been the work of the Bigs, or others like them. This confirmed that it was definitely Luce they were after when they paid their call at the offices of Pymander Productions and Monad Management, and they'd been after her for years. But why? I had the feeling that I was standing at the edge of a vast, tangled web; here and there were a few strands I recognised, but they vanished into the darkness at the heart of the tangle. Or no, I thought. I'm not standing at the edge of it any more, I'm in it and being drawn deeper by the minute.

'What do you think happened?' I asked Karen.

'Faulty wiring, that's what the police said.'

'You don't think so?'

'I don't know.'

'But you suspect . . .'

'If you're suggesting that Lou and Frankie did it themselves, no, I don't think that at all, though somehow they'd realised it was going to happen and got everyone out of the way. If a fire had started with a hundred people there, someone would have been hurt, that's for sure. The thing is . . . I think I may have seen who did it. I didn't go to the police, obviously, because it would have led to questions about why I'd left town so suddenly that night, and with whom. My evidence was pretty flimsy anyway, only my own feelings and impressions, and by then they'd decided it was an accident, case closed.'

'What feelings and impressions?'

'First of all, that afternoon a new person had turned up. New people came along all the time, but mostly brought by friends. This guy appeared on his own. Not unheard of, but the location was so out of the way, not many people just wandered in. Then, he didn't fit, he didn't look right. He was too smooth and neat.'

I interrupted to enquire about his hair.

'Yeah, funny you should ask. His hair was all wrong. Like he'd come from the barbershop, not a hair out of place. Mr Brylcreem. And he wasn't enjoying himself. He hung out on the edges, not participating. Someone handed him a tambourine, but he didn't seem to know what to do with it. He just stared at everything with a blank expression on his face. Everybody, and I mean everybody, became happy at Awarehouse. Different kinds of happy: serene happy, bouncy happy, sweet happy, wild happy, quiet happy, even sad happy, if you know what I mean. You could see it happening to them, gradually or suddenly breaking out of them, dissolving all the shit. It's how we're meant to be. It's our true nature. Like we were in Eden – that's what it means, that lost paradise story. It means the natural state of the human is happiness, and it's not far away in the distant past, or for that matter the future. It's . . . available all the time, it's only a matter of knowing where, inside your own mind, it's to be found. Because that's where it is, not out there in the material world.' She waved a dismissive hand. 'Adam and Eve left the garden, and went to live in the world of separation, the world of matter. Then they invented a God who'd banished them, and decided to worship him. But the door's right here.' She tapped her forehead. 'Just go back to the garden.

'But that guy, that strange, too-neat guy, I could tell he didn't have a garden to go back to. It was like he was empty. No home inside him, no Eden, no happy. I felt sorry for him, so I went and tried to talk to him. I thought maybe it really was in there, but so well hidden I hadn't seen it, and I could help him find it. I said something like, "Welcome to Awarehouse". He didn't

129

say a word, but he gave me such a look it rocked me back on my heels. It was cold, utterly cold and dead. He made me feel like I was less than a cockroach to be stepped on. All of a sudden I didn't feel sorry for him any more, in fact I felt scared of him. I don't know why, he was just a creepy little guy and I was surrounded by about thirty good friends, but he had nasty vibes. The nastiest vibes I've ever encountered. It was making me feel sick to be near him. This weird, awful feeling was oozing out of him – horror and dread and misery.' A shudder passed through her body. 'I really thought that if I didn't get away from him I'd pass out right there, so I practically ran away. I had to go outside to clear my head. He'd really shocked me. No one like that had ever come to Awarehouse before.

'After a little while the strange guy left, and I felt a huge relief. Lou and Frankie had been doing other stuff and at the time I didn't think they'd seen him. But now I believe they had. I think they probably also noticed that I spoke to him, and my reaction. Something about his presence told them it was time to get out. The reason I think that is because I saw him again in the street as I was driving away that night. I know it was the same guy because as I passed him I got a chill that felt just like the look he'd given me, and a wave of that queasy sense of dread like I'd felt before.'

'You think he's the one who started the fire.'

'Well, I suspect it. Nasty person appears. Nasty thing happens. Hard not to imagine a connection.'

I knew then that I'd have to tell Karen everything, but I wanted to hear the rest of her story first, to learn about that time with Lou and Frankie in the house at the edge of the desert.

7

Not Like You and Me

❧

*Desert Days and Nights. She Makes the Waters
Flow. Dancing into the Desert. Don't Photograph
Her Face. Frankie's Unfortunate Luck at Cards.
Certain People Are Interested. They Take Her Away.
Persecution, Liberation and the Zeitgeist.*

L ou and Frankie had spent only three weeks in Warm Springs
(16 September–7 October 1964), not the months I'd guessed
from Jay's account. Lou's hair, Karen had been astonished to
observe, grew exceptionally fast, at a rate of about an inch a week.

'Lou loved it there,' Karen said. 'We had no TV or radio, but
we made up stories and songs to pass the nights. Frankie played
my mom's old piano – we had to get it tuned, nobody had played
it since Mom died.'

I recalled that the springs had started flowing again at about
the same time they got there, in September of 1964, according
to the brochure I'd read.

'Yes, so they did,' Karen said. 'The day after we arrived, to be
exact.'

'Are you implying there's a connection?'

'We went for a walk in the hills the first evening there. I was telling Lou about my great-uncle Abner who'd been famous for being able to find water underground. A water diviner. He told people where to drill their wells. So suddenly Lou stops and points to the ground. She says there should be water flowing right below us, but it's got blocked. She stamps her foot, and says There, that's fixed it. And strides off, bounding up the cliff. She could climb like a goat. I stayed on the lower track and watched her run along the ridge. And the next day the old pools had filled and were overflowing.'

I asked about the reports of visions and miraculous healings. Karen shrugged. She'd heard of them, but since they'd stayed so briefly, the whole thing hadn't developed into much. Living several miles out of town, they had heard only vague rumours. She was astonished when I told her how the town had grown, how busy it was, how well known.

Warm Springs has since faded again; its renaissance was brief. The healings were shown to be almost all delusion. I say almost, because the first ones, those occurring in late September and early October 1964 (during Lou's presence), remained unexplained despite thorough investigation. The spring retained its full flow for only a few years; by 1970, the owners of the 'Spa', as it had then become, were surreptitiously augmenting the flow with water from their own well.

There can be no doubt that in some instances, Luce intended to have the most radical effect on people's lives, but intentionality on her part is not necessary to explain every extraordinary event she left in her wake. These visions and miracles may simply be the result of an undirected influence that intersected each life, each mind, in a unique way, transforming in a unique direction – just as everyone who encountered her art was affected in a manner particular to themselves. You touch something like that and you're changed. You may never know what hit you, or you may attribute the effects to causes of your own invention.

I'd put the Golden Square photos on the floor between us. Karen looked through them slowly, lingering on the image of the lone figure, arms outstretched, that had become the cover of the album. 'I took this the first morning, when I woke up to find she was gone. I ran out in a panic and saw her dancing off into the desert. I knew not to go after her, so I went and got my camera instead. She was being so . . . I don't know. So intensely *herself* that it hurt, it actually hurt me here.' She made a stabbing gesture towards her heart. 'That was when I began to realise that she was out of reach, then and always. So I took the photographs instead. I wanted something for myself. Silly me. She danced, and I took pictures.'

Karen turned to the one on the porch that almost showed Lou's face. 'I should never have taken this. I knew she hated having her face photographed. At Awarehouse, Frankie always kept an eye out for people with cameras. He'd been on my case right away because I'm always taking pictures, and it was natural for me to want to photograph Lou. So I knew better. Several times I saw him exchange words with someone who'd gotten too close, which ended with them giving him the roll of film. He could be very persuasive. He never had to use force, of course – the vibe there was so mellow. But I always had the feeling he could if he wanted to, and he would if it was necessary. I never understood why it was such a big deal. I figured it was just her personal phobia, an idiosyncratic form of shyness. Lou could look so innocuous if she wanted to – she had this ability to efface herself, blend into a crowd, go unnoticed. One minute she'd be blazing, fizzing with energy and magnetism, the next she'd go all anonymous. She'd disappear. And if there were cameras about, that's what she'd do. People would come looking for this magical person they'd heard of, this alchemist of sounds and images and mind-blowing experiences . . . and if she didn't want to be seen,

133

she could move among them all incognito. Then you'd hear something, and turn around, and there she'd be in a corner, playing her guitar, weaving astounding tapestries of sound, and everyone would turn towards her like flowers to the sun and she'd play, and then when we looked up she'd be gone again.

'It never occurred to me that she had reasons for hiding her face, but when I took this picture,' Karen tapped it with her finger, 'I'd really overstepped the mark. Frankie asked me what other pictures I'd taken, and I said only some long shots of Lou in the desert. He started acting suspicious of me and my motives, and wanted to destroy the film right away. I resented his attitude, I resented him telling me what to do and I didn't understand his argument, which seemed to be that the photographs put us all in danger, though he wouldn't explain how or why. At the time I had no idea what had happened to Awarehouse.

'Frankie and I were both being pretty stubborn so we appealed to Lou. She resolved the argument with a compromise. We'd get rid of the film, but it should not be destroyed because, she said, the photographs might yet have a purpose. As indeed they have, haven't they? When I saw one on the album cover I knew I was right not to let Frankie destroy them. We put the roll of film into a box and sent it to a Mr Greyling at a place called Golden Square in London. Is that where you found it?'

I confirmed that it was. Greyling again! As I'd suspected, he knew very well who the tenants of the upper floors had been. Here was proof that already in 1964 he had been connected to and trusted by Luce.

'After that,' Karen continued, 'Lou always managed to slip off unnoticed into the desert. She'd be gone for hours, sometimes all day and night. I got the impression that solitude gave her something no human company could. I asked her one time about what she did out there, but she hated being asked to explain herself, and even if you didn't ask, she'd sense that you wanted something –

134

explanation, reassurance, whatever – and she'd give you a look, the briefest look. It said, You can't own me. It said, I don't belong to you. It wasn't an angry look, or even a cold one. It was a beautifully kind and loving look, but it indicated that an unbridgeable gap lay between us. And I knew that was true even as I pretended it wasn't. I'm no dummy. I could see what she was saying. I chose to pretend she didn't really mean it, or she did, but *under* it all she didn't. Under it all, after it all, when she was done doing whatever it was she had to do, and for sure she had to do something, anyone could tell she was just burning with some great purpose, though she never said what it was, but when it was accomplished she'd become what I wanted her to be. God, I was so full of shit.'

'Do you think Lou was happy?' I asked.

'Happy? I don't know. I know she was capable of huge joy, and ecstasy was always just a whisper away. Almost anything could tip her over into it. But happy, like you and I are happy or unhappy about this or that . . . I don't know. There was a deep sorrow in her, and sometimes I caught a glimpse of it. One night I couldn't sleep and walked out onto the porch. She was sitting on a rock, gazing out at the desert. The look on her face was of such terrible sadness it made me cry, I couldn't help myself. What *is* it? I asked her, what *is* it that hurts so much? but she made no answer, just a smile, a shake of her head that seemed to mean . . . everything. The human condition. Separation, loneliness, loss. The necessity of bearing the unbearable.

'I'd hoped she would stay a long time. I thought it would be good for her – restful and inspiring. I thought *I'd* be good for her. I thought that I was what she needed. I'd look after her, help create a beautiful home for her where she could be free to paint and sing. In the ambience that *I* would create, she'd make her greatest art, she'd compose the music that would transform the world and all because of what *I* gave her . . . oh, what a load of crap.' Karen made an impatient gesture. 'It still makes me so angry at myself that I was there with her and all I thought about was *me me me*. If I thought of her, all I saw was my idea of her, which was just more *me me me*. I wish . . . I wish I hadn't wasted that time, because it didn't last long.

'It was Frankie who brought it all to an end. Lou, I believe, truly enjoyed the peace and quiet, the beautiful desert nights, the simple way of life. But Frankie, you could tell, got tired of it. He was more of a city person. He was bored. Tonopah doesn't offer any amusements to someone like him. I teased him, saying he'd *love* Las Vegas, which of course I hate. He acted like he'd never heard of it. He said, What's Las Vegas? so I played along, explaining that it was a big city a few hours away, with lots of shops and restaurants and casinos and nightclubs. Well, that was it, he had to go, so we piled into the VW van and drove down there.

'Frankie was like a kid in a candy store. The first thing he had to do was buy himself some snazzy new duds. We'd been hanging out in jeans and T-shirts, but he hated being so casually dressed. He pawned one of his rings – he wore lots of rings – and I was astonished at how much he got for it. Two hundred dollars. The guy said it was a very good emerald, can you imagine? I never realised he was wearing that sort of serious jewellery. I thought it was just a chunk of green glass. Anyway, he got the money and bought himself a new outfit, the best he could find. Gabardine suit, silk shirt, fine leather boots. Even silk socks. Lou and I helped him choose a silk cravat and matching pocket handker-chief. He got so much pleasure out of those clothes, I had to laugh. You could see how good they made him feel. Once he was dressed to his satisfaction, he wanted to go to a casino to gamble. We went in to Caesar's, the biggest casino on the Strip, and he asked where to find the faro table. No one had ever heard of faro but we managed to figure out that it was similar to blackjack, so he bought a bunch of chips with the money left over from his clothes binge and settled in at a blackjack table.

'Lou and I wandered around for a bit, then went for a drink at a bar which was set in a sort of colonnade along the edge of the gambling floor. I had a glass of lousy, overpriced white wine and Lou earned some dirty looks from the waiter for ordering only a glass of water. It came with ice cubes, a slice of lemon, a slice of lime, a slice of orange and a maraschino cherry, two straws and a paper parasol, and cost as much as my wine. The place was bright, glittering and depressing, and all I could think about was how long I'd have to endure it. Lou sat there quietly, withdrawn into herself. She'd get like that when there wasn't much going on that interested her. But then gradually we became aware that something *was* going on; people had begun to gather around the blackjack table where Frankie was playing. The next thing we knew, two large men in suits were marching him away. They took him through an unmarked door at the side of the room. Lou and I looked at each other. Oh shit, she said. I asked what we should do; she thought for a moment, then said we had to wait, he was OK.

'I didn't know what to think. Had he been arrested? For what? Was he trying to cheat, and they'd found out? I asked Lou this, and she looked horrified. He didn't cheat, she told me very firmly. He was just extremely lucky at cards, always had been. So I thought it would be all right, they'd find out he wasn't cheating, let him go, perhaps ban him from the casino. That was the worst they could do. We agreed it was best to wait for him in the van so we headed back to where I'd parked in a side street a few blocks away. I was wishing so much that we'd never come, I was pissed off at Frankie for getting us into this mess, I just wanted us all to be back home.

'We sat in the van. It got dark. I went off to a deli and bought some sandwiches and coffee. I ate, Lou didn't. We sat in silence for a couple of hours, then Lou started up suddenly and said Shit. He's in trouble. He's afraid.

137

'I knew then that she really was connected to him, there was some kind of psychic link; she could tell what he was feeling. She was so agitated, I'd never seen her like that. Another ten minutes passed. She sat very still, very tense, as though listening hard. If she'd been the sort of person who chewed their nails, they'd have been bitten to the knuckles.

'I suggested that we contact the police, find out if he was being charged, get a lawyer, et cetera, but Lou said it wasn't a matter for the law and he was not in the hands of the police. She wanted to leave it at that, but when I pushed for an explanation she said that certain people were interested in him because of things in the past, and if they realised what he was, they'd never let him go. It struck me that she'd said *what* he was, not *who* he was, and I asked her what she meant. He's a lot stranger than he looks, was all she said.

'Suddenly she gasped and went white. She looked like she'd been shot. I asked what had happened and she said He's gone. Do you mean he's dead? I asked. No, not dead, she said, but they've done something to him, something bad. She climbed out of the van and told me to drive straight back to Warm Springs. I was to obliterate all signs of her and Frankie's presence and paint over the murals. She had to go and find Frankie, she said, and since she didn't know where he was the only way was to get "them" to take her, too.

'It felt like the ground had dropped out from under me and I'd fallen into some sort of a nightmare. Things were moving too fast. I had no idea what was going on, or why it had got so heavy all of a sudden. All I knew was that she was slipping through my hands, I was losing her – I'd already lost her. She thanked me for putting her and Frankie up, for putting up with them. She even made a little joke of that word play. She couldn't have been kinder, but she was leaving. Nothing I could do or say would change that. She kissed me. I knew it was the last time. Then she turned and walked away.

'I wanted to run after her but she'd only tell me to go back, to go away. She might even get angry with me. I didn't think I could bear that, but neither could I bear to let her go, so I followed. She headed straight to Caesar's, bought a one-dollar chip and went to the nearest roulette wheel. Soon a crowd gathered and I heard people saying that the ball had dropped on the one three times in a row. The croupier announced that the wheel was closed and the same two men came and took Lou away. She didn't resist, she didn't look around, but I thought I glimpsed a small smile. She'd accomplished her first goal. In that moment I was able to believe that somehow, she'd be all right.

'I went back to the van and drove home. On the drive I had a chance to think, and it came to me that I'd had it all wrong from the start. I'd always thought that Lou's remoteness, her distance, was her way of keeping some little part of herself private. I'd imagined that I understood, that it was generous and kind of me to be so tolerant. But it was the other way around. It was the part that had touched me, connected with me, that was the small part, the tiny part. Who she was, was so much bigger than I'd ever conceived. It was the rest of her life that was real, and she'd vanished back into it without me.

'So I did what she asked, or I tried. I cleaned the place, burned the few clothes she and Frankie had worn. As Lou should have realised, Jay wasn't going to let me paint over the murals. I'd never seen him so upset since he was told he couldn't play football any more after he broke his ankle. We argued all day but he wouldn't let me into the room. If he blocks a door, it stays blocked. He slept on the floor in front of the door and announced his intention of doing so until I left. And so I left.

'When I got back here and learned what had happened to Awarehouse, I began to wonder about connections between that creepy, too-neat guy, the fire, the men who'd searched for Lou here at Waller Street and those "certain people" she'd spoken of, who were interested in Frankie because of "what he was" and who would likewise be interested in her. Because of what she did at the roulette wheel.'

'You really think she made the ball fall on the one three times in a row in order to get herself arrested?'

'There's no other explanation. Haven't you ever heard of telekinesis?'

'I've heard of it, but I'm not sure I believe in it. And levitating a table or moving a matchbox a few inches is not the same as controlling the fall of a roulette ball three times in a row.'

'Isn't it? Maybe there are other ways to relate to the material world than the usual so-called laws that most people abide by. I know, and I think you know too, that Lou is not like you and me. There was her ability to take all that acid. And how she unblocked the springs. And how she can affect people – that most of all. She can make you feel things, know things. Why are they after her? The very fact that Awarehouse burned down, the house in Warm Springs burned down, creeps in suits came looking for her proves it. There's something really different about her. And whatever Frankie is, I'm sure it has something to do with the . . . oddities of Lou's nature. That's why she had to do what she did – in order to get the attention of "certain people" who are interested in those sorts of oddities. Is it any wonder we don't hear about people with unusual abilities? I mean the real ones, not the frauds. If I realised that "certain people" were interested in me, I'd take care never to show what I could do. But for Frankie, Lou did. She had to.'

Karen had clearly given the matter some thought, and I could not argue with her conclusions. More weird shit had happened to me since I'd started looking for Luce than in the entirety of my hardly uneventful previous life. Telekinesis seemed a fairly modest addition to the collection.

'Eventually,' Karen said, 'I gave up trying to figure her out. She passed through my life and it was wonderful. That's all that matters. When the *Human* album came out I could tell that was Frankie playing on it, so I knew she'd found him and he was OK.'

'And you've never heard from her again?'

'Oh yes, I have, I'm sure I have. She sent me a card a week later, and others since.' She went to her room and came back with a cigar box, from which she took four picture postcards. The first had a cartoon of a cactus wearing a sombrero and the words, 'Greetings from Taos, New Mexico'. It was postmarked 14 October 1964 (a week after the Las Vegas episode). The next was a picture of Mount Everest, postmarked Kathmandu (December 1964), then the Eiffel Tower (January 1966). The latest was from London – Buckingham Palace (February 1967). On the back of each no words, only a drawing of an open eye, the iris depicted as the pinwheel of a camera's aperture blades. 'That's me, the camera,' Karen said. 'It's her way of saying that I did mean something to her after all, she'd seen and understood. She knew me better than I knew myself.'

I gave Karen the strip of negatives from Golden Square and she tucked them carefully into the cigar box with the postcards. It meant a lot to her to have them, I could tell. We'd been talking for hours and both felt an urge to get out of the house, so we bought a bottle of wine and headed up to the top of Buena Vista Park to watch a hazy sun set slowly in the west.

Karen's story had had a powerful effect on me. More than once as she spoke, I felt that I was seeing and feeling Luce through her eyes and senses, and through the intensity of her love. As her tale grew stranger it grew at the same time more familiar, more inevitable. For the first time I could put the events of Golden Square into a context. An outlandish one, to be sure, but the only one that offered even a glimmer of understanding.

As we sat on the hill, high above the muted clangour of the city, I told Karen everything that had happened at Golden Square

141

– Greyling, Mr Big, Tweedledee and Tweedledum, the fire. The terms with which she'd described her reaction to the nasty-vibe guy at Awarehouse – the nausea and dread – reminded me of that weird, sickening fear Mr Big and his minions had provoked in me. I told Karen how I'd taken to calling them demons, and about Ambrose's theory of astral entities.

'I know what you mean.' She shuddered. 'Whatever they are, they definitely don't mean well. They're not people like you and me – they can't be. They're not . . . human.'

But then I also had to tell her about Mrs Big and the NOHRM, and how the fire at Jay's house plus the tampering with my camera had led me to suspect that I'd been followed from London to Warm Springs, and that it might be my fault the house had burned down and Jay was nearly killed. If I'd expected comforting reassurances, I didn't get them. Karen thought it was quite likely that I had, indeed, been followed. The fire itself wasn't proof, because it could so easily have been an accident, though the timing was certainly suspicious. But it was my missing roll of film that made her certain.

'She told me to paint over the murals, didn't she? She knew that if they found them, they'd have to destroy them, and fire seems to be their favourite method. So it's Jay's own fault the place burned down. If he'd let me paint over the walls I believe they'd have left it alone. They can't possibly go around burning down every room she was ever in – it's her art they're after. And that's because it has such an effect on people. It's *alive*. It gets into you and changes you in ways they obviously don't like, so they have to destroy it and they don't care who gets in the way.'

'Jay thinks one of the painted figures woke him up and guided him out.'

'It must have been the one he called his angel,' Karen said. 'Lou painted it specially for him. He said she'd seen it in his head. Perhaps she knew he'd need it.'

Our talk of demons had made me uneasy; I kept looking around, scanning the passers-by for that tell-tale bland neatness, and scanning my inner weather for any hint of the fear that signalled their presence. If despite my best efforts to lose them they were still following me, I was endangering anyone I was with.

Karen saw what was worrying me. 'No use getting paranoid,' she said. 'What they seem to be after is Lou herself, and her art. They want to stop her influencing anyone, affecting people as we know she can. "Certain people" are interested in her. Who could that be? FBI? CIA? Your NOHRM, whatever that is? Probably people we've never heard of. But she carries on, doing what she has to do. And she gets away with it, doesn't she? She got the *Human* album out and staged those secret gigs. She's adopted guerrilla tactics, hit and run. Who knows what she's going to do next? If we don't know, we can't lead them to her, so I wouldn't worry too much. But do try not to be followed, in case you stumble upon something.'

❧

The image that came to mind was of a great mailed fist reaching for Luce, snatching and missing time and time again. In Las Vegas, they'd snatched and grabbed . . . and, as I was soon to learn, got their fingers burned.

Why were – why are – the pioneers of consciousness always so persecuted? What makes them so feared and hated that, for example, Richard Nixon called Timothy Leary, Harvard professor, 'the most dangerous man in America'? He hadn't killed or hurt anyone, merely suggested that it might be useful, personally and socially, if people were to do some serious – or fun – investigation of their own mind-sets and of the nature of reality in general. 'Turn on, tune in, drop out,' he said. This, in many different forms, has always been the Gnostic's message: an encouragement to search for ultimate reality within, rather than among the

143

outward manifestations of material existence. Some people feel threatened by the merest suggestion that the material world in which they so devoutly believe is not the entire reality. The unknown scares them; they don't want to hear about it, they don't want to read about it and they definitely don't want to encounter it. When this fear is aroused in a person of low intelligence and high insecurity, it leads to a desperate need to squash any blasphemy that might undermine the fixed definitions of reality to which, like mindless barnacles, the masses cling. In this context, it is no surprise that Luce, who could open people's minds with a word, an image, a touch, was seen as the greatest imaginable threat.

As I tracked Luce's art and life, I began to sense an agenda – a consistent, fuck-with-your-head agenda – developed in San Francisco in 1964 and continued in the secret London gigs of 1967. And LSD played its part. The chemical had the status of a sacrament in many of the new religions, or the new takes on very old religions, that were springing up all over the place. 'Liberating elixirs are a crucial element facilitating entry into the mysteries of many religions. These entheogens ("generating the divine within") are known by different names and are based on diverse substances, but all have the same purpose: to release the initiate from the limitations of ordinary consciousness and open the way to the apprehension of a "higher" level of reality, the one inhabited by God or the gods.'*

Lou's programme of mind-alchemy can be seen in the context of a tradition that ranged from koan-posing Zen masters to Shakespearean jesters and my own dear Alice in Wonderland. In the context, as well, of the widespread belief that the world was in the process of radical, unprecedented change. Of course,

* Curtis B. Nathan and Henry P. Delahaye, *Traditions of Initiation* (Cambridge: Cambridge University Press, 1983), p. 178.

any student of history knows that this sentiment recurs regularly, which is not to say that it isn't in some way true every time. The world into which Luce's (and my) generation had been born believed itself to be uniquely fraught with fears and uncertainties, cut off from the comfortable securities of the past, ravaged by wars both hot and cold. The threat of nuclear Armageddon lurked over the horizon, driving humanity in a panicked herd towards a future where it seemed that the only options were annihilation or transformation. The notion that things would carry on as usual – good and bad, hope and despair mingled or alternating – was the unbelievable thing. As opportunities for annihilation multiplied, so too did self-proclaimed agents of transformation. Charismatic leaders, world teachers, heralds of the new dawn sprang up like mushrooms, started socio-political movements, spiritual cults, magical orders, mystery schools, then faded to obscurity, died in a brief blaze of glory or were discredited and expired in ignominy.

A popular anthem of the times was 'The Age of Aquarius', from the musical *Hair*. Due to the precession of the equinoxes, the planet enters a new Age or Aeon every 2,600 years, as delineated by the signs of the zodiac. This idea blended in the common imagination with the vast Hindu cosmic cycles, according to which we're in a Kali-Yuga, a Dark Age of ignorance and suffering. Many people took comfort in the idea that our situation was *objective*, not our fault, and therefore nothing could be done about it: we just had to grit our teeth and bear it until the new Age dawned, finding salvation or at least consolation where we could.

So much for the zeitgeist. On my quest for Luce herself, things were about to get even stranger.

Now.

All this reminds me of Richard the Mad Reichian. Many years ago, I met a chap inside who'd started on his road to madness as a devotee of Dr Wilhelm Reich - now there's someone who really got persecuted. One must, therefore, conclude he was on to something. What particularly interests me is his theory of Fascism - why some people become oppressors. Reich believed that the neurotic need to control others was due to the sex instinct being repressed in childhood and the profound alienation that ensues, but I think it's deeper than sex.

If there's one thing I learned from my study of Luce's life and powers, it's that we're not the isolated brain-boxes we, in our ignorance, believe ourselves to be. No, we are minds, and as minds we exist in a sea of consciousness, from which birth abruptly parts us and to which we always long to return. Sex, if you're lucky, can only emulate that sublimely connected state.

As infants, we're cut off and our natural telepathy

- our natural *connection* - is ignored. Sooner or later we come to realise we've been abandoned, like an animal captured in the wild and locked up alone in a cage with none of her own kind. The young Luce, I was told, used to communicate in some mysterious way with tiny babies. Maybe she was reassuring them, comforting them in their confusion.

Without the sustenance of connection, we grow fearful and uncertain, desperate to touch but constantly thwarted. What's real is denied; what's false is exalted. So we learn to suppress our own awareness; we *turn ourselves off*. If your entire concept of who and what you are is based on this cruel delusion of separation, and someone comes along to *turn you on* - well, you can either go with it joyfully or fight it to the death, for it will destroy your illusions. There are many, as Auden says, who would rather die than change. Leave it all behind, said Jesus. Be as little children and follow me. Turn on, tune in, drop out, said Leary. Open your mind to reality, say the Gnostics, and Luce.

Richard the Mad Reichian (his offences related to 'public decency'; his refusal to recant got him an indefinite sentence) had a great secret: his time in the Orgone box had given him a peculiar sort of tele-kinetic power that applied only to certain fruit. He could make an orange roll towards him from a distance of up to six inches, a grape from about a foot.

He was canny enough not to go around displaying this ability, but when I finally gained his confidence he swore me to silence and gave me a demonstration. I wasn't surprised to hear that he'd been taken away for 'tests' after having foolishly demonstrated his powers to a nurse. 'But when I got there I felt afraid, I didn't like the doctors, and I heard Dr Reich's voice in my head saying, *Hide, Richie, hide!*

'So I pretended I'd only been pretending. When they asked for a demonstration I didn't *really* do it, but - this was clever, don't you think? - I pretended to believe that I *had* actually done it. They decided I was just ordinary crazy and sent me back.'

He tried to describe how it worked. 'We're all in a sea,' he said, making floating gestures with his arms and bobbing buoyantly up and down. 'And we're made of the same sea - me, the oranges, the grapes, everything. So I feel them, I know what it's like to *be* them, and if I love them, and ask them to come to me, they do. Because they love me, too.'

8

A Wandering Troubadour

§❧

Waldo Seton Smith's Story. Harold Childe. The Enchanter with the Blue Guitar. She Sings Their Souls. Enter the Robots. The Eschaton.

San Francisco to Taos, May 1967

By the time I'd finished telling Karen my story, the sun had set and a soft evening mist was drifting in from the sea. We strolled towards North Beach, where she knew a good Moroccan restaurant. On the way we stopped into City Lights. Karen chatted with a friend of hers who worked there; I browsed the shelves of what was, even then, one of the world's great bookshops. In the Avant-garde Fiction section a slim volume caught my attention because its distinctive cover, though a woodcut rather than a photograph, reminded me of Karen's picture of Lou: a solitary, androgynous figure seen from the back, silhouetted by the stylised rays of a setting or rising sun, walking into the distance. This one had a guitar slung over its back. The book's title, *Petra Lumis*, also intrigued, sounding as it did so like a variant of Lou Peterson. I bought it and, as we waited for our dinner in the restaurant, leafed through it with Karen. We soon became convinced that the title character, Petra Lumis, had to have been inspired by Lou Peterson some time before Karen met her in San Francisco.

The book had been published in 1964 by Coyote Howl Press of Santa Fe, New Mexico. It was not destined to be an immediate success; in fact it was a total flop, remaining entirely obscure until 1993, when it was cited by Johan Sorenson in his acceptance speech for that year's Nobel Prize for literature, as his most important influence. Its author, Waldo Seton Smith, never wrote another work of fiction, though his poetry and essays are highly regarded. He's now best known as the founder of the Taos Temenos, a writers' workshop and retreat centre at Taos, New Mexico, wellspring of the 'Southwest School' of American literature and incubator of numerous National Book Award and Pulitzer Prize winners.

The narrator of *Petra Lumis* (subtitled *An Eschatological Fable*) is an eleven-year-old boy named Harold Childe, a reference to Byron's *Childe Harold's Pilgrimage*, source of the novel's epigraph:

> To such as see thee not my words were weak;
> To those who gaze on thee, what language could
> they speak?

In the poem, 'Byron expresses the view that man's greatest tragedy is that he can conceive of a perfection which he cannot attain.'[*] The glory and the tragedy of Harold Childe's life is his encounter with a strange person called Petra Lumis.

Harold was abandoned by his parents at birth due to a mysterious condition, a never-specified deformity, anomaly or aberration. Although he says he's blind, he appears to see perfectly well. He also claims to be deaf, but recounts everything he hears. He

---

[*] Jerome McGann, ed, *Byron: The Complete Poetical Works* (Oxford English Texts series, 1980–1993), p. 104.

frequently describes himself as a cripple, but he walks and runs and, on occasion, swims. He says he's dumb, but he speaks and, once, sings. Harold Childe's disabilities, then, may be taken as metaphors, pertaining to his mind or his soul rather than his body.

The story begins at dawn on Harold's eleventh birthday (a magical moment of transition in many old stories and fairy tales). Harold hasn't slept all night. 'An antsy kind of tear-ache, a long-night longing that wouldn't let me rest' drove him outside, where he 'sat gnawing scabby knees on the grimcold grimy stoop' of the orphanage in Tophet, Indiana, where he has lived all his life. (In the Old Testament, Tophet is the place where children are taken to be slaughtered.) A wandering troubadour strolls past and Harold's life is changed.

> She was thin and wonderful clean, hair angel-pale, quick fingers trilling the strings and the frets of her guitar. Above her head a bird fluttered in and out of the incandescent air, whirring bright wings, and the scent of roses curled in heady whirls from her heels. She's singing a song about laughter, about water that flows like burning ice, about another place where I could live, if only, if onlyonlyonly. I'd never seen anyone like that and what could I do but scream inside, shriek, howl and cry? With one look she turned me inside out. I abandoned my maimed and empty past, I stepped into the sparkling stream, I followed her.*

Her name is Petra Lumis. She carries a blue guitar† slung across her back on a red cord, with a tassel 'that dusted the dusty air

---

* All quotations from Waldo Seton Smith, *Petra Lumis: An Eschatological Fable* (Santa Fe: Coyote Howl Press, 1964), by permission of the author.
† 'And they said then, "But play, you must,/A tune beyond us, yet ourselves,/A tune upon the blue guitar/Of things exactly as they are."' Wallace Stevens, 'The Man with the Blue Guitar'. Waldo acknowledged that it was he, not

with seducing to and fro'. She and her accordion-playing sidekick Chico (a diminutive derived from the Spanish form of Frank, Francisco) are walking across the country. 'A chancer, a trickster, an enchanter, a will-o'-the-wisp, a slip-slider between the humdrum ticktocks of the clock,' as the star-struck Harold describes her.

At first the novel seems to promise a light-hearted, whimsical road-trip. Petra, Chico and Harold encounter eccentric characters and get into and out of scrapes. Everywhere that Petra and Chico stop to play, people gather. Petra keeps them spellbound with her singing; the songs, Harold realises, are made up on the spot, inspired by the listeners' own lives, 'spun from their dreary days, melded with mythical metals, burnished into true fables'. Petra somehow knows each person's secret loves, their long-forgotten hopes. 'She drew their squandered dreams from the farfar back of their eyes, sang them into poetry that turned upon them with sweet loving kiss of waking.'

Things grow stranger as they head west into a semi-imaginary American hinterland. They encounter speaking trees, mobile boulders, huge piebald storm-crows, fire-foxes with flaming tails, triple-headed river-snakes, a pipe-smoking dung-beetle the size of a cow. The natural world becomes a character in the unfolding drama: an obliging asteroid delivers a telegram, a hailstorm courteously marks the path out of a deadly maze.

The tone darkens; Harold notices that they are being followed. For a long time it's only a vague feeling, but he starts watching closely and soon catches glimpses of ominous figures, visible at dusk and dawn 'as though extruded from the chaos chasm between night and day'. Although these figures resemble humans, Harold describes them as 'robots'.

One night in the middle of nowhere, while they're camping
_____
Petra, who was quoting Wallace Stevens with this reference. Petra's actual guitar was a plain brown Gibson.

in a 'bitter-red desert land between the long-dead river beds', Harold dreams that the robots attack, killing Chico and Petra and leaving him tied up and helpless: 'they wrap me in a frozen cocoon of dread, IcannotmoveIcannotspeak'.

A meagre day dawns; Harold wakes up alone in a blasted world. Everywhere he looks, there is devastation and destruction. Petra and Chico have vanished. It's not just his own soul that has been severed from its beloved, the whole world is dead or dying. He wanders around for a while and sees only corpses and ruins. It's the end of the world, the eschaton. He dies.

Possibly the unalloyed pessimism of the ending had something to do with the book's lack of immediate popularity.

&

The next morning I called Coyote Howl Press and arranged to interview Waldo Seton Smith two days hence at his home. The address they gave me was, intriguingly, a few miles from Taos, New Mexico, source of Karen's postcard. I didn't want to leave a trail of airline bookings or car hire, so – doing our damnedest to make certain we weren't being followed – we drove all night and half a day in Karen's sturdy VW van, arriving at Taos mid-afternoon.

Waldo Seton Smith was a homely, gawky man of about thirty, with large ears and a weather-beaten face. He looked less like the author of an avant-garde novel than a farmer, which is what he was, having inherited the family dairy ranch. His comment, as we shook hands, was the somewhat ungracious 'The publishers said I had to talk to you.' Nevertheless, he showed us into a large, cluttered kitchen, shifted a somnolent tabby cat from one chair, a pile of farm machinery catalogues from another, and indicated that we should sit. A young woman with a gurgling baby at her hip came in, was introduced as his wife Miriam, and served us coffee and cake. The loving look with which Waldo

153

greeted their appearance suggested that his reserve with us did not indicate a temperament cold by nature.

To put him at ease I began an ordinary interview, expressing my admiration for the book (which I'd read on the way), asking about his literary influences and so on. When I enquired about possible autobiographical elements he denied that the book was based upon any actual experiences whatsoever, insisting that he'd made the whole thing up in his bedroom upstairs.

'See, it says right here.' He pointed to the page. 'Any resemblance to persons living or dead is purely coincidental.'

The only way to get him to open up, I saw, was for Karen and me to be completely open ourselves. Karen took over the conversation, telling the story of her friendship with Petra Lumis and Chico, whom she knew as Lou and Frankie Peterson. When she came to the Las Vegas bit and told them about Lou's telekinesis at the roulette wheel, Miriam, who'd been pottering quietly in the background, came and slipped into a chair next to her husband. Karen showed them the postcard from Taos; Miriam studied it closely, then handed it to Waldo with a small smile.

Then I explained that Lou Peterson and Petra Lumis were Luce of Luce and the Photons, whose story it was my mission to tell, and Chico was the keyboard player on the *Human* album. A look of wonder gradually replaced the tight-lipped reticence on Waldo's face. He and Miriam exchanged glances. By the time I got to the part about the demon-simulacra in Golden Square, they were both rapt. The clincher, I think, was Karen's and my description of the paralysing, nauseating fear they evoked, so similar to the 'frozen cocoon of dread' that enveloped the helplessly dreaming Harold Childe when the 'robots' attacked.

Dishonesty had been a great strain on him, and Waldo was clearly relieved to acknowledge that *Petra Lumis* was indeed based on real events and encounters with a real person. I didn't yet understand why he'd been so determined to deny it. Waldo knew that Petra wasn't her real name, though he'd never known what that was. The time that he'd spent on the road with her had changed his life, and now it was a great pleasure to speak of those days with others who'd known her.

Waldo had gone east to university, having won a scholarship to Brown, where he'd studied, of all things, Old English. He could recite *Beowulf* in the original, which he proceeded to demonstrate, much to the amusement of the baby, whose name was Petra. After graduation he undertook a *Wanderjahr* or two, tramping the byways of America, taking up jobs and leaving them, staying in workers' dormitories or bleak, cheap rooms or sleeping in the open, scribbling poetry in dozens of notebooks which he discarded as soon as he'd filled them. Somewhere in Missouri in the summer of 1962 he'd met Petra and Chico. For over a year they wandered the back roads of America together, heading south in the winter, north in the summer. The events of the novel, though fantastical and symbolic, were all, he insisted, based on things that had really happened.

'Petra had a way of attracting intense people,' he said. 'Or, I should say, a way of bringing out some intensity in them that I'd missed. I'd been bumming around for more than a year, and nothing much had happened to me. The people I'd met had all been completely ordinary, nice or not so nice, kind or unkind, clever or stupid, but all of them very ordinary. When I was with Petra, everything was different.'

Talking about Petra made Waldo light up; his guarded demeanour melted, he sat forward, hands gesturing. 'The people we met were so real, so vivid. They shone, they sparkled. And I don't mean they were all nice or bright. They shone with themselves, their good and their bad. All their humanness was lit up, but it was Petra who made it happen. I was seeing them through the lens of her presence. She opened my eyes to their reality, which I'd never seen before. That's what I meant when I made Harold Childe blind and deaf. He hadn't been able to see. I hadn't been able to see.'

'Did Petra and Chico tell you anything about their background?'

Waldo laughed. 'Petra said nothing, but Chico said lots, a different story every day. He said they'd been stowaways on an alien spaceship, now stranded on Earth. They were refugees from a country called Arcadia, where an evil dictator, Generalissimo Archon, had seized power. They were orphans, abandoned on a church step. They were wealthy English aristocrats, travelling in this manner for pure pleasure. They were bank robbers on the run.'

I asked about the novel's enigmatic climax. What had really happened?

He sighed and shook his head. 'I don't know. What I said in the book was true about my feelings, but as to the real cause? Were the robots real or figments of my imagination? Petra and Chico vanished one night while we were camped near Winslow, Arizona. I was asleep and I had a nightmare, just like in the book. Of course, when I woke the world wasn't literally in ruins, but it felt that way to me because Petra and Chico were gone.'

'But the story didn't end that night, did it?' I said. 'Petra and Chico – Lou and Frankie – arrived in San Francisco in May 1964 and stayed until September, then went with Karen to Warm Springs. Three weeks later they disappeared from Las Vegas and a week after that Lou sent this postcard from Taos. She was here with you, wasn't she?

Miriam and Waldo exchanged another meaningful glance; then she got up and left the room. Waldo excused himself and followed her. When they returned a few minutes later Waldo announced their decision: they would tell us the rest of the story under the condition that their identities remain secret during their lifetimes. Their condition has been honoured. Waldo died in 2009, Miriam the following year.

9

The Harrowing of Hell

Miriam's Story. The Experiments. The Child in the Chair. Phantom Limb. Death of a Doctor. Escape by Station Wagon. A New Life. A Bird without a Cage.

After Petra and Chico vanished, Waldo returned in desolation to the family ranch. His father had fallen ill and he was needed at home. He wrote *Petra Lumis* over the course of six hard months as his father died, painfully, of stomach cancer. He'd sent it off to publishers less in the expectation of getting it published than with the desire to expunge a traumatic chapter of his life. He settled in with the cows, rode out every day over his twelve hundred acres, mended his fences and had no ambitions beyond increased milk production. He was astonished when Coyote Howl accepted the manuscript. *Petra Lumis* came out in September 1964.

And then, on 9 October, Petra herself appeared with Chico and four others piled into a station wagon.

'Where had they come from?' I asked.

'They'd come from Hell, she'd rescued them from Hell. That was all any of them would say at first. They seemed to be in a daze. Petra said that they needed some peace and quiet, and could I take them in for a while? Of course I said yes. I was so happy to see her. I'd told her about the place and she said she'd visit some time, but I hadn't really expected it.'

'Who were the others?'

'That's it, you see. They didn't know who they were. They were pretty out of it – some of them could barely speak. They didn't even know their own names, just what they'd been called in Hell: John25, Bob14, Jane19 and Nancy27. Chico was the worst case of all – he was nearly catatonic. He'd walk if you pulled him along, sit if you pushed him into a chair, eat if food was put in his mouth. It used to tear my heart to see Petra feed him, talk to him, walk him around the yard, try so hard to coax him into life.'

Karen and I exchanged glances. I knew she was picturing the suave, enigmatic, attractive man who'd charmed all the girls. This must be what Lou had meant when she'd said Frankie was 'gone'.

'So I found them all places to sleep,' Waldo said. 'I made food, soups and stews, good nourishing food. Tried to take care of them. They were pale and weak, as though they'd spent a long time indoors. They'd break down in tears at odd moments. They stuck together, comforted each other. Whispered to each other before any of them would ever speak to me. At first they seemed numb, then afraid, gradually a bit less afraid. For a long time, I learned, they suspected that everything was an act, part of a mind game someone was playing with them.'

'How had they got like that?'

'Hell,' Waldo said. 'Hell made them like that. They'd been there, some of them, for years. Bit by bit they got better and began to talk about what had happened to them. But none of them was ever able to remember their life before Hell. They'd been . . . experimented upon. Against their will. With drugs and . . . other things.'

159

Miriam had tucked the sleeping baby into a crib and was listening intently as Waldo spoke. She shivered and reached for a shawl that was draped over her chair. 'They were lab rats, human lab rats,' she said. 'They were kept in boxes, lights controlled, temperature, everything controlled, even their thoughts and emotions. Even their will. Drugs, experiments. Some caused terrible pain, unbearable feelings. They messed with memory, with sleep, with dreams.'

'But why?' I asked. 'Experiments for what purpose?'

Miriam and Waldo shared a long look, then she spoke. 'Some people have unusual abilities. What Lou did in the casino. You knew it was telekinesis. That's one ability – it's pretty rare. There are others. And there are people who are interested in studying and using these abilities.'

'What people?' Karen asked. I knew she was thinking of the 'certain people' Lou had mentioned.

'People who have power, and who want to keep it,' said Waldo.

'You probably think this is a crazy fantasy,' Miriam said. 'We're deluded, or we're making this up to play a trick on you, sell you some tall tale for a joke. I wouldn't blame you. It sounds like a Hollywood movie. Or a trashy science-fiction story.'

'Actually, I do believe you,' I said. 'It makes sense of something else.' I turned to Karen. 'Doesn't it remind you of the painting Lou did in your house at Warm Springs, the child strapped into the chair?'

Miriam inhaled sharply; Waldo took her hand.

'It does sound just like that,' Karen said.

We described the painting to Waldo and Miriam: the wires and needles, the evil doctor looming, the pain and the helpless fury of the child.

Miriam's eyes brimmed with tears; she brushed them away.

Something suddenly became clear to me. 'You were there, weren't you? In Hell. You're one of the ones Petra rescued.'

She glanced at Waldo. 'Yes. I was there. I was Jane 19. I have one of those special abilities they were researching. Astral travel, etheric projection, whatever you want to call it. It's something everybody does when they're asleep, but most people aren't able to control it and don't remember it when they wake. I can go out of my body any time, remember what I see and hear, then return and tell it. That's what they trained me to do. They'd drug me, then the Controller would take over. Someone would enter my mind and direct me, send me places, make my astral body do what they wanted it to do.'

'But how did you end up there in the first place?' Karen asked.

Miriam pulled her shawl close and gazed into the distance. I could tell that she was steeling herself to remember things that she'd no doubt spent a lot of time trying to forget. 'I don't know. A few fragments of my past have come back to me, though not enough to trace where I came from. There was an ocean, and playing with another child, who I think was my sister. A garden with flowers. I was talking to the flowers and they were talking to me, then there was a bright light everywhere and the next thing I knew I was in a hospital. Then a long gap where I don't remember anything at all, then I was in the lab. In Hell. I don't know for how long. I don't know how old I was when I got there. They were trying to breed us. I had children, I think three or maybe four.'

'Christ. What happened to them?'

'I have no idea. They were taken away at birth.'

We were silent for a long time; none of us could think of anything to say. My eyes were drawn to the baby asleep in her crib; when I looked around, I saw that we were all gazing at her.

'Who did this to you?' I asked. 'Who were these people?'

'I don't know. They didn't wear *name tags*, you know. They didn't *introduce* themselves.' Miriam's tone was biting. 'They were just . . . the ones in control. Doctors, nurses, technicians, guards. The US government had something to do with it, I assume, because the guards wore US Army uniforms. The doctors weren't all American, though. It was a very international outfit. We often had foreign doctors. I call them doctors because that's how we were told to address them, no names, just "Doctor", but I don't know what sort of doctors they were. Not the kind that help you if you're sick, that's for sure. Several were English, some were Japanese, I think, but maybe Chinese or Korean, I can't tell. And a couple Germans, or maybe Poles or Swiss or something like that. A French guy, or could have been French-Canadian. I'm only guessing from their accents. They'd come, run their experiments on us, collect their data and go. Then others would come with other experiments. Some of the drugs they gave us really messed with time-perception, so it's impossible for me to remember in what order things happened.'

'There were you four, plus Chico . . . was that all of you?'

'Yeah, that was all of us right then, though at times there had been more, maybe ten or twelve. Not huge numbers. We were an exclusive little group. Some people were newer than me, and some who'd been there before me weren't around any more. I suppose they got transferred, or maybe they died. Sometimes people arrived from other labs. I don't think they ever let anyone go. Once they had you, there was no exit. Or,' she gave a small laugh, 'only one. I assumed I'd die there, when they were done with me, or if some experiment went wrong.'

Dusk had fallen as we talked, accompanied by the lowing of the cows as they made their way to the milking sheds behind the house. The horrors of Hell lurked just beneath the surface of this idyllic little family scene, and the absolutely ordinary had never looked so rare and precious to me. Waldo got up and turned on the lights.

'Then one night,' Miriam said, 'they brought in a new man. Chico, as it turned out, though of course I didn't know his name.

162

He was in a wheelchair; they'd already done something to him. They parked him in the corridor while they worked out what room to put him in, that's where I saw him. The doctor came out and seemed very pleased to get him, but angry when he saw the state he was in. Maybe he'd had a bad reaction to some drug they'd given him to keep him quiet during transport. I'd seen that happen before. It can happen if you go out of your body, then while you're out they give the body a new drug they want to test, and then when you come back the patterns are so disrupted that you can't get yourself lined up, so you're locked out. The body doesn't die, it maintains a sort of animal existence, but you can't live in it any more. That's how Chico seemed to me, totally out of it.'

'Tell them what happened when Petra came,' Waldo said. He waited for her to speak, watching her face, a look of deep tenderness in his eyes.

'It was some time later that night. I was strapped in and hooked up to the usual drips and sensors that kept me in hypnagogic sleep – that in-between state when you're neither awake nor fully asleep. Theta-wave range, in the jargon. My lights suddenly came on and a person came in. I sensed their presence before my physical senses woke up, and I knew right away that it wasn't a doctor or a nurse or a technician. What I felt coming into my room was . . . goodness, intense goodness. I can't describe it any other way. It was a sense of prayers answered, of salvation. I was being saved, somehow I knew that, and my heart woke up and in a rush my mind ripped through the drugs and leapt up to meet her. She disconnected me and told me to get dressed and follow her. That's when I saw Chico again, he was shuffling along after her. We went into the other rooms and I helped her unhook the others and get them dressed. She asked if we didn't have shoes, and I said no, only slippers. Then for some reason I found that incredibly funny. I started laughing and couldn't stop. I

163

hadn't laughed for years, I'd forgotten what it was, I scared myself. Then I started shaking and couldn't stop that, either. She took my hand for a moment and I calmed down right away. She gathered us all together and led us down the corridor. I was helping Nancy27, who'd had a foot removed.'

'A foot removed? Why?'

'For a phantom-limb experiment. Heard of that?'

'Isn't that when a person continues to sense a limb that's been amputated?'

'Right. It's their astral limb they're sensing. An interesting phenomenon, they'd done several experiments on it. Luckily not yet on me. We hadn't got very far when one of the nurses appeared. Petra said something to her in a whisper, just a few words like, "You want to help us." And she did. She took Nancy27's other arm and put it over her shoulders and helped her. We encountered another nurse, a lab technician, a cleaner – and the same thing happened. Petra spoke to them and they came along with us. But then a doctor appeared, the one who ran the place. His experiments were the worst. I really don't want to talk about the experiments.' Her hands clenched, then she made a swift gesture, as though batting something aside. 'That's definitely best forgotten.'

'You don't have to go on if you don't want to,' Karen said.

'Oh, but now we're getting to the good part. Before Petra could speak, John25 charged at him, grabbed him around the throat, had him down and was throttling him and banging his head against the floor. It was all over in about two seconds. I don't know what killed him, the strangling or the smashed skull.'

'Blimey. What did Petra do?'

'There was nothing anyone could do. I was afraid the nurses would react, would now try to stop us, but it was like they were hypnotised. Petra said, "Come on, let's go," and we left him lying there in his blood. It gave me such a feeling of satisfaction to step over that pool of blood, and look down on his dead face. I only wished his death could have been very slow and painful. He didn't deserve such a quick end. I tried to spit on him but my mouth was too dry. We came to a door, one of the nurses unlocked it, we went along a corridor and finally we came to the outside door, where there was a guard. Again, Petra spoke to him, he smiled and opened the door and came out with us. She asked if there was anyone left inside. He counted us, checked his clipboard and said, "Just Dr Anderson," and Petra said, "I think he's staying."

'I hadn't been outside in so many years, I couldn't take it in. I hadn't breathed real air in so long I'd forgotten what it was like. And the hum had stopped, that steady hum of machinery and electricity. And I could see more than a few yards. I could see more than walls and floors and ceilings. It was the world, and it went on and on. I had to keep checking to be sure I was in my physical body. It was nighttime; I think if it had been daytime I couldn't have borne it. The sensation of air on my skin, a breeze, the smell of tarmac and earth and . . . everything. I was overwhelmed, I think we all were. Except Chico, who took no notice of anything. Petra had him by the hand and was pulling him along. It was too good to be true and all at once I was filled with fear that it was all a delusion, a trick, that we were about to be stopped, shot, I don't know. I had an urge to run back to my room and hook myself up before they caught me, but the door had closed.

'We walked to the parking lot. There were a few cars, mostly small sedans, one station wagon. Petra asked whose it was. One of the nurses said it was hers so Petra said, "You want to give us this car," and the nurse said the key was in the ignition. We got in and Petra drove away. She stopped the car on a little rise, got out and stood gazing down at the place. It was a low, feature-less building next to an airstrip with only flat, scrubby land in all directions. There was a flash of light and the building collapsed almost silently into itself. I knew she'd made that happen. She got back into the car and drove for a few minutes until we came to a fence and a guard post. She chatted with the guard, he opened the gate and let us out. None of us dared speak. The sun came up behind us, so I knew we were heading west. We drove all day, stopping only for gas and sandwiches. We drove on into the setting sun. Then we arrived here.'

Waldo took up the story. 'I realised pretty soon that they'd escaped from somewhere, I thought probably a mental hospital.' He laughed. 'It was the slippers. I had no idea why Petra was doing this, but it didn't matter. I was glad she'd chosen me to help. We hid the car in a barn, and she took it apart herself, every nut and bolt, and buried it. I had to account for the sudden guests, but that wasn't too difficult. The nearest neighbour is more than a mile away. I'd been living alone since Dad died, just a couple of old hands coming in to help with the cows. I told them the newcomers were writer friends of mine from the east coast. Everybody knows that people from the east coast are crazy, not like regular people at all. Since I'd been there and become a writer, it was understood that I was a bit crazy, too. Anyway, people round here mind their own business.'

'After a couple of weeks with no drugs and no experiments we were a lot better,' said Miriam. 'We chose new names. It felt like a rebirth; we were like children, discovering who we were, what we wanted to do. None of us wished to go back to our previous selves, even if we could have remembered who we'd been. There were no memories to guide us, or almost none. The best thing was to lie low, not call attention to ourselves.'

The back door of the house opened, sending a gust of cool, farmyard-fragrant air across our faces. Hell receded; the ordinary world marched in with the farmhands. Cheerful voices emerged from the passage as they took off boots and coats. Miriam got up briskly and went to the stove where she stirred a big pot of something, lifted a tray of potatoes out of the oven, took down a stack of plates.

'You'll stay for supper,' she called over her shoulder to us. 'Plenty of food.' She'd resumed her happy role as farmwife, one could see with what relief. All that had grown tense and tight as we spoke of her time in Hell was now released and I realised what it had cost her to remember.

The farmhands came in, washed their hands at the sink, received plates of food, took places at the table and were introduced as Waldo handed round bottles of Schlitz. There were two men, Lance and Christopher, and a woman called Sarah who walked with a limp.

Waldo caught my eye, saw me make my guess and gave me a small smile. I studied the farmhands covertly. Which was John25, I wondered, the one who'd killed the doctor? Chris was a wispy fellow of perhaps eighteen or twenty, with a slight tic in his eye and a shy, somewhat nervous manner. It had to be Lance – fortyish, grizzled hair and beard, economic of movement. He had the build to tackle a man and bring him to the floor, and his large, rough hands looked quite capable of strangling. And he'd chosen a warrior's name. *Well done you*, I thought to him, *and good luck*. He glanced sharply up at me and I remembered that the reason he'd been there in Hell in the first place would have been due to some 'special abilities' he possessed. Including, apparently, telepathy. I raised my beer in salute.

After supper Miriam invited us to stay the night, but one didn't need to be telepathic to sense that she'd rather we went on our way. Our presence was a reminder of all that she most needed to forget. Karen and I decided we'd make a start on the drive back to California. As Miriam and Waldo walked us out to the VW I asked what had happened to Petra and Chico.

'Chico wasn't getting better,' Waldo said. 'He was like someone in shock. Petra didn't understand what was wrong with him, and that was really upsetting for her. At first, I think she believed she'd be able to fix him, make him himself again, just by *willing* it. When she spoke to him, she called him Francis, not Chico. I think that must be his real name, and she was trying to get through to him by using it. But nothing she did seemed to work, though he knew her, that's for sure. He'd look up when she came into a room, and generally was happiest when she was near. About a week after they'd arrived, I woke up one morning and they were gone. The night before, Petra had told me how grateful she was for my help, and I realised later that she'd been saying goodbye.'

'In December 'sixty-four,' said Karen, 'I got a card from Kathmandu. With an eye, like the first.'

'We got one from there, too,' Waldo said. 'All it had was a drawing of a bird, but we knew it was from Petra. We get another one every now and then, just a bird. A bird without a cage. We know what it means.'

'If you see her,' said Miriam, 'tell her we're all fine. Tell her . . . tell her we thank her more than words can ever say.'

Karen gave Waldo and Miriam each a long hug. Being English, I confined myself to a brief one, but no less fond. We drove off into the night, promising to visit some time, though we understood that they'd be perfectly happy never to see us again. We'd come, we'd taken their story, and we'd left. They'd use us as part of the forgetting, the getting rid of, the leaving behind. What we took away with us they released gladly, and some part of their burden was shed.

We drove in silence for a long time. Around midnight we stopped for gas and coffee at a twenty-four-hour truck stop. As we sat nursing our cups in the bright, almost empty diner we kept looking at each other, sensing a similar state of speculative rumination and dropping back into our own thoughts, pondering what we'd heard. I'd entered that phase of my quest for Luce in which every bit of information I acquired increased my uncertainty. As a journalist, I was accustomed to using facts to pin down my subjects, each item leading to a sharper focus, a more fixed definition. But with Luce, each 'fact' sent me off in a different direction, I lost focus and Luce continually slid out of my grasp. Who was she? Rock star, artist, multi-media wizard, LSD priestess . . . these fitted together. This was the Luce I'd set out to find. But then we get telekinesis, mind control, daring rescues, evil doctors, demon-simulacra and The Government. We get the Bigs, the NOHRM and secret psychic research programmes. It was beginning to do my head in. If I'd had any sense it would have sent me running in the opposite direction as fast as I could, but I had that casual disregard for consequences that is a result of the delayed entry into adulthood characteristic of my generation. I realised I'd developed a tendency to divide Luce into two persons, and had continually to remind myself that the two must be reconciled.

Did she, too, struggle with this necessary reconciliation? In 'O Mephistopheles', Luce sings of a 'dance with the dark angel of necessity, gravity, destiny'. What necessities governed her life, her choices? When you have certain extraordinary abilities, it must be that sooner or later, even if you most heartily wish to live an ordinary life, you will be brought to a situation in which you must become who you are. And then one thing will lead to another.

Finally Karen spoke, and it was clear that our musings had covered the same ground. 'Lou's painting of the child strapped down in the chair.'

'Yes,' I said. Was that Luce herself?

'The numbers.'

'Yes.' What had happened to the earlier Johns, Bobs, Janes and Nancys? How long had the programme been going on? How many people had been involved, how many prison-laboratories?

'She had been there, or another place like that.'

'Yes, she must have been. As a child.'

'Because she has those special abilities they're interested in. I wonder how they found her, where she'd been before. Who her family is. Who she really is. Does she know herself? Or was she left like Miriam and the others, with no memory of her past?'

'Children were born there, too . . .'

'Was *she* born in a lab like that? Bred from others? And then got away, or was rescued?'

'And who's Frankie? *What's* Frankie? Is he really her brother? Maybe they escaped together from one of those places.'

'Frankie's still a mystery to me,' Karen said. 'I always thought he had something to hide; now I know it's for a good reason. He loves Lou and she loves him and they look out for each other. That's all that matters.' Then she changed tack. 'You're a journalist. Are you going to write about this?'

The thought had crossed my mind, as I listened to Miriam's story, that I had the scoop of a lifetime: a secret government programme to research psychic powers, that kidnapped and imprisoned people, experimented upon them and even bred them. I'd basked in the glory of journalistic fame for about two seconds before I realised it would never be published. The evidence I'd need, the testimonies of witnesses . . .

'They'd squash you like a bug,' Karen said. 'Like a bug. You'd disappear and no one would ever hear from you again.'

'I know I can't write about it.'

'And Lou?'

'What could I write? I keep on not finding her. I have a feeling there's a long way to go before I'm ready to tell her story.'

'And your work for the NOHRM?' Karen had a way of putting her finger right on the nub.

I'd given some thought to the fortnightly reports that Mrs Big expected from me. If I'd been followed to Warm Springs, she would know I'd been there, but now that the paintings had been destroyed, there was nothing I needed to protect. Karen believed that she herself was in no danger, and it didn't seem that Jay had been deliberately targeted. The most important thing was for me to conceal from the Bigs the fact that I knew it was Luce and her works they were after; if I lied about Warm Springs, it would be a dead give-away. In due course I reported that I'd searched in Nevada and found some paintings that I thought might have been by Luce, but which were unfortunately burned in an accidental house fire before I could photograph them. The house's current occupant had told me that the paintings were made by someone who'd rented the house briefly several years ago, and left no forwarding address.

Karen dropped me off at LA airport. I'd decided to go on to Kathmandu, to see if I could find any trace of Luce/Lou/Petra and Frankie/Chico/Francis. I was already halfway there and, if I needed further encouragement, there was the thought of my brother's wedding in London. An excellent reason to be on the other side of the planet. I sent him a card, the cheesiest I could find, citing urgent business far away.

Now.

Email from Karen today, with photos of her wedding.
After thirty-five years together, she's finally been
allowed by the state of Nevada to marry her long-time
partner Wendy. They look ridiculously happy. They
say, 'Wish you were here,' and I think they do mean
it. I've sent them a tandem bicycle as a wedding
present, and here they are on it. Grinning like idiots.
Karen's a bit on the heavy side now and her wild mane
of hair is all white, but her face is as open and kind
as ever.

They're going to Hawaii for a honeymoon. I find that
sort of faith in normality very touching, though only,
I've noticed, when it's practised by people about whom
I care. Mostly it's just tedious, but Karen's been a
good friend and she can do what she likes. She used
to visit me in hospital, then when I was let out on
overnight leave, she'd have me to stay – she and Wendy
were living in the house at Warm Springs by then, with
Jay, who'd rebuilt it just as she'd foretold. When I
was moved 'into the community' it was Karen who helped

me furnish my flat. She brought seeds and a trowel and got me started growing vegetables in the handkerchief-sized garden. I rarely ate them, but I never told her that. And it was Karen who persuaded me to get a glass eye. She knew I didn't believe I had a right to look 'normal'. So if Karen feels the need to marry, and to have a honeymoon, even in Hawaii, all I want to do is wish her well.

10

Into the Mountains

❦

Frontier of the Mind. The Moon Garden. The Portrait. Giorgio Servadio's Story. The True Satsang. The Journey. Gauri's Story. The Healing of the Blind. The Blizzard.

Kathmandu, May 1967

I'd been to Kathmandu once before and it wasn't until I climbed into the twin-prop at Patna for the last leg of the flight that I remembered I'd sworn I would never, never fly into that town again, no matter how long and arduous the road journey threatened to be. The landing strip (I cannot dignify it with the term 'runway'), approached by tacking this way and that through narrow gorges, is the barest sliver of tilted, potholed concrete tucked into a steep valley. It permits no second thoughts, no second chances. The pilot cannot pull up or veer aside if there is, as happens not infrequently, a yak in the way. One lands, avoiding the yak as best one can, or one crashes into the mountain.

Ten minutes from landing a sudden storm arose and all my premonitions of disaster seemed about to be realised. The plane was swooping and lurching like a drunk on a trapeze. Trapped in a rain-lashed window seat I closed my eyes tightly as we touched down with such a gut-wrenching bump I was sure we'd crashed and ghastly impact with mountainside was milliseconds away. The fact that several seconds passed without death occurring I took for the subjective slowing of time that's said to occur as one is about to die. When the plane finally came to a stop it took ages to persuade my fingers to loosen their grip on the armrests.

Kathmandu had the feel of a frontier town, which is precisely what it was. But a new frontier had arrived of late, a frontier of the mind, as spaced-out hippies confronted the reality – the immense and unfathomable unreality – of the mountains. To Western, city-crowded eyes, the ever-changing unchangingness is a right old mind-fuck. I'd known people to get hypnotised by the mountains, the vision of purity becoming addictive as a drug. The vast distances, the whiteness, the eternal cold: were these not the real realities they'd always sought? So easy to sit and contemplate the far, shining peaks, to imagine a life of icy cleanness, of freedom from the grubby, cluttered world.

And then there was that other drug, that other snowy whiteness. A lot of people found that when they couldn't manage the pure life in the mountains, some surcease was to be obtained in one of Kathmandu's kindly back-street doss-houses, where for a tiny amount of American currency, you could get a bed and a fix as a package deal.

Some time had passed since Luce's postcard (sent in December 1964), so although Kathmandu was, in essence, a small town as far as Western travellers were concerned, I wasn't overly optimistic about finding traces of her. Then again, she'd proved to be highly memorable in the past, and if she was travelling with a companion in a near-catatonic state she'd be even more distinctive, so I reckoned I had about a one-in-ten chance. The first few days, as I trawled bus depots and markets, hotels, cafés and hostels, were unproductive. I showed everyone I met Karen's photo of Lou, which admittedly didn't provide the clearest possible likeness. My enquiries were complicated by all that I'd learned about Luce's ambiguous appearance, changeable hair and variable names.

By the end of my fourth day I was ready to give up. Tomorrow, I decided, I'd take the bus to Patna – not, under any circumstances, risking another aeroplane trip – and head for home. Tired and thirsty, I stopped into a little restaurant called The Moon Garden, in a back street off Durbar Square, found a table by the window and ordered a beer and a bowl of rice and dahl. It proved to be better than average, which wasn't saying much. I drank my beer and ate my food and was debating with myself whether it was worthwhile to get out the photo and show it around when a small voice at my elbow asked if I wanted my portrait drawn. A little girl of eleven or twelve held a large drawing pad and a clutch of ballpoint pens.

'Five rupees only, very cheap. Gauri good, Gauri very very good! Look-see, look-see.' She showed me her drawings, and what I saw astonished me. The pages were filled with beautiful, elaborate geometries, trees and stars, angels and birds and strange part-human, part-animal forms. It seemed so like Luce's work that I assumed she must have got hold of a notebook of Luce's when Luce passed through Kathmandu. I asked if she knew the person who'd made these drawings.

'I make,' she said. 'Gauri *artist*. I show.' She hopped up on the chair opposite me, turned to a clean page and began to draw. She stopped after a few seconds and looked at me with a grin. 'Five rupees, okeydokey?'

'OK,' I said. 'Show me what you can do, Gauri.'

Her hand moved swiftly over the paper, the pad tilted towards her so I couldn't see. I waited, bemused, still sure that the drawings I'd seen had been done by Luce. I'd studied her work on

176

the *Human* album, at Golden Square and the house in Warm Springs; her style and imagery were distinctive. It was only polite to let little Gauri finish the portrait, but then I'd have a good look at the others. Maybe I could buy them. I'd offer her fifty rupees for the lot, going up to a hundred if necessary, or two hundred. Actually, I'd go as high as she liked; it was a pittance to me, and the opportunity to own original Luce drawings was not to be missed.

Gauri took longer than I'd expected. It grew dark and the proprietor brought an oil lamp to the table, pausing to look at Gauri's work and giving her an approving pat on the head. He came back with another beer for me. 'On the house,' he said. 'For being patient with our little artist.' He spoke in Italian-accented but fluent English, and I learned that his name was Giorgio Servadio, a former shoe salesman from Rome who'd washed up in Kathmandu after years of wandering and now worked as the night manager of the café. He had a classic Roman nose, receding hair and the beginnings of a paunch.

The portrait, when Gauri finally showed it to me, set all my assumptions on their heads. The same artist, the same hand, had undoubtedly made it and every other drawing in the notebook. Using ballpoint pens in four or five different colours, she'd drawn me in half-profile, looking pensive, my embroidered jacket morphing into a background of exploding pinwheels, stars and snaky lines. Curiously, she showed me wearing a hat with a peacock feather. I did have a hat with a peacock feather; in fact it was rather a trademark of mine, but I wasn't wearing it in Kathmandu.

I looked closely at the grinning Gauri, half expecting her to reveal herself to be Luce . . . but that truly was impossible. I reminded myself that Luce was at least five foot ten, and Gauri no more than four foot eight.

'This is wonderful, Gauri,' I said. 'But why have you given me this hat?'

She shrugged skinny, eloquent shoulders. 'Gauri draw what Gauri see,' she said, tapping her forehead. 'You like? Five rupees, please.'

'Yes, I like very much,' I said, handing her the money.

Giorgio came to the table and studied the drawing over my shoulder.

'How did she learn to draw this way?' I asked. 'Did someone teach her? I'm asking because I know a person who draws like this, and who was here about two and a half years ago. That's who I'm looking for.' I took the photograph of Luce from my bag.

It was clear that Giorgio recognised Luce immediately, but something about seeing the picture so affected him that he couldn't speak. He groped for a chair and sat down, never taking his eyes off the photograph. Gauri whispered, 'Lukas.' Giorgio put his arm around her and hugged her as he wiped his eyes.

'It's Lukas,' he said. 'We know him. We know him very well, don't we, Gauri?'

'He make me see,' Gauri said, touching her eyelids. 'He make me *artist*.'

'Gauri was born blind,' Giorgio said. 'Lukas healed her.'

ॐ

Giorgio, now turned thirty, had been one of the earliest of the wave of Western questers who abandoned their moribund churches and cathedrals, their dead saints, rigid creeds and tasteless wafers, in search of a more immediate, more visceral and simpler route to higher wisdom. Imbued, like all Italians, with Catholicism from infancy, his idea of higher wisdom was inextricably bound up with conflicted notions of the feminine and surreptitious hopes of unearned salvation. I think he was probably homosexual, though he didn't acknowledge it. His passion for the person he knew as Lukas was spiritual, certainly, but with a distinctly erotic tinge.

178

Giorgio had been wandering from ashram to ashram for nearly four years, from the beaches of Mahabalipuram to the Kashmiri hills. He was consistently disappointed, his thirst for enlightenment unquenched, his faith in human nature eroded. And then he met Luce: on her way, with the still nearly catatonic Francis, to Nepal. Her appearance in Giorgio's life caused the sort of immediate upheaval I'd come to expect from people's encounters with Luce.

'I was staying at Swami Satchitramananda's ashram, which was far from the worst place I'd been. It was called Prashanti Nilayam, which means "Abode of Highest Peace". I'd concluded that was meant as a joke, or a wish so long unfulfilled that it turns into a joke. The closer one gets to one's spiritual nature, it seems, the worse one's character becomes. Wars all the time between the old disciples, who came with their wives and mothers, their beds and baskets and babies, and the new ones, the stupid children like me, with our backpacks and mosquito repellent. They shat happily in the hole; we protested, and cleaned, and complained, and ordered new equipment which always broke down. They were happy and thrived; we were sick and miserable. They loved their guru with childlike devotion; we wanted things explained to us over and over again.

'But these were the petty wars. In ashrams the real war is the war of power and proximity, waged with gossip and innuendo, tale-telling, back-stabbing and spiritual sabotage. All gurus, I'd discovered, play their devotees off against each other, giving and withholding, beckoning one night, dismissing the next. Who was more enlightened? Whose practice was more perfect? Who was closer to Guru? Who really understood him? Who would succeed him when he died? Everyone fighting for influence through clenched teeth and saintly smiles.

'So no wonder I was fed up with India, and thinking of going home. I only lingered because I'd got used to the life and wasn't sure I could manage any other. I didn't really fit in India, but Europe was like another planet to me. And then one evening, Lukas and Franz came in to pass the night – the ashram always offered travellers free food and a place to sleep.'

'Was Franz a tall man with reddish hair?' I asked.

'Yes, that's him.'

'And was he OK? How did he seem to you?'

'Physically he was OK, but Franz was . . . not all there.' Giorgio made a circling motion next to his head. 'Drugs, I think, but that's just my guess. Like he'd blown the circuits. Lukas took great care of him. During dinner I went and sat next to them and introduced myself. There was something about Lukas that drew me, that pale hair, his eyes that changed colour . . .' Giorgio saw my look and said, 'Oh no, it wasn't . . . I'm not. I am trying to say . . . that he shone. He stood out like a lamp in the darkness. I was like a moth, I wanted to be close to it. I asked where he'd come from. He said, "*Da lontano*", from far away. He spoke fluent Italian. He spoke a lot of languages – eventually I realised that he spoke to everyone in their own language.*

'After dinner everybody had to attend satsang.† I sat near Lukas and Franz at the back. Swami took his usual place on a dais at the front, the senior devotees on the steps below. One favourite to lead the chanting, another to recite from one of Swami's books – a chapter on the purification of the senses.

'We were about halfway through the reading when a powerful fragrance of roses suddenly filled the air, although there were no

* An extraordinary facility with languages is a common characteristic of avatars and other mythic super-beings. 'Throughout history and legend, from Africa to Alaska, India and China, the god-men are noted for their ability to speak every language.' M. L. Hutter, *Language, Thought and the Rise of Civilization* (New York: Harper and Row, 1978), p. 288.

† Sanskrit, 'association with good men'. A spiritual discourse led by an enlightened guru or teacher with the purpose of making, for each participant, a direct link with the divine.

rose-bushes anywhere. It grew stronger and stronger, all around us, as if we were in a vast rose garden where thousands of roses had all decided to bloom at once. The smell was so beautiful, it was making visions in the air, it was making people cry. No one was listening to the reading any more; the smell was too marvellous for anyone to want to do anything other than inhale it. The reader didn't know whether to give in to the pleasure of the scent or fight it in the name of order and duty. Swami was getting red in the face as though with pent-up rage. The devotees looked worried. I started laughing. I couldn't help it, they looked so funny, but I wasn't mocking them. The weird thing is that my heart was overflowing with affection for them – they seemed like children who'd misplaced their toys and took it for the end of the world. Others were laughing too, which made Swami even angrier. He was staring around, looking for who was to blame. How did he know? He must have had some genuine spiritual insight in order to recognise the source of such disturbing beauty. He pointed straight at Lukas. Two of the devotees came down through the crowd, took Lukas by the arms and led him out. He didn't resist – he was laughing too hard. Franz followed and I hurried after them. Lukas was being told to leave the ashram at once. I ran and got my things and caught up with them at the gate.

'I've often wondered what he did, how he made that smell of roses appear – was it really there, in the air, or was it in our minds – did he cause us all to hallucinate the scent? And why did he do it? I think just for fun, because everybody, especially Swami himself, was taking Swami so seriously. It was a game for Lukas – a game in the sense of a light-spirited and compassionate engagement with life that can only happen when you know it for illusion. What they call *lila*. I realised it was what I'd been looking for. When I'd first started to study Hinduism, it was the concept of *lila* that had captivated my heart. But I'd never found even a glimmer of it in all my time in ashrams.

'An American couple joined us, running along the road to catch us up, whooping like children escaped from school. Kevin and Sheila. In an instant we were best friends, brothers, sisters. We'd all glimpsed the same thing and we felt like we had jumped off a cliff and discovered we could fly. Why not others? Why didn't everyone get up and leave that false satsang and follow the true one? But no, not everyone can. It's not the right time for them. It's one thing to get a glimpse of . . . something from that other dimension, but then you have to recognise it, seize it, trust it, overcome your fear, surrender to it. You have to be ripe enough to fall from the tree as it passes. Because you have to be willing to drop everything and go with it, whatever it is.

'We went on foot as traditional mendicants. People gave us food and shelter. If one of us needed a coat or new shoes, someone would always provide it. Along the way, three others joined us: a pair of Danish twins, Mathias and Elias, and an older guy, Jason, from Canada. I'd run into Jason before, at an ashram in Karnataka. I was sorry to see that Kevin and Sheila, Sheila in particular, started acting superior because they'd been with Lukas longer. I hope I didn't. No, I know I didn't, even though, strictly speaking, I had been the first to follow him. I was so full of Lukas, of being with Lukas, that I had no spare emotional energy for game-playing. I loved everyone the same, because I saw them through Lukas.

'He did nothing to distinguish himself from the rest of us, and only later, as I tried to remember every detail of those first days, did I realise that I had rarely seen him eat, and never sleep. He was treated . . . I was going to say, with reverence, but that is the wrong word. More than respect, yet not worship, certainly, because that would have been to make an object of him, but all along, throughout everything, we knew him as a . . . special being, a window, a door. He was transparent, that's what I'm trying to say. It's not what he was, but what he wasn't. He made an opening, a space, in the . . .' Giorgio sketched a wide gesture that took in tables and chairs, the people, the city, the world, his hand returning to thump his own knee. 'In all these . . . things.' Tears filled his eyes and slipped slowly down his face. He wiped them with his sleeve. 'It's hard to put into words, but I've been trying to write about it.' He touched his pocket, from which protruded a thick, dog-eared notebook.

'It's curious how no one thought beyond the day, no one worried about where our next meal was going to come from or whether we'd find a bed for the night. It's such a relief, you know, not to fret about tomorrow or regret yesterday. We all had the same sense that we were sailing into a new life, a truer one. *The* true one. With Lukas the world was transparent, open. It let you in, and it got into you. Not this opposition all the time,' he rapped the table, 'between *me* and *it*.

'The odd thing is that this didn't surprise me, me who'd worked so hard learning to meditate, learning that it's incredibly difficult to detach from the material world, that it's difficult and rare to experience, really experience, the bliss, the higher reality, whatever you want to call it – nirvana, samadhi, moksha. Heaven. I'd always been taught that it was far off, accessible only after long discipline, concentration, hard work, being good. If then. One might never be good enough, and all one's work might be in vain. Tiny unnoticed errors might creep into one's practice, ruining the whole thing. I realised that if you define your goal as elsewhere, that's where it always is. No matter where you go, or what you do, no matter how hard you try, you never find it because *by definition* it's always over there, never here.' He gave a deep sigh and got up to fetch us each a beer from behind the bar.

'Did Lukas tell you about his background?' I asked, when he returned.

'I never questioned him. To me he seemed so perfectly in and of the moment that a past would have been incongruous. But

183

Sheila really pestered him. One day he told her that he'd been born in a concentration camp. Perhaps he said that just to get her off his back – it certainly shut her up.'

'And where was he going?'

'He was heading to Nepal to see a holy man, a hermit who lived in the mountains. That was all he told me or anyone. It only later occurred to me that the purpose of the journey may have had something to do with Franz, that he was its focus, rather than merely tagging along. Maybe the hope was to help him, to heal him. I don't know. He was like a shadow, staying close to Lukas, always holding his hand or the edge of his cloak.

'Several times Lukas told us the way ahead was very difficult and urged us to leave him, but we refused. As we passed through Kathmandu we came upon Gauri, begging outside the bus park at the edge of town. Little kid, thin like a twig, hands reaching up and these blank, blank eyes.'

Across the table Gauri smiled and blinked her bright dark eyes. 'When Lukas come I see him,' she said. 'Not with eyes, but with . . .' she tapped her forehead '. . . with inside. Like dream. Never I see person while not sleep.'

'She came running after us,' Giorgio said. 'Such a strange sight, this little beggar-child, obviously blind, coming straight at Lukas, bumping into people, bouncing off, pushing them aside . . .'

Gauri grinned. 'I rude, yes?'

'Yes, very rude.' Giorgio ruffled her hair affectionately. 'She grabbed hold of his hand and wouldn't let go. Franz had to yield his place. I saw that she *had* to be with Lukas, just like the rest of us. That night we stopped at a farm, where they gave us dahl and chapati and a place to lie down by their hearth. The others were asleep but I was still awake, watching Lukas. He was sitting quietly in that peaceful, self-contained way of his, face hidden by a fold of his cloak. Gauri climbed into his lap. He kissed the top of her head.'

'Then I sleep,' Gauri said. 'Not like other sleep. I feel . . .' She waved her hands slowly in the air and looked questioningly at Giorgio.

'Floating?' Giorgio said.

'Yes, I floating. I think maybe I dead, and my spirit leave my body. But I happy, very very happy, I not care if dead or life.'

'I fell asleep,' Giorgio said, 'and woke at dawn when this little one,' he poked Gauri in the stomach, 'let out such a shriek the whole household came running.'

'I make noisy because I wake,' Gauri mimed stretching and yawning, eyes squeezed tight shut, 'and I rub,' she passed her hands vigorously over her face, 'and I open eyes,' she opened them wide with an astonished expression, 'and I see!'

'So there was a big to-do,' Giorgio said, 'and everyone talking about miracles. Lukas said that his little friend had only had a bad dream but now she was awake. Everything calmed down, people went about their daily chores. We walked on, Gauri clinging to Lukas with this big smile on her face.'

'I think if I look always at him, I see. If I look away, I maybe blind again. Long time I think I have always to look at him.'

'We headed north into the mountains,' Giorgio said. 'For the first two weeks, the path went along a river and the ascent was not too rapid. Because it was so late in the year, there were no Westerners about, just the local people and their animals. Then we started climbing. Now there was only the occasional un-occupied shepherd's hut to camp in, no more villages. Everyone we met was headed the other way. Lukas again told us to return to the valley, but we would not. Clouds came down and hid the high peaks. It snowed from time to time. We climbed. One day Mathias had a touch of altitude sickness, so he and Elias turned back. The rest of us believed we could stay with Lukas, but we were wrong. That night there was a blizzard. No one thought they'd be able to sleep – the wind was howling and snow was coming in through gaps in the roof – but somehow we all dropped off. When we woke in the morning the storm had ended but Lukas and Franz had disappeared. Gauri would have run out in search of them – we had to hold her back. It was impossible to guess in which direction they'd gone.

'By mid-morning the snow was melting. A caravan came down the path, laden yaks ploughing through the snow. We tried to ask the yak drivers if they'd seen anyone, but couldn't make ourselves understood. They obviously thought we were crazy to be where we were, and with gestures persuaded us to accompany them down. I felt so sad, like I'd lost everything. As we descended we left the snow behind, the clouds parted and the evening sun shone on Annapurna. Suddenly my heart lifted. I felt Lukas near, though I knew he wasn't physically near at all. But his presence was. I saw him everywhere, even in the stones of the path.' He reached into his pocket and showed me a pebble. 'I saw him in this. I took it with me so that I'd never forget.'

The little group returned to Kathmandu and there parted company: Kevin and Sheila went back to America, Jason to Australia. Giorgio stayed in Kathmandu, hoping that Lukas would come through town again. Gauri, who'd attached herself to him when her first choice became unavailable, had begun drawing everywhere and on everything until he bought her pads and pens. Now she made a good living as an artist; already her portraits had earned her a reputation among the hippie travellers.

When Giorgio asked, finally, about my own interest in Lukas, I had to exert some effort to resist the temptation to dazzle him with the information that his Lukas was (*inter alia*) the world-famous Luce of Luce and the Photons, whose music one heard on the radio even here in Kathmandu. Clearly that was not a healthy association; the last thing I wanted was for him to draw the attention of the demons, the NOHRM or anyone looking for Luce. I hastily made up a story that was an echo of Giorgio's own: I'd encountered Lukas before (I was vague about where and when) and yearned to find him again. That was easy for Giorgio to understand, and he was so wrapped up in his own cloud of devotion to the Lukas he'd known that other people, other Luces, didn't make much of an impression.

As I'd listened to Giorgio and Gauri's stories of Lukas, odd things had happened to those other Luces in my mind. I'd been operating on the assumption that Karen's Lou Peterson was the real Luce, at times taking other identities, but this was only because that's what Karen believed. Maybe Lou Peterson, born in Bethlehem (how had I missed that joke?) as the atom bomb fell on Hiroshima (surely too archetypal to be actual, even as it may be true), was as much of a mask as Luce the masked rock star, Petra Lumis or Lukas Steiner. Maybe none of the personae I'd yet encountered was the real one. I had a sudden sensation of vertigo as all the Luces flew up into the air and hovered, unwilling to resume their former configuration and not yet able to drop into a new one.

Now.

I google Giorgio and find a big, slick website. Well, well. He wrote that book after all, and another, and another: *Walking With L*, *Talks with L* and *Living with L*. I download them.

The encounter with Lukas - and I have to respect him for this - turns out to have been the cornerstone of the rest of his life, and though the story he developed out of it is in large part fiction, and though he failed to resist the lure of being the First Disciple (he uses capital letters with abandon), I know that true feelings lie at the heart of it.

He tells how L, a mystical Teacher in the manner of Carlos Castaneda's Don Juan, chose him (Giorgio) to be his Special Disciple and the Recorder of his Teachings. L, he tells us, is meant to represent Light, Love and Life as well as evoke the Hebrew and Arabic terms *El* or *Al* (usually translated as 'God'). Giorgio's L, unlike the reticent Lukas he'd described to me, is positively brimming over with Teachings that take the form of Insights, Instructions, Talks and Parables.

For example, the chapter called Healing the Blind tells Gauri's story, taking Lukas's apparently offhand comment that his 'little friend had a bad dream but now she was awake,' as the basis of a Teaching on the subject of the Delusory Nature of Ordinary Consciousness (the blindness experienced by the 'little friend', which is the ego or small self) and the possibility of awakening from it into Reality as from a bad dream.

In his account L vanished from a mountain top in a blazing column of light, but only after imparting enough Teachings to last for several volumes and appointing Giorgio *alone* to be their Custodian and promulgator. Apparently L still visits Giorgio regularly In Spirit, thus ensuring that the Fount of Wisdom continues to flow unabated.

Giorgio stayed in Nepal and now runs a centre outside Pokhara that offers retreats, courses and workshops. The most popular seems to be a ten-day Meditation Trek during which participants can experience Walking with L themselves for $699, airfare not included. He has 64,850 followers on Twitter, where he emits a steady stream of positive aphorisms.

I email him and get a warm and friendly reply right away that makes me feel a bit ashamed of my sneering. Of course he remembers me, hopes I am well and so on. He says he is still in regular communication with Lukas, and promises to pass on my regards.

I ask about Gauri, and he sends me a link to her website. She has a gallery in Los Angeles that shows contemporary Nepali and Tibetan art and has an international reputation. Her portraits are highly sought after, too, though she undertakes few commissions these days. Her fees are very steep.

The drawing she did of me in The Moon Garden has lain hidden all these years in Luce's box; it's a bit grubby and creased. How strange to see it now: me as I was, but not as I was. Chimera Obscura in the peacock-feather hat, as seen by Gauri's Luce-opened eyes. I must get it framed.

11

Der Wunderbare Wandmalereien Haus

Encounters with Luce. A False Luce. Disinformation.
Übermensch and the Orb. My Baby Browning.
Charlie and I Attempt the Cairngorms. The Ruined
Croft. Theft among the Vegetables.

London and Scotland, June–August 1967

Back in England I was in deep disgrace for having missed my
brother's wedding, which I made worse with my patently
insincere attempts to pretend I was sorry. I ended up giving the
impression that I had absented myself without leave for the sole
purpose of insulting everyone. I had not realised what a prominent
role they'd expected me to play in the elaborate, pretentious
choreography of synthetic sentiment that comprises our society's
nuptial rites . . . and how very distressing and unsatisfactory were
the last-minute adjustments forced upon them by my unannounced
absence. My card had not arrived until several days too late.

My fascination with Luce continued to grow as I wrote up
what I then knew (or thought I knew) about her . . . or him. I'd
begun to have doubts about Luce's sex as well as her name. If
one can pass as either, what better way to slip into a new mask

191

than by adopting a different sex? I'd decided even then that the book would have to be told from many points of view if a true picture of Luce was to emerge. As to who she *really* was . . . the more I'd learned, the less I understood, but I was sure my path would cross hers again. In the meantime, my life resumed its picaresque: I travelled and frivolled, experienced and experimented, wrote my columns, articles and essays and finished my book. *Strange Worlds: The Culture of Counter-Culture* came out that December to general approbation and gratifying sales. I pictured it on coffee-tables throughout the land, a subtle, covert disrupter weapon aimed at the mind of Middle England.

As time passed, Luce and the Photons' fame increased rather than faded. In the absence of any hard information, the band was catapulted to mythic status. People deciphered the lyrics, played the tracks backwards, discerned mysterious coded messages in sequences of chord changes. Wild rumours circulated about the next album, which was awaited like the Second Coming. There were occasional reports of sightings of Luce; the fact that some people were convinced Luce was female, others male, led to a certain amount of acrimony among the band's devout fans. I recorded several personal stories of such encounters (which took place in London during the period of the secret gigs) and include three of the most typical.

፨

On 16 February 1967 Melanie MacGregor, twenty-one, a junior graphic artist at an advertising agency, had been sent to the British Museum to look up Egyptian motifs for possible use in the advertising of cigarettes. She found herself transfixed by the imagery, the colours, the gods and goddesses and strange animals, the mysterious inscriptions. Standing before a sarcophagus in a far gallery, thinking she was alone, she'd murmured out loud, 'I wonder what it says.'

'It says, "Yours, O Osiris, is the barque that sails the night of Amenti, the boat of millions of years,"' said a voice beside her. It belonged to a young man with long, pale blond hair beneath a grey fedora. He was wearing an old, rumpled flannel suit, plimsolls and blue-tinted glasses that hid his eyes. Oddly, she wasn't startled by his presence, although, looking back, 'it's like he materialised out of thin air'.

She'd been listening to the *Human* album, and carried on with a quotation from 'The Dream of Osiris': '"The boat of millions and millions of years, that sails the bittersweet sea of tears."'

'"And brings me here to you, sweet Isis,"' the young man said. He took her hand as he said this and spoke with such intensity that she knew he wasn't just quoting a well-known song but was speaking from the heart. He really did mean her, and him, right there and then, as though the universe had arranged its billions of happenstances precisely so that he, and she, should be standing together at that moment, in that place. It was utterly improbable; it was inevitable.

That's when she knew it was Luce, and he was just as she'd always pictured him. She'd seen one of the videos but had never been to a gig. She danced to his music every night in her bedsit, alone, and it always filled her with joy.

'It's you, isn't it?' she said.

He didn't answer, but he kissed her. Just once, just lightly. She touched her lips as she told me this. 'No one will ever kiss me again,' she said. 'Not like that.'

She had returned to the office in a daze, handed in her notice and applied to study Egyptology at University College. She'd recently learned she'd been accepted.

Melanie MacGregor is now a professor emeritus of Egyptology at Cambridge. Her many publications include *Nights of Amenti: Poems of the Afterlife*; *Isis the Philosopher*; *The Path of Isis*; *New Kingdom Gods and Demons*. Under the name Barbara Winstanley, she writes hugely popular novels about an intrepid female Egyptologist sleuth, set during the Second World War.

&.

Edwin Chalford, forty-three, encountered a white-haired young woman in Hyde Park on 4 April 1967 at five a.m. in the rain. He'd been kicked out of the house by his wife, because he'd lost his job, because he'd been rude to the boss, because he'd been fed up, so fed up, and tired, but tired in a way that made him angry, but he wasn't *allowed* to be angry, so he'd just been sad, until it had all blown out of him, he'd said what he thought, pushed over a desk, burst into tears, locked himself in the toilet and refused to come out until the police threatened to cut the door down and arrest him for criminal damage.

He'd been drinking, quite a lot, and had just finished off a bottle of whisky. He was sitting on a bench, getting soaked, not caring. Someone sat down next to him and the rain stopped. Or, no, it didn't stop, he could see it was still raining nearby, but it was as though the person carried a large, invisible umbrella and extended it over both of them. She – he decided it was a she though he hadn't been sure at first because she was wearing a long, loose coat and a fedora with the brim pulled down – wasn't at all wet, not even her shoes.

She seemed to radiate a sort of warmth, and he realised he'd been very cold. Sitting next to her was like sitting next to his granny's fire when he was little. She'd always ask him to read her the stories he'd written; no one else ever did.

'She made me feel like somebody really saw me. Me, the real person that nobody let me be. That I didn't let myself be. That was what Gran made me feel, and that's what this person made me feel.'

He'd begun to be ashamed of himself, his condition, and in a feeble attempt to be hospitable he offered the stranger his whisky, only to realise, to his chagrin, that the bottle was empty.

'That's all right,' the stranger said. 'Try some of mine.' She took a silver flask out of an inner pocket and passed it to him. He took a sip. It tasted like plain water, but the effect was strange, indescribable, marvellous.

His words, which had been something of a torrent up to this point, stopped. He was silent for a long time as I waited.

He shook his head and looked at me. There was a smile deep in his eyes but he still didn't speak.

'I . . .' he said, then shook his head again and gave it up. He laughed, and though it was only the smallest of chuckles, I caught an echo of the laughter that Luce had given me at the secret gig. 'Can I take your hand?' he asked.

I held out my hand and he took it between his. 'I'll try to show you,' he said. He closed his eyes. It might have been my imagination but it did seem as though a gentle wavelet of light flowed from him to me.

'There,' he said, opening his eyes. 'Did you feel that?'

'Yes, I did.'

'That's just a tiny fraction of what she did.'

'How did you know it was Luce?'

'She said so. I asked, "Who are you?" She said, "My name is Luce."'

She disappeared as silently as she'd come, but the rain had stopped, it was almost dawn and the strange water from the flask had washed Edwin's drunken despair right out of him. As the sun rose and the birds began to sing, the empty space inside him filled with joy. 'It wasn't the end, it was the beginning. I suddenly knew who I was, simple as that. I was forty-three years old and I'd never been myself, not for one instant, since those childhood nights with Gran. I was like a little kid again, filled with sheer delight.'

Now, three months later, he had an air of calm purpose. He'd gone on the dole for a few weeks, then got a job in a library. His wife was divorcing him, at which he felt sorrow, but mainly relief. He was writing stories, though he wouldn't show me. 'Not good enough yet,' he said. 'But I think maybe they could be, one day.'

Edwin (E.B.) Chalford (1924–2002) wrote eleven novels and four collections of short stories, and won the Booker and Whitbread prizes.

&.

Jeremy Ethan Powell, eighteen, formerly a pupil at Eton College, had by sheer luck stumbled upon the second secret gig. It was his first acid trip, and he'd entered such a state of ecstasy that when he got back to school he abandoned discretion and told his friends. Word got to the prefect, and his housemaster, and he was sacked. It was, he said, the best thing that had ever happened to him. 'That place might have killed me.' He'd found a squat in Kennington and got a job at a record store.

He'd seen Luce before dawn on the morning of 8 April 1967, on the Thames. He'd rowed at Eton and had friends at a rowing club on the river at Chiswick, who let him keep a single scull there in exchange for helping out. He liked to start the day with a brisk row up to Twickenham and back. He had just rowed past Oliver's Island when he saw someone walking on the water. As usual at that time of day, there was mist clinging to the surface of the river, but he knew this stretch like the back of his own hand. It was near high tide; the water was many metres deep. The figure strolled across to the island, climbed up the shore, sat on the dock next to a derelict skerry and lit a cigarette.

He'd abandoned rowing in astonishment, and found himself drifting back towards the island. He could discern a long, light-coloured coat and a fedora and at first thought it was a man but, as he drifted closer, he decided it was a woman. She looked at him and waved, and in that instant he knew it was Luce.

'How did you know?' I asked.

'It was the way she waved at me, like we knew each other, like we'd arranged to meet at that time, in that place. It triggered a memory. I remembered that at the gig in Brompton, I'd seen an image – I thought it was in one of the films they were showing on the walls – of someone sculling on a river in the mist, and someone waiting for them on an island. And I realised it had been of this exact moment.

'She was sitting on a heap of rusty iron chain; I noticed that it had left reddish marks on her coat. She smoked a cigarette – I could tell from the smell that it was Turkish tobacco. She smiled at me. It wasn't a very big smile but she was just brimming with joy and that infected me. Of all the things I might have said to her, all I could think of was, "Did you just walk on water?"

'She gave this little rueful laugh. "Sorry," she said. "One of those temptations. I always wondered if I could. Felt I ought to, but also ought not, you know? Anyway, it's no big deal. Anyone can do it. Just re-imagine the relationships between the electrons. Cheerio!" And she strolled back across, climbed the bank, gave a farewell wave and vanished into the trees.'

He was teaching himself to paint because, he said, 'She put this seed in my head and it keeps on sprouting, images and colours and forms and such amazing pictures I just have to . . . have to . . . try. It's all rubbish so far, but I think, if I keep at it, I might be able to give people a glimpse of what she showed me.'

In reviews of his 2007 Tate retrospective, Powell was described as 'one of Britain's most important living painters. Relentlessly defying genre, his work consistently excites and inspires . . . powerful, luminous and exalting.'*

*Henry P. Lambert, *Great British Artists: Turner to Powell* (London: Thames

I was a bit put out to see that a rival of mine had a big spread in *Rolling Stone* about Luce, but relieved to discover that he'd been taken in by an imposter, a fumble from which his career never fully recovered. His Luce turned out to be a young man from Lewisham, real name Nigel Tubbs, a not untalented and unquestionably audacious local lad who, with his band the Tubbles, had previously made a modest living playing covers on Saturday nights at the pub and doing the occasional wedding. He took in quite a few people for a while and got a record contract, which was renegotiated though not rescinded when his true identity was revealed.

My rival's experience inspired me, however, to engage in a modest programme of disinformation. Positioned as I was, with contacts in every walk of life on several continents, I was well placed to release a number of plausible red herrings into the ever-swirling seas of rumour and speculation that collected around the enigmatic figure of Luce. 'Those who know, say nothing,' has long been a motto of the mystery schools. Saying nothing is difficult for me; I found it more amusing to say misleading things. They too serve who only lie and deceive.

The letter I'd sent to Greyling had been returned; there was, apparently, no redirection of the bookshop's mail. The Land Registry revealed that number eleven Golden Square was owned by a company called Aleph Investment Network based in Switzerland, with a Basel post-office box for an address. I couldn't find out anything about them from the usual sources; they seemed to operate, if they operated at all, with exemplary discretion. They did not reply to my written enquiry. Greyling, I saw, would not easily be tracked down,

---

Press, 2010), p. 323.

yet I had a feeling we'd meet again – denizens, as we both were, of Synchronicity City.

The fire at Golden Square was declared an accident due to the unfortunate juxtaposition of leaky paraffin heaters with dodgy electrical outlets, neither particularly unusual in London buildings at that time. The authorities continued to maintain that no bodies had been found.

My contact with the NOHRM had resumed – if it had ever been interrupted – as soon as I'd returned to London. I'd been back in town for less than twenty-four hours when, returning to my flat, I saw the green van parked in front. The fear struck at once, a toxic cloud emanating from Mr Big as he stepped out to intercept me on the pavement. But now I knew what to expect and was able to fling up a mental – or, as Ambrose would have put it, an astral shield. The terror was still there, gnawing at the edges of my mind, but it didn't overwhelm me as before. The thought of Luce illuminated my consciousness like a distant lightning flash; she would never be intimidated by Mr Big, and neither would I.

He said nothing, just fixed me with his dead-eyed gaze, handed me a blank white envelope, climbed into the van and drove off.

The visit informed me, as I can only suppose it was meant to, that the Bigs knew I'd left London and knew I'd returned. But had they followed me every step of the way or tracked my movement through passport controls, airline bookings, currency exchange, credit card? If I was to have a chance of evading them in the future, my *modus operandi* would have to get a lot cannier.

The envelope contained what I expected: another fortnight's stipend, plus a reminder that my first report was now due. I was ready for this, and had a strategy. From then on, Mrs Big received my reports regularly and on time; I was a hard-working, obedient agent of the NOHRM. But I made mistakes, got facts wrong, names mixed up, dates confused. I repeated myself and

199

contradicted myself. Spelling and grammar deteriorating with each report, I pushed them along in a calibrated decline from silliness to stupidity, from foolishness to sheer idiocy, all the while maintaining a portentous style of earnest, mind-numbing verbosity. They were, I hoped, unreadable.

But perhaps I was being too subtle; I failed to deter Mrs Big. The blank white envelopes appeared regularly on my doormat; invariably, after that first encounter, delivered by unseen hands without benefit of stamp, postmark or return address. Each contained my loathsome stipend as well as requests for reports on topics of special interest to the NOHRM. One, I recall, had me investigate a performance art group known as the Orb, which turned out to be an acronym concealing an esoteric secret name: the Ordre de la Rose Blanche, legendary eighteenth-century Rosicrucians (the hidden powers responsible for the French Revolution, among other things), a fictional group that many people believe is real and active to this day. Another assignment was a proto-electro-rock band called Übermensch, who enjoyed some small glory in the London club scene during the autumn of 1967. They dressed in stylised Nazi uniforms, quoted Nietzsche and Bulwer-Lytton and sang about the 'Coming Race'. Greater prats never walked the earth, and I derived a perverse pleasure from the marriage of my by then perfected style of utter inanity with a subject matter of infinite imbecility. I was gratified, as well, to see some of my own Lucian red herrings come swimming back to me in directives from the NOHRM. Naturally I investigated these as assiduously as the others.

Although Mrs Big's interests ranged across a wide terrain encompassing most aspects of culture, the arts, mass movements and fringe politics, the nature of her requests convinced me that Luce was of particular interest and that she knew Luce might appear under other names and in other guises than as a rock star. My assignments tended towards topics such as psychic or

200

superhuman powers (Übermensch an example, albeit a facetious one), occult-inspired political dissidence (the fictitious but influential ORB), anything spoken of as 'transcendent', unusual new art forms, back-to-the-earth new tribalists, Luddites, Libertarians, inexplicable healings, charismatic figures, religious cults. Although she soon lost interest in the old dears who inhabited the dusty corridors of the venerable Theosophical Society and the Society for Psychical Research, she did find druids quite interesting for a while.

Since there was a lot of all this sort of stuff going on, I was kept busy. And since the vast majority of the people involved in these enterprises were run-of-the-mill wankers, self-satisfied, self-deluded and entirely ineffective, I knew that reporting their activities to the NOHRM would bring them no trouble. I did encounter the occasional drop of gold, but there was so much dross it was easy to hide it.

I deposited my fortnightly stipend in the Palestinian refugees' collecting box in Ahmet's café.

I saw no more of Mr Big (except, perhaps, occasionally, out of the corner of my eye and at a distance) but I became aware that I was being watched and followed by one or another smooth-faced, neatly coiffed, blank-eyed simulacrum. Without doubt, my flat was searched a couple of days after my return, though they missed the artistically dust-strewn removable section of floorboard under the kitchen dresser where I'd stashed everything to do with Luce. I started doing things I'd read about in spy thrillers: I stuck a hair across my desk drawers (if someone opened the drawer, the hair would fall off. It always worked for James Bond) but when sometimes the hair was dislodged, sometimes not, I concluded that it could easily have fallen on its own, due to the warmth of the room or the movement of air caused by a draughty window. I went everywhere by roundabout routes, doubling back on myself frequently to discomfit my demons, and

201

told no one my plans in advance. My flat had a rear window that looked out onto a small paved area, separated from my neighbours by half-rotten fencing panels. Three houses along, a tiny alley led through to the next street – it involved a bit of a scramble, but I worked out a route over and through the fences. I have always found it comforting to know that I have a back door should I need to disappear fast.

I decided I'd feel a lot safer if I had a gun, so I acquired a Baby Browning from an underworld contact of a friend of a friend (not as difficult as I'd thought it might be). My reasoning went like this: whether the Bigs were physical or astral, the next time someone waved a gun in my face I wanted one to wave back. No more meekly putting my hands up and backing off. If they were actual people going around with guns threatening to kill other people, it was simple self-defence, and only sensible to be prepared. If, on the other hand, they were astral simulacra, I'd wave the gun's astral counterpart just as effectively, if not more so, with a physical one in my hand to enhance my powers of concentration, as Ambrose would say. Again, only sensible to be prepared. (I sought out Ambrose soon after my return, hoping to grill him about demons and their power to affect the physical world, but he'd gone to Finland to study astral projection with a famous guru.)

I'd never even held a gun before, but Charlie took me out to his country place and taught me how to use it. I practised on tins lined up on a fence and though I found the noise and the kick deeply unpleasant, he said I had the makings of a half-decent shot. He, along with the rest of his family, had of course been merrily shooting animals large and small since he was old enough to hold a shotgun, but Charlie had always had a particular affinity for guns. In 1958, when we were at university and I was conducting experiments into the nature of consciousness, he'd been runner-up British fifty-yard pistol champion.

Charlie seemed to have developed a Luce-fascination of his own and his wide range of contacts regularly tossed up leads of varying degrees of improbability. My own red herrings returned in this way, too. My activities in the field of disinformation, along with almost all of what I knew about Luce, I kept secret from everyone, even Charlie. Not that I distrusted him, but he was the most indiscreet person I've ever known. Something you'd told him in strictest confidence would flit into his mind, provoked by God-knows-what random association, and out it would come in front of God-knows-who, most probably the very last person you would wish to hear it. He was like a magpie in reverse: not collecting and hiding the bright, shiny things, but flinging them wantonly out of concealment at every opportunity. Later, when you reminded him that he'd revealed a secret, he'd be mortified. But he'd do it again, until finally one learned not to tell him anything one didn't want the world to know. In response to his eager enquiries about what I'd discovered at Warm Springs, I gave him the same story I'd prepared for Mrs Big: that I'd found some wall-paintings that might have been by Luce, etc. I omitted all mention of Karen and, of course, Waldo and Miriam.

Nor did I question his assumption that Luce was a man. At first afraid that I'd slip and refer to Luce as 'she' in conversation, a habit I'd acquired from Karen, I was surprised at how easily I adapted. Some part of me, it seemed, had continued to think of Luce as the man I'd taken him for at the secret gig. The shift in perception was retroactive as well as prognostic: my memories of Lou Peterson, vividly pictured as female while I listened to Karen's stories, now drifted subtly towards the maleness of the Luce for whom Charlie and I searched. My conception of the 'real' Luce was becoming quite detached from notions of sex and gender; this is a necessary mental leap for anyone hoping to understand Luce's true nature (or indeed their own).

Charlie and I followed up all the leads we got, my fictive

contributions no more outlandish than many others. None led to Luce or any trace of him, until one evening in mid-August when an otherwise uninteresting friend of Charlie's called, I think, Des, mentioned in the course of a long and implausible story involving a red-headed girl and her irate father, an incontinent dog, an ounce of Acapulco Gold and a dead pheasant, that he'd come upon a place with astonishing wall-paintings. One night in early June, while fleeing the dog – or maybe it was the father – his car had broken down, stranding him on an uninhabited stretch of road in the Cairngorms. He'd glimpsed a light that he thought might be a house and headed for it, but a fog had descended suddenly and he'd wandered for what felt like hours in eerie, murky silence before coming upon the tumbled walls and gaping roof of an abandoned croft. Too tired to go further, he decided to take whatever shelter it had to offer and remain until daylight could reveal a path.

To his surprise, the interior of the ruin was tidy and free of rubble. In a corner he found a simple lean-to roofed with branches and bark. A mound of pine boughs and dried bracken made a welcome bed; he lay down and fell asleep. He had amazing dreams which he promptly forgot because when he awoke he saw the paintings on the walls. As he described them and their effects, Charlie and I exchanged glances. He'd heard my account of the painted room at Golden Square, and this sounded very similar: complex, shifting geometries; colours that changed as you looked at them; figures that were simultaneously animals, trees, people, stars; a sense of falling into infinite depths; disconcerting time-distortion. What really excited me was Des's opinion that the paintings had been done not very long before his visit: the colours were vivid and fresh.

We obtained the best description Des could manage of the location of the place. He never did figure out how he'd got there, but was able to tell us that he'd departed in a westerly direction (in order not to have the morning sun in his eyes) and come upon a road about an hour later which proved to be the B970. He'd got a lift to the nearest hamlet, Auchgourish, from where he was able to telephone to a garage in Nethy Bridge. His own car was eventually discovered four miles away on an unnamed, unnumbered and unpaved track between Aviemore and Loch Morlich. His recollections of his trek included impenetrable pinewoods, a treacherous scree slope, a black-water tarn, several icy burns, at least one bog (it might have been the same one he encountered more than once) and a boulder shaped like Winston Churchill's head. (It turns out that most boulders are shaped like Winston Churchill's head when viewed from the correct angle.)

By then it was three in the morning; a perfect time, Charlie declared, to drive to Scotland. He'd got a new car, a sleek blue Aston Martin DB6, that he was eager to try on the open road. Charlie was by this time familiar with my need for elaborate procedures to 'shake off the demons' that persisted in following me, which he resolved in this instance by driving at 140 miles an hour most of the way. No one could possibly have followed us.

We got to Auchgourish at about nine on a lovely bright morning, parked the Aston in a layby and set off into the hills with the sun in our eyes, equipped with a compass (broken, though we didn't know that), an Ordnance Survey map (which neither of us could read and which we later realised was for the adjacent square), a pair of Brobdingnagian binoculars, whose weight increased exponentially with every yard we ascended, a packet of ham sandwiches, a flask of tea, a flask of brandy (to be saved for life-and-death situations), plenty of hash and a large umbrella. I had my camera, of course, every sort of film, a flash outfit with spare battery and a tripod. If the paintings really were by Luce, I was determined to make and keep a photographic record.

It would be tedious to relate the route by which Charlie and I stumbled, staggered and limped to the ruined croft. Suffice it to say that it took three hours and forty-nine minutes, involved all of Des's vexations and several of our own. The umbrella and the binoculars were claimed by the third bog, much to our relief.

Upon arriving, midge-bitten, peat-stained, sweaty, torn, bruised, filthy and absolutely knackered, we were astonished to discover that we were not alone. A pair of immaculate German tourists, lounging in front of the croft, greeted us with annoying cheerfulness and confirmed that this was indeed the place we sought: *'der wunderbare Wandmalereien Haus'*. The paintings were already famous; they'd heard of the old croft and its wonderful murals at the hikers' hostel in Aviemore.

Charlie and I collapsed and administered sips of brandy to each other. When we'd recovered our strength, we discovered we were ravenous. Tepid tea and stale ham sandwiches sounded like nectar and ambrosia, but it was not to be. The flask had cracked along the way, or perhaps been cracked to begin with; the tea was laced with shards of glass and smelled very bad. The ham sandwiches had become permeated with bog and were inedible.

Hansel and Gretel, our German new best friends, came to the rescue. They turned out to be exactly as well prepared as you'd expect. From their rucksacks they produced an astonishing amount of food. Sensibly not trusting the provisions available in rural Scotland, they carried their own *wurst* (four kinds), black bread and hard cheese to supplement the local fare, which consisted of pasties, porridge oats, kippers, a jar of strawberry jam, four bottles of Guinness and a pint of pickled herrings.

While luncheon was being laid out I went to look inside the croft. I had to know whether we'd come all this way for nothing; the arduousness of our journey and the sheer number of ludicrous misfortunes attendant upon it had, by then, induced a certain pessimism. It was with immense relief and joy that my first glance assured me the paintings were definitely by Luce.

'So are these his?' Charlie caught me on the verge of falling into the first one.

'Yes, of course they are,' I said. I thought it was odd he couldn't tell just by looking at them; to me they blazed with Luce-ness like thousand-watt beacons.

Reluctantly, I let Charlie draw me back outside to eat; I had the irrational fear that incendiary demons lurked in the shadows of the pinewoods behind the croft and would emerge to torch the place the minute I turned my back.

After a restorative lunch I returned to the croft with my camera equipment, determined both to seize the experience and to wrest from it a permanent record. The demons apparently believed that even photographs of Luce's art were dangerous: twice they had destroyed my film, but this time I would thwart them. I was pretty sure I could get a full-colour spread in *Rolling Stone*, if not in *Life*. I wanted as many people as possible to see the paintings and have a chance to be affected.

Luce had clearly planned for the murals to be ephemeral; they'd been done in egg tempera right onto the few areas of smooth plaster wall that remained in the house – one in the passage, one in the kitchen and three in the front room. The one in the passage had already caught some rain. The paintings were far smaller than the others I'd seen, which had filled walls and indeed entire rooms. These were no more than about two feet by three.

I pictured the place as it had been when Luce stayed here – not more than a couple of months ago, if Des had been right about the freshness of the paint he'd seen in June. The lean-to stood in the corner, as he'd described it – had Luce built it for himself? I'd learned that he didn't need much in the way of bodily comforts, could thrive on no sleep, little food. A burn tumbled down the slope beside the croft; that would have supplied his water.

The limited size of these paintings and their medium suggested an economy of means: all one needs for egg tempera are eggs, water and dried pigment. I pictured Luce wandering the land, a rucksack on his back in place of the guitar, or maybe a guitar, too, why not? A few ounces of pigment would make dozens of paintings. Placing them in abandoned buildings meant that, even if the demons found them, no one would be in danger when they burned. And serendipity could be trusted to send along the right people at the right moment to see what they needed to see.

The light was not very good and one had to peer at the paintings quite closely, which served to hook the mind. Although one's physical eyes had, perforce, to stop some distance from the wall, one's inner vision seemed to carry on into the image, which expanded temporally as well as spatially. Like Luce's earlier work, it provoked experience, not merely visual perception. What appeared to the inner senses to have lasted anywhere from ten minutes to half an hour proved to have taken only one or two minutes of external time.

But also like the earlier work, it was difficult to retain a conscious memory of what had happened in there. The dynamic linearity of the acutely personal story or journey that the paintings initially evoked resolved first into discrete images, like a flowing stream cohering into beads of water on a string; these in turn dissolved, along with the words that had arisen to describe them, into a lingering, amorphous gestalt of emotion, colour, flavour, texture and tone that faded over the course of a few hours, like water draining from a sponge.

The following day I could remember only a feeling as of something important and beautiful that I'd forgotten: the presence of absence in the form of a light-filled void, a crystal-lined geode in the darkness at the back of my mind. Nevertheless I knew that Luce's art had once again penetrated and permeated me like an alchemist's elixir. It had grown more powerful as it had become more concise; it slipped deep into my consciousness . . . where it continues to emit its potent signal.

I spent an hour going from painting to painting, looking and absorbing, then another couple of hours taking photographs in colour and black-and-white. Charlie, after all our efforts to attain the place, was oddly indifferent to the wonders we'd found. He looked around once in what seemed to me, in my raptures, a most cursory way, then went back outside and fell asleep in the shadow of a big rock.

When I emerged it was late afternoon. Hansel and Gretel were making preparations to spend the night. A tradition of passing a night in the ruined croft had already sprung up, a spontaneous resurrection of the ancient tradition of temple-sleep. Although I was in favour of staying, Charlie refused on the not-unreasonable grounds that we had no camping gear, no food, no insect repellent, no warm clothes and no desire to enter into greater intimacy with Hansel and Gretel, who had laid claim to the lean-to. I decided that I'd go with Charlie back to London, get my film processed and safely hidden, then return alone and better equipped for a night with Luce.

Hansel and Gretel gave us directions and even drew a little map. It turned out that the spot where we'd left the car was a scant hour away along quite a decent track, which we'd contrived to miss altogether in our previous perambulations. From an inner pocket Charlie produced a gram of coke I hadn't known he'd brought, and with its aid was able to drive us all the way back to London. I dozed, my shoulder bag with its precious load of exposed film hugged in my lap.

Back in town, Charlie stowed the car in his basement garage and we went up to his study. Clement brought us brandy-laced Earl Grey tea and buttered toast. We'd been gone just twenty-four hours, but it had felt like a trip to another world, and I don't mean Scotland. Charlie soon went off to bed but I was too excited about what we'd found to sleep, so I sat up waiting for seven, when the lab would open and I could take in my film.

I left Charlie's house at six thirty. It was a lovely, pearlescent morning. I walked through dewy Green Park and along Piccadilly before turning into White Horse Street. I was hungry, and knew a fruit-and-veg stall would already be open in Shepherd Market, which was on my way to the lab in Conduit Street. Although the demons couldn't possibly have followed me to Scotland and back, by habit I kept an eye open for unnaturally smooth-looking people. There was hardly anyone about; those who were tended towards the out-all-night roughness of experienced party-goers heading home or the ordinary roughness of labourers on their way to work.

The little veg stall was already busy; it supplied not only local workers and residents, but also the small-scale needs of several nearby cafés. I selected a banana and an apple, and as I fished in my pocket for silver, an emphatic jostle from behind caused me to lose balance and pitch headlong onto the piled pyramids of fruit and vegetables, which collapsed and rolled everywhere. I flailed about, trying to regain my feet, which kept sliding out from under me. Apples and potatoes, lemons, limes and melons were like ball bearings; the soft fruit such as peaches, grapes and berries serving to lubricate the mass.

Amid cries of dismay and gales of laughter, several pairs of hands reached for me and helped me to stand; this operation caused the collapse of further boxes of vegetables, adding carrots, turnips, parsnips and tomatoes to the mix. It was all so complicated and so embarrassing that it was several minutes before I stopped apologising and remembered that it hadn't been my fault; someone had bumped me from behind. A split second later it occurred to me that it might not have been an accident. I pawed frantically among the spilled vegetables, crawled under the cart and around people's feet but my shoulder bag with its precious film was gone.

I thought I was going to explode with fury. The people who a moment before had been joking with me as they helped to wipe the squashed fruit from my clothes must have thought I was deranged as I suddenly let out a howl and ran back and forth shouting, 'Thief! Thief!'

It was with grim fatalism that I returned to my flat, changed into clean clothes, went out to buy new photographic gear and hired a car for the drive back to Scotland. I was not surprised to find that the ruined croft had suffered a fire. There was nothing that could burn except the lean-to; its wood and bracken had been piled against the paintings, which were scorched and blistered beyond recognition. The place was littered with beer bottles and trash. In Aviemore, they said Glasgow hooligans were likely responsible.

Any plans I'd entertained, involving tramping all over Scotland looking for other ruined buildings that Luce might have graced with his art, evaporated. I couldn't figure out how the demons had followed me, but I had to concede that it was possible. It would be far better to refrain from finding any more of Luce's paintings.

Now.

An idle internet search reveals a mention of the 'Miraculous Murals Found at Aviemore'. The article (a couple of paragraphs in the back pages of the *Inverness Herald*, 29 July 1967) describes the paintings, or tries to, and relates the story of a deaf hiker who spent a night in the ruined croft and awoke with his hearing restored.

I find it oddly disconcerting - though undeniably useful for research - that the past has so prolifer-ated. Online archives scan and publish more by the second. What once dwindled and shrank - sensibly, naturally, one might even say elegantly - as books went out of print and recollection faded from the minds of men, is now continually resurrected, on and on, like a dying man given shock after high-voltage shock. Won't we suffocate under the sheer weight of all this information? Every word I ever wrote is available in bootleg downloads; serves me right, I suppose.

Luce is everywhere; her (or his - there's still a

lot of argument about that) fame has scarcely faded with the passage of time. Cyberspace has fomented a strange brew of groups, lists, Facebook pages, fan clubs, scholarly societies, etc., dedicated to Luce and the Photons. I'm joining them all, launching a small flotilla of clever pseudonyms.

Here's a group who gather to worship on a hilltop in west Wales where Luce ascended to Heaven on a horse made of fire and smoke. They wear Japanese masks and honour Luce as the harbinger of planetary apocalypse. They keep getting themselves arrested for playing the *Human* album at ear-shattering volume through loud-speakers directed at the walls of the Bank of England, the MoD, Buckingham Palace and, for some reason, BT. They believe that the music contains hidden frequencies designed to bring down the institutions of oppression.

Someone with the moniker 'Monkey Mind' has created a very engaging comic strip with Luce as a super-cool superhero and the Photons as a gang of shape-shifting, trans-dimensional beings who help him save the world with music and light. Every week. A chap called God N. God, who has two left hands and a third eye in the middle of his back, plays a prominent role as a double agent. His black poodle Mephistopheles is really an enlightened robot from Alpha Centauri. A minor character, famed for non sequiturs so enigmatic as to be entirely opaque, is called Kim Darke. If that isn't a play on Chimera Obscura I'll eat my fedora . . . and the peacock feather.

There are tribute bands all over the place and an album of Luce's songs as performed by the stars of today – try as I might, I can't imagine Madonna covering 'Immortality', but there it is. No way will I pollute my ears with it, but it can't be a bad thing if hearing that song, even in a garbled form, leads people to the original. Some power was and is invested in the music as created: it interacts with individual consciousness in a unique way that has to be experienced, and is every bit as powerful and transformative now as it was in 1967.

People claiming to be Luce post messages from time to time on one or another of the groups I'm following. Most are instantly identifiable as imposters, but a few could just about be Luce. I wonder - have they learned to imitate Luce through repeated doses of her art? Or is it someone who's been genuinely inspired by Luce at some point in the past, perhaps by attending a secret gig, like me, or another encounter? Or is it actually Luce, still transmitting from the astral plane or wherever, undimmed by death? For dead I know she is, though that does not seem to stop her speaking to *me*. I'm hearing her voice quite often now, as though she's watching over my shoulder as I write. Once or twice - all right, more than that - she's corrected some detail that I (or someone I'm quoting) has misremembered. Of course I take her word for it when I hear it; I always have.

12

L'Age Atomique

໕

The Solarised Twin. Fission and Fusion. Bootleg It.
Paul Asher's Story. An Adopted Child. An Escape
Artist. A Born Autocrat. Pointless.

Paris, October 1967

The next time I saw Luce was in Malcolm's, my local record shop. I was flipping through the second-hand bins, looking for my fancy of the moment: obscure French jazz bands of the fifties. Her face leapt out at me from an album cover: a photograph of a young person, typically androgynous, leaning against a mirrored wall. At first I thought it was two people standing back to back. The reflected image had been solarised in the printing, giving it an other-worldly dark radiance. Luce is wearing a white three-piece suit and a broad-brimmed Panama hat tilted low over the eyes. A long-fingered hand (recognisable as Luce's to anyone who'd seen her play the guitar) has just removed a stubby, unfiltered cigarette from her lips; she's exhaling a thick coil of smoke. The face, shadowed by the brim of the hat and partially obscured by the smoke, is smooth, with a certain delicacy, yet there's a firm line to the jaw that's not especially

215

feminine and the strong nose that I recognised from the photo Karen took on the porch at Warm Springs. I gazed at the image of Luce with her dark reflection and felt myself drawn into the photo, standing back to back with her: she in a white suit, I in black, each of us with our wide-brimmed hat, our smoke-screen, our mirror.

The album, called *L'Age Atomique*, was by 'Pierre Lumière'. It had been produced in 1959 by a small Paris-based record label, Disques Cybellines, that was known for experimental jazz. The sleeve was quite tattered and had a dark stain across one corner as though someone had spilled coffee on it, but of course that wasn't going to deter me. I bought it and hurried home to play it.

One could immediately hear the link with Luce and the Photons' work of several years later – *L'Age Atomique* has a similarly original palette of instruments and textures. Although mostly instrumental, there were some vocals in a language I didn't recognise. The voice or voices had been treated in the studio, double- and triple-tracked, so that it was impossible to be sure how many people were singing, or whether they were male or female. This uncertainty, combined with the incomprehensibility of the language, helped to induce a dissociated state.

Unlike *Human*, *L'Age Atomique* is not divided into songs: each side of the album is a single twenty-three-minute track, one called 'Fission', the other 'Fusion'. In the evolution of Luce's music it precedes the highly individual and personal effects of the troubadour Petra Lumis, the public, interactive Awarehouse experience and the sophisticated Luce and the Photons' album and gigs. In each progression Luce expanded and perfected her techniques and became more adept at affecting the consciousness of her listeners.

I played it over and over, all night. I lay on the floor in front of my hi-fi and let Luce soak into me, the music acquiring greater depth and subtlety every time. By the fourth or fifth repeat, I noticed that it was generating imagery, which grew clearer and clearer as I listened. By the seventh or eighth time, it had evolved into something very like the intense dream-voyage that one can sometimes experience with good acid.

By the tenth or eleventh time, as I ceased trying to analyse and just surrendered, I began to feel as though it was me who was making the music, not merely listening to it; creating the experience, not merely watching it unfold. And then with an odd little click at the back of my head I found that I'd entered the dream. I could act within it, make choices, explore, have an effect. When the record ended, the dream ended. When I played it again, it started again: a bit more coherent each time. I had no terminology for this state at the time, though I speculated that I might have wandered into an obscure corner of Ambrose's astral plane. These days, it's called lucid dreaming.

Over the course of the following weeks I tested *L'Age Atomique* on a selection of friends. About eighty per cent never got a coherent dream-experience, just a fascinating journey through amorphous thoughts, feelings and sensations. Of the twenty per cent for whom a cogent experience developed, there was considerable variation of intensity and coherence, as well as content. All, however, perceived themselves as the protagonists of the narrative.

Naturally I tried to contact Disques Cybellines, but found no listing for them; I learned that they'd gone out of business. That would have left me with another dead end, but I noticed that the cover photograph was credited to Paul Asher. Of course I knew the name. Paul Asher had been a highly regarded portrait and fashion photographer since the 1930s, when his daring shots of models in ripped couture gowns caused a sensation. He'd remained at the cutting edge for the last three decades, pushing the boundaries of fashion by his use of 'ordinary people' as models, and the boundaries of portraiture with collage and multiple exposure. Of late he had ventured into landscape photography, producing images of hallucinatory beauty. He exhibited at top international galleries and in recent years had done almost no commercial work. A little research revealed that he was half English, half American, and had lived in Paris for many years. A favourite of the gossip columns, he'd been linked to what sounded like an interesting assortment of women – an opera diva, a socialite-philanthropist, a professor and a jazz violinist, among others. I wondered how a tiny record label like Disques Cybellines had got the world-renowned Paul Asher to do the album cover, and how Luce had come to be making an album in Paris in the first place, three years before she appeared as Petra Lumis on the dusty highways of America.

I obtained Paul Asher's Paris address and phone number, telephoned and spoke to an assistant, who told me Monsieur Asher was shooting today, not available, but I could call back the next day, Saturday. I booked a flight. People are far less able to decline a request made in person.

Before I left London I took *L'Age Atomique* to Malcolm at the record shop and told him that Pierre Lumière was Luce. He played it and at once concurred. We made a master copy on his reel-to-reel, and agreed a division of the profits on the thousands of bootleg cassettes he was sure to sell. It's only because of this single criminal act of ours that *L'Age Atomique* became known to the world. Of course there was controversy, with some calling it a forgery, an attempt to cash in on Luce's fame. As a piece of art, it's not terribly accessible and more than one impatient and unperceptive critic has simply been baffled.

❧

The Paris afternoon was smoggy and cool. Atelier Asher occupied a cobbled courtyard reached through an archway off a narrow street in Montparnasse. It was past three o'clock, though it does not do to underestimate the Parisian's commitment to *déjeuner*, as a sign on the door indicated. But I caught sight of a figure through the window, tried the door and found it unlocked.

I entered a room whose high white walls were lined with huge blow-ups of some of Asher's most famous portraits. Garbo, Callas, Woolf and Monroe looked down on me from one side, Bogart, Sartre, Ali and JFK from the other. Dark wooden floor, red leather chesterfield sofas, a pretty girl of thirteen or fourteen in a tiny polka-dot dress sitting on a desk, swinging her feet in their lime-green Mary-Janes and chattering on the phone. She rang off, hopped down, seated herself on the chair, arranged her features into what I took to be her best shot at professional-receptionist demeanour and greeted me politely.

I showed her the *L'Age Atomique* album and explained that, since Paul Asher had taken the photograph, I hoped he could tell me something about the person in the picture.

'Ah,' she said, 'that's Lucienne. But I've never seen this record before.' She glanced at the date on the back. 'No wonder. Nineteen fifty-nine, I was only four. How beautiful she is, so chic, don't you think? She's my sister, you know. She's fantastic. Do you think I should cut my hair short like that?'

Her sister? Had I stumbled upon the real Luce at last?

'No, I like it a bit long, as it is,' I said. 'Maybe try a fringe? Do you know where your sister is now? Does she live in Paris?'

'Oh no, no one ever knows where she is.'

That didn't surprise me. 'When was the last time you saw her?'

The girl tilted her head and thought. 'A couple of years ago, she came by on her way somewhere. She's always on her way somewhere.'

'Where was she going? Kathmandu?'

'No, she'd just been there, I think.'

This fitted with Karen's sequence of postcards: after Kathmandu had come one from Paris.

'Is Monsieur Asher here? I'd love to ask him about this picture.'

'Of course he's here. I will call him.' She picked up the phone, stabbed a few buttons at random, then abandoned it, got up, went to a door and shouted, 'Papa, someone to see you!'

Papa? Here was yet another twist. If this girl who was Luce's sister was Paul Asher's daughter, Paul Asher himself had to be Luce's father, or perhaps step-father. This lead was proving to be far more exciting than I'd imagined.

Up to this point I hadn't pictured Luce as anything other than a fully formed being, self-generated and self-sustaining. All that I'd heard about her had enhanced this iconic quality. The notion that she must have been, at some point in her life, something so ordinary as a child, was startling, disconcerting and oddly thrilling. What on earth sort of a child would she have been?

A minute later Monsieur Asher emerged. In his early seventies, he was still a very attractive man, with his grey-white hair and keen photographer's eyes. I introduced myself, saying that I wanted to interview him about Lucienne for a book I was writing on Luce and the Photons. The shadow of wariness that immediately fell across his face I put down to the famous person's inevitable response to being waylaid by a journalist. However, when I showed him the *L'Age Atomique* album and explained that I'd come across it in a record shop in London, his look changed to one of utter astonishment. At the time I didn't know why.

I thought he might quite justifiably enquire about my credentials or bona fides, but his question took me by surprise. 'Do you like the music?' he asked.

'Oh yes, I love it,' I said, and went off on a bit of a rave, even telling him about the dream-state that it had, over time, begun to induce. Whatever I said seemed to have passed his test: he agreed to talk to me then and there. I now understood the reason for his initial response. If he was Luce's father, he might well be aware of the dangers that threatened her and would naturally want to protect her. Perhaps he, too, was perpetually on his guard against demons. Had he suspected me of being one myself? That explained why he'd asked, not about my qualifications as a journalist, but about my response to the music. No mere simulacrum would love it or be able to feign love convincingly.

Monsieur Asher – 'Please, call me Paul' – led me along a corridor papered with his *Vogue* and *Harper's* covers and up the stairs to a vast room that spanned three buildings, with windows looking out in every direction. At the far end, rolls of seamless paper, light stands and tripods, then desks and drawing tables, a grand piano, clusters of old sofas, worn rugs, low tables, bookshelves. An assistant came in, received instructions about some printing, went off to comply. Paul made coffee on a little Turkish stove and served me himself. The girl from downstairs, now introduced as his daughter Juliette, wandered in and out, brought us biscuits from the patisserie across the road and obtained from her obviously indulgent papa some money to buy an absolutely necessary new frock.

Although it was no doubt an all but automatic gesture on his part, I was flattered when he asked to take my picture. He held his Leica up to his eye in the one-handed grip that only someone for whom the camera has become an organ of his own body can manage. I'd never seen it before. He could focus, click the shutter and advance the film with one hand in a single smooth motion. It was beautiful to watch.

Given what I'd learned of his reputation, I expected a slick seducer, an egotist, probably a secret misogynist, and was surprised to find him relaxed and natural and fun to be with. That, perhaps, was the secret of his undeniably very real charm. People fell for him because he fell for them – at least in the moment. He gave his undivided attention and made one feel that one was the most interesting person in the world.

If it was all calculated to smooth the way for the lies that followed – well, the lies were in a good cause that was my cause, too: the protection of Luce. Lies, if you know how to read them, cannot help but reveal truths, and the experience of being charmed by Paul Asher was not to be missed. I did wonder why he agreed to talk to me at all, and concluded that, in his place, that is exactly what I would have done. It was the only way to exert any control over what I wrote. If he refused to say anything, an ordinary journalist would take that as licence to ferret out God knows what and say whatever they chose. He'd present a coherent, consistent and thoroughly believable narrative, but I didn't plan to believe everything he said.

'Why do you seem so astonished to see this album?' I asked.

'It was never released. There was a fire at the record company, their whole stock melted the night before the album was to go to the distributors. I didn't think any had survived.'

'How extraordinarily unfortunate,' I said, though I'd almost expected to hear something of the sort. Here was proof that the demons had been after Luce's work long before Golden Square, even before Awarehouse. *L'Age Atomique* was the most endangered and dangerous object I'd ever touched – or it would have been, if I hadn't already arranged for copies to be made and widely distributed. It gave me enormous pleasure to realise that through my actions the demons had, eight years on, been foiled. I'd paid them back, in my stumbling human way, for all they'd ruined or stolen. It was clear to me now why Luce had created the *Human* album anonymously and in secret, and surreptitiously distributed it herself. It didn't matter that the numbers were limited; she knew it would be bootlegged and would get out there.

Paul was pleased to learn that I'd had *L'Age Atomique* copied and it was well on its way to being widely, if illegally, sold. I offered to send royalties to Lucienne if he'd give me her address.

'Oh, I don't think that'll be necessary,' he said. 'After all these years. But do please send me a cassette.'

I agreed, of course, and considered how best to approach the interview – which cards to show, which to hide. There were so many questions to pursue, but I had to tread carefully. I didn't want to reveal that Lucienne was, to me, anything other than the mysterious masked rock star of Luce and the Photons. And it's a general rule that the best interviews happen when your subject remains largely unaware of what you know or suspect: people paint best on a blank canvas.

I decided to start with the widest possible opening gambit, and see where it led. 'So Lucienne is your daughter?'

'Adopted daughter, to be precise. Do you mind if I ask how you know that? Did Lucie tell you?'

While it was certainly tempting to claim personal acquaintance with Luce, I didn't think I could pull it off. Perhaps it was a test to see if I lied. 'No, I learned it ten minutes ago from Juliette, downstairs, when I showed her the album. I'd thought I recognised the person in the photo as Luce, and then when I played the album I was sure. I saw that you were credited for the photograph, so I came here to ask you about it.'

Paul's expression was bemused; he'd been tricked, but not by me, just by circumstances. He was also, I saw, relieved to have an explanation that did not involve other parties. He launched straight into the prepared narrative.

When an infant, he told me, Lucienne had been left on the step of a church in Ploërmel, Brittany, with a note saying her parents were both dead, but nothing about who they were. It was 8 January 1940, St Lucien's Day, hence she was given the name Lucienne. She spent the war in an orphanage; Paul and his Swiss wife Inès adopted her in 1946.

This account of Lucienne's origins gave me a powerful frisson of connection. I, too, was an orphan of unknown parentage; I,

223

too, was adopted. That quality Luce had, of standing alone in the world, a quality with which I'd so easily identified, is characteristic of the never-quite-belonging frequently felt by adopted children. In the darkest days of my childhood, when I was completely under Neil's thumb, I – like many a persecuted child – dreamed of another family, my real family where I truly belonged. My particular dream-family always included a twin from whom I'd been separated at birth. One day, I'd tell myself, we were destined to meet. The feelings that Luce aroused in me were echoes, I'd always recognised, of a child's yearning. I had no reason to suppose that what Paul Asher told me was true in any literal sense, though the fact that it was part of Luce's story I took as further proof that we were linked.

Inès Asher was the professor-wife, an archaeologist whose work involved lengthy periods of residence at the sites of excavations in far-flung corners of the globe. She had usually taken Lucienne with her on these foreign sojourns. I gathered that, due to their professional commitments, Paul and Inès had lived largely separate lives throughout their marriage; they divorced in 1953. This had little effect on Lucienne's life; she continued to accompany her mother most of the time, with occasional periods of residence in Paris. It occurred to me that Lucienne might be Inès Asher's illegitimate child, the 'adoption' a convenient (and common) fiction to hide what was in those days an unacceptable situation.

Naturally I was eager to learn more about the peripatetic Professor Asher. Paul readily provided me with her address, care of the Nationalen Institut für Heuristische Linguistik in Switzerland. He smiled as he did so, and I later surmised that he'd been enjoying a small private amusement, imagining the mincemeat his ex-wife would make of me.

With all this travelling, I wondered about Lucienne's schooling and learned that Professor Asher disapproved of mass education:

Lucie had a private tutor who accompanied them everywhere. He was an Englishman named Stephen Aubrey, now semi-retired and living in Paris. This address, also, was obtained with such ease that I knew he'd be trusted to present the same story.

When I asked what Lucienne was like as a child, Paul relaxed a bit and let his fondness show. Speaking of events in the distant past couldn't harm Luce now, or lead the demons to her. Nevertheless he was careful about what he said. Paul's Lucienne could be highly intelligent, a musical genius, a precocious eccentric, but unusual powers and psychic skills would never come into it.

She was, he said, 'devastatingly clever in some ways, terrifyingly naive in others. Amusing, disconcerting, infuriating. Frequently impossible. Impossible because she wouldn't behave like a child, though she managed to make me feel that it was my attitude, not hers, that was out of line. She had the strongest aversion to authority – or no, that's not quite right. Not an aversion. She simply didn't recognise the right of anyone to exercise any authority over her, at any time, for any reason. A born autocrat. If she didn't want to do what you . . . suggested, she'd refuse. If you tried to compel her with threats, she would ignore you. She never pleaded, never complained, never negotiated. She simply did what she wanted. Even locking her into her room didn't work. She picked locks, climbed out of windows, over roofs, along gutters, down drainpipes. Children are cunning animals and amazingly agile, but Lucie was in a class by herself.'

'I suppose she learned all that at the orphanage,' I said.

'Oh, ah, yes, I suppose she did. At the orphanage. But she never did anything bad, you understand. She wasn't a little criminal, like some of the kids you see these days. Her . . . deprivation didn't damage her in that way. She has always been someone who would, who *could* only do what *she* chose to do. Nothing could stop her. All her great escapes were just so she could take a walk, or sit on the roof, because that was what she wanted to do at that moment. We soon saw it was futile to put obstacles in her way.'

We were briefly interrupted by Juliette, displaying her cunning and agility in obtaining another twenty francs for a pair of shoes to go with the new frock. She danced off, blowing kisses.

I asked about Lucie's friends – did she have playmates?

'Playmates?' Paul laughed. 'Lucie didn't play like children play – make-believe or hide-and-seek – trivial games or time-wasting amusements. She'd lived in so many different places, seen so much of the world by an age when most kids have done nothing but go back and forth to school. Kids bored her, although I've seen her have long conversations in some sort of gibberish with quite small babies, whom she seemed to find more *simpatico*. But it wasn't only children she found boring. Her favourite expression was "pointless", delivered deadpan, in a dry, indifferent tone. I've seen her say that to the most self-important persons. It punctured people wonderfully well. I got into the habit of contriving encounters with anyone I thought could do with a little taking down. She was my secret weapon, and she knew exactly what she was doing.

'I remember one time when she was about eight or nine, I'd been reading a newspaper at the breakfast table. She watched me turn the pages and then she put her hand on mine, stopping me, and stared seriously into my eyes, shaking her head slowly. "Pointless," she whispered, like she was confiding a great secret. And winked at me.

'She was very funny, though not in the sense of making jokes or poking fun. No, it was subtler than that. She could make me laugh just by glancing at me. It was like she was enjoying a state of constant amusement at everything and everybody, and in an instant she could give you a glimpse of it. Not an unkind amusement – it wasn't as though she was secretly taking the piss. No, it was that she made me see . . . how beautifully funny everything is. I can't quite get that feeling back.' He sighed. 'She travels all the time now, I hardly ever see her. I miss her, she was great fun to be around.'

I'll bet she was, I thought. 'What did Lucienne like to do?'

'She was happiest when she was making something, or painting or writing stories. Or music, of course. She would sing to herself, making up the melody and the words. You'd walk into a room, and there she'd be, singing and dancing. All by herself, as though in a trance. She could play any instrument you gave her – she'd somehow know what to do with it. I used to buy every odd musical instrument I could find, old ones, foreign ones, the more bizarre the better. I wouldn't even know, sometimes, which end was up – and this seven- or eight- or nine-year-old would pick it up, like she'd handled it a thousand times, and play it.'

'Did she have formal training?'

'We tried various music teachers, but she outgrew them all. It became apparent very quickly that she had a talent way beyond their scope. Although she could learn any piece of music almost instantaneously, and sing it or play it note for note, she was bored by the idea of reproducing other people's compositions. "Pointless," she would say. What she really loved was to make it up as she went along. It was like there was an endless stream of music in her; all she had to do was turn on the tap and it would flow. She liked to busk by the river – she had a favourite spot on the Pont Neuf. The *flics* would move other buskers on, but since she was so young – this was when she was ten, twelve years old – they looked out for her instead.'

It was interesting that Paul didn't mention Francis, also known as Chico, Franz and Frankie – Luce's 'brother' or companion through every guise. Since I'd seen him myself at the Camden gig, I could display knowledge of him without revealing other sources.

'Do you know her keyboard player, Frankie?' I asked.

Paul looked blank.

'Or Francis?'

Paul's sudden guffaw was quickly turned into a cough, though I could tell that he was barely able to restrain his hilarity. 'What's so funny about Francis?' I asked.

'No idea who you mean,' Paul said. 'Must be a friend of hers from the Conservatoire.'

If he could muster a straight face to retail this obvious lie, I could accept it in like manner. 'The Conservatoire?' I asked.

Paul, clearly delighted to move onto safer territory, explained that when she was eighteen Lucienne had got a place at Paris's famous Conservatoire Rameau. The next year she'd made the *L'Age Atomique* album. 'I gave her her own flat in the building across the courtyard; I saw very little of her.'

I asked to see the space, and he obligingly escorted me down stairs, along passages and up other stairs. Since moving here in 1946, he explained, he'd gradually bought up the whole courtyard and now it was a warren of interconnected apartments used by his family and his various businesses. We passed down a corridor lined with doors, several of which stood open revealing art studios; Paul had turned one building into an artists' co-operative.

'It's just a storeroom now,' he said, opening a door into a long attic room, with dormer windows looking over the rooftops towards the Panthéon. Stacked boxes, a rolled carpet, an old wardrobe, steamer trunks, a tailor's dummy, a collection of odd chairs and other bits of spare furniture. There was no sign that Luce had ever lived here. I walked forward slowly, feeling for her presence, not getting anything. I'd hoped for wall-paintings or some relics of her life, but the room was barren, neutral. The walls, the ceiling and even the floor were all cleanly painted white, yet I thought I could sense the memory of burning. I wondered if there had been a fire here, too, that had, like the others, eradicated all traces of Luce.

'Do you have any of her early work, paintings or . . . ?'

A brief pause. 'No,' Paul said, with such firmness that it reinforced my suspicions. He took the opportunity to bring the interview to a close, saying that he had work to be getting on with.

'Do you know where Lucie is now?' I asked.

'No idea,' said Paul. 'Haven't seen her for ages. Travels a lot, never stays in one place very long. Patterns set in childhood, you know. She seems to be most comfortable on the move.'

'Any idea what her future plans are? Another album . . . ?'

'I really wouldn't know.'

'And you wouldn't tell me if you did.'

He laughed. 'Quite right.'

13

She Knows No Fear

&.

Stephen Aubrey's Story. The Nomadic Life. An
Atrocious Student. She Speaks Every Language.
Chess, Shakespeare, Movies.

The next morning was Sunday; enquiries at the Conservatoire
Rameau would have to wait until the following day, so I
decided to call on Stephen Aubrey. His concierge told me
Monsieur Aubrey had taken his dogs for a walk but usually
returned within the hour. A modest restaurant called Le Poulet
d'Or occupied the ground floor of the building and I settled
down to wait with a coffee and a croissant at a window table. In
the slightly run-down but perfectly genteel heart of the 14th
arrondissement, not far from Paul Asher's atelier in Montparnasse,
the area had a village-like ambience. It was the sort of neighbourhood where everyone knows everyone else. A stout old
woman, who I guessed was the restaurant's owner by the way
she bossed the young waitress, sat at the next table doing her
accounts. I asked if she knew Monsieur Stephen Aubrey; indeed
she did and in due course pointed him out: a slight, sprightly
man in his mid-sixties, pulled steadily along the pavement by

two pugs on leads. He wore a Burberry mac with a purple paisley scarf tied at his neck.

I approached him as he entered the building, introduced myself and my mission and told him that Paul Asher had given me his name.

'Oh yes,' he said. 'Paul rang to say you might call.' He'd be happy to talk to me, though he couldn't see me now. He had a student coming (he worked as a private tutor in Latin and Greek) but invited me to dinner that evening.

I went along at eight, stopping to buy a bunch of flowers and a bottle of good wine. Stephen Aubrey had an old-fashioned, courtly air that made one want to observe the courtesies.

He lived on the top floor of the building. I contemplated the six flights of worn stone steps and decided to risk the ancient lift. Creaking, glass-walled, redolent of onions and stale cigarette smoke, it ascended in shudders and jerks, stopped at every landing for no apparent reason, and could only with difficulty be persuaded to let me out before it groaned, twitched and heaved itself downward once again with a discordant clang.

Mr Aubrey (he did not invite me to address him as Stephen) greeted me at the door wearing a blue velvet smoking jacket, perfectly pressed grey flannel trousers and red Moroccan slippers with upcurled toes. He accepted the flowers and wine with evident pleasure. 'How very kind of you. Most young people are so dreadfully casual these days.'

He led me down a candle-lit corridor, past spindly gilt-legged tables loaded with Sèvres figurines. The pugs jostled and snuffled around our ankles, claws clicking on the parquet.

Mr Aubrey showed me into the sitting room, then went off to find a vase for the flowers. Chintz-covered sofas and chairs clustered at one end of the room; at the other, a table had been set for two. There was no doubt that he was well prepared for my visit, and while his gracious-host routine felt genuine, I suspected he'd be just as much in control of his tongue as Paul had been.

Flowers arranged, wine opened and left to breathe, Mr Aubrey poured us each a glass of sherry and explained that, as he didn't cook himself, his meals were brought in. Our dinner was a bit late, but it would surely be along in a moment. We had a very English conversation, chatting about the weather (I have found that expatriate English have a craving for the subject), the countryside of France versus England, the increase of motor traffic in Paris. It turned out that we shared the distinction of having been sent down from Oxford, though in his case the reason may have been of a more personal nature – he quickly changed the subject back to the weather before I could ask.

I showed him *L'Age Atomique* and he expressed the same bemusement as Paul, though not the sheer astonishment. 'Paul said you had a copy. How extraordinary. We thought all had been lost, you know. It was such a tragedy.' Like Paul, he was delighted to hear I'd arranged to have it copied onto cassettes and asked me to send him one.

I heard the door at the end of the passage open and close as someone let themselves in. 'That will be our dinner,' Mr Aubrey said, and hastened to lend a hand to a portly old woman bearing two baskets and a bulging string bag. I recognised her as the proprietress of the restaurant downstairs. She apologised for the delay: the sous-chef, an Algerian – she should have known not to trust him – had run off with one of the waitresses, her own great-niece Madeleine, that ungrateful girl, and hadn't she always said that La Madeleine was too pretty for her own good. (I suspected this was the girl who, that morning, had been on the sharp end of her boss's temper.) As a consequence of this unimaginable betrayal, everything at the restaurant was in a state of disarray. That was why she had to bring the dinner herself; there was no one to send, but she was always glad of a chance to exchange news. She and Mr Aubrey chattered and gossiped like old friends as she unpacked bread and several cheeses, a terrine, a salad in a glass bowl, a casserole and an apple tart.

As she turned to go, the photo of Lucienne on the album cover caught her eye. She peered short-sightedly at it and gave Mr Aubrey a questioning look. 'Isn't that our Lucie?'

'Yes, that's Lucie,' I said, and brought the album over to her. 'I'm writing a book about her. Do you know her?'

'Ah, it's you,' she said. 'And I see you have found your friend Monsieur Stephen.' She tapped the photograph fondly with a gnarled finger. 'Do I know her? She's like my own daughter.'

Her name, I learned, was Madame Boucher, and she had been for many years the Ashers' cook-housekeeper. She was not in the least surprised that Lucie was now to be the subject of a book; she'd always known she was special. She bustled off; I decided I'd seek her out later for a further word.

My interview with Stephen Aubrey was very pleasant and, while providing some fascinating detail, was in its way as circumscribed and cautious as Paul's account, repeating in suspiciously similar terms much of what Paul had told me. Paul, I decided, was far slicker, and would have been entirely convincing if I hadn't known how much he omitted. Mr Aubrey, an altogether more ingenuous soul, revealed in numerous ways that the narrative he spun for me was running alongside another, truer one in his head. He had, nevertheless, a good technique for diverting my enquiries: initially taking to a subject with enthusiasm, and giving every impression that he was eager to discuss it, he would seize the earliest opportunity for digression and hare off in an irrelevant direction with the same gusto.

Paul's description of the nomadic life lived by his wife and adopted daughter had been no exaggeration. I learned that Professor Asher and Lucienne, accompanied only by the faithful Mr Aubrey, had at various times between 1947 and 1957 resided in Egypt (Siwa, Saqqara and Luxor), Morocco, the Sudan, Kinshasa, Rangoon, Chiang Mai, Jerusalem, Baghdad, Beirut, Madras, Rishikesh, Kyoto and Kathmandu. Professor Asher (Mr Aubrey never referred to her without the title) was a specialist in ancient languages. Luce, as I already knew, had a remarkable facility for languages. Just before a long, unstoppable digression into semantics and semiotics, Mr Aubrey made a revealing comment.

'Lucienne seemed to be able to acquire new languages whole. She learned not in a linear way, like anyone else learns a language. We'd come to a new place and she would immediately begin conversations with people. I watched this happen many times. She'd go from no words to twenty in two minutes, to hundreds in a matter of hours. And not only vocabulary; she'd get the whole structure, the grammar, verb tenses, everything. It was as if she got it from the inside out, not the outside in, as if she absorbed it directly from people's minds.' He seemed at that moment about to expand on Lucienne's special abilities, but stopped himself.

On the subject of Lucienne as a student Mr Aubrey was more forthcoming; here he was on safer ground and could let his natural affection loose, for it was clear, throughout his ditherings, evasions and discursions, that he had loved his charge very much indeed. He could control his tongue, to some extent he could control his thoughts, but he could not control the deep light that kindled in his eyes when he spoke of her, and the warmth that crept into his cool, schoolmasterly voice.

'If you define a good student as one who does what she's told and learns what you've set her, then she was not a good student. An atrocious student, rather. She had her own ideas of what she wanted to learn. Where she lacked interest, she was an absolute mule. It was not a matter of *teaching* her, rather of *equipping* her for intellectual expeditions, then offering a variety of tempting journeys. Of course we did the usual things, the classics, poetry, literature. Latin, Greek, Hebrew. Ovid, Chaucer, Milton. She liked chemistry and botany, mathematics and physics. I had to get in special tutors for her on some subjects – the sciences are not my strong suit, and in mathematics she outpaced me in no time at all. She went through a chess phase, progressed to quite a high ranking before she suddenly quit and took to Shakespeare instead. For about six months, when she was eleven, it was Shakespeare morning, noon and night. When I asked her, "Why so much Shakespeare?" she told me she was trying to understand what it was to be human. She learned every play and acted them out, taking all the parts herself. She would put on shows. She has an extraordinary memory, what's called an eidetic or photographic memory. Every image that enters her awareness is imprinted for ever; she can summon it back at will, even whole books.

'After Shakespeare, she developed an unaccountable fondness for detective stories, spy thrillers and science fiction, which she would devour at the rate of three or four a day. I'm not sure I want to know what *that* was teaching her about being human. Then it was the cinema. She'd sit in there all day, see the same film over and over. What films? Oh, let me think. Resnais – *Hiroshima, Mon Amour* especially. *Night and Fog*, that grim one about the concentration camps. Renoir, Cocteau, Buñuel, Ophüls, Bresson, *The Wizard of Oz*. The Marx Brothers, Charlie Chaplin, Buster Keaton.

'Sitting still was hard for her – she must have really loved those films to spend so much time in a seat, indoors. Usually she was extremely active and energetic, though she hated sports. Pointless, she called all that. She hated any sort of organised activity; if it had rules, she wasn't interested. That was why she got bored with chess. She liked the calculation and the combat, she liked the disciplined exercise of the imagination, but in the end she had to step off the board. What I think she most loved was to walk. She could walk and walk and walk, through city streets, up and down hills, mountains. Deserts, especially. She was like a camel – she could walk all day without pause, without even water. There was no way anyone could keep up with her. In Siwa, the Bedouin adopted her, she'd go off with them for weeks. They called her The Pale One. Odd, you know, that even with her colouring, that very fair hair and almost translucent skin, she never sun-burned. She'd slowly, very slowly, turn golden. Me, I went red and stayed that way, except for the white patches of zinc ointment.

'She had a physical toughness that continually surprised me. I'm prone to everything from sea-sickness to sprained ankles; she was never sick a day in her life, never suffered even the most minor injuries such as all children get. And she'd fling herself at things, no calculation, or none that I could see, along the lines of *can* I do this? *Should* I do this? Am I sure I really *want* to do this? that most of us use to talk ourselves out of taking the least risk. She simply didn't worry about things. She knew no fear. When we were in Morocco, this was when she was thirteen, fourteen, she took up rock-climbing, on those bare red cliffs in the Atlas Mountains. We'd camp at one of the oases near the foot of the cliffs, and she'd go up and down the rock face alone, no ropes, no special shoes, no guide. She'd just go at it, hand and foot. I'd watch through binoculars, my heart in my throat the whole time. Why didn't I stop her, you wonder? Ha. There was no way to stop her. The first time she did it I had no warning – one of the *fellahin* pointed her out to me, halfway up the cliff. I nearly died, I really did. When she came back, not a scratch on her, I was beyond terror, beyond anger. I was in tears, because I'd been so afraid of losing her. That was what I realised, as I watched her climb. That it was all selfish, it was all about what *I* would lose if she fell off the cliff. She, I

236

had to acknowledge, was perfectly fine, and more than capable of looking after herself.'

I asked about the mysterious Francis and got a response so similar in wording to Paul's that I knew they must have discussed the subject. 'Francis, you say? Hm, no, I don't think I ever met a Francis. Must be a friend of hers from the Conservatoire.'

One of the pugs chose that moment to be incontinent in the hallway. Mr Aubrey mopped it up and scolded the dog, but also apologised to it for being late with evening walkies. The dog, he said, was too old to control his bladder as well as once he could, and 'One can't be too hard on the poor old boy, can one, because there but for the grace of God, et cetera, my dear.'

He fastened the dogs onto their leads and we walked down the stairs together, parting company with a warm handshake and a promise to keep in touch. He turned one way and I the other. When he had disappeared around the corner I doubled back.

14

She Reads People's Minds

&a.

Madame Boucher's Story. A Peculiar Child. The Nightmares. She Wanders Off. Lord Francis, the Imaginary Friend. The Escape of the Birds.

The windows of Le Poulet d'Or glowed with warm lamplight beneath a golden neon chicken. It was just before eleven; the last diners were finishing their meals with leisurely coffee and liqueurs. The disarray occasioned by the unplanned absence of sous-chef and waitress apparently surmounted, the lady herself presided from a table at the back, keeping an eye on the comings and goings of her staff.

She was thrilled to be asked to contribute to the book. Clearly, no one had told her to watch her tongue on the subject of her darling Lucie. A peremptory order sent a young waiter scurrying off to fetch a bottle of wine. It was no *vin ordinaire* but a mellow Merlot, reserved, she told me, for her most special customers.

The restaurant was a family enterprise – all the staff were nieces or nephews or cousins. Except for that Algerian; what a mistake that was, and good riddance to him. Madame B had lost her husband and her two sons early in the war; her daughter, active in the Resistance, had died in a prison camp. After the war, things were terrible, terrible; Madame la Professeur Asher saved her from destitution and despair. All this was recounted brusquely; it had to be explained because young people had no idea of how awful things had been, but it was not to be dwelled upon, and certainly not to be used as an inducement of sympathy.

Madame B had gone to work for the Ashers in 1947, a year or so after they'd adopted Lucie. Her memories of those days, even the vexations of dealing with such a self-willed and unbiddable child, were all good; those had been the best of times and she was happy to speak of them. Interviewing her was easy; the simplest question would spark long chains of reminiscence, not all of which were particularly interesting or informative. Luce's special qualities notwithstanding, there are some ways in which all children are alike, and hence boring to all but their own doting relations.

Much to her regret (though she had no great liking for untrustworthy foreigners and their unhygienic lands), she did not travel with Professor Asher, Lucie and Mr Aubrey, and had Lucie only during her limited sojourns in Paris. These times, nonetheless, had expanded in her memory into a veritable golden age.

'What was Lucie like as a child?' I asked.

'Peculiar, yes, you could certainly call her peculiar. It was her upbringing, of course, all those uncivilised places where she lived. It made her not quite like a child, more like a little adult, always finding her own way, not being told which way to go. Some people might say obstinate. But very kind and sweet-natured, very considerate of others. It was as though she knew what you were thinking, or about to think, even before you did. I often had the notion that she was reading my mind. For instance, just when I was thinking about how very dear she was to me, she would say, "Oh, Bouchie" – that was what she called me – "I love you too." Or I'd be thinking about what to make for dinner, and she'd say, quite out of the blue and in the midst of doing something else, "Not turnips, Bouchie, please not turnips today." She was so particular about what she'd eat, no meat or even fish. A vegetarian, can you imagine? And that wasn't easy in Paris after the war – far easier to find a black-market pig than a bunch of bananas. That was why it was turnips all the time. And potatoes, many potatoes. Lucie used to take me to the North African market in the Goutte d'Or where you could get dates, she liked dates, and almonds and all sorts of strange fruits and spices. She would chatter away in Arabic to the merchants, and I had no idea what they were saying. It sounded like she was telling them stories – they'd listen for a bit, with occasional oohs and aahs, and then a lot of laughter at the end, like she'd delivered the perfect punch line. They all found her very amusing. She taught me how to make some of the heathenish dishes she ate when she was gallivanting around those foreign places. She liked to cook more than she liked to eat, that was the thing. She'd never eat much of anything. "It tastes so good, Bouchie, I only need a little," she'd say.

'She was just as fussy about what she wore and would always dress herself. She wouldn't let me help her bathe or even brush her hair. All that had to be private. I wanted to be able to dress her up and do her hair, like I used to when my own daughter was little. All those sorts of things that mothers want to do with their daughters. Not with Lucie. She'd lock the bathroom door in my face. That was another way in which she refused to be treated like a child. And she didn't like to be petted, though she'd happily give you a hug and a kiss. On her own terms, when she wanted, not when you wanted. Never for duty, you see, never *submitting* to it like children do, with expressions of distaste and endurance on their little faces, but that was what made her signs of affection so dear. What she did, she did because she meant it, not because she was supposed to.

'Most children, you see it in them, no matter how they're brought up, they want to please you, they want to obey. They may protest, but really they want rules to follow. It's when you don't guide them that they become unhappy and afraid. They let you decide for them how a child should be. This is where Lucie was different. She met you as an equal – if you could, that is. She'd be your friend but not your pet. And to be her friend, well, that was a fine thing. To have her smile and laugh, and talk to you, sing to you. She was always making up songs for me, little songs about my life. She'd sing to me while I was cooking. It was a bit uncanny what she seemed to know. I never told her what had happened to my children, but she understood what I'd lost, and the hole it had left. She even understood, I think, that letting me love her was filling it. Even though she was the child, and I was the one who was supposed to take care of her, we both knew it was the other way around. She was my source of strength.'

'Was she happy?'

'Oh, yes. Mostly. I think so.' Madame B paused and sipped her wine. 'To tell you the truth, I don't know. I know she was very happy sometimes – anyone could see how happy she was when she was playing music, or singing or dancing. A wild joy would come over her – her face would shine with it. It was like she'd dived into a sea of happiness. And she'd get so happy and excited about all sorts of things. A flower, or a bee, or a person's face, or the river, or a tree, or the wind, or the sunlight on the table . . . anything could make her explode with joy. For a minute or two. "Look, look, look," she would say. "Bouchie, look at that! Isn't it beautiful?" And it was, for that moment. She would seize my hand and somehow convey it to me like an electric charge, and even tired old Bouchie with her bunions and her backache could feel it. But there were times when I had the impression that she was hiding something from me, something that made

241

her sad. She'd put on a smile and I could see her push away the dark thought that had crossed her mind.

'I remember when I first came to work for the Ashers, Lucie was having terrible nightmares. She would toss and twist as though struggling to escape from something tying her down. It was so distressing to see, and so difficult to wake her and soothe her. "Let me go, let me out," she would say, over and over. And "No, no, no," as though in pain, as though something awful were being done to her. This impression was so strong that I asked Madame if she had been in hospital, perhaps had an operation or some sort of painful but necessary treatment – though I have to say she was the healthiest child I have ever known, not even colds or runny noses, not even toothache or earache or measles.'

'What did Madame say?'

'Nothing. She said nothing. But I think there was something she would not talk about, because a look came into her face, a tight, grim look. She was angry, but not with me. She was angry about something in the past. Later she came to me and said that she knew I loved Lucie very much and was giving her exactly the care she needed. And it was true. I loved her from the moment I saw her. The nightmares gradually ceased. When she was a bit older I asked Lucie about them, but she said she didn't remember any nightmares.

'The first time she disappeared, I was terribly upset. I'd only been working for the Ashers for a week and one night Lucie didn't come to dinner. No one else was bothered about it. Finally I asked Madame where she was and she said she didn't know. No one knew. Madame said not to worry, she was always going off on her own without telling anyone. I suppose they'd got used to it, but when she still hadn't come back at ten o'clock, I was beside myself with worry – she was only seven years old. But apparently she did it frequently. Madame made a joke of it and said if she wasn't tied down she'd wander off, and if she was

242

tied, she'd untie herself and then wander off. I sat up all night, and when she still hadn't come back by dawn, I was for calling the police, and I would have, too, if Madame hadn't strictly forbidden it. "She would never forgive you," Madame said. "She would hate to waste their time." And sure enough Lucie turned up that afternoon. She was perfectly fine, made nothing of it. She said she'd gone for a walk, that was all. I said, "Won't you tell me next time before you go?" and she said she didn't know in advance what she was going to do, so she couldn't, but I was not to worry, everything would be all right.

'Monsieur Stephen said it was the same when they were in other places, and he'd had to get used to it. He told me something strange. He said that she'd offered to take him along with her, not physically, but if he went to sleep, she'd make him go along with her in a dream.'

'In a dream?'

'Yes, that's what he said.'

'Did Monsieur Stephen try it?' I asked.

'He said he did, and it was so vivid and real, like it was happening to him, and yet he knew all along that it was really happening to her. Well, quite frankly I thought he'd gone a bit mad. He smokes hashish, not that that's so bad, I think, compared with the drinkers, but I wondered if it didn't make him a bit . . . fanciful. More fanciful than he was already, that is, with those pagan gods of his and foreign poetry. But he said he only tried it the one time, it was too strange. Even for him, too strange. So I don't know if it really happened. Lucie came and went as she pleased and wasn't going to answer to anybody, not to Monsieur Stephen or her parents and certainly not to me.'

I asked if Lucie had a friend named Francis, and got an interesting answer.

'Francis? You must mean *Lord* Francis. Oh yes, I'd say he was a very close friend.' Madame B laughed fondly. 'I couldn't see him, you understand. I suppose he was what they call an imaginary friend. Most children outgrow their imaginary friends, but Lucie never did. He would come for tea every Tuesday; I had to set a place for him. She explained that he was a great lord and expected things to be done just so: a proper English tea with linen and silver and the best china. She would tease me by describing everything he did, what he wore, what he said. "Look at Lord Francis," she would say. "Isn't he fine today? He's wearing the green silk coat with gold embroidery, there are silver buckles on his shoes and diamond rings on his fingers. He's telling me about his famous sea voyage, how he was set upon by pirates and shipwrecked on Aphrodite's Isle, where he met the love of his life, the great enchantress Rosalba." She was always telling me stories about magic and mysteries and miracles. Monsieur Stephen, as I've said, was full of such things.'

'Did Monsieur Stephen attend these Tuesday tea parties, too? Or Lucie's parents?'

'Not usually. They were Lucie's parties, but they might stop by.'

'What did they think of Lucie's imaginary friend?'

Madame B shrugged. 'Well, I suppose they were quite used to him. They pretended to see him, and treated him as one of the family.'

So Paul Asher and Stephen Aubrey had lied to me; they knew at least as much about Francis as Madame Boucher, though Paul had been genuinely startled and hugely amused to learn that he was going by the name of Frankie, and was Luce's keyboard player. The fact that this subject was worthy of outright lies indicated its importance, but shed no light on the mystery of who and what Francis really was. It would be years before I found the final pieces of this puzzle.

The restaurant emptied of diners. Le Poulet d'Or's neon sign was turned off and the street changed colour, dropping abruptly into a gentler shade of night. From the back came the clink and clatter of dishes being washed. A young lad turned the chairs up onto the tables and began softly to sweep the floor. Madame Boucher flicked a glance at him, noted that he was not neglecting the corners and gave a small, satisfied grunt. She refilled our wine glasses and sat for a time turning hers in her hands, gazing into it with a far-off look in her eyes. When she spoke again it was with an air of decision, and I had the impression that she'd been debating whether or not to speak of something.

'One day I took Lucie to the Ménagerie at the Jardin des Plantes. It was soon after I'd come to work for the Ashers. I'd accompanied Lucie on one of her walks by the river and I thought it would be a nice place to stop. I didn't know her well then or I'd never have suggested it. She was very quiet as we walked in, and later I realised it was because she couldn't understand the place at all. "Why are the animals in cages?" she asked. She had never seen a zoo before, you see, and it shocked her to the core. I explained what a zoo was, but she looked very upset, with her lips tight shut, and shaking her head like she couldn't believe it. She was always close to animals – we had to take in every stray cat and dog. I couldn't swat a fly. It had to be caught – ever so gently – and let out. She even made friends with a rat that used to nose around the rubbish bin. She asked who owned the animals. I said the city did. She said we should buy all the animals and set them free. I tried to explain that you couldn't do that. They were dangerous, and even if they weren't dangerous, they'd be unable to look after themselves. She said we could leave their doors open, so they could come and go as they pleased, and we'd put food out for them where they could find it so they wouldn't bother anybody. I'd run out of arguments and was coming round to her point of view. I found myself wondering how much it would cost to buy all the animals; I told her we'd ask her parents about it when we got home. We were passing the aviary then, which was full of all sorts of bright, chattering birds. I'd always thought it was so commodious, with trees inside and a pond for the water birds, but now I was seeing it from their point of view: the iron frame, the glass, the steel mesh were terrifying and oppressive. It made me think of the Nazis. Awful feelings were washing over me, desperation, futility, constantly suppressed urges to fling myself against the barrier that I knew was impenetrable. I was holding Lucie's hand and I realised that she was making me feel what the birds felt, she was translating their suffering to me. I saw that they were in prison, through no fault of their own. They'd committed no crimes, but they were going to die behind those bars, and suddenly it was my daughter I saw there in the cage, she was going to die in prison and never be free again.'

Madame B paused and brushed away a tear. 'You see? Still, still it makes me so upset. I am so ashamed that we have such places, that we do such things.' She drew a handkerchief from her sleeve, blew her nose, wiped her eyes and sighed. 'So I was standing there, thinking of my daughter, with the tears running down my face, holding onto Lucie's hand for dear life. Lucie was very still, her other hand gripping the rail, staring past the bars. One of the zoo-keepers had gone into the aviary to put out food or clean it or something; Lucie was watching him with a very intent expression on her face and whispering to herself, though I couldn't make out the words. He did his little jobs, made his way back to the door on the far side, opened it and stepped out. And then he walked away. He'd left the door open and didn't seem to notice. In a minute or two one of the birds flew out and perched in a tree a few metres away. Other birds followed. Lucie led me away then, and she was smiling. The next day it was in the papers: "Miraculous Escape of the Birds." Some were recaptured, some never left the safety of their cage, but some got away. It turned out the cockatoos and the ducks were the boldest. That's why there are flocks of wild cockatoos now in Paris, and Chinese ducks in the marshes. They're all descended from the ones who escaped that day.'

'Do you think it was just a coincidence that the keeper left the cage open?'

Madame B gave me a long look.

I recalled Miriam's account of how Petra had made the nurses at the laboratory help them. Merely by saying a few words, she had caused them to change their perception of the situation, their attitude and behaviour. I thought of Ambrose, and the effect his mild efforts had had upon Clement. He'd claimed to be a novice, which had made me wonder what an expert could do. I was finding out.

'Do you believe Lucie somehow influenced him?'

Madame B shrugged and looked away. Her hand moved to the crucifix at her throat and she touched it lightly, then looked back at me. 'Yes, that is what I believe. I believe that she could read people's minds and influence them, too. I don't think she *liked* to do it, and I don't think she did it often, but sometimes, yes, she did.'

Now.

A couple of cracks have appeared in my bathroom, between wall and tub. Also, the bathroom door doesn't line up any more, it sticks and has to be kicked. Maybe the building is subsiding. Or it could be ordinary, typical shoddy construction.

I report it at the office; they tell me not to worry about it. I know that tone well; it's obvious they think I'm deluded. They ask if I'm taking my meds, and make an appointment with the GP so that I can 'discuss' the 'situation'. Naturally I evince mild acquiescence, as though I truly believe in the power of SSRIs (blessed be their many names) to underpin a sinking edifice.

I mention the cracks to one of my neighbours; he tells me that 'everything fucking subsides these days; it's just how things are. They don't build things like they used to, everything is crap, crap, crap.' His helpless, acerbic moroseness is infectious.

Another neighbour is more sympathetic; she's noticed them too, and they're getting worse. She takes me to her flat (an appalling mess, through which I tiptoe as fastidiously as I can) and shows me a crack running along the base of her wall. 'It's the world,' she says, and cackles malignantly. 'Crack, crack, crack. Can't happen soon enough for me.' She tells me to look on the internet. 'Google "cracks",' she says.

I do, and find a number of intriguing articles about fissures opening in the earth. A crack has appeared in an Essex back yard, between the garage and the buddleia; in a car park behind a McDonald's in Brighton; in a field in Shropshire (the sheep look unimpressed).

On YouTube, a clip of a crack in the very act of cracking. The person had been videoing a children's party – coloured balloons, cupcakes, lots of squealing. Then all the children start pointing at the ground and the camera follows. In the middle of the bright green lawn a dark line has appeared. It's about a foot long and slightly curved. Some kind of steam or smoke issues from it, blurring the edges. Scared voices tell the children to get inside; the camera is dropped, picked up again. We back away, then zoom in closer. The crack lengthens gradually, at a rate of about six feet a minute, but remains only a couple of inches wide. Its edges are obscured by the smoke or steam, which seeps lazily across the lawn, clinging to the ground, then dissipates in the bright sunshine. The crack enters a flowerbed, negotiates a rose-bush and comes to a stop next to a naff cast-concrete statue of a naked girl coyly draped with her own long tresses. This is in Oklahoma; there are others from all over the planet. So far only a few minor injuries and one fatality – an old lady in China had a heart attack when a crack appeared beneath her as she sat shelling peas in her garden.

They seem unable to determine how deep the cracks go. In California, someone sent down a little camera probe but it broke before they found the bottom. They tried again, but concluded that some sort of magnetic signal was interfering with the camera's electronics.

Nor is anyone offering an analysis or explanation of the smoke or steam that is frequently observed emanating from the cracks. I think of the hallucinogenic gases seeping from fissures in caves that the seers of the ancient world got high on - the oracle at Delphi most famously. I wonder if anyone has tried inhaling the vapours of these new cracks.

15

The Only One

§❧

Conservatoire Rameau. A Falcon among Geese. An Orchestra to Play with. René Laverre's Story, Part 1. She Turned Him into a Toad. Disques Cybellines. A Molotov Cocktail. The Demon in the Alley. The Blood-stained Album. She's Only Been Playing with Us.

Paris, October 1967

On Monday morning I called at the Conservatoire Rameau, in a magnificent eighteenth-century building off the Boulevard Haussmann. It took some persistence, but I finally wangled ten minutes late that afternoon with the director, Madame Dubois.

I arrived promptly, waited twenty minutes, then was shown into a grand office, all Louis and gilt. Impeccably dressed and tastefully bejewelled, Madame Dubois, an eternal fiftyish, regarded me with distaste. I didn't take it personally. I gathered at once that Lucienne had made a strong impression, largely negative; the fact that Madame Dubois said anything at all was explained, I decided, by the brittle defensiveness she clearly felt about the failure of the Conservatoire adequately to mould what had seemed, at first, such a promising student.

251

'This is a post-graduate institution, and we normally do not accept students before they are at least twenty-one,' Madame Dubois said, as she gestured me to a hard chair some distance from the furthest edge of her highly polished desk. Her tone was blunt; she spoke in a brisk monologue that permitted no interruptions and took no trouble to conceal that she intended to get this ordeal over with as soon as possible. She would say what she had to say, no less and certainly no more.

'Mademoiselle Asher came to us when she was only eighteen and completely lacking in formal training, though the skills she demonstrated in our extremely stringent entrance examinations meant that she simply could not be turned down. I was the sole vote in opposition, I have to say, and was overruled by the other assessors. I feel that one must always weigh the talent against the character of the applicant. My initial concerns were that such a young, inexperienced girl would suffer from shyness and inse- curity, but it soon became apparent that Mademoiselle Asher, far from being timid, was one of the most self-willed people I have ever encountered. As for the talent, she was very gifted, of that there can be no doubt. The violin was her best instrument, though she could easily have made a career as a pianist. Or a singer for that matter. She has a very fine voice with an aston- ishing range. I regret to say that she seemed to prefer the . . . electric guitar.' Madame Dubois' mouth twisted as though the name of that dreadful instrument was almost too galling to pronounce.

'But it was in composition that she really excelled, and it was as a composer that I expected her to make her mark. Though hardly in the sort of music in which it appears she has attained fame. Rarely have I met a student with such a thorough and refined grasp of orchestral arrangement. Naturally I hoped that she would develop in that direction. It was a great disappoint- ment when she left before completing her degree. Of course

I wish her well, but I fear she has wandered down the wrong path.'

This was all I could get from the disdainful Madame Dubois. As she showed me out of her office, I asked if she could put me in touch with any of Lucienne's friends, but she said she no longer remembered who they had been. Her secretary, a mousy middle-aged woman in a brown suit that might have been fashionable in her mother's day, waited until Madame Dubois had retired behind her closed door, then turned to me with a shy, conspiratorial smile and introduced herself as Anne-Marie Beaumaire, the school secretary.

'I knew Mademoiselle Asher,' she said. 'Or, I should say, I knew who she was. Really, there was no one like her. She was a falcon among geese and ducks. Everyone else tried so hard to fit in. She stood out. She acted like a buccaneer and dressed like a boy. Some people thought she was just arrogant. I heard that she threatened to turn one of the professors – a pompous man, I must admit – into a toad. And he did fall ill, quite ill, for a time. Of course, he might easily have fallen ill at any time – he was old and, I believe, drank rather more than was good for him. But there were those who were quite prepared to believe Mademoiselle Asher had put a curse on him.

'She ignored the instructors when it suited her. All she wanted, I think, was to have an orchestra to play with. In her first year – her only year, unfortunately – she won both the composition prize and the school's grand prize of the year for her opera. No first-year student had ever won either.'

I asked if the score was available.

'No, and that is something of a mystery. Every copy of the score has vanished from our files. I think it was the other students. Some loved her but most hated her. It was envy, pure envy. Although perhaps,' she added, 'envy is never pure. They did what they could to sabotage her – even going so far as to damage

253

instruments in an attempt to ruin a performance. All made to seem like accidents, of course. And it didn't work – the improvised arrangements that had to be made at the last moment only added to the vitality of the work. But you should talk to René Laverre. He was her leading singer in the opera. And I think also a close friend. He teaches here now. His office is on the third floor. Good luck.'

I made my way up the grand staircase, wandered down a few corridors and was finally guided to the voice department by the sound of singing. A passing student directed me to Professor Laverre's office, where he was preparing to leave for the day. Elegant in tweed and suede, René Laverre was in his early thirties, with wavy black hair and soft brown eyes. I introduced myself, explaining that I was writing a book about Luce and the Photons, and had learned that he'd known Luce when she was Lucienne Asher. At the sound of her name a twinge passed over his face, but he agreed to an interview and suggested the café across the road. While I sipped one coffee, he downed Pernods. I lost count of how many.

At first he spoke lightly, as though of a casual acquaintance, though I sensed that he was skating over stronger feelings. He kept sidling up to the subject, then skittering away. I had to hear, first, about the Conservatoire, what a strange hothouse it was, all those talented and egotistical kids jostling for praise and position, most quite young for their years because of their music-oriented upbringings, still adolescents, full of blazing self-obsession and dire self-doubt, intimidated by and rebelling against the teachers, who were themselves torn by envy of their students' youthful promise and bitterness at their own failures, which had brought them back to school as teachers . . . and how odd it was to find himself employed there now, he never thought he'd end up a teacher, but strangely, he liked it; it was a relief after the anxious years trying to make it as a singer, not knowing when

254

the next job would appear, being passed over for roles he could have . . . ah, never mind. Having got all that out of the way, and with Pernod stoking the fires of reminiscence, at last he allowed himself to circle in on the subject of Lucienne.

'She fascinated me from the start. I'd never seen anyone like her. I'd had a romantic fantasy that people like her existed, somewhere out there in another land, but I'd never met one. Everyone I knew was so boring. My father is a dentist. His father was a dentist. My older brother is a dentist. My younger brother is a dentist. My mother is a housewife, and the most exciting thing in her life is black-spot on her rose-bush. For me to be interested in music was all but incomprehensible to them. And they weren't always kind about it.

'Lucie was like a character in a book – or no, what I want to say is that she was more real than anyone I'd ever met, and the only encounters I'd had with such real, vivid people – people I could truly love – had been in books. She made everyone else seem like dim, dusty half-persons, pale little ten-watt bulbs, and she came in blazing like a Klieg light. When she walked into the room I got such a jolt, it was like I woke up from a doze. I looked around and suddenly I saw that everybody else was in a box, they'd spent their lives making it and fitting themselves into it, and the more they thought their box resembled everyone else's the better pleased they were. She was not in a box. She was simply *there*, herself, more real and alive than anything I'd ever seen.

'It was her first week at the Conservatoire; I was in my final year. She came straight into the most advanced voice class. No first-year student had ever been put into that class before. I thought she was a boy, because of how she dressed, but also how she acted. The self-assurance. Girls, and I see it all the time, even the most stupendously talented ones, the ones you know could be great, always have something apologetic in their manner.

They hope you like them, they look down, they look aside, they smile ingratiatingly, they close in on themselves when they should step boldly out. Lucie . . . Lucie stepped boldly out. The range of her voice, and the feelings she was able to evoke with it – I'd never encountered anything like it. It was almost as though, when she sang, she put me into a trance and poured her thoughts right into my mind through my ears. To try her, the professor gave her a song by Purcell. 'Fairest Isle'. I can still hear her now.'

He paused, head tilted, eyes half closed, a look of intense concentration on his face. I waited, until – I supposed – Lucie finished the song, then René picked up where he'd left off.

'Afterwards, she saw how I'd been affected and invited me for a coffee. That's partly why I assumed she was a boy, because a girl wasn't likely to do that. Girls in those days didn't ask boys out, they fluttered around and waited to be asked. And it was disconcerting, because I was so attracted to her. I was relieved to realise that she was a girl, not that she ever acted like one. And not that I ever got anywhere with her. But we were friends, certainly.'

'Do you know her family?'

'Her family? Not really. I know she's adopted. Her father is the photographer Paul Asher, but I only met him once, briefly. She had her own flat in Montparnasse in a building he owned, around the corner from his atelier, but I was never invited. You have to understand that although sometimes she was the most alive, accessible person you could imagine, at other times she'd withdraw, pull herself back inside. She'd become silent, and then you'd look around and find she'd left. It was as though she'd stepped out of the scene and closed it up behind her. Like it was a stage, and she made her exit while the rest of us were stuck in the play, and we only saw her when she chose to enter again. Oh, I'm sorry, I'm running on. She still does that to me.

Oh God.' He summoned the waiter and ordered another drink.

'What was I saying? Oh yes, how she was *there* with you one minute, more *there* than anyone, so *there* it almost hurt to be with her. And then not. And part of her *not* being there was that she never talked about her past, like one does when one is friends, or getting to be friends with someone. See, like you and me. Already you know a lot about my past, don't you? And that's a good thing, but with Lucie it never happened. There was always a barrier, and no one could cross it. Lots of people tried, lots of people wanted to be her friend. I think I was closest, but that's not saying much.'

I asked him about Lucie's compositions, and he set off on a rhapsodic exposition involving motifs and counterpoint, asymmetrical metres, chromatic scales, polytonality and so on. It went right over my head. I asked what it was like to sing in her opera, and he fell silent and looked away. When he turned back to me I was astonished to see tears in his eyes.

'It was . . . wonderful,' he said.

The opera, I learned, was called *Le Seul* (The Only One). René played a Faust-like character who had two lives: one as a Renaissance alchemist and the other as a contemporary poet. In both, he's seeking knowledge but is constantly being seduced by delusions. Other characters appear, summoned by his dreams or his incantations: his mother, his sister, his lover, his old teacher, the ghost of his father. Choruses of demons and angels tempt and torment him. Then a doctor enters, and one realises the whole thing has taken place in a madhouse, and all the characters are insane. But in the last act one sees that the doctor was no more real than the rest, and they were all figments of the poet-alchemist's imagination.

I was fascinated to hear this account of what was surely Luce's first large-scale art work, for the achievement of which she was prepared to put up with the strictures and conventions of the

Conservatoire. Despite being confined to the linear narrative format of live opera, Luce was already playing with the nature of reality. I tried to picture her, a home-schooled eighteen-year-old, androgynously beautiful, exploding with musical talent. If not exactly spoiled, certainly accustomed to getting her own way. Precocious, exotic, eccentric, charismatic and not afraid to flaunt it. I asked René about the professor she'd threatened to turn into a toad.

He laughed and shook his fingers in the gesture indicative of having touched something very hot. 'She despised Professor Joubert – music theory was his subject – not because he was old, or because he was wrong about everything, but because he knew he was wrong and would not admit it. And it was his treatment of another student, not of Lucie herself, that enraged her. He knew he had the power to help and encourage; he also knew his criticism had the power to destroy. He was a sadist, and I'd already seen that each year he'd pick one or two students and vent all his contempt on them. That year it was Emil Wildstein, a rather frail, sad young man, one of the scholarship kids. A gifted oboist, but so insecure. Joubert needled him and needled him and one day he cracked. He fell apart in class. That was when Lucie threatened to turn Joubert into a toad if he didn't apologise at once. Of course he didn't – he couldn't, being who he was. She stood up and pointed her finger at him. She didn't say a word, but he went red in the face, sputtered and gasped and croaked like a toad. We thought he was having some sort of fit. A doctor was called and the class broke up in some confusion. He was very ill, and was out for several weeks. When he came back he was a different man. Something had changed in him, and while he was never exactly nice, he was a lot less nasty after that. He apologised to Emil, though in private. I'd have liked to see a public apology, but you can't have everything, I suppose. It made a difference to Emil. He was a lot more sure of himself after that, and he's now first oboe with the Strasbourg, so it ended well for him.'

René summoned another Pernod. 'And then there was the dogs. I used to call her St Lucie des Chiens. We Parisians love our dogs and treat them at least as well as our families, but occasionally you do get someone who's not being kind to their dog. Lucie would notice right away, no matter where we were or what we were doing. She'd stop and stare at the person, who would feel her look and glance around, and she'd catch their eye. Then she'd go up and talk with them. I have no idea what she said to these people – she never let me accompany her. Sometimes it worried me when the people she approached were real toughs, and obviously drunk. In most cases, after a bit of conversation, they'd go off with their dog in a state of peaceful mutual affection. Lucie never explained what had gone on. But one time she came away with the dog. All she said was that they'd agreed it would be happier elsewhere. It was a handsome Alsatian; a friend of mine fell in love with it at once and took it on.

'Another time – it was January – someone's little dachshund slipped on the icy bank by the Île de la Cité and fell into the river. The poor little thing was desperately trying to get back to the shore, but the current was carrying it away. We all ran back and forth uselessly. Before anyone realised she'd done it, Lucie had jumped in and was climbing back out with the dog. She hadn't troubled to take off her coat so I took it off her and tried to wring it out. She was annoyed that water had got into her cigarette case and ruined her Gitanes. By the time I'd finished wrestling with the coat the rest of her clothes were dry. Her hair, too. I mean entirely dry. I asked how she'd done that. She shrugged and said something about having a high core temperature.'

This is reminiscent of a Buddhist practice called *tummo* (inner fire). Practitioners of this advanced meditation technique compete to see who can dry out the greatest number of soaking wet cloths draped over their naked bodies, while sitting outside in freezing weather. Generally considered to be one of the pointless *siddhi* (psychic powers) that impede the seeker of enlightenment, evidently Luce found it useful on occasion.

I asked René if he knew a friend of Lucie's called Francis.

'Francis?' He frowned. 'There was a François at the Conservatoire, a cellist, he had some good solos in *Le Seul* but he wasn't a particular friend. Oh, wait, there was someone, a very strange guy. I only saw him once, briefly, then he . . . disappeared.'

'Disappeared?'

'Yes, vanished. I mean I saw him for a few minutes, then he flickered like a bad TV picture and disappeared. I thought I'd imagined him because I'd taken some acid. LSD, you know?'

'Oh yes, we're old friends.'

'Well, you know that one sees things that aren't there. At first I thought this strange character was a hallucination. He was dressed like something from the court of the Sun King, gorgeous frock coat, lace, all that.'

'"Silver buckles on his shoes and diamond rings on his fingers"?' I quoted Madame Boucher.

'His edges were a little blurred, so I didn't notice details, but yes, that sort of thing. Then Lucie spoke to him and I realised she could see him too. They had a very odd conversation. She said, "Francis, I think it's working." And he said, "Ah, I thought it might." They spoke in English, which was another oddity. Lucie asked me if I could see him, and I said I could, which pleased them both very much. They began laughing, and I started laughing too, though I had no idea why, but they were clearly so happy about something, it was infectious. He began flickering then. The last thing I saw of him, before he disappeared, was his grin. Like the Cheshire Cat. You know, Alice in Wonderland? Lucie introduced me to that book. It was one of her favourites.'

Aha! I could not help but think. There was by now an inevitability about it; I'd have been surprised to learn that book was not one of her favourites. 'When was this?' I asked.

'Spring 1959. Lucie and I were working on a . . . project together. She was teaching me things about music I'd never imagined at the Conservatoire, and she got me to take some LSD to help me sing better.'

'Did it work?'

'Oh, yes. It was . . . well, I can't describe it. Everything came alive, the music and the air and the light . . . I learned more about my voice in a few hours than I had in all those years of training.'

'Where did she get the acid? It wasn't easy to find in those days.'

'From this wild character called Alex Trocchi. A mad poet. They were friends of a sort. They'd have these staring sessions, when they'd sit for an hour, not moving, staring into each other's eyes. Then Trocchi would go off and write a poem. When I asked him about what he did with Lucie, he said he was "taking dictation from Barbelo."* I asked, "Who's Barbelo?" but he just winked at me. The poems were pretty good, I thought, with stories that curled in on themselves and beautiful imagery. Not like most of his other stuff, which I have to say never did much for me. He was really into the drugs, any and all drugs. He was the first person in Paris who had LSD. He'd brought a huge amount of it with him from New York.'†

---

* According to Wikipedia, Barbelo is 'the first emanation of God in several forms of Gnostic cosmogony'.
† Alexander Trocchi (1925–84). Described by William S. Burroughs as a 'cosmonaut of inner space', Trocchi played an important role in introducing LSD to the intellectual and cultural avant-garde of Paris, London and New

'Did Lucie take it, too?'

'She tried it, but said it had no effect. Trocchi thought that was impossible, and kept giving her higher and higher doses, until he finally gave up. But she understood it, I'm sure. She knew exactly what it would do for me. It was like a key – it unlocked me.'

'What was the project you were working on with her?'

'Oh, just an idea she had. I was so happy she'd asked me, but it . . . it didn't end well.'

'Was it *L'Age Atomique*?' I took out the album and showed it to him.

He went white with shock. 'I can't believe it,' he whispered. 'Can it be? Oh God, oh God, oh God.' He took it from me, touched the brown stain with tentative fingers, laughed softly in amazement. 'Where did you get this?' he asked, and I repeated the story of how I'd found it in London.

He gazed at me with a look of wonder in his eyes. 'So it's come to you, and you've brought it here. How strange is fate. I never imagined I would see it again.'

'Tell me all about it,' I said, but he needed no encouragement.

'Lucie began the album that spring, during the last semester at the Conservatoire. *Le Seul* was in rehearsals and she was working with us singers and the orchestra, but she never seemed to sleep. She'd spend all night on the album, then come into the Conservatoire next day bright and sharp.'

'Mademoiselle Beaumaire, the secretary, said she thought all Lucie wanted was to have an orchestra to play with. That was why she'd enrolled in the Conservatoire.'

'I think that's true. Anne-Marie is a sensitive woman behind that tidy, repressed facade of hers. For the last month or so, Lucie only came to the Conservatoire to work on *Le Seul* – she'd

---

York during the fifties and sixties.

262

given up on the professors and the classes. A friend of hers, a French-Lebanese called Eduard Gemayal, had a record company, Disques Cybellines, and she was spending most of her time in the recording studio. She laid down all the instrumental tracks herself.'

'What are the instruments? It's hard to tell, because none of it sounds exactly like any instrument I recognise.'

'That's because she treated the tracks as raw material and played about with them in the studio. There were dozens of instruments – most of the orchestra, plus a lot of odd foreign ones and a synthesiser that she built herself. The music was created in the mix. The studio had an Ampex eight-track, one of the very first, and she got hold of another and somehow connected them. I had no idea she possessed all these technical skills, and I'm not sure she did, either. I believe she was making it up as she went along. The whole thing was like a chemical formula, she told me one time, when I asked how she decided what track to put where. I was thrilled that she wanted me – she needed a second voice, a different timbre, she said.

'She'd set me up in front of the mike, then put me into some kind of a trance. I don't know how she did it but the song would come, I'd open my mouth and it would flow out. I hardly even knew what I was doing myself.'

'Wasn't there a score or a text?'

'No, nothing like that. And no preparation, no rehearsal. I stood there and . . . let it happen. I got out of its way, if you know what I mean. I didn't have to think.'

'Do you mean Lucie used you like an instrument?'

René considered that. 'No. I don't think she controlled me at all, or the music. I don't think she knew what would happen herself. The music just . . . came.'

'Were you tripping?'

'Oh, yes.' He paused, staring into his Pernod. Whatever he

found in that glass of odd, radioactive-looking liquid, I suspected that it would never touch the highs of those times with Lucie.

'I couldn't understand the words,' I said. 'What language is it?'

'Lucie said some people called it Enochian, and used to believe it was the language of the angels, back in the days when people believed in angels. She had a theory that it might be the ur-language, the first language, the one that shaped the human mind, and that by using it, we could touch people's consciousness at a deeper level than ordinary languages do. It would act as a key, in the same way as LSD.'

'Do you know what the words mean?'

René shook his head. 'It's a strange thing. I remember,' he tapped the side of his head, 'I remember that *while* I was singing, I understood perfectly. But afterwards, no. I ceased to know what the words meant. I asked Lucie, but she said that translating it into French or any other language would only get in the way.'

'In the way of what?'

'Of what she intended it to do, which was to open people's minds. Sounds, she said, just sounds, frequencies, harmonies arranged in certain ways could penetrate people's shells and wake them up. She knew it didn't work for everyone, and she knew she couldn't control how much or in exactly what way it would work when it did. That was the problem, she said, with recordings. What she really wanted, I think, was to be with live audiences, creating an experience within each person that would act like a chemical on their minds.'

This explanation shed a lot of light on the strange, dream-like state I'd entered when listening to the album, and I wasn't surprised to learn that Luce had intended this effect. I described it to René; he said he'd never had the chance to hear the whole album all the way through. I assured him that the effects could be obtained from the cassette, and promised to send him one as soon as I returned to London.

When I told him I'd been to one of Luce and the Photons' secret gigs he smiled sadly. 'I wish I could have been there, seen her again. When the *Human* album came out, it was playing everywhere. I knew right away it was her, as soon as I heard the first few bars. Luce and the Photons. No room for me in the Photons, apparently.'

He summoned another drink and shrugged off the moroseness that had come over him. 'All water under the bridge,' he said. 'Water under the bridge. I never had any reason to think I'd have a permanent place in her life. Still, it was great while it lasted.'

'You said it didn't end well.'

'Could hardly have been worse. All burned down, not one disc left. Except this one, this single miracle. The master tape that Lucie had spent months creating, burned to a cinder.'

'How did it happen?'

'It was one night in the middle of June. The records had just been delivered to Disques Cybellines from the presser and Lucie invited me along to celebrate with Eduard. The company occupied a small, one-storey building out in the twentieth, not the most fashionable of neighbourhoods. There was a receptionist's office at the front, with a door and a window onto the street, then Eduard's office, then the recording studio, which had no windows, and then the storeroom with a window and door onto a parking area at the back, accessible from the adjacent street. You'll see, there's a reason I'm describing the layout. The staff had all gone home and we three were the only ones there, drinking champagne, smoking Eduard's excellent hashish, talking, having a good time. Lucie played the upright piano and Eduard was teaching us Lebanese folk songs. We were a little drunk and very happy. *Le Seul* had had a triumphant run at the Conservatoire's end-of-year show. Lucie had won the grand prize and received a lot of interest from the press – she was so young and so . . .

interesting. She was being hailed as a genius and compared with Mozart. I'd had a few job offers. Things couldn't have been better. Suddenly we heard a crash from the front room. We ran to look, and saw that the window onto the street had been smashed and something thrown in that spilled a burning liquid all over the floor. Only a few seconds had passed, but already the carpet and the curtains were on fire and the room was filling with smoke. The way out was blocked by flames, so Eduard slammed the door and we retreated through the building towards the storeroom, which had a back exit. That's where Lucie's records were all packed up ready to be sent out the next day, and others besides – the company's entire stock. But smoke was curling from under its door into the passageway, and we didn't dare to open it. Eduard led us back to his office, which had a window onto a side alley that led to the parking area.

'I wasn't all that afraid at first. OK, so there was a fire, but we had an escape route. I wasn't thinking yet about why someone had thrown what appeared to be a Molotov cocktail through the window. Of course, when we discovered that the storeroom was on fire too, it was worrying, but still, it seemed there would be no great difficulty in getting out. Eduard took charge, and although he was cursing and swearing, he wasn't panicking. After all, it had been barely a minute – how fast could a fire spread? But it was spreading a lot faster than I'd thought possible, and coming at us from two directions now. It began to seem less like random vandalism and more like a concerted attack on Disques Cybellines, or Eduard, or maybe the owner of the building. I remember my mind darting around between political arson (was Eduard involved in Lebanese politics?), gangsters (did he owe somebody a lot of money?) and insurance swindles, all jumbled together over the course of a few seconds as he struggled to get the window open. It had locks to deter burglars, and I thought they were going to trap us inside. Eduard finally found the right key and got the window open.

'We climbed out, first Lucie, then me, then Eduard, who'd grabbed the copy of Lucie's album that he had in his office, the one he was keeping for himself. The only one that was not burning in the storeroom. This one.' René tapped my copy of *L'Age Atomique*. 'Why, out of all the things he thought to save from the fire, did he choose that? Maybe because it was near to hand. Maybe he realised that all the rest were lost. Maybe so that one day it would come to you, so that you would show it to me, so that I would tell you its story. Maybe because he was far more deeply devoted to Lucie than I'd realised.

'As we dropped down out of the window the noise of the fire cut off and I remember thinking how silent it had become. Then a man appeared at the end of the alley. We hurried towards him, Eduard calling out that there was a fire, we had to summon the fire brigade.

'That was when the terror started. It came in waves and I thought I was going to be sick. I couldn't understand it – we'd escaped the fire, no one had been hurt, all we had to do was call the fire brigade to come and put it out. But it was as though a monster had grabbed me by the throat, a monster made of pure fear. I was choking with fear. I couldn't move. I've never felt anything like that fear. The man came towards us, and I realised the fear was coming from him, but he seemed to be just an ordinary man.'

'Can you describe him?'

René stared at the table as though he was watching the events unfold on the checked tablecloth between the ashtray and my coffee cup. 'Middle-aged, middle-sized, suit and tie, an ordinary businessman-type. Smooth and neat. Like an insurance salesman. It was dark, of course, and I couldn't see his face, but his manner was odd. He didn't seem interested in the fire, or why we were in the alley. And what was he doing in the alley in the first place, I remember wondering, if not coming to help us? The alley didn't go anywhere. He didn't respond to Eduard's call, just walked towards us like a robot. When he was about three metres away he lifted his arm and pointed at Lucie. That was when I saw the gun. It had a silencer on it, and somehow that pushed me over the edge, because it meant this was no ordinary street robbery, and no mere threat. I've never been brave. I'm afraid I fainted. The last thing I saw was Eduard launching himself at the man, there was a bright flash, then everything went dark.

'I think I came to as soon as my head hit the pavement. Eduard was slumped against the wall of the alley, one hand clutching his shoulder, the other still holding onto the album. Blood was running down his arm. This blood.' René touched the brown stain on the album cover. 'Lucie tied up his wound with her scarf, then she came to me and helped me to stand. The awful fear had gone, but I was weak and shaking and there was a blinding pain where I'd hit the side of my head on the cobblestones. We got Eduard onto his feet and made our way out of the alley. There was a dark form lying on the ground. It was the man. I don't know what had happened to him, but it seemed obvious that he was dead. His face was turned upwards, like he'd fallen flat onto his back. I looked into his eyes as I passed. Wide open, utterly dead. When we got to the end of the alley I looked back, and his body was gone.'

'Gone where?'

René raised his eyebrows. 'That's a good question. There were no doors or windows onto the alley, other than the window we'd come out of at the far end. The next building had windows only on the first floor, well out of reach. I thought I was imagining it, my perceptions probably not very reliable after what had happened. Perhaps he was lying in shadow and I couldn't see. I reasoned that hitting my head must have affected my vision. But nobody ever found a body.'

'What do you think happened to him?' I asked, remembering

the demon-simulacra at Golden Square, whose bodies had also vanished.

'Well, one must try to be logical,' René said, ordering another Pernod with a click of his fingers. 'It's most probable that he wasn't dead after all, only unconscious. I didn't see him when I glanced back, that once, because it was dark and I was stunned. Then later he recovered, got up and left.'

'You don't sound convinced.'

He laughed. 'No, I'm not. I know I was in shock, but that only heightened my perceptions. I can still see it so clearly. He was lying dead in the alley. When I looked back, he wasn't there. Maybe he was a hallucination from start to finish, though how a hallucination could have shot Eduard I don't know.'

'Maybe he was something else. Not a hallucination in the sense of a visual delusion, but not exactly a real person, either.'

'You think that's what he was?' René leaned forward and addressed me confidentially, exhaling a warm and potent cloud of Pernod. 'It crossed my mind, of course. One hears of such things, doppelgängers, phantoms, golems. Because even before he vanished so mysteriously, there was something extremely strange about him. Like a creature from a nightmare.' He sat back with a shudder. 'Thinking of him makes my skin crawl.'

'What did Lucie have to say about it? Did you ask her?'

'I did, though not right then. I couldn't even speak at that point, and the main thing was to take care of Eduard. By the time we made it around to the street, the fire had been noticed and someone had already called the fire brigade. We found a taxi and took Eduard to hospital. The bullet had gashed the fleshy part of his shoulder. They cleaned it and bandaged it and gave him a shot of penicillin and some pain-killers. They wanted to keep him in overnight, but he insisted on going back to Disques Cybellines.

'From the first sign of the fire Lucie said hardly a word, but

I could tell she was very angry. Some people, when they get angry, make a lot of noise. Some go very quiet. Lucie had gone so quiet it was scary. It was like how she'd been with Professor Joubert, but ten times stronger. A hundred times stronger. He'd gone all red and gasping when she'd pointed her finger at him, and had been ill for weeks. Then I remembered the flash of light I'd seen, much too bright to have come from a gun. Something had killed that man in the alley – it hadn't been me, it hadn't been Eduard and it certainly hadn't been an accident. Suddenly it was like I was seeing Lucie for the first time. There was something in her, something I couldn't have imagined. The thought came to me, She's not like us, she's only been playing with us. At that moment I loved her more than I'd ever thought it was possible to love someone. And yet at the same time it broke my heart, because I saw the great divide that lay between us and I knew I could never cross it. The illusion that we'd been special friends was destroyed and I'd never felt so alone.' René gazed at me with sad eyes and pressed his hand tenderly to his heart: still broken, he wanted me to know, still aching. Then his hand moved with instinctive relief to his glass, he drank deeply and resumed the story.

'We were standing outside the hospital, waiting for a taxi for Eduard, smoking cigarettes. Until then, I'd been functioning on automatic, doing what needed to be done. Now I began to think about what had happened, though it was already slipping away like a bad dream. If I hadn't seen Eduard, with his arm in a sling and the album still clutched in his hand, I would scarcely have believed what we'd been through. Lucie had taken him aside and was speaking quietly to him. I couldn't hear what they were saying, but when the taxi came, he gave her the album, got in and drove off. Maybe she was telling him what to say to the police, and what not to say. He never brought Lucie or me into it. He told the police there had been a burglary as he was working late, alone – a struggle, a shot, an accidental fire. Obviously no burglar was ever caught. Eduard left Paris shortly afterwards.

'Lucie told me to go home and forget about the whole thing. She apologised for getting me involved, but that only made me more confused. I didn't want to leave her – something had changed and I was afraid that if we parted, I'd never see her again. No further taxis came along, so she set out to walk back to her flat and I tagged along. Although she never seemed to hurry, I had the feeling that she wanted to get there as fast as possible, and had only lingered out of concern for Eduard.'

'So what happened to the album?' I regarded it with awe, its scruffy corners and faded brown stain testament to the strange events it had witnessed.

'On the way to Montparnasse Lucie broke into a record shop – she was good at that sort of thing – and left it in the second-hand bin. She said it was the safest place she could think of.

'I was beginning to emerge from the daze that had numbed my brain. My head felt like a jumbled jigsaw. Nothing connected with anything else. Certain memories stood out – the gun, the blast of light, the body lying dead – but none made sense. One minute we'd been ordinary people enjoying some of life's little pleasures, the next we were actors in a nightmare scenario and I'd never seen the script. I had so many questions I didn't know where to start, but I knew that if I didn't ask now, I wouldn't get a second chance.

'I asked who that man had been, and why he'd wanted to shoot her. She laughed and said it must have been because she was doing something right. She tried to shrug it off, but I wouldn't let her. I felt that I was owed an explanation. After all, I might have been killed, in the fire or by that . . . whatever he was. All I'd done was faint like a sissy. It was Eduard who'd acted, Eduard who'd suffered for her, and he didn't have any complaints, but a sense of grievance built up in my mind. She knew what it had

271

all been about but she wasn't telling me. I pestered, I demanded, I accused her of not caring about anybody but herself.

'She stopped and looked at me and I felt ashamed. I knew it wasn't true. "I don't understand," I remember saying, in a small voice like a child's. Even though she's five years younger, that's what I felt like – a child dropped all unprepared into a grown-up world, with no idea of what was going on or what any of it meant. She took my arm, and drew me along, and we were walking together, like we had so many times before. Just walking like that made me feel better. We stopped for a few minutes on the Pont Neuf to watch the water flow. It started raining, a light, sweet summer rain. She kissed me, but I knew it was a goodbye kiss and it made me sad as well as happy. I didn't even try to tell her I loved her; there was no point, but I should have. I should have anyway.'

'Did she explain about the man in the alley?'

'No. She said that in the future, whatever she did, she'd do it more discreetly. And so she has. Hardly anyone knows who Luce is. You, and me, and even we don't really know, do we?'

I agreed that we did not.

'We smelled the burning from the bottom of her street. Lucie's concierge came running up to us, dreadfully upset. There had been a fire in Lucie's flat. No one had been hurt – the fire had been extinguished by the fire brigade, though the water had done some damage to the ceiling below. We learned that it had begun about ten p.m. – half an hour before the attack on Disques Cybellines. Lucie and the concierge headed up the stairs and I followed. It was the first time I'd come in with her.

'The door to the flat stood open and a man was there who turned out to be her father, Paul Asher. He gave her a big hug, like he was overwhelmed with joy and relief to see her. They went into the room and stood there in silence, gazing at the mess. It looked like the fire had gone around the outside of the room, because while all the walls were badly scorched, the furniture wasn't burned, only soggy from the water. A couple of fellows who, I gathered, were neighbours in the building were already at work with mops and buckets, and they saluted Lucie cheerfully. Lucie told her father about the fire at Disques Cybellines and they gave each other a long look, very grim. Monsieur Asher said, "They've found you," or something like that.'

'Did he say who "they" were?'

'No. At that point he noticed me. Lucie introduced us, we spoke for a minute or two, and when I looked around, she'd disappeared. And that was it. She was gone.' He made an abrupt gesture as of something blown away. The waiter, interpreting a summons, brought another Pernod.

'Have you heard from her at all since then?' I asked.

René reached into an inner pocket, took out a soft leather wallet, unfolded it and withdrew a stack of postcards. He passed them to me still warm from his body, softened and shaped by much handling. The first had come from London, dated August 1959, a couple of months after the fires. Then one from New York City – April 1960. There followed ones from New Orleans (December 1962, during Petra Lumis's wanderings), San Francisco (July 1964, coinciding with Awarehouse), Kathmandu and London again. The last two were dated at the same time as those received by Karen. On the back of each was a drawing of a bridge over a river, without doubt by the hand of Luce.

I asked what he thought the bridge meant.

'I don't know. We used to walk together – Paris has lots of bridges. Sometimes I think she's trying to tell me something . . . but then I think it just means that she's far away and beyond my reach.' He sighed and lit a cigarette. He seemed tired now, wrung out by reminiscences. I gathered up my things and prepared to leave, but he had one more thing to say.

'After she disappeared I thought about her constantly. And the more I thought about her, the less I knew her. In the end, I realised I'd become obsessed with my image of her, not her at all. And that made me feel even worse – that I'd had the chance to know her, but . . . I looked right at her and didn't see her.'

☙

I left Paris with an immensely richer harvest than I'd expected. Although I had not uncovered the 'truth', the contact with Luce's family and early friends had taken me deeper into the layers of myth than ever before. Paul Asher and Stephen Aubrey had presented a united front and a coherent, consistent account of Lucienne's early years. Although I was fairly certain that the broad parameters of their story were fabricated, the anecdotes with which they had dressed their narrative had an undeniably authentic ring. They'd given me a delectable glimpse of Lucie as child and teenager to add to my images of Luce and Lou, Petra and Lukas.

I could have confronted Paul Asher and Stephen Aubrey with what I'd learned from Madame Boucher and René, but I had no desire to press them further, or reveal that I knew they were lying. In total contradiction of good journalistic practice, whatever story they had concocted I, too, would maintain. As I still do. The ones who knew the truth undoubtedly had good reasons for obscuring the details of Luce's early life – and it is known to be *de rigueur* for avatars' origins to be cloaked in mystery. 'Circumstances surrounding the parentage, conception and the birth of an avatar always have powerful mythological significance which is enhanced rather than diminished by contradiction, ambiguity and uncertainty.'*

* John Greyling, *op. cit.*, p. 89.

Now.

I've acquired a hi-fi with a turntable so I can play
my original *L'Age Atomique* album, but the experience
is not the same as it was the first time. The images
that come to me now seem all, or almost all, to be
memories, though whether they're memories of lived
experience, dream or trip I'm not always sure. One in
particular has been dominating towards the end of the
'Fusion' side: I'm riding a horse by a lake. I can't
tell where it is but I know it's summer because it's
warm, and I know it's late afternoon because the sun
is low in the western sky. Every time I play the album,
that image becomes stronger, clearer. It's accompanied
by an intense, poignant feeling, like coming home. Of
course I have various memories of riding horses, and
of lakes, but I can't recall the two in conjunction.
I'm wearing my fedora with the peacock feather, which
would date it to the mid-sixties.

I've had Gauri's portrait of me in that hat framed
and it's hanging over my desk, so perhaps that's
affected my imagination. If I stare at it with

unfocused eyes, its abstract swirls and geometries look a bit like a horse's head (the alert ears, the gleaming eye), a lake, a setting sun. I wonder if that was there all along and I'd never looked at it in the right way . . . or whether I'm projecting it now from my own imagination, stimulated by *L'Age Atomique*.

The image has the unmistakable flavour of existing in a continuum, yet I can't remember what preceded it and what followed - how I got there, and where I was going. That would suggest it might be a fragment of a dream, but I've found that as time passes, certain memories of 'real life' become as isolated as dream-fragments. Mundane context washed away, they're like those steep lava cones whose surrounding sedimentary rock has eroded, revealing the abandoned pinnacles of ancient eruptions standing lonely in the landscape.

I've searched all the discussion topics on the *L'Age Atomique* internet forum, going back over six years; no one's mentioned its dream-inducing effects. I wonder whether the mp3 format, in which everyone now hears it, has the same potential extra dimension as the LP and the cassettes we made. It's possible that the reduction in file-size has caused the critical factors, whatever they are, to be lost - but it may simply be that, given the tiny attention spans of people these days, no one's listened long enough.

I post a message on the forum, describing the sort of effects I get from it and urging everyone to try for themselves, suggesting they give it at least ten or fifteen continuous repeats. I also drop the tiniest of hints (an offhand mention of 'the cover') that I possess an actual LP. I can't help myself, and after all, I'm preparing the way for *The Book of Luce*.

16

An Interview That Was Not

&

Professor Inès Asher at the NIHL. The Spinster-academic Look. Luce's Mother Understands Me. I Am Comprehensively Bamboozled.

Switzerland, November 1967

I wrote to Professor Inès Asher at the Nationalen Institut für Heuristische Linguistik and received a prompt and cordial reply, offering an appointment the following week. I booked a flight and girded my loins. Paul Asher and Stephen Aubrey had spoken of this woman with unconcealed respect and indeed deference; that, combined with the fact that it was she who'd evidently set the terms of Lucie's upbringing, led me to suspect that I was approaching the true creator of the well-crafted fictions they'd presented. I had no wish to challenge her, but hoped that by assuring her of my good intentions I might elicit some greater confidences.

It was drizzling when I arrived at the elegant headquarters of the NIHL, outside Thun. Burnished wood floors, rya rugs, discreet lighting and well-chosen contemporary art, including a huge tapestry depicting the Tower of Babel. A decorous coming and going of tweedy academic types, with the occasional be-suited gent to add an air of gravitas . . . and money. I gave my name to the receptionist, and after a few minutes a slim youth in red roll-neck and tortoiseshell glasses came to escort me to an office on the third floor. Professor Asher, he said, would be with me shortly.

The room was large, silent and cool, plushly carpeted in rich forest brown, with framed prints by Klee and Kandinsky on the walls. A long walnut desk held an immaculate blotter, empty in- and out-trays and a pair of pens in a marble stand. No photographs or personal paraphernalia whatsoever. It had the ambience of a stage set rather than a real office that someone used. Beyond the plate-glass window lay a serene vista of primordial pinewoods, the blurred grey waters of the Thunersee and distant cloud-shrouded peaks. A pair of Eames chairs bracketed a curvy coffee-table. On one wall hung a large mirror, which struck an incongruous note and caused me to wonder whether provision had been made for observing a visitor prior to meeting them. Perhaps I was just being paranoid. I strolled about the room, attempting to convey relaxed and friendly innocuousness.

Inès Asher emerged from a door in the same wall that held the mirror and greeted me graciously, apologising for keeping me waiting. In her middle fifties, she was tall and thin, with an aquiline nose and deep-set, hooded eyes. Her grey-streaked hair was pulled back into a tight, professorial bun. I looked at once for a resemblance to Luce, and thought I noticed a similarity in the line of the nose, the set of the jaw. Though she spoke perfect English, her speech was appealingly idiosyncratic, overlaid with shreds and shadows of all the other languages, ancient and modern, among which she dwelled. She wore a shapeless tweed suit, sensible shoes and not a speck of make-up. It was hard to picture her with Paul Asher, who even at seventy-something exuded a potent if somewhat ironic sensuality. But she moved with grace, and I wondered if the spinster-academic look was, at least partly, a mask. Perhaps she, like Luce, had evolved mechanisms of disguise, protective colouring, smoke and mirrors.

We sat at the coffee-table. Professor Asher asked about my column, my essays, my other interests, and gradually guided us onto the subject of my prospective book on Luce and the Photons. I recalled how my evident love for the music had persuaded Paul to speak to me, so I thought it was a good strategy to go on at length about the *Human* and *L'Age Atomique* albums. That led quite naturally to the secret gig, and I couldn't refrain from telling Professor Asher about how Luce had chosen me to eluci-date her story, and that was now my life's purpose.

From there it was easy to ramble on about my increasing identification with Luce, my dawning certainty that our lives were intertwined. Professor Asher seemed fascinated to hear all this, which encouraged me to explain how I felt I'd been fated to find that strip of film in Golden Square, and what had happened there, and how I'd followed the clues in the photo-graphs to Warm Springs . . . and so on. Before I knew it, I'd spilled out the whole story, all the stories: demons, arson, the Bigs, the NOHRM, psychic powers, government laboratories . . . everything. It just seemed the right, the easy and natural thing to do. I didn't think twice about it; I'd ceased to think at all.

By the time I left, three hours later, I was sure that Inès Asher understood me as few people ever had. It was so gratifying that my deep connection with Luce was accepted and valued by her own mother. Wrapped in a cocoon of maternal approbation, I felt so warm and cosy, so deeply at peace, that it wasn't until later that evening, returning to London, in the back of a taxi stuck in traffic on the A4, that there arose in my mind the faint tickle of a notion that . . . what was it? Oh yes, I'd gone to Switzerland to *interview* Professor Asher. I tried to recall the interview but found, oddly, that I could not remember a single thing she'd told me, though I had a general feeling that it had gone well.

At least, I reassured myself, I have the tape. I then discovered that I'd forgotten to turn on my tape recorder. It finally dawned on me that I'd been mugged: manipulated so thoroughly that I hadn't even known it was happening. I began to recall how much I'd said, and how little she had said. I'd learned nothing at all.

At the time, I found it incredibly difficult to *think* these things; I felt as if I was forcing my thoughts through treacle, fighting an almost irresistible tide of languor and contentment on which Inès Asher had set me drifting while she picked my brains. I made myself write down then and there every single thing I remembered about her and our 'interview': it was pitifully little.

Later, I was struck by similarities between Professor Asher's manipulation of my mind and Mrs Big's, though Inès Asher was the more skilled. She had done it so adroitly that no defences had been triggered, whereas I'd been on to Mrs Big's efforts fairly soon into our encounter. But the main difference was in my own response: Mrs Big had evoked fear and revulsion in me but, try as I might, I found that I had only respect and affection for Inès Asher. She was welcome to the contents of my humble mind, and I trusted that she had learned I was on Luce's side.

❦

My contact with Luce's family made me wonder what it must have been like to parent such a child – knowing that she was special beyond all measure. It is one thing, not uncommon, for a parent to see their offspring overleap them (which may be a cause for satisfaction, resentment or their bittersweet commingling) but quite another to know that she is, by any definition, more than human, with a destiny far beyond the power of merely human love to shape. Perhaps, seeing her all too clearly, they'd sought to protect her from herself as much as from others.

Although Luce's true history remained ambiguous, everything I'd learned convinced me that something traumatic had happened during early childhood. This was surely the horror depicted in the painting of the tortured child at Warm Springs. I was now certain that she had been a bird in a cage: an inmate of a laboratory like the one described by Miriam, though whether she'd been born there or was captured and brought there I did not know.

Luce's putative parents had, despite their best efforts, convinced me of exactly what they'd intended to hide: they knew who and what she was. Why else would they have crafted such a seamless, impenetrable fiction? Whoever Luce had been prior to 1946 vanished; what emerged was Lucienne Asher, orphan, adopted child of Paul and Inès, who arrived in Paris as a precocious, strong-minded child with nightmares uncannily similar to the ones that had haunted me at around the same time.

Paul and Inès Asher surely knew what had happened to Luce in the past, but I suspected they were as much in ignorance about her present whereabouts and future plans as everyone else. Young Juliette had said it: 'No one ever knows where she is.' Luce had been taken by surprise in Paris; the attack at Disques Cybellines, the arson there and at her own flat had utterly changed her. No more would she go blithely into her life, reaping the joys of expressing her creative genius. Already cloaked in the initial layer of pretence, the one called Lucienne Asher, from that day on she would add layer after layer. Her years of masks had begun.

Now.

Well, it's certainly gratifying to have an effect. My last post has stirred up the sleepy backwaters of the *L'Age Atomique* forum. The place is buzzing. I'm astonished to see that hundreds of people have woken from their lurking slumber and tried my suggestion, with remarkable results. Some report the effects kicking in after just three or four continuous repetitions. Have people grown more sensitive, or is this simply a larger sample than my original group of friends? Or – who knows? Maybe the mp3 format has enhanced rather than diminished the effects.

All describe the usual mind-bending synaesthesia and time-distortion, and quite a few – a far higher percentage, it seems, than in my first sample – have had lucid dreams. A few claim to have had out-of-body experiences of remarkable vividness and duration. And several have posted to say that in the out-of-body experience they encountered Luce.

I'm feeling a bit envious – why haven't I had an out-of-body experience? Why haven't I encountered

Luce? I have a feeling SSRIs may be to blame for my dulled perceptions, and resolve to wean myself from the Seroxat.

The repeated listenings have also renewed interest in the language, and several long-dormant threads have reawakened. I find it extraordinary that no one has twigged it's Enochian, but these are self-consciously highbrow, intellectual types and that sort tend to be very snobbish about the so-called 'occult'. They go round and round, arguing about tracks played backwards or spliced or speeded up, Latin, Hebrew, Ancient Egyptian, pre-Mandarin Chinese or proto-Indo-European. I can't resist. 'Anyone considered Enochian?' I post, with a nice smiley.

17

Daily Life in the House of Ghosts

❦

V's Story. A Pentecostal Childhood. Prophecies and Visions. Two Men in Suits. A Special School. The Seamy Side. A Prostitute at Seventeen. Suicide. Rescue by Tugboat. An Education. Timothy Leary. The Murder of Mary Pinchot Meyer.

London, November 1967

The only clues I had about what Luce did and where she spent the years between the burning of Disques Cybellines in June 1959 and Waldo's encounter with Petra Lumis in the summer of 1962 were the postcards René had received during that period (from London and New York), and Karen Cooper's recollection that when Lou arrived in San Francisco in May 1964, she mentioned having known Timothy Leary on the east coast. I knew it was during those years that Leary had begun to work with LSD and suspected Luce was somehow involved. Dr Leary himself did not reply to my various letters; I doubt they ever reached him. He was, at the time, very busy being persecuted. In November 1967, however, I came across a brief memoir written by a woman who had been a graduate student at Harvard working with Leary

284

in his LSD research, recently and anonymously published (the author is identified only as 'V') by Freedom and Fortitude, a short-lived and very political Chicago underground press. *Daily Life in the House of Ghosts* describes, *inter alia*, V's encounters with two people who, I was certain, were Luce and Francis.

A particular incident in V's childhood, recounted early in the book, is worthy of interest for the light it sheds on Waldo and Miriam's story. I was reminded, also, of Karen's observation that one doesn't hear much about people with genuine psychic powers because they've learned, perhaps the hard way, that it's best not to reveal them.

V was born in the mountainous backwoods of an unnamed southern state of the USA. Her family were members of an extreme Pentecostal Christian sect, the sort that go in for healings, speaking in tongues, prophecies and miracles. From a very young age, V showed astonishing gifts. She could see ghosts and spirits in their thousands, inhabiting, as she puts it, 'their own side of the world' while physical people plodded around this side, passing right through them without noticing. At first she assumed everyone could see them; for her it was just daily life, and for all her life, she says, she has 'dwelled among the spirits in a house of ghosts', though in order to survive she soon learned to pretend that she did not see them.

Her earliest memory was of being dressed in 'scratchy nylon lace and ruffles, hair tormented into ringlets, mouth smeared with pink lipstick, chubby cheeks with rouge, placed on a chair on a table and made to prophesy'. People came from miles away to see the Child of Miracles, as V was billed. As her fame grew, so did the congregation and the donations. Her father became the preacher. Her mother, as preacher's wife, had 'attained a status sufficiently gratifying to compensate for her husband's affairs'.

V's life changed one sweltering summer Sunday in 1948 when she was eleven. Two men came to the church and watched her prophesy. Later she saw them talking with her parents; they wanted to test her. In return for a sizeable donation her parents agreed and shut her into the back room with the two men, who asked her questions about what she saw and how she saw it and gave her some simple tests, like knowing their mother's name, or what was their first pet, or what had happened to their grandfather, easy things like that.

They seemed quite pleased with her, gave her some candy and sent her off to play while they went to talk to her parents. She tried the candy but didn't like it, so she spat it out. Instead of going to play she crept around the side of the house and hid in the forsythia bush outside the open kitchen window, her best spying spot. It was one thing, she'd learned, 'to know what people were thinking or feeling on the inside, but it was also useful to know the sometimes opposite things they said and did in the outer world'.

The men were sitting with her parents at the kitchen table, saying what a special girl she was and offering her a place at a special school. Unfortunately it was quite far away, in another state, so she'd have to go and live there some of the time. V, listening, thought that might be all right, but her parents said they wouldn't allow it; they couldn't bear to be parted from their little girl because they loved her so much. V knew that was a lie. Then the men said that of course she'd be allowed to come home for holidays. V could tell that was a lie, too, and was confused. Why wouldn't she be allowed to come home for holidays, and why would they lie about it? V began to see that the men were after something more than they let on.

Her parents said they couldn't afford to let her go even part of the time as she was responsible for the church being so successful and people making donations in gratitude for what the Child of Miracles told them, which enabled the church to do so much good work. They were planning a mission to Africa, though that was the first V had heard of it. In fact, her father said, the whole community depended upon their beloved Child. The men said they understood that, and perhaps some compensation might be made. V sensed her parents' 'greed awakening like a sharp-faced fox'. One of the men took out an envelope stuffed with money.

V watched as 'a thick black cloud flowed from the man, through the money, a poison cloud of evil'. At once she saw what she must do. If this transaction was not stopped, 'misery and horror would follow, and a tormented death'. She had no great love for her parents, she knew them too well, but she couldn't allow them to sell her to these men, for 'it would be to sell their very souls'. So she ran away and kept on running, and never returned.

The next part of the book describes the path that, fourteen years later, would lead V to Luce. It's a gruelling read. The account of V's wanderings across America provides a glimpse of the not-very-pretty underbelly of the post-war American Dream. With a few notable exceptions, 'the kindness of strangers was not much in evidence'. Nevertheless V counted it as a great achievement that, during those years, she learned how to shut down her visions. It was 'a matter of psychic survival'.

But her life was on a downward trajectory; at seventeen she was a prostitute in New York. She'd had four abortions, twice overcome a heroin addiction only to succumb once again, been charged with the attempted murder of her pimp (the charges were dropped when she told them her true age and threatened to reveal the names of her clients among the city's bigwigs), and tried to commit suicide by jumping off the Brooklyn Bridge.

This was the turning point. A passing tugboat pulled her out of the water, the captain befriended her and took her home to his wife. They were in their sixties, childless, and V became the daughter they'd never had. Although not an educated man, the captain was a great reader and with his guidance V discovered books; she had been barely literate before. She spent six months reading in her tiny upstairs bedroom in the captain's semi on

Staten Island. Books led to a love of learning that fed her soul as nothing else ever had. She sat the high-school equivalency exams and the Scholastic Aptitude Tests, getting top marks in both. She was admitted to Barnard College in September 1956 and obtained a BA (*cum laude*) and an MA in psychology. In 1961 she entered Harvard as a PhD candidate.

In March 1962, she was one of three graduate students who accompanied their professor, Dr Timothy Leary, on a visit to a remote farmhouse in upstate New York. The house, a few miles outside Woodstock, belonged to a friend of Leary's, the artist Claudia Baumann.* She'd invited him to meet her houseguests, two English brothers who were, like Leary, experimenting with LSD.

Leary had tried LSD for the first time a few months before and found it immensely more powerful than the psilocybin and mescaline he'd been researching. He had already come to understand that it's not the drug that causes the experience: it merely opens the way for an experience that is determined by 'set and setting'. The purpose of their visit was to learn whatever these Englishmen knew about tripping, and also to find a new source of LSD, since although LSD was not illegal then, and was widely used recreationally in intellectual and artistic circles as well as in psychotherapy, the CIA had begun to regulate and control its manufacture.

They arrived at twilight on a rainy afternoon. As they approached, V felt something 'stirring at the back of [her] mind,

* 'Claudia Baumann (1911–98) grew up in an orthodox Jewish family in the Bronx, New York, to parents of Polish descent. She studied at Cooper Union and the Art Students' League, specialising in printmaking, though it was as a painter of huge, intensely colored canvases that she became best known. Throughout the forties, fifties and sixties she was an acknowledged leader of the Abstract Expressionist movement, though her deliberate use of impermanent materials has led to her work being largely forgotten.' Crayston, Fielden and Schmidt, eds., *Encyclopedia of American Artists* (Princeton: Princeton University Press, 2002).

pressing against the door' behind which she'd shut her inner perceptions. She told herself it was merely nervousness at the thought of her first experience of LSD, but as they drove up the long, rutted driveway 'a picture began to form in [her] mind of a figure made of light, dancing in a whirl of energy'. They pulled up to the house; a young man stepped from the porch to greet them. All at once V's inner senses reopened with a bang and she knew that he was the dancing figure she'd seen. 'At last [she] was not alone in [her] inner world; someone was with [her], someone who knew his way around.'

Luce was calling himself Piers Lightfoot; his 'brother', called Dermot, was certainly Francis/Frankie/Chico. In a small laboratory in an outbuilding, Dermot produced LSD of the finest quality and purity while Piers guided trips for the scores of people who came to see him, brought by word of mouth to 'pay court to the young Englishman with his uncanny ability to open minds'. At any given time, there would be half a dozen or more house-guests, including many of Claudia Baumann's artist and writer friends from New York. Leary's group spent several days there, Leary afterwards telling his students that he'd learned more in those days than in all his previous years of research.

Piers taught him how to guide an LSD voyage using sounds and imagery, reducing the reliance on verbal communication that had been found to cause more problems than it solved. V describes a set of cards Piers made with 'geometric patterns designed to unlock the frozen parameters of conditioned consciousness and conduct the fledgling true self through a series of experiences to induce, enhance, stimulate and strengthen self-knowledge and self-actualisation'. (This is what psychology PhDs sound like. Gnostics, more succinctly, call it 'knowledge of one's own god-nature' and Buddhists, the most succinct of all, call it 'awakening'.)

Leary first worked alone with Piers, then each member of the group had a session guided by Piers with Leary observing. V's first LSD experience was utterly transforming. For the first time in her life her inner and outer worlds were at peace; for the first time, she was not torn. She had not realised that she'd been living in a state of constant pain until it ceased. The inner world, once a chaos of cacophonous spirits, resolved into order. She understood it all; she felt it all; she was one with all. And for her, the revelation did not fade, as the astonishing insights of LSD often do. Although her fellow students had experiences of great beauty, power and significance, the luminosity was destined to be lost because they were trying to be 'scientific'; they remained wedded to the materialist view. They thought it was all happening in their *brains*; they failed, she believed, to take the further step of realising that 'the brain, indeed all of material reality, can best be described as a fluctuating projection of consciousness'.

Over the course of the next two months, V returned to Baumann's house as often as she could, sometimes with Leary or other colleagues, sometimes alone, until one day in May 1962 when she arrived only to learn that Piers and Dermot had departed and left no forwarding address.

V's account was tantalising. I felt sure she knew more than she'd put into the book and finally, through friends of friends of friends, I managed to contact her. She was living under a false name in Canada, but I learned neither this name nor her real one. She was just V. Nor did I ever learn the reason for this caginess. I had to telephone V from a randomly chosen phone box some distance from my flat. The number I was given to call was obviously also a phone box.

I explained that I was writing a book about Piers Lightfoot, and would appreciate any further details about him and his brother Dermot that had not found their way into her memoir. In contrast with the chary nature of the contact arrangements, her manner was almost immediately quite open and friendly; I soon realised that this was because she'd read me at once.

'Piers? Oh Lordy, how strange. Or not, I suppose. He used to talk about synchronicity. Listen to this.' The muffled background noise suddenly increased – she'd opened the door of the phone booth – and I heard the final chords of Luce and the Photons' 'Synchronicity City'.

'The radio in this bar,' V said. 'How 'bout that?'

I was momentarily silenced.

'Hello?' she said.

'Sorry. The synchronicity of that rather took my breath away. I didn't think anyone else knew that Piers Lightfoot was Luce. How do you know? Did he stay in touch with you?'

'No, no, he didn't. But I recognised him in the music, and the art on the album. And the lyrics, the ideas, the feelings. And the figure on the front. Obviously him. Once you know someone, you know them in everything they do. That wasn't his real name, you know.'

'I know.'

'Do you know what it is?'

'I doubt it.'

'But you're writing a book about him.'

'I'm writing a book about the versions of him. I don't claim to know the truth.'

'You have a lot at stake in this, don't you?' V said. 'Personally, I mean.'

I was silent.

'That's all right,' she said. 'I understand. You're connected, I can tell. I'll help in any way I can. What would you like to know?'

'Oh, anything. Everything you can remember.'

'OK, I'll try. The first thing you have to understand is that he was absolutely not like anyone else. Most people are made of reflections of other people. He was made of himself only. A singularity, and therefore the point about which everything else revolves. Whatever he did, he did it with his whole being. No one else I ever met had that much power of focus. Like a laser in a world of smoky candles. A different kind of light. Sorry, all this is perhaps a bit esoteric. I've got my own language for understanding things, and it doesn't always make sense to other people. But I don't want to make it sound all high-and-mighty serious. There was a lot of fun going on all the time. Laughter, lots of laughter. The atmosphere was playful. Unlike in academia, with Piers it was understood that knowledge and joy go together. There's an ecstasy in discovering a truth, in seeing a connection. Sorry, there I go again. But this is how I see things. Is there anything in particular you'd like to know?'

'Did Piers and Dermot say anything about their background?'

'Dermot was always telling tall tales, but one wasn't meant to believe him. Piers never said anything to me, but Claudia told me he and Dermot were English, illegitimate children of someone so important their name was never mentioned. She thought probably a royal.'

'Can you tell me what Piers did during the course of an ordinary day?' I asked, feeling like Jay Cooper, for whom only actions occurring within his field of vision constituted reality. I longed to picture Luce doing ordinary things.

'Ah, the mundane man. You think that's where truth resides? Well, perhaps you're right. Some truth, anyway. As far as I know, he didn't sleep. All I ever saw him eat was fruit or rice, perhaps some vegetable soup. Claudia used to make big pots of vegetable soup. He smoked smelly French cigarettes. He played a beat-up old guitar and sang with a thousand different voices. He didn't drink or do drugs at all, not even pot. LSD had no effect on him. He could access any state of mind at will without chemical assistance. I think that's what convinced Leary that Piers knew something no one else did about how the mind worked. And I think Piers respected Leary, recognised something very true and sincere and brave in him.'

'What did Piers look like at that time?'

'You mean on the outside? Yes, I suppose you do, and Piers would be the first to agree that the inner makes the outer, therefore the outer must carry some truth, however distorted. I call him *he* because that was how he presented himself, but the real Piers – or whatever his name was – like the real anyone, is of course not male or female. So, what did *he* look like? Tallish, thinnish, very still and economic of movement when he wanted, but this was simply to counterbalance the vivid dance going on inside him. He seemed awfully young to be as wise as he was, but sometimes there was a look in his eyes as ancient as anything. He wore his hair – very pale hair – rather long for 1962 and he liked soft, loose clothes, baggy linen pants and rough-spun smock sort of tops. Hats, he liked hats, especially a floppy old fedora. He had very beautiful hands.'

'What was it like to have a trip guided by him?'

'Well, there I draw the line, I'm afraid. I said in the book as much as I'm prepared to say. Some things are too important to speak of.'

'Oh . . . sorry. I know what you mean.'

'Do you?'

'Yes, I do.'

There was a moment of silence as, I suppose, we each contemplated the infinite, ecstatic depths of ourselves that Luce had shown us.

I was curious about Dermot, Piers's chemist brother. It was during this time that he made the transition from Lucie's 'imaginary' friend Lord Francis, invisible to Madame Boucher and briefly glimpsed by the tripping René as a flickering, frock-coated apparition, to the fully materialised being known by Waldo as Chico and by Karen as Frankie. To show I was not the utter dolt I suspected V took me for, I asked if Dermot had been entirely visible when she knew him.

She laughed. '*Touché*. I won't underestimate you again. Dermot was a very strange being, perhaps unique. He was different from other people, but not in the same ways that Piers was. I couldn't get a clear reading of him. He wasn't trying to evade me, he didn't even know I was probing, I'm sure. He was not telepathic, like Piers was. Piers knew what you were thinking and feeling before you did, instantly and completely, without effort. It was part of his view – he couldn't help but *see*. Dermot had no psychic abilities that I could detect – he simply didn't resonate to the same frequency as everyone else. He really was a master chemist, though. He produced the best LSD ever. He took it constantly himself, and I mean constantly, several doses a day, though it didn't make him trip in the usual way. One day I asked him why he took so much if it didn't alter his state of consciousness. He said it *was* altering his "state of consciousness" – he mocked my prim academic terminology – but not in the same direction as it altered other people's because he was starting from a different place. When I tried to get him to explain he quoted Shakespeare at me: "There are more things in heaven and earth, Horatio, than are dreamt of in your philosophy."'

'What do you think he meant?'

'I've given the matter a lot of thought,' V said. 'He knew what he was doing, he wasn't just messing around. I think he and Piers had discovered more properties in LSD than were apparent to the rest of us. We know that LSD works by creating a viable, conscious interface between our outer and inner worlds – this is why it can open the way to a spiritual or religious experience, and why it's so useful in psychotherapy. For human beings, it allows a great flow of inspiration and understanding to enter one's life, a flow that for most has been blocked up since childhood. I think that Dermot was not really human, which was why I couldn't read him. He was some sort of an in-between being. For him, the effect of LSD was to enhance the coalescence of his physical form at the subatomic level. It was making him human, which I guess is what he wanted to be.'

'Were the two men who came to your parents' church human?'

'What an odd question. Yes, they were.'

'You said in the book that you felt they were hiding their true purpose. Have you given any thought to what that might have been?'

'Well, it was obvious that it had something to do with my abilities. Is there a reason you're asking about them?'

I told her briefly about Miriam, of course mentioning no names.

'That doesn't surprise me,' V said. 'I was so young and so ignorant, though I saw so much. I knew they were bad, that's all.'

'You didn't eat their candy.'

'It only occurred to me much later that it may have contained a drug to make me compliant. Even just a bit of Valium would have made it impossible for me to resist.'

'Did you ever encounter them again?'

'During my first few months on the run I thought I'd spotted them a few times, and several times I had to run away from a place when people told me that somebody had been asking about a child of my description.'

'So you never saw them, or anyone like them, at Woodstock?'

There was a long pause. 'I didn't, but Claudia did. She told me that two men – she thought they were some sort of plain-clothes policemen or maybe FBI agents – had come looking for Piers and Dermot, who'd left a few days before. The men insisted on searching the house, and gave her the impression that Piers was wanted for some major crime, though they didn't say what.'

'Do you have any idea why Piers and Dermot left?'

Another pause. 'Yes. I'd been there the previous week when Leary appeared with a woman named Mary, who wanted to learn how to guide trips. She was beautiful and glamorous, and Leary always was a sucker for rich, powerful people. He told me she was a big deal in Washington and made out there was some huge secret about her. He was very coy. She had a session with Piers, from which she emerged quite wrung out. She stayed overnight, and Piers played music for her, and she slept. In the morning she looked like another woman, something childlike and beautiful in her eyes. But then a car came for her, with dark windows, and a chauffeur in a cap and sunglasses, and as she drove away I had a premonition of danger, though whether it was danger *to* her, or *from* her, I couldn't tell. I told Piers, and he said he knew, he'd known she was big trouble from the instant he saw her. I asked why he hadn't sent her away, why he'd gone ahead and worked with her, and he said, "There's a chance she can do some good." I had no idea what he meant, but as it turned out, those were the last words he said to me, because I went back to Cambridge with Leary and the next time I came to the house, Piers and Dermot were gone. Mary turned out to be Mary Pinchot Meyer. If you don't know who she was and what happened to her, look it up. Look up the Washington newspapers for October 1964.'

That was all V would say, and it was clear she felt the interview was at an end, so we rang off.

I looked up the papers she'd suggested and learned that on 12 October 1964, Mary Pinchot Meyer was shot twice at point-blank range (once in the back, once in the head) by an unknown assailant while walking along a towpath near her home in Washington, D.C.

Since then, more has come to light. At the time of her visit to Piers, Mary Pinchot Meyer was a soignée Washington socialite, recently divorced from a prominent CIA official, and the mistress of John F. Kennedy. In his autobiography (published 1983), Leary tells how she approached him, saying she had a very important friend who, impressed by her own accounts of LSD experiences, wanted to try the drug. Leary suggested that this friend come himself; this she refused, saying he was too well known.

Leary quotes her as saying, "'The guys who run things – I mean the guys who really run things – are very interested in psychology, and drugs in particular. These people play hardball, Timothy. They want to use the drugs for warfare, for espionage, for brainwashing, for control . . . But there are people like me who want to use drugs for peace, not for war, to make people's lives better.'"

Leary goes on to say that he had a call from Pinchot Meyer soon after Kennedy was assassinated (22 November 1963) during which she sobbed and said, "'They couldn't control him any more. He was changing too fast. They've covered everything up. I gotta come see you. I'm afraid. Be careful.'"*

Mary Pinchot Meyer's biographer, Nina Burleigh, confirms Pinchot Meyer's own use of LSD, her involvement with Leary during his tenure at Harvard, and that this involvement occurred at the same time as Pinchot Meyer's intimate association with President Kennedy. 'Mary's visits to Timothy Leary during the time she was also Kennedy's lover suggest that Kennedy knew more about hallucinogenic drugs than the CIA might have been telling him. No one has ever confirmed that Kennedy tried LSD with Mary. But the timing of her visits to Timothy Leary do coincide with her known private meetings with the president.'†

Her murder remains unsolved.

* Timothy Leary, *Flashbacks* (London: Heinemann, 1983) p. 130.
† Nina Burleigh, *A Very Private Woman: The Life and Unsolved Murder of Presidential Mistress Mary Meyer* (New York: Bantam Books, 1998); *New York Times* excerpt: http://partners.nytimes.com/books/first/b/burleigh-private. html.

Now.

So much of what I learned from V and from Waldo and Miriam seemed far-fetched at the time, though I never doubted their honesty and sincerity. Only when the revelations about Project MKUltra were published did I realise that there was nothing in the least far-fetched about the idea of a secret government programme that kidnapped people and subjected them to experiments, torture and psychological manipulation . . . and murdered anyone who might expose it.

Every state that has ever existed has deemed it necessary to control the shaman, the witch, the magus, the seer: the ones with the knowledge and power to navigate other planes of existence, to converse with gods and spirits, angels and demons. If they cannot be made to serve the state they must be silenced - imprisoned, declared insane, burned at the stake, crucified . . . shot.

The facts of the CIA's mind-control programmes leave horror, fantasy and science fiction far behind. The original files - the few that were accidentally overlooked when CIA director Richard Helms ordered all records destroyed - are now available to read online; they're proving a fascinating way to pass the sleepless hours. There are thousands of pages, hugely redacted and mostly dealing with expenses, but here and there I'm catching references to an outlier programme, called MKTheta (perhaps named after theta waves, the frequency of brain waves linked to astral consciousness?) to which certain subjects were sent. Searches on 'MKTheta' yield nothing, but the very thorough Wikipedia entry on MKUltra cites as a reference a book called *Astral Wars: The CIA's Secret Psychic Operations* by someone called Allyn Q. Ranklowics. I can't find the book anywhere online, but the British Library has a copy, so I order it up.

At the Library I collect the book - in an eye-wateringly bright orange dust jacket - and settle at a desk to read. I'm disappointed: it seems to be largely a rehash of various articles and books on MKUltra, with a pinch of Illuminati, a *soupçon* of extraterrestrials and a generous shot of Nazi occultism stirred in.

Perhaps it's the overwrought language of the author, or maybe the undeniably sinister subject matter, but within a few minutes I'm beginning to feel distinctly uneasy. I'm getting a prickle in the back of my neck and I sense I'm being watched. I turn around casually as though stretching, but no one at the nearby desks is paying me any attention. I look up to the balcony; several people are standing at the railing, gazing down at the readers below. Yes, the feeling's definitely coming from up there. Could there be a demon about? I can't make out much detail of the faces or clothes; they all look extremely ordinary from here. I don't dare switch to my distance glasses and peer around. I settle back into my chair, outwardly calm but inwardly very agitated indeed. The lurid orange of the book cover glows like a beacon and I have the thought, stimulated no doubt by the conspiracy theories I've just been reading, that the book is a decoy and I've walked into a trap.

Nonsense, I tell myself. It's the bloody Seroxat withdrawal - it's making me hyper-sensitive. Nevertheless, I have an irresistible urge to get the hell out of here. Presence of mind not altogether deserting me, I switch to my other glasses under cover of gathering my things and preparing to leave, giving the balcony a casual scan. With a twinge of dread I identify one figure as a likely demon: a female in a beige trouser suit and blue shirt, pale, pasty face, short, neat hair and a blank expression. She's looking right at me and, as our eyes meet for one awful second, the surge of fear that washes through me is unmistakable. I make myself go calmly to the desk, hand in the book and walk out. The open space of the plaza in front of the building is such a relief my knees go weak. I sit on a bench to catch my breath and watch the doors. Beyond the reflections on the glass wall of the lobby I think I see Beige Suit walking purposefully towards the exit. I bolt to the street, scurrying as fast as my shaky old legs can carry me. I jump the queue boarding a bus on the corner of Euston Road; as it pulls away, I glimpse a beige-suited figure standing on the pavement, watching.

I used to find this sort of thing almost fun. Not any more. I feel queasy, my heart is behaving oddly,

300

I'm cold and sweaty and all I want to do is crawl into a hole and hide like some hapless field mouse. I must look as bad as I feel; someone offers me one of the seats at the front of the bus, suggested for 'the elderly'. I'll be insulted another day; now I sink gratefully into it. Beige Suit is left behind as the bus pulls away. I've just about regained my composure when, at the next stop, Beige Suit or another one very like her is waiting in the queue to board. I leap to my feet and push towards the back doors, managing to time my exit precisely with her entry. I duck into a newsagent's, spend a few minutes browsing the magazine racks, then buy a newspaper and step cautiously outside. The pavement is crowded: lots of ordinary-looking beings going this way and that with blank faces. They can't all be demons. Can they? I treat myself to a taxi home and return, with relief, to the past.

18

The Secret Society

&.

*Lucifergus Lights. A Request for Help. Charlie
Drives Us to Devon. John Greyling and the Avatar of
the Aeon. Not Exactly Human. The Reality of Evil.
The Scribe. Fergus Meakin's Story, Part 1. A Medical
Miracle. Blindfold Chess. The Downy Old Bird.*

London, December 1967

The instant I saw him behind the controls of the light show
at a Roundhouse concert in early December I recognised
the man who'd worn a Frankenstein mask at Luce and the
Photons' secret gig. About my age, small in stature but wiry, he
had watery blue eyes, a sharp nose and a full, reddish-blond
beard. Although not now masked, there was something very
distinctive about the way his hands moved over the key pads,
the dials and sliders – he was playing the board like an instrument.

I hung around when the concert finished. Assisted by a young
Asian woman with a thick black pigtail, he packed up his equipment (stencilled 'Lucifergus Lights', with a lightning-flash logo),
and I considered how best to approach him. If he'd gone to the

trouble to be masked at the secret gig, it might spook him to know he'd been recognised. Most of the people who'd associated closely with Luce had good reason to be wary. In the end I just introduced myself, gave him my card, explained that I was writing an article on the evolution of the light show from Plato's cave to the present and would love to talk to him. I thanked him for a great show and said good night. If he contacted me, well and good. If he didn't, I was confident I'd run into him again in Synchronicity City.

My confidence was well placed. At two in the morning I was awakened by urgent knocking at my door. I pulled on my dressing-gown and peered out of the spy hole, but all I could see was a hunched figure. 'Who is it?'

'Hi, awfully sorry to bother you, it's Fergus. Fergus Meakin. From Lucifergus Lights. You gave me your card, and I . . . was just passing. Look, it's raining, could you let me in, please?'

When I opened the door he gave a quick glance up and down the street, ducked in and closed the door behind him. I'd turned the light on; he flipped it off, moved to the window, checked that the curtains were tightly closed, then said, 'You can put a light on now.'

I put the light back on and offered to take his wet coat, but he said he couldn't stay long. He lit a cigarette; his hands were shaking.

'Sorry,' he said. 'I'm a bit, er— Someone's been following me. I'm pretty sure I've lost him, but I daren't go back to my place and it's too early to get a train. I was wandering around in the rain and then I remembered I had your card in my pocket. Hope you don't mind. You seemed like a good person, so . . . Look, I need to get out of town for a while. You don't happen to have a car, do you?'

'No, but I can easily borrow one. Give me a sec to get dressed.' I scrambled into some clothes, slipping the gun into my pocket.

I'd got into the habit of carrying it everywhere – after all, what was the point of it if it sat in a drawer?

Back in the sitting room, I discovered Fergus had found my drinks cabinet and helped himself to a brandy. 'Help yourself,' I said.

'Thanks, I will.' He poured another and downed it in one gulp, followed by a raucous and prolonged fit of coughing.

When he'd recovered I offered him the choice of front or rear exit. Without hesitation he chose the rear, despite being warned that it was something of a steeplechase. I saw I'd met my match in paranoia – or, as I preferred to think of it, the taking of sensible precautions.

Charlie (wide awake at that hour, as I knew he would be – he'd got into coke in a big way) declined to lend any of his cars unless he could come too. Twenty minutes later (we all had to do a couple of lines and Clement had to prepare a flask of coffee) we emerged from his basement garage in the Aston Martin.

'Where to?' Charlie asked.

'South-west,' Fergus said. 'I've got an uncle in Devon – near Manaton, you know it?'

The rain eased as we headed out of town. Fergus kept looking behind us and insisted on a circuitous route. Charlie was familiar with such manoeuvres. 'You got demons on your tail, too?' he asked Fergus.

'What?' said Fergus, looking startled.

'Never mind,' I said. 'Private joke. Who's following you, and why?'

'Long story. I really appreciate the lift but, quite frankly, you don't want to know.'

I suspected I did know, but that was all he'd say on the subject. As we wended our way through south-west London we chatted about light shows, music, the weather. I was wondering how to introduce the subject of Luce when I heard the sound of snores from the back seat. He was out cold, or doing a very good job of pretending to be. I'm not sure I could have fallen asleep so soon after doing coke.

Charlie was, as ever, gleefully oblivious (or so I thought) to everything but the fun to be had from the present moment. The reasons that one might find oneself in any given situation were immaterial, as were its consequences. Just now, the fun was in trying to roll a joint with one hand while whipping the DB6 at seventy miles an hour through the roundabouts between Hounslow and Staines with the other.

'I could roll that for you,' I said.

'No thanks, I've been practising this. One of those important life skills, you know. My dear mother is always reminding me that I lack life skills, so I thought I'd better lay some on.'

And he did, in fact, manage with very little spillage, though the joint was a bit wonky. A later one, undertaken on a long, straight stretch of the A303, was almost perfect.

The sky had begun to lighten as we neared Manaton. I woke Fergus and he directed us out of the village, along narrow country lanes and down a steep driveway. We pulled up outside a substantial farmhouse, wide-windowed and ivy-clad. The air was clear and cold, with a drift of mist across the lawns.

We climbed out, Fergus unfolding himself stiffly from the back seat. The porch light went on before he could knock and the door was opened by an old man in a tartan dressing-gown.

'This is my uncle John,' Fergus said, introducing Charlie and me.

'How nice to see you, Mr Greyling,' I said.

'Aha,' said Greyling. 'I had a feeling we might meet again.'

'You two know each other?' Fergus asked.

'From Synchronicity City,' I said.

'Do come in,' said Greyling. 'I'll put the kettle on.'

He led the way down a tiled passage into a warm kitchen,

filled a kettle at the sink and put it on the Aga. 'Anyone hungry? Fancy some scrambled eggs?'

We discovered that we were famished.

After food came repletion; after that, an irresistible desire for sleep. Charlie crashed on the kitchen sofa while I climbed heavily upstairs with Fergus, who pointed me to a tidy little bedroom under the eaves. I kicked off my shoes and collapsed onto the white chenille bedspread.

I was awakened by the sun on my face. The grandfather clock on the landing struck noon as I made my way downstairs. In the kitchen I encountered a cheerful middle-aged lady in gingham apron and Marigolds: Mrs Yates, the daily. I prodded Charlie; he rolled over with a grunt. Fergus was still asleep and Greyling, I learned, had gone for a walk. Mrs Yates made me a cup of coffee and I took it across the hall into a bright, book-lined sitting room, whose windows looked out over a tidy garden to a meadow. Half a dozen fat white sheep were arranged just so on the green-sward and a pair of buzzards circled lazily above. Beyond the meadow a slow brown river flowed between banks overhung with hazel.

I perused the bookshelves. Poetry and novels, some philosophy, a fair bit on the natural sciences. Anthropology, art history, comparative religions. The complete works, as far as I could tell, of C. G. Jung, snuggled up next to Goethe, both in the original German. A wide-ranging selection of the later Jungians. At the end of the row, a slim volume entitled *The Reality of Myth: Evolution and the Avatar*, by John Greyling, MD, PhD. The bio blurb mentioned that he had trained with Dr Jung, was in private practice as an analyst, and had written several novels and a collection of short stories in the 1920s and 1930s.

Settling into a comfortable armchair, I flicked through the book with mounting interest, for although he spoke hypothetically, citing many different mythological traditions and several pertinent case histories, it was clear to me that Greyling meant it literally: myth had become real; evolution had taken a leap; a being with god-like powers actually lived in human form.

I heard a door open and shut at the back of the house as Greyling came in, accompanied by the scents of wood and meadow. I had planned to approach him delicately, revealing as little as possible of what I knew and extracting as much as possible from him, but when I saw him I couldn't help myself. I held up the book. 'So you already knew what Luce was in . . .' I checked the publication date '. . . 1955.'

He raised his eyebrows; evidently he too had been expecting a more oblique me. 'Good afternoon,' he said mildly. 'Did you have a refreshing sleep? I see Mrs Yates has given you coffee, excellent. And you've made yourself at home. How nice.'

He eased himself into a chair, took a pipe from his pocket, tapped it briskly into an ashtray and began to fill it from a leather pouch. When he had packed it to his satisfaction he struck a match and puffed slowly for a while. I'm sure he really did want a pipe, but I suspected that these tactics were designed to keep me hanging and regain the initiative in this meeting. I lit a cigarette and waited, determined not to be provoked into impatience. I'd begun smoking Gitanes, Luce's brand, and I noted that Greyling clocked the distinctive scent of the Turkish tobacco with a twitch of his nostrils and a glance at the packet I'd placed on the coffee-table.

At last he saw fit to address me. 'I usually require at least four serendipitous encounters before I reckon someone is of interest, but we've had three quite good ones. Tell me, do you have any recurring dreams?'

This was an unexpected manoeuvre, yet altogether apt. I told him about the Dream of the Cavern, which had stayed with me ever since Luce's Camden gig. He seemed very taken with it. 'Yes, yes, following a single thread into the unknown. Underground, darkness, the unconscious. And you say you feel no fear. That is excellent. It shows you have a mind that is not irredeemably closed. Some cracks, you know?'

'Yeah, cracks,' I said. 'No shortage of cracks. But I'm no longer quite the idiot I was when we last met. At the time, I was a bit confused and didn't know what to ask.'

'And now you do?'

'Oh, yes.' I riffled through the long list of questions stacked up in my mind and decided to start at the beginning. 'At Golden Square, did you really shut those two . . . people in the building, make them burn in their own fire?'

'Yes.'

This ready acknowledgement set me back somewhat. I'd expected to have to press him quite hard on this point. His casual annihilation of Tweedledee and Tweedledum obviously caused him no moral qualms. 'They were not human beings, were they?'

'Not exactly, no.'

'Were they astral entities?'

'You could say that.'

'What did they want?'

He thought for a moment, then replied with a question of his own: 'Are you prepared to believe in the reality of evil?'

'That depends. Would you care to define your terms? Believe, reality, evil?'

'Cambridge?'

'Oxford.'

'Well, then. Humans are far from perfect, but let's posit that we have the ability to become better, as individuals and as a species – more intelligent and aware, wiser and freer, more loving, more enlightened, however you define it. There is in us a tendency towards the good but there's also a pull in the opposite direction. There is love and kindness, but also hate and cruelty. There is a will to hurt and destroy just as there is a will

308

to heal and create. You may think that concepts such as good and evil are outmoded in our subtle, complex age – or, at best, are philosophical qualities with no application to the so-called real world. But I tell you, as someone who has lived through two world wars, they are utterly real and relevant. They're at war in everyone, and they're at war in the world. The beings we encountered were soldiers in that war, as am I.'

I was having a hard time reconciling Greyling's kind, professorial demeanour with this rather wild talk of good and evil. Perhaps as a Jungian analyst he could not help but think in the grand archetypes. He was, as well, a writer of fiction – attracted, no doubt, to the dramatic concept, the evocative phrase. Or it could be that he was a bit cracked himself.

'You're now beginning to wonder if I'm crazy,' he said.

'You do have a rather extreme point of view.'

'Why are you really here?'

'Fergus showed up at my door and asked for help.'

'Why did he come to you?'

'I—'

'Why were you at Golden Square in the first place?'

'I was looking for Luce.'

'Why?'

'Because Luce made me see something, feel something so . . . so wonderful. Words can't do it justice. Beauty? Ecstasy? And ever since then, all I've wanted was to find it again.' I laughed to cover the tears that sprang to my eyes. Greyling passed me a box of Kleenex – shrinks always have them to hand. I blew my nose and lit another cigarette. 'So what *am* I looking for?' I asked at last. 'Why does this feeling drive me so?'

'It is the love of the good,' Greyling said.

'Of the good? That's an idea. I'm looking for a specific person.'

'They're the same.'

I was pondering that when Mrs Yates stuck her head into the

room to announce that lunch was ready. We crossed the hall to the dining room as Charlie emerged, sniffing vigorously, from the downstairs loo. 'Fresh air!' he exclaimed. 'I love the countryside.'

'See a lot of it, do you?' asked Greyling.

'I hope to.' Charlie grinned. 'One day.'

Lunch was tasty and, after all the talk of good and evil, surreal in its ordinariness. Greyling managed the conversation adroitly, steering us around a series of well-trodden mundanities. Roast chicken with gravy, mashed potatoes and peas: the weather. Sliced cucumbers with salad cream: the foibles of local worthies. Apple crumble and clotted cream: the eccentricities of old houses. After lunch Greyling, citing his venerable age, retired for a nap. Charlie wandered off – perhaps he really did venture outside. Mrs Yates having left for the day, Fergus and I washed up.

We chatted about art and film, light shows and music; I steered the conversation gradually around to Luce and the Photons. Until Fergus spoke of Luce as 'she', I wasn't sure whether, to him, Luce was a man or a woman. My conversation with Greyling, while suggesting that he knew Luce very well, had given no hint. The avatar referred to in his book was, by definition, androgynous.

The companionable activity of washing up together had relaxed Fergus and seemed to loosen his tongue. I confessed that I'd recognised him from the Camden gig, told him something of what had happened to me there, and explained that I was researching a book about Luce.

'Oh, you're the one who writes as Chimera Obscura, aren't you? Luce calls you the Scribe.'

I was at once astonished to hear that Luce knew of me and not in the least surprised.

'All this makes sense to me now,' Fergus said. 'As I was wandering around in the rain last night, a bit scared and not sure what to do, she told me to go to you. I . . . probably you'll think this is silly, but I hear her voice once in a while. In my head. Not very often. She told me to look at the card, your card that was in my pocket, and to go to that person.'

'Not silly at all,' I said. 'I know what you mean. She's got into my head, too. And I'm glad.'

Our eyes met with a true sense of connection; we shared a bond, and the bond was Luce. I had again that feeling of really *knowing* somebody I'd only just met. The phrase 'brotherly love' came to me, and I understood it in a way I never had before. After that, it was easy to talk about Luce. I asked how he'd got involved with her in the first place.

'Family connection. I know Luce through Uncle John. He's an old friend of her parents.'

So was this Lucie Asher I was encountering again? 'Have you met the Ashers?'

'No. They live in Europe. I didn't meet Luce until 1958. August 1958. She completely changed my life. You wouldn't think to see me now, but I was a cripple. Spinal cord severed. They'd told me with absolute certainty that I would never walk again.'

'Christ. What happened?'

'Car crash. I was sixteen. Dad was drunk. As usual. He and Mum were fighting. As usual. He wrapped us around a tree. Not so usual. He and my brother and my sister and my mother died. I was paralysed from the waist down. When I got out of hospital Uncle John took me in. The following summer Luce came to stay for a couple of weeks. My God, she was so glamorous. So continental, so sophisticated. She was the coolest person I'd ever seen or hoped to see. It was like she was from another planet, a far, far nicer one. It was heaven just to watch her exist. I was terrified of her. I mean, can you picture me, a cripple, living with my elderly uncle? Awful clothes, terrible haircut. Spots. Wheelchair. I prayed for her not to notice me.

'But she ignored everything that was wrong with me. She sat and talked, and got me talking too. It was as though we were old friends, or she was my brother and my sister combined, they'd only gone away for a while, and now . . . we were together again.'

Fergus washed the roasting dish slowly, turning it with care, not missing anything. I waited, tea-towel in hand.

'She used to wheel me around with her. We couldn't go very far or very fast, but she didn't seem to mind pushing my chair and I loved it. I couldn't believe how happy I was. I'd resigned myself to never being happy again. One day, we took some sandwiches and a flask of tea and went a little way upriver to a picnic area and swimming place where I used to go with my brother and sister. It was very hot. We sat in the shade and ate our lunch. There were a few other people about and as I watched them running, jumping, diving, swimming, all the happiness drained out of me. I saw it for what it was – a temporary delusion. I'd only borrowed it. It wasn't mine. When Luce left, the happiness would leave, too.

'I sat there feeling sick with envy and self-pity. Before Luce had come, I'd been trying to accept my condition, to look on the bright side as the doctors were always telling me. Trying to focus on what I could do, not what I couldn't. If I couldn't be happy, I could get along. Things would never be great, but they'd be OK. Now I saw through all that. I'd been kidding myself. What was real was despair, and nothing else could ever be real for me. It was a bottomless pit; it was where I lived and I would never get out. I knew, right then, that I would kill myself as soon as I could arrange it. That's when Luce got up and said, "Let's go for a walk, Fergus." I thought she was teasing, but it was a cruel tease and that wasn't like her. I laughed, but really felt like crying. And then I was crying, like I hadn't cried since the weeks after the accident. All the rage and frustration and despair was boiling out of me. I was so embarrassed. I put my head in my hands and tried to control myself. And then she did it.'

'What did she do?'.

'Damned if I know. She touched me, that's all. Just once, on the top of my head. It was like a lightning bolt. At first I thought she'd killed me. There was a flash of indescribable pain, then a burning all over, almost unbearable. It was followed by pins and needles in my legs, or really I should say daggers and knives. I wanted to scream but it hurt so much I could barely gasp. When the agony eased off a bit I noticed that my toes were twitching, then my legs. I couldn't believe it. Luce helped me to stand and I took a few steps, then fell over. I was laughing so hard I just rolled around for a while. She helped me up again and I walked. I was weak, of course, couldn't do more than stagger a few steps while she held me. But my muscles got strong again. And there's nothing wrong with me now, nothing at all. I'm what they call a medical miracle. I don't know what she did, or how, or why. I don't think I'll ever know. She never spoke of it, never explained. Some things simply can't be explained. You can believe it or not, as you like. Or you can say, like a girlfriend of mine used to, that it was love that cured me. Of course I was in love, far more thoroughly than my little teenage mind could comprehend. It was like she'd seized my soul. I never told anyone, but of course Uncle John saw it. And somehow it didn't matter that she went away. I'd get postcards from her every once in a while, no words, just a drawing of a lightning bolt. That's how I know they're from her.

'Years passed. I did a degree in electrical engineering – I nearly got married a couple of times. Then at Christmas in 1965, she showed up here with . . . Wingbow and Jukebox and the Holy Ghost. And it was like no time at all had passed – our lives had flowed apart for a while, and now were flowing together again. She had a big project in mind and she needed me. I can't begin to say how happy that made me. She had it all worked out like a military campaign. The *Human* album, the films and the gigs. We set up headquarters in Golden Square. She had some weird ideas about sound engineering – I don't think I could explain it to anybody, but it worked. She designed the studio, I built it. All the time I'd been doing my degree I'd had a notion that I was learning all this for some purpose other than just having a trade at which I could make a living, that no matter how bored I got, I had to persevere. I finally understood why. She also taught me some strange stuff about sound and light and time. How you can use them to influence each other. A kind of harmonic thing. Hard to explain. Wingbow claims to understand it – she says it's like Buddhism, but that doesn't explain anything, at least not to me. We all read your column where you talked about listening to the album tripping, how it flips the subject/object thing. Wingbow says, that's Buddhism. I say, that's Luce. She designed it to do that, she knew lots of people would play it while tripping.'

In that 'Night Eye' column, written a month after *Human* was released, I'd reported my own experience, backed up by an informal survey among my friends. I'd noticed that when I listened to the album while tripping an inner shift would occur at some point; instead of hearing the story of the god who came to Earth, one realised that one was *oneself* the god who came to Earth.

My column led, immediately and gratifyingly, to a huge increase in the number of people tripping and listening, seeking and getting the effect. Needless to say, it was an immensely powerful experience of almost unbearable exaltation, despair and everything in between. It proved a bit too much for a few people I knew, who went about shattered for days. A whole book could be written just on that phenomenon, which was the first and, as far as I know, the only time most people took acid with any

314

purpose at all, other than to have a good time. And yet I hadn't realised, until Fergus told me, that Luce had engineered the music specifically to work with the drug. Had she known her Scribe would promulgate the message? It made me feel that I'd been part of the plan all along, an agent so covert even I hadn't known what I was.

'Who else was on the team?' I asked Fergus, sure that there had to be at least ten people involved.

'Ha! It's a matter of need-to-know, don't you know.' He tapped the side of his nose with a sudsy forefinger, gave a mock-salute, then fell about laughing. He wiped his nose on his sleeve. 'The Secret Society, that's what we are. Code names only. I'm Rufus, Luce is Primus. The Holy Ghost plays keyboards. And . . .' he counted on soapy fingers ' . . . Jukebox, Crocodile, Bamboo, Dandelion, Pinocchio, Marmalade, Sentinel, Jabberwocky, Scooter, Badger, Houdini, Obelisk and Wingbow, but even I don't know everybody's real names.'

I took a shot in the dark. 'Is Jukebox the theremin player?'

'That's right. She's some sort of a cousin of Luce's. Cool chick, very cool. Amazing musician, plays lots of instruments.'

'And Obelisk – is that Bobby Fisk the set builder from Notting Hill?'

'Oh, you know him?'

'He claimed not to have had any idea who'd hired him.'

'He's a good bloke, Obelisk.'

'And the Holy Ghost is Francis, right?'

'He's Luce's cousin too, or something like that. Related, anyway. She used to call him Grandpapa, but that was a joke. Francis is the strangest man I ever met, and I've met some strange ones. I mean, we're all on one trip or another, and people say the weirdest things, but he's in a class of his own.'

'I've heard some odd stories about him,' I said.

'Yeah, he collected strange stories like a magnet. Told some,

315

too. Late one night he told me this long story that he said was the story of his life, and that explained why he was the way he was. I was tripping at the time, and it made a vivid impression, even if it didn't make a lot of sense. It was like one of those fantastic *Arabian Nights* stories. It was all about a key and a door, an island on a lake, a book in code, the Stone of the Philosophers, the elixir of immortality, a doomed love, a fateful mistake – oh, it went on and on. There were so many tall tales going around about the guy, I doubt anyone knows the truth. He cut a dash, that's for sure, dressed up to the nines in his frock coats and lace.'

We finished the washing-up, made a pot of coffee and sat at the kitchen table. I rolled us a joint. How much did Fergus know, I wondered, about his uncle? Did he know what Greyling had done at Golden Square . . . what he could do? Did Greyling speak to him about good and evil as he'd spoken to me? Possibly not. This sort of thing was generally best handled with discretion. I decided to avoid the subject unless Fergus raised it himself.

'What about the painted room at Golden Square?' I asked. 'Luce made that, right?'

'You went in there?'

I nodded.

'Blow your mind?'

'It did.'

'How she does that, with just paint on walls, I don't know.' Fergus shook his head. 'If she wasn't such a laid-back, peaceful-minded person, she could conquer the world. Before breakfast. With both hands tied behind her back. If she wasn't so nice she'd be very, very scary.'

He paused for a moment, staring out of the window at a flock of sparrows twittering in an old apple tree. 'I'd heard that she'd been a good chess player when she was a kid. I play a bit, fancy myself not bad, go to tournaments from time to time, sometimes make it past the first round. So I persuaded her to come with me to an exhibition where this famous Russian grandmaster was going to play against the thirty best British players simultaneously. The guy somehow recognised Luce, who'd got herself up in beanie hat and sunglasses. I wouldn't have recognised her. The Russian came over and they spoke for a while. In Russian. The pair of them were chattering away, obviously old friends, though he seemed to be calling her Petrushka – maybe that was a nickname. I could tell that he was trying to persuade her to do something and she was laughing and saying no. *Nyet* I understand. But eventually she was won over. The Russian went to the organisers and they had a hasty confab. Then an official of the chess federation came and blindfolded her. Another one checked the blindfold. I realised she was going to play a game of blindfold chess, I thought perhaps with the Russian. Then I realised she was going to play thirty-one games at once – the original thirty players plus the Russian. She made her moves as fast as they told her her opponents', sometimes not even waiting to hear what the opposing player's move had been. She won all thirty-one matches. It would have been the world record, but since it was all so impromptu, it didn't get recorded properly. Afterwards, when everybody was clamouring to talk to her, she disappeared. I mean literally, out from under everybody's eyes. You won't believe me, but I swear I was looking at her – she was shaking the Russian's hand while being congratulated by one of the officials. I'd been standing on a chair at the side of the room – it was one of those hotel ballroom places, vast, and as the games progressed it had become absolutely packed with spectators. I was watching her hat, in the middle of this sea of heads and bodies. Then I blinked and it was gone. The Russian and the officials were at the centre of a scrum of players, all converging on a point that had vanished.'

Vanishing, I'd already learned, was one of her specialities. I asked Fergus if he knew where Luce was now. He shook his head. 'Like I said, need-to-know. And that's something I don't need to know right now. But maybe soon . . .'

'Maybe soon what?'

He winked. 'Vow of silence, sorry.'

Greyling came down from his nap; Charlie breezed in from the garden. Fergus was planning to stay for a few days, so Charlie and I headed out to his car. As I was getting in, Greyling dropped several small, hard things into my hand. They were bullets, the bullets from my own gun. Downy old bird indeed.

'Have a safe journey,' he said. Fergus waved from the porch.

On the way back to London Charlie was uncharacteristically silent, and I mulled over what I'd learned. Once again, with the acquisition of additional 'information', Luce had become more mysterious, not less. It was like putting together a jigsaw puzzle when you don't know what it's meant to be, and each new piece contradicts the previous ones.

Much against my will, I found my thoughts returning to Greyling's discourse on good and evil. The black-and-white nature of those terms was distasteful to me; they seemed archaic vestiges of a primitive past, repulsive in their absoluteness. Artificial, too, like panto characters, Punch and Judy puppets. The world I inhabited, or thought I inhabited, was a nuanced world of ambiguity and uncertainty, of interwoven fictions and metaphors, alive with subtle currents and cross-currents of meaning and suggestion. Was I too sophisticated to see what was right in front of me?

Now.

It's a real shame that one can't get decent acid any
more. As I discovered back in 1967, it unlocks a whole
other dimension of the *Human* album, inaccessible to
people today. Even I wouldn't dare take a tab of whatever's being sold as LSD now. Although I see that,
very recently, tentative new shoots of serious research
are emerging. So someone must be making good stuff.
In the old days I'd have known how to find it.

This aspect of the album seems to have been forgotten;
I can find no mention of the subject on the various
internet forums where *Human* is discussed. People
regard it, and rightly, as of huge artistic importance, but if you know how to use it, like all of
Luce's art, it can take you places and show you things
far beyond the surface. That's why the demons tried
so hard to destroy her work in all its forms - and
why I try so hard to thwart them. People should know,
and it's my job to tell them. *The Book of Luce* will
reveal all, but in the meantime, I feel the need to
stir things up. For the sake of the greater good, and

319

because I'm well hidden behind a pseudonym, I'm posting
on the album's Google-group, alt.fan.human, the
suggestion that, if good LSD could be obtained, it
might be worth devoting a trip or two to listening to
Human, giving the vaguest of hints that another dimension might become available. As a source, I cite a
certain 'Night Eye' column from January 1967.

19

The Masquerade Ball

≀▲

Red Lion Square. Harlequin. An Edgy Vibe. Coke
and Coke. It's Her! Chaos and Confusion. A
Stampede for the Exits. A Catastrophic Car Crash.
Clement's Revelations. Charlie's Very Own Demon.

London, December 1967

A couple of days after our little excursion to Devon I received
an invitation to 'Melchizedek's Magical Masquerade Ball', an
event I'd been planning to attend in any case. It was to be held
on the twenty-second – the night of the winter solstice (and the
anniversary of the *Human* album's release). The invitation was
unsigned, but a Monad drawn in the corner told me who it was
from, and a note on the back said my name was on the guest list.
A dozen bands were on the bill including the Move and the Pretty
Things, plus a few I'd never heard of: Spheroid Banana, Canticles
Sunday, Metatrix, the Elohim Swim. Could one of them be Luce
and the Photons? Fergus had hinted that such a thing might be
planned. When I told Charlie I thought Luce might put in an
appearance, he decided to delay his departure to his family's
Warwickshire estate for the holidays in order to attend.

The ball was held at Conway Hall in Red Lion Square. It was a cold night, with a hint of snow in the air. The curse of costume parties in winter is that either the costume is warm in itself (a bear or gorilla suit, for example), eliminating the need for a coat but unpleasant indoors and ridiculous for dancing, or you put your ordinary coat on top, squashing the costume and ruining the effect of your entrance. I elected to freeze on the way there and worry about how to get home later. I went as Harlequin in a black-and-white patchwork tunic, green suede boots, a long-nosed mask and a curly blond Harpo Marx wig. I took a tab of acid that I'd been saving for a special occasion – really good LSD had become much harder to obtain. As I was leaving the house I rang up Charlie to arrange a meeting place, but he said he'd been struck by a stomach bug at the last minute and was staying at home.

Conway Hall was packed and throbbing with sound. Hundreds were dancing on the main floor, hundreds more crowding the balcony that wrapped around three sides of the auditorium. I observed all the usual amusing and not so amusing consequences of no one being very sure of who anyone was. Including, perhaps, themselves. I kept forgetting that I was masked and failing to recognise myself in mirrors.

The stage was hung with a backdrop depicting a giant full moon over Stonehenge and a massive trilithon – papier mâché, one assumed, though quite realistic – stood in the middle, amps and drum kits arrayed at its base like lesser megaliths. Thick streams of dry-ice fog flowed from the wings, swirling around the musicians' knees and spilling onto the dance floor. Bands came on, played their sets and were replaced with others. The musicians were masked and costumed like the rest of us, but it was easy to tell that they weren't Luce and the Photons.

Fergus, masked but recognisable despite having trimmed his beard into a devilish goatee and dyed it black, was at the control board; he was working hard and there was no opportunity to speak to him.

There was a weird vibe – edgy and argumentative. Quarrels broke out over mistaken identities, spilled drinks, trodden toes. I began to regret doing the acid. The hallucinations I was getting weren't the usual gorgeous colours and delightful embellishments – instead everyone appeared cloaked in shadows, their masks shape-shifting in the flicker of the strobes. I had one of those odd moments when you completely lose any sense of identity – it's like there's a void where you are, a cut-out, a gap . . . and then you click back into existence and everything's real again.

I bought half a gram of coke from a Crusader Knight, which helped in one direction, and a rum and Coke from the Warlock bartender, which helped in the other. I smoothed out nicely. At around eleven thirty I was up on the balcony watching a set change on the stage below. I noted the equipment being arranged by masked roadies – one of whom had a long black pigtail. There were tape decks and mikes, foot pedals, three keyboards, a synthesiser that I thought I recognised from the Camden gig. An auburn-haired, gold-masked figure came out and sat at the keyboards. A froth of lace at throat and wrists, a white frock coat: it had to be Francis, the Holy Ghost. And that one in the clown suit with the violin, just stepping up to a mike was surely Jukebox – yes, I spotted the theremin at one side. A rhythm track began to roll, embellished by synth riffs, entwined with the smooth, insistent legato of the violin.

And now from the shadows came a tall, slim figure in a silver space-suit and helmet, eyes hidden behind a dark visor. In her hands – her beautiful hands – the distinctive black Stratocaster. It was her; at last I was seeing her again! I leaned forward, gripping the rail of the balcony. She looked up and saw me, I'm sure she did. There was a brilliant thread of laser-light connecting us, humming with rainbow colours.

323

She stepped up to the mike and sang the opening words of 'Human': 'I found you or you found me in this beautiful darkness, beloved human, dark heart of life . . .' Shrieks erupted in the hall as people realised who it was and surged towards the stage – and then all hell broke loose: bangs and flashes, sparks and smoke and chaos. The stage became an indecipherable melee of scrambling figures falling over each other. I dashed for the stairs, but so did everybody else, and I wasted precious minutes trapped and trampled among panicking masqueraders. By the time I made it to the main floor the Stonehenge backdrop and the trilithon were on fire and there was such a stampede for the exit that I was swept along.

I talked to quite a few witnesses that night, as we gathered, shaken and confused, in a nearby pub while fire engines and police cars jammed into Red Lion Square. No one was able to agree with anyone else about what had happened. There had been several loud bangs, which some took for firecrackers but others thought might have been gunshots. Someone was convinced that the amps had exploded, another that smoke bombs had been thrown at the stage. One girl, who'd been right at the front, told me that as the bangs occurred – she believed they were gunshots, three or four – the frock-coated musician had leapt in front of the space-suited one. She'd seen him fall, clutching his chest, and vanish in the clouds of dry-ice fog.

I tried to return to the building, but although the fire had soon been extinguished, no one was allowed in. I said I was worried about a friend who might have been trampled and was told that the injured had been taken to nearby University College Hospital. There I learned that a dozen people had been treated for cuts and bruises, minor burns, sprains, concussion, one broken leg and two broken arms. No gunshot wounds.

☙

When Clement phoned me in the early hours of the morning to say that Charlie was in hospital, I assumed his digestive complaint had worsened, but Clement told me there had been an accident: Charlie had crashed the DB6. I went straight to the hospital and, pretending that Charlie was my brother, managed to see him. He'd just come out of emergency surgery: head-to-toe bandages, drips, bleeping machines, wires and tubes. The only part of him that was visible was one badly bruised hand. He had some chance of survival, they told me, though not a very good one.

Knowing that extensive use of cocaine can have a deleterious effect on various bodily functions, I thought I should make the doctors aware of his predilections. But it was I who'd been uninformed. High levels of heroin had been found in Charlie's blood and many needle tracks revealed on his arms and legs, some long-abscessed and infected.

I sat with him and held his hand and wept for the Charlie I had known.

His mother arrived from Warwickshire. (Not his father, who was too frail and, in any case, had been gaga for years.) Lady Kelmont had always treated me as one of the family, so my cover with the hospital wasn't blown. Since she would stay in town while Charlie remained in hospital, I decided the most useful thing for me to do was make sure the London house was ready for her. I could at least hide the drugs.

I should have known Clement would have all that well in hand – he'd even swapped his usual bright *dashiki* for a sober suit and tidied his dreadlocks into a snood. I helped him turf out the last hangers-on and, aside from the psychedelic murals, the place looked disturbingly normal.

The crash had occurred at Hyde Park Corner, not far from the house. I walked there in the grey dawn light. The wreckage had been cleared, but shards of glass and bits of metal were scattered over a wide area at the base of the Wellington Arch in the centre of the roundabout. Scorch marks reached thirty feet up.

An all-night coffee van traditionally occupied the north-west corner. I crossed to buy a cup and have a word with Mervin, the wizened and usually taciturn proprietor. Not at all taciturn this morning, he was quite pleased to have an audience for the story.

Given his location, it was no surprise that he knew his cars, and had recognised Charlie's DB6 right away. It was not uncommon for cars like that to take the roundabout rather fast, and though he didn't know Charlie by name, he knew that the owner of that particular car was a lover of speed and a skilled driver. But this time he could tell right away that the car was going too fast.

'I knew they were gonna lose it,' Mervin said. 'Christ, that was a beautiful car. It makes me sick, it really does. Rich folk, don't know what they got. Throw it all away. Pair of nutters want to kill themselves, fine by me, but no need to destroy a beautiful machine like that.'

'Pair?' I asked. 'Are you saying there was a passenger?'

'Sure there was.'

I questioned him closely, but he knew what he'd seen. Two people, driver and passenger. He couldn't say if they were male or female, young or old; they were going too fast for that. But definitely two people in the car.

A couple of shop girls came by for coffee and he started from the beginning, relishing the details, polishing his story. It was destined, one could tell, to become a high point of his life. The crash had occurred on the opposite side of the monument (unfortunately for the story, though I sensed later versions might improve on this regrettable circumstance) but the noise had been unbelievable, and the fireball had nearly blinded him. The police had arrived within a minute – a patrol car was habitually parked just up the road, and another had been cruising along Piccadilly.

And then a fire engine, an ambulance, more police. He'd temporarily shut up shop and gone over to see, but the police weren't letting anybody close.

A new lot of customers arrived; the story began again.

I bought an extra cup of coffee and took it to the young officer in the police car which was parked in its usual place at the top of Grosvenor Crescent. I asked him if he'd been on duty when the accident occurred, and it turned out he had. The crash had happened at midnight – about half an hour after the shooting at Conway Hall. Maintaining the story that Charlie was my brother, I cajoled him into telling me about it.

'I wasn't looking when he whizzed past, but I heard him. He entered the roundabout very fast, skidding a bit but in control. There wasn't any point in trying to stop him – I'd never catch him up. But I'm afraid it was no accident. You may as well know, it's all in the report. He turned. Right there.' He pointed to the spot where Constitution Hill enters the roundabout. 'And drove straight at the monument. Bang. I got the fire extinguisher out of my boot and ran – it was faster than starting my car and turning around and driving there. Another patrol car arrived and we pulled him out. He can't have been in there more than a minute, but there was quite a fire. I hear he's in a very bad way . . . I'm so sorry.'

I asked about the passenger, but he was certain there had been no one else in the car. He didn't appear to be lying and anyway, why would he? Perhaps Mervin the coffee-van man had been mistaken.

Back at Charlie's, I helped Clement decide what food to get in for Charlie's mother. When I asked if anybody had been with Charlie in the Aston Martin, he shrugged.

I settled down to wait for Lady Kelmont – I thought she'd appreciate a friendly face, and if there was anything she needed me to do she could tell me at once. Clement pottered around;

327

I wondered if he was nervous at the prospect of a new regime in the house. He dawdled in my vicinity and several times seemed about to speak. Although always extremely polite, Clement had never been especially chatty, and we'd had few conversations about anything other than what I wanted to drink, smoke or eat.

'Is there anything you'd like to say?' I finally asked.

There was. He thought that maybe, after all, he did know about a man who might have been in the car, a man who'd been 'running Charlie's life'. A well-groomed, smooth-faced man with cold, dead eyes like a fish's. He rarely spoke, but if he looked at you . . . well, that was best avoided. Clement thought he was the front man for some new kind of Mafia. Whoever he was, he was hand in glove with the police, who never gave any trouble.

Fear crawled over my skin from my scalp to the soles of my feet. Could this be Mr Big? What was he doing with Charlie? 'Is that who Charlie was getting his smack from?' I asked.

Clement looked at me like I was an idiot. 'Getting his smack? Oh, yeah, I'd say that's where he was getting his smack. He never wanted you to know, but I thought you'd figure it out. He always says you're so smart. Don't you know he was dealing? And not just a gram here and there. He was dealing kilos. Uncut, you know, kilos of pure. Most of what gets into London comes through here. How do you think he paid for that fancy car? And for all the parties? He used up Granddaddy's trust fund long ago.'

I felt like the wind had been kicked out of me. 'Does this Mafia man have a name?' I asked.

Clement smiled an entirely humourless smile. Once again, it was clear, I was an idiot. 'The fellows like that,' he said, 'don't go by names.'

'Why didn't you leave, Clement? You could have got into big trouble.'

He looked down and shifted uncomfortably. Emotion vied

with dignity. 'Somebody had to look out for Charlie. But I didn't do a very good job.'

'Neither, apparently, did I.'

I pressed him for a description of the Mafia man and got more about the expressionless face, unnatural complexion, tidy hair, innocuous clothes. I knew then that Mervin the coffee-van man had not been mistaken, nor had the policeman lied; Mr Big had been with Charlie in the car. He had vanished and left no body, just like Tweedledee and Tweedledum, just like the demon-simulacrum René had seen in the alley behind Disques Cybellines. And the crash was not merely a wild suicide attempt as the police believed, but attempted murder as well, if that was the right word for killing a demon. Perhaps extreme exorcism might be a better term.

It suddenly became urgent to know which of us had been the demons' first prey. Did Charlie bring them (and their kilos of heroin) into my life, or had I brought them into his? This is something I have never known. Clement could not pin down a date for the first appearance of Mr Big, but it was more or less at the same time as my first contact with him at Golden Square.

My obliviousness appalled me. I thought I'd been a good friend to Charlie, but obviously I'd failed him utterly. How could I have missed his descent into heroin addiction, the major criminal operation going on under my nose . . . and the demon-simulacrum 'running his life'? Why hadn't he told me? He always thought I was so smart, Clement had said. Did he think I'd noticed but hadn't cared enough to speak? Or was he ashamed? I scanned my memories, looking for clues I'd missed, and came up with a catalogue: unexplained absences, oblique replies, casual enquiries brushed off, steady weight loss (he said he'd taken up squash – I should have known how ridiculous that was), lack of appetite (he always said he'd just eaten), long sleeves with cuffs always linked (he said he was going for a more debonair look). I concluded that Charlie had taken some trouble to make sure I didn't know. But that was no excuse. Friendship should have seen through his most devious manoeuvres. Friendship should have served him better. I could not help but feel that I bore some responsibility for the car crash Charlie had made of his life, but it was too late, it had happened, and it was far worse than anyone could have imagined.

Greyling's terminology had become terribly real to me. The demons – for that is what they truly were – had penetrated the very heart of my life and I found myself dealing with something quite outside the usual run of my experience. It no longer seemed so silly to call it evil. The word had repelled me, but now I could not get it out of my mind.

'Good' is, on the face of it, easy. It's a common term – we use it every day. But only when we consider it as the opposite of evil do we glimpse its rarer essence. Evil is a word rarely encountered; it lurks, cloaked, behind ordinary things. Good is right out there – it's a sunny day, it's the smile on a friend's face, it's tasty food and pleasant company. Evil carries its meaning like a hidden dagger; it's a word you don't want to find under your bed in the middle of the night. It's a scary word and I was scared to use it, as though by using it I would allow it to exist within me.

But of course it did, it does exist in me. And not as a vague concept but as real, lived experience. For the first time the notions of Heaven and Hell, which I'd always dismissed as ridiculous fantasies, clicked into meaning for me. It had nothing to do with religion. Heaven was the experience of good, Hell the experience of evil. The indescribably beautiful state that I'd entered into at Luce and the Photons' secret gig – that was what it felt like to touch the good. The sick, disabling fear I experienced when a demon was near – that was what it felt like to touch evil.

Now.

Following my LSD suggestion, things went rather quiet on alt.fan.human. A few people posted indignantly, chastising me for suggesting something illegal and 'dangerous'. Really, the demons have so little to do these days; people control themselves into tighter and tighter zones of correct behaviour, speech and thought. I suppose there's nothing to be done; most people have always been beyond help. But perhaps the quietness indicated that others were seeking to implement my suggestion. A few have now posted enigmatically, some merely replying with a thumbs-up emoticon, others with veiled hints that something has happened. Now if I can just find out where they got the acid . . .

A knock at the door. I know who it is. Some idiot has signed me up for the chess club at the local library and cannot accept my demurs, which have progressed from polite to cool to cold to downright rude. I go to the door and, without opening it, croak that I'm too sick to come out.

'It's me, Weirdo. Had no idea you were ill. You OK?'

Christ, it's Neil. Reluctantly, I open the door. His round face is creased with concern.

'You OK? Flu?'

'I'm fine. A sniffle. What brings you here?'

His expression relapses into sheepish amiability. 'Nothing, nothing special, just wanted to . . . hang out.' The slang stumbles awkwardly from his mouth. 'You know, like we used to.'

We never, *never* used to 'hang out', unless you count the time he tied me up, hung me by my collar on the hook behind my door and left me to wriggle helplessly for an hour. What, I wonder, has gone so very wrong with his life that he regards 'hanging out' with me in my tiny Enfield flat as a nice thing to do on a Sunday afternoon? Poor chap. I feel sorry for him in a whole new way.

'Cup of tea?' I say, and he smiles gratefully.

I go into the kitchen and make tea, hoping that when I come out, he'll have disappeared.

Shit. Not only has he not disappeared, neither has my life. I forgot to put it away when I answered the door. Luce is everywhere. The albums, the magazine covers, all my notes and transcripts. *The Book of Luce* is open on my laptop. No, I won't scurry around like a mouse, trying to hide the evidence. It is what it is. It is what *I* am. I've just got to brazen it out.

Neil takes the cup of tea I hand him. 'Oh, Weirdo,' he says, pudding face collapsed in sorrow. 'I thought you'd put all that behind you. It's not . . . well, you know. Really. Oh, Weirdo.'

'What?' I say. '*What?*'

'All this.' He gestures. 'Your obsession. This Luce person. Come on, you let all that go years ago. That's

332

what they said. The idea that you knew the greatest rock star in the world, he was God, he was your special friend, all that nonsense.'

Ah, he can't help it. Contempt and revulsion are creeping back into his voice. I won't be drawn. Meek and mild, I tell myself. Harmless old nutter, that's what I am. I shrug, smile. 'It's just a hobby. Everybody has a hobby. Would you like a biscuit with your tea? Chocolate digestive, or wait, maybe I have some short-cake, let me check.' I retreat to the kitchen, wishing with redoubled fervour that he'll be gone when I return.

No such luck. 'Sorry,' I say, 'no biscuits after all.'

Eventually he leaves, forgetting to drink his tea but not forgetting to remind me, in careful, reason-able tones, that the notion of a higher, wiser and benevolent power influencing me for its own ends is only the reverse of the coin of my paranoia – the long-held delusion that demons were out to get me. I doubt he'll be back. Let's hope he's cured of any desire to 'hang out' with me.

With immense relief I return to my real life. *Luce*, I say, *if I could get some good acid I'd be able to find you, but till then, give me the strength to put up with Neil.*

20

Astral Vision

❧

*Wingbow's Story. Out of Lo Manthang. Thobo
Rinpoche's Miraculous Cure. Francis Reborn: A
Handful. The Journey West. The Rhododendron
Grove in Hyde Park. A Demon on the Embankment.*

London, December 1967

About noon on the day after Charlie's crash I awoke gritty-eyed
and stiff-necked. I'd fallen asleep in an armchair waiting for
Lady K, who, it turned out, had chosen to make her London base
at Claridge's instead. Clement brought me coffee and rolled a joint,
which we smoked together in silence, then I made my way through
grimy drizzle to Conway Hall. Tidying was sure to be under way,
and I hoped to pick up more information about what had happened
the previous night. I was far from alone; the place was crawling,
often literally, with people looking for things they'd lost in the
previous night's scramble, plus the roadies of several different bands
trying to untangle and extract their equipment from the monumental
jumble of instruments, amps, packing cases, stands and leads.

I heard a dozen new variants of the stories I'd collected the
previous night, and looked for bullets. I found none, which told

me either that none had been fired or that they'd ended up lodged in someone's body – or merely that they'd already been swept away with the rubbish. I was just leaving when a van pulled up and two people got out. One was the Asian woman with the long black pigtail I'd seen helping Fergus at the Roundhouse gig, the other I recognised as Bobby Fisk, the set builder.

'Hey, Obelisk,' I said.

He greeted me with a wary nod. 'Do I know you?'

'I'm the Scribe,' I said. 'We met a few months ago. Primus and Rufus know me. What happened last night? I was too far away to see. Is the Holy Ghost all right?'

'All we know is that he got shot,' the woman said. 'Primus and Jukebox took him away. We haven't heard anything since. I'm Wingbow, by the way. I saw you a couple of weeks ago talking to Rufus at the Roundhouse. He told me who you were.'

We shook hands. Obelisk, after a moment's hesitation, shook hands too. They'd come to pick up Lucifergus Lights' equipment. I helped them load the van, then invited them for a drink. Wingbow accepted; Obelisk said he had other plans and drove off. I suggested the pub on the corner but Wingbow said she didn't drink, didn't like pubs, and would rather take a walk. I, too, tend to prefer walking to pubs and drinking, so we set off companionably for Hyde Park. I asked how she'd got involved with Primus and the Pymander Productions gang and she told me a fascinating story, one that serves as well to fill a gap in Luce's history. It begins in Nepal, some time after Luce left Giorgio, Gauri and the others behind to venture, with Francis, further into the mountains.

Wingbow was from the remote community of Lo Manthang, on the border of Nepal and Tibet. Her family, like most, were illiterate peasants. She'd been born with a squint, believed to be a very bad omen, and had therefore been abandoned in the mountains to die soon after birth. But a holy man found her, healed her and returned her to her parents, who accepted her miraculous recovery as phlegmatically as they'd earlier forsaken her. She herself had no memory of this, it all having happened when she was an infant, but the story was passed on and she'd grown up hearing it. It had given her a feeling that she might be a bit special. The holy man was called Thobo Rinpoche. He had lived alone, in a tiny stone hut high in the hills, for as long as anyone could remember. His needs were few – tea and yak butter, *tsampa* and occasional roots or vegetables – and gladly supplied by the villagers, whose minor ailments he deigned to cure.

Wingbow (motivated by economic necessity but also by that belief in her own specialness) had left the village at thirteen to seek work in Kathmandu. A job cleaning offices at a college led to a desire to learn, and with her employer's help she began a course of study that took her, eventually, to university in New Delhi. She completed a master's in cultural anthropology and in June 1965 returned to Lo Manthang for the first time in fifteen years. There she encountered Luce and Francis, who were now preparing to leave. They'd arrived the previous winter, seeking Thobo Rinpoche's help for the strange malady that had afflicted Francis since his capture in Las Vegas. The villagers believed he was suffering under the curse of a powerful magician, which had separated his soul from his body. They were not surprised that their own great Thobo Rinpoche had been called upon to help in this trickiest of cases.

Lucha (as Luce called herself there) was already well known in the village, having come with her mother and an Englishman (Stephen Aubrey, I recalled, had listed Nepal as one of the places Professor Asher had sojourned) some years before to visit Thobo Rinpoche. Lucha had made a strong impression as a pale-haired twelve-year-old who was always going off into the mountains alone, once coming back with a leopard. The villagers were so alarmed that they wouldn't let her near, so she sat down at the edge of the

336

village and had a long conversation with the beast, at the end of which they embraced and the leopard had loped off.

'As soon as I met Lucha,' Wingbow said, 'I got the strangest feeling, like I knew her very well, had known her for ages, had always planned to meet her at that time and place. At university I'd become very Western in my thinking, but as soon as I was back in the mountains I was a Buddhist again. It was as though I'd simply worn Western materialism as a garment, and now I shed it. Gladly. It seemed obvious to me: Lucha – and Francis too, of course; his connection to her ran deeper than I could fathom – and I had been friends in other lives, in many other lives, and now we were together again. There was so much we had to do, so much we'd been working on for all those lives. And that was how Lucha treated me, too. Old friends, long-time companions. We were connected here.' She tapped her heart. 'I think you know what I mean.'

'Yes, I do.'

'So it was the most natural thing in the world to set off with them, with no more than a pack on my back. Thobo Rinpoche's treatment – I never knew what he did – had been effective. Francis's soul had been restored to his body, but some time would be needed for him to grow fully into himself again. Having passed through infancy – I'm glad I missed that stage – he was like a five-year-old when I met him. An intelligent, articulate and very strong-willed one. And since he was, in form, a healthy man of six foot two, he was quite a handful. For the next six months, as we travelled across Asia and Europe, he matured. He hit adolescence as we were crossing Afghanistan. That was awkward because for a few weeks he imagined himself in love with me, but by the time we reached Istanbul he had outgrown it.'

'Can I ask a materialist question?' I said.

Wingbow laughed. 'Go right ahead.'

'How did you deal with practical matters, like borders and

passports, tickets and money?' This had bothered me ever since I'd heard Giorgio's account of his journey with Lukas.

'First of all, where we went, on the old tracks used by herders and smugglers, borders aren't apparent. There are no fences or control posts, sometimes just a cairn or a small sign. Usually not even that. One does encounter officials now and then, but if someone asked to see our documents Lucha showed them any old scrap of paper. The official would examine it, hand it back and wave us on. She can do that sort of thing so easily. Tickets we didn't need because we generally walked, or were given rides by people. If we had to cross a large body of water, we'd find a boat going where we wanted, Lucha would ask them to take us, and they would.'

'What about food and shelter? And clothes and shoes?'

'People gave us everything we needed. You have to understand, it wasn't a struggle. It was easy. Everyone was glad to see us and helped us in every possible way. Wherever we went, Lucha had passed that way before, she knew everyone by name, and their families. There's hardly anywhere she hasn't been – she spends most of her time just walking around the world, you know. And helping people. We were always meeting someone she'd cured of something, or people whose disputes she'd resolved, friends who used to hate each other, allies who used to be enemies. People regarded her as a saint and her presence as a blessing, whether they were Buddhist or Hindu, Jain, Muslim, Christian, whatever. Francis and I just sailed along in her wake.'

I'd seen this aspect of Luce already in the form of the itinerant troubadour Petra Lumis, as well as the various odd stories of encounters with Luce that I'd collected in London. It dawned on me then that the amount of time Luce spent in one location, making art that was fixed in time and place, was by far the lesser part of her life.

At Marble Arch Wingbow stopped at a phone box, saying she

338

wanted to find out if there was any news about the Holy Ghost. She came out shaking her head. 'I just spoke to Fergus. He doesn't know where Primus and Jukebox went. He's been sitting by the phone, but hasn't heard. He's really worried.'

Something in her voice when she spoke of Fergus reminded me of his tone when he'd spoken of her. 'Are you guys together?' I asked. 'You and Fergus?'

'Yeah, we are.' She gave me a shy grin. 'For a while now. Luce – I mean Primus – brought us together, but we were both so in love with her that it took us a while to notice how we'd come to feel about each other. I hope Francis – the Holy Ghost, I mean – is all right. Poor Jukebox. She hasn't told him yet, but she's pregnant with his child.'

'With Francis's child?'

Wingbow nodded. 'That's another slow-burn romance. When he recovered and was fully himself again – I mean a grown-up in a grown-up body – he set out to enjoy himself to the full. He's a very attractive man; he had lots of girlfriends. And then one day it was like he and Jukebox saw each other for the first time and they fell in love. Fell hard and deep. That was just a few months ago. She was going to tell him about the baby after the show last night. Well, maybe she has, maybe they're fine and happy somewhere right now.'

We entered the park. In the murky twilight the great lawns were windswept and drab. Low grey sky, wet grey pavement, a wet grey dog dragged along by a grim-faced walker. The Wellington Arch, where Charlie had crashed, was visible to the south. Illuminated by spotlights, the chariot of war and the angel of peace floated eerily above the mist. Charlie wasn't fine and happy, that I knew. I glanced at my watch; evening visiting hours would soon begin.

'I need to go and see a friend,' I said to Wingbow.

'Have you got a few more minutes? We're nearly there.'

'Nearly where?'

'You'll see.' She led me across the soggy grass towards a thicket of oak and rhododendron enclosed by iron railings. We helped each other to climb over, then pushed through the dense undergrowth and past a brick shed to emerge in a small clearing.

'What are we doing here?' I asked.

'Primus showed me this place. It's . . . special. Just be quiet for a minute and listen.'

I tried to listen, but in fact it seemed that the noises of the city had ceased. It was unnaturally silent. Dark, wet rhododendron leaves encircled us, bare-branched oaks loomed into the clouded sky.

'Listen to what?' I asked.

'Shh.' Wingbow smiled and tilted her head, and raised one finger.

And then I heard it: a faint hum, at the very edge of perception. As my attention caught the sound it increased and I discerned several strands, many strands, flowing and intertwining. The more closely I listened, the more distinct the sounds became. It was music, but not like earthly music, made on material objects for physical ears. And I saw that the music was also light, coloured waves and ribbons of light swirling and weaving, making and releasing patterns, and the light was also scent, but not of any earthly flower. The colours, the shifting geometries, the synaesthesia – it was like being inside a living piece of Luce's art . . . or, no, it was like being inside Luce's mind. This was how she saw things, I realised: these were the astral patterns beneath the physical forms.

I don't know how long we stood there; after a time Wingbow took my hand and led me out. As we moved away from the spot, the sounds and lights and scents faded; ordinary reality reasserted itself. Traffic growled past on Bayswater Road, horns hooted. A hardy jogger trotted by. I was in a daze. Wingbow looked at me and said, 'You need to eat something.'

340

She was probably right. I couldn't remember the last time I'd eaten. We went across the road to a café, ordered coffee and cake.

'London was so hard for me at first,' Wingbow said. 'Culture shock. As you can imagine. The people, the noise. The way the surface of everything is so hard. But if you know where to look – how to look – you can find the places where things open up. That's one of those places, a big one, a centre. Primus showed it to me. She wanted me to understand why we were here. There are patterns within everything, she said. If you know them you can use them. Like swimming in a current. You can't see it, but you feel its effects. If you go with it, it's easy; if you go against, it's rough. We always found an ideal space for a gig exactly where we needed it to be.'

For Luce, Wingbow said, these living geometries were always seen and felt. She didn't need to go anywhere special. The strings of the invisible world were at her fingertips; she played it like an instrument. And to perfect the chord, the final string needed to be struck. 'She'd always planned the Conway Hall gig as the last one. It was meant to complete the harmony, then Luce and the Photons' work would be done.'

'What work? What would have happened if they'd managed to do that last gig?'

Wingbow smiled. 'A sudden outbreak of enlightenment? I don't know. I don't think Luce knew, for that matter, except that it would be good. She can't foresee the future, you know – at least not usually, and not exactly. Too many variables, she says. Just like the rest of us, she has to make guesses, take chances, choose, act, hope for the best, deal with the consequences.'

'So what happened? Who shot at them?'

'I don't know. I don't even know if it was Luce or Francis they were aiming for, or somebody else. I was up in the booth with Fergus. No one knew Luce and the Photons were going to play.

We used another name, Metatrix, and we arranged the whole masquerade ball as a cover.'

Someone obviously did know, I thought. I'd known, or at least had a strong suspicion, and I'd told Charlie; therefore many, many people might have known . . . including the Bigs. Why, I wondered, if there had been demons about at Conway Hall, hadn't Luce sensed them and dealt with them? Come to think of it, if there had been demons about, why hadn't I sensed them? I might have been too high to tell; everyone had looked dodgy to me, and I'd felt uneasy all night.

'Did you ever see anybody suspicious hanging around?' I asked. 'Following Luce, or watching her? Somebody who didn't look right or feel right?'

'Well, yes. I think maybe I did. A couple of nights ago we were walking on the Embankment, Luce and Fergus and I. It was about five in the morning, no one about. We'd been up all night tinkering with the equipment for the gig. I thought I glimpsed someone following and at the same time it was like a cold draught passed over my heart. Fergus said he was feeling very queer. Later he told me it was the same feeling he'd had that night when he came to you for help, when he'd thought he was being followed and hadn't wanted to lead them back to me . . . or the equipment. Luce told us to walk on ahead, she'd catch us up. I wasn't sure I wanted to, but Fergus always obeys her. He grabbed my arm and pulled me away. As I looked back I saw a figure step out from behind a tree. Luce beckoned it to come to her, which it did. I never saw its face, or even whether it was a man or a woman. When it got close, she spoke to it; I couldn't hear what she said. Then she touched it and it vanished. Like a soap bubble that's been popped.' She clicked her fingers. 'When Luce caught up with us I asked who that was, but she didn't say.'

Now.

I have to go to that place Wingbow showed me, find out if it's still there. Just to be on the safe side, I take a roundabout route via several buses and the tube. Although I see a number of people who look suspiciously bland, I get no definite feeling of a demon's presence.

I arrive in Hyde Park at about dusk and make my way to the thicket, enclosed by its iron railing. The rhododendrons have grown huge and dense. It's a warm evening, lots of people still about - I don't dare climb the fence. I sit on a bench and try to remember the feeling, the vision, but although I sense it may be near, I can't quite get it. I'll have to go inside.

When it's full dark I try to climb in. Apparently I'm not as agile as I think I am. My jeans snag on the rusty iron spears of the railings and I become stuck, unable to go forward or back. Naturally, when you want to be left alone people pester you to death; when you need help, there's no one about.

The policeman might not have seen me, but I'm so

glad to see anyone that I call out to him. Any embarrassment, even the risk of arrest, is preferable to
this painfully suspended state. To my relief (mixed
with a little disappointment), he finds me pathetic
and amusing, not dangerous. I blather on about how
I'd always wanted to see what was in there, then
realise he doesn't care. I don't need elaborate
excuses. I am old and harmless and quite possibly a
bit dotty - someone to be helped kindly on their way,
gently scolded and warned not to go 'wandering about
and climbing fences at your age'. He walks me out to
Bayswater Road. Suppressing an urge to kick his shins,
I smile meekly and head towards Marble Arch. He watches
me go. I wave bye-bye.

But I never was someone who went away when told. In
the late-opening shops of Edgware Road I buy a hoodie
with a Kraftwerk logo and a new pair of jeans - of a
different colour - to replace my torn ones; also a
length of sturdy rope and a pillow. I return to the
rhododendron grove where I contrive a pair of stirrups
from the rope, hook them to the railing and place the
pillow over the spikes. In this manner I scale the
fence with ease if not actual grace. I hide my gear
and push through the thick shrubbery towards . . .
towards where? It's not like I remember it, there's
several buildings instead of the one small shed.

Just listen, I tell myself. *It's here somewhere.*
Which way? I feel myself drawn ahead towards a gap
between two sheds, then left, then right, and all of
a sudden I'm in the spot. The oaks lean protectively
over me, lush-leafed and rustling in the summer night.
I wait, and listen, and try to still my erratically
thumping heart . . . and then it comes, that hush,

344

that silence into which the first clear sweet strands of light emerge. I close my eyes to see them better.

Ah, body. It's stiff, it's chilled, it's getting wet because it's started to rain. It's hungry, it needs a pee. Too soon, far too soon, it needs to go home. But just before I turn to leave the clouds break, the moon shines through and in the pale shaft of light I see Luce, with that enigmatic smile I remember from our last meeting, stepping towards me as she did then, her hand reaching to touch mine . . . then the clouds close over the moon and she's gone.

I make my way out, shaking a bit with cold and tiredness, fall awkwardly over the railings and twist my ankle . . . but I did it, I got in and I got out. No fence can stop me! My watch tells me I was only there for ten minutes but it was worth it. I look up at the sky; the clouds are thick, dense and low. No moonbeam could have penetrated that lot. The moonlight was only as real as Luce - but she's as real as it gets. And I know she knows who I am, she knows what I'm doing: I'm Chimera Obscura, the Scribe, the Elucidator, the Scaler of Fences, the Indomitable. I treat myself to a taxi home.

21

The Secret Masters

§

Did I Kill Him? Ambrose Has Been Contacted.
A Rumour of a Shooting. The Avatar Must Be
Everywhere. Her Most Vulnerable Moment.
A Blood Clot on the Brain. Luce's
Final Resting Place(s). Demonology in
the British Library.

London, December 1967–February 1968

Charlie was a mess: mangled intestines, broken ribs, punctured lung, crushed spleen. Right leg too badly smashed to save, amputated above the knee. Left leg broken in six places, held together with a forest of steel pins. Relatively simpler fractures of both arms. Severe burns, especially to his face. Right eye lost. Jaw to be reconstructed later, if there is a later. Extent of spinal damage, too early to tell.

My thoughts ran round and round the same, remorseful loop: I wished he'd told me what was going on. If I'd been a better friend, I would have known; he wouldn't have had to tell me. Clement was right – I should have figured it out.

On the second night after the crash I was alone with Charlie,

346

Lady K having gone back to Claridge's for dinner, when he murmured, groaned and opened his eye.

'Hey, Charlie,' I said.

I don't think he recognised me, but he seemed to be trying to say something. I leaned closer to hear and pushed the button for the nurse. He was mumbling and groaning, then he said, quite clearly, 'Did I kill him?'

I thought he meant, had the crash killed Mr Big? I wasn't sure if astral entities did actually die, but reassuring Charlie was the most important thing. I said, 'Yes, you did.'

He moaned and drifted out of consciousness. The nurse came and summoned a doctor, but by then Charlie was gone again and they warned me not to get my hopes up. I'd just settled back into my chair when Ambrose appeared.

I was very glad to see him. He was one of the few people who'd known Charlie before his glamorous London life had attracted so many superficial friends. He was also the only person with whom I felt able to share my thoughts about the demon in Charlie's life, though it was not a conversation to have at the bedside, with all the coming and going of doctors and nurses. Ambrose pulled up a chair and sat quietly on the opposite side of the bed, watching Charlie through his donnish specs. His face was unreadable. Was he remembering our university days, recalling Charlie's escapades? Was he rueing his own failures of friendship, as I rued mine, or was he silently condemning Charlie for wasting his life? When visiting hours ended, we adjourned to a pub nearby.

Feeling the need of fortification I ordered a whisky, but Ambrose requested water only. When I asked if he'd stopped drinking he said something about preserving psychic purity. This, I should have realised, was a warning sign. But I didn't heed it, being eager to spill out all my concerns and conjectures to someone who, at least, would not think I was crazy.

347

The last I'd heard, Ambrose had been in Finland, studying astral projection. It had occurred to me, as we sat by Charlie's bedside, that if his studies had been successful I might get him to investigate things on the astral plane for me. I needed to find out who these demon-simulacra were, where they came from, what they wanted, and why they'd targeted Charlie. I also hoped for some tips on how to deal with them; specifically, whether shooting them would work.

'So, have you mastered astral projection?' I asked, not wanting to beat around the bush when Charlie's life was at stake.

Ambrose smiled and seemed almost to preen himself, which was such an uncharacteristic attitude for this formerly least vain of men that I did a double-take. Yes, definitely a preen.

'I have,' he answered, after a suitably dramatic pause.

'And is it . . .' I struggled to come up with an appropriate adjective. Nice? Scary? Interesting? 'Is it all you'd hoped?' I finally asked.

'More. More than I'd hoped. You have no idea.' He leaned forward confidingly. 'It's vast in there, simply vast. The further in you go, the bigger it gets. Realms upon realms, kingdoms within kingdoms, millions of worlds. Infinite worlds, and all . . .' he opened his hand and gazed at it in wonder '. . . in the palm of my hand.'

'Really?' I put my whisky aside; Ambrose was behaving so oddly that I wanted my wits about me.

He turned his gaze on me. Behind the mild-mannered spectacles, his eyes had a strange gleam. 'Yes, really. You may not think so to look at me, but I've been *contacted.*'

'Contacted?'

'By the Secret Masters.'

'Oh, Madame Blavatsky's lot?'

He made a dismissive gesture. 'Helena was a feeble vessel, prone to exaggeration, ridiculously conceited and deluded about her own importance. So were all the others – the snivelling Mathers, a mere clerk; old Aleister, just a slouching beast with pretensions, who never made it to Bethlehem. No, the Masters have done better now, far better. They've met their match in me, a peer of the realm, and they know it.' He sat back with a harrumph of satisfaction.

'It's good to have friends in high places,' I said, which could be taken either way.

'Yes, they find it so.' In Ambrose's universe, apparently, a Marquess of Great Britain ranked higher than Secret Masters of the Astral Plane.

I trod cautiously. It was not hard to present a demeanour of awed astonishment, though I had to be careful not to give in to the urge for parody. 'I'm . . . honoured to know this, Ambrose.'

He nodded graciously. Parody, I realised, would whizz right by unnoticed.

'You should also know,' he said, 'that I am the avatar of the aeon. The Secret Masters have confirmed it.'

'Oh, so *you're* the avatar. Congratulations.'

'Thank you. But this is not a meaningless title, in these dire times. Danger is everywhere.'

'Christ, yes.'

'An imposter. A true avatar of the aeon would not die such an ignominious death.'

'Maybe that was another aeon.'

'That is true.' Ambrose conceded the point magnanimously. 'Primitive times, primitive people. Human evolution has moved on.'

'To you.'

'Indeed. Being the avatar of this aeon requires far greater power than fishing by the sea or feeding the peasants.'

'Oh, I should think it requires simply lashings of power.'

'More than you can imagine. The forces of the anti-avatar are arrayed against me, but I will conquer them all. It's my destiny. They've told me. If I do my own true will, none other shall say me nay. I paraphrase Aleister, of course. He was no avatar, scarcely even a prophet, but he did have a way with words.'

'You'll certainly not get any nays from me,' I said. My whisky looked quite appealing now; I drank it down and rose to get another. When I came back to the table Ambrose's next move took me utterly by surprise.

'What happened at Conway Hall?' he asked.

'At Conway Hall?' I was too startled to do anything other than parrot the question.

'There was a shooting . . . wasn't there? Do you know if anyone was hurt, or died?'

I became very wary. 'How would I know?'

He frowned. 'Weren't you there? Charlie said you were going.'

If Ambrose was asking these questions, incongruous as they seemed, perhaps he knew more about what had happened there than he was letting on. Well, I was an old hand at that game. 'I did hear a rumour about a shooting,' I said, 'but apparently the police don't think so, or they'd have made some sort of announcement.'

'I thought you might have heard from your friend, what's his name? Fergus, Charlie said.'

'Hardly my friend, I've only met him once. What makes you think he'd know anything?'

'He has that light company, doesn't he? Lucifergus, clever name. He was doing the sound and light at Conway Hall, Charlie said.'

Charlie, it seemed, had said quite a lot. It was unkind to think ill of someone so ill, but I wished he hadn't blabbed so much. And that was such a typical thought to have about Charlie, Charlie at his indiscreet best, or worst, that it cheered me. If I could be annoyed with him, surely he was going to live. But why on earth was Ambrose interested in Conway Hall?

'I'm astonished to find you so well informed about such trivial matters as masquerade parties, Ambrose.'

'The avatar must be everywhere.'

Everywhere? Was it possible he'd gone himself? 'Doesn't it sully the psychic vibrations to attend that sort of a shindig?' I asked, testing.

'Oh, I have means of purifying myself.'

Astonishingly, he did not deny being there . . . but why would he have gone? Surely not for the fun of it; he would never find it fun. His idea of fun was browsing for incunabula in antiquarian bookshops.

'That's a relief,' I said, 'though I'd scarcely have thought you'd find it worth the trouble. I, obviously, went because it was just the sort of frivolous thing I love, but why did you go?'

'The Secret Masters said I was to keep an eye on Charlie, but we got separated.'

'Charlie *went* to the masquerade ball?'

'He had to see this rock star you're both so enamoured of – what's he called? I find it so hard to keep track of these pop bands. Loke? Luke?'

This obfuscation rang so false that it told me its very opposite: Ambrose, I realised, knew exactly who Luce was. 'Do you mean Luce?' I asked.

'That's it. Luce. Charlie said he would be there.'

'Well, I'm sorry you had to go to all that trouble to sully and then re-purify, Ambrose. I've no idea if Luce was there – everyone was masked.'

'But then who was shot?'

'Was anyone shot?'

'That's what I heard.'

'I think if a famous rock star had been shot we'd know about it, don't you?'

'Maybe the shot missed.'

'Maybe it did.'

'You carry a gun, Charlie told me. Are you carrying it now?'

'I am, as a matter of fact.' Christ, I really did wish Charlie had kept his mouth shut.

'Can you hit anything with it?'

Was he trying to suggest that *I* was the shooter at Conway Hall? 'I've only attempted tins so far, and I killed a fair few of them.'

'I'd be careful. Sometimes people can . . . shoot themselves.'

Ambrose had begun to scare me. 'I'm always very careful,' I said, standing. 'It's been a long day, Ambrose, I think I'll head home now. Good to see you again . . . and best of luck with this avatar business.' I left him sitting there, glass of water in his hand, gazing imperiously about the nearly empty pub as though it was his throne room, thronged with devoted courtiers.

I walked home through a biting wind, feeling frightened and very alone. My old friend Ambrose would be no help – it was obvious he'd gone quite mad. No doubt occult practices had unhinged him; he was scarcely the first to succumb to delusions of grandeur. But his delusions seemed fixated in a peculiarly relevant direction. Reluctant as I was to face the implications, I made myself work systematically through the things I'd learned.

Why had Charlie lied to me? He didn't want me to know that he was going to Conway Hall. Why was Ambrose so keen to find out if Luce had been killed, or if the shot had missed? Charlie – I made myself say it out loud, because the thought was so awful. Charlie was a very good shot.

I'd been wondering why, at Conway Hall, Luce hadn't sensed that there were demons about and dealt with them as she'd done in Paris at Disques Cybellines, or latterly on the Embankment in Wingbow's account. And then I had a revelation. Whoever was running this show had learned that demons couldn't get close to her; with the acuteness of her astral senses she'd be aware of their presence, and with her command of psychic powers she could neutralise them before they did any harm. But a human assassin, hidden among hundreds of other humans, striking when her attention was fully engaged with her music and she was at her most vulnerable . . . .

I remembered what Charlie had said in his delirium – just before Ambrose appeared, in fact: 'Did I kill him?' Was he referring not to Mr Big but to Luce? Had *he* been the shooter? Was that why Mr Big had corrupted him, made him into a junkie, entangled him in a deadly criminal enterprise, controlled him by debt and addiction? Poor Charlie, driven to murder and attempted suicide. Poor Ambrose, so easily deluded. His Secret Masters were demons, using him as they used Charlie.

I examined other persistent mysteries in the light of what I now knew. I'd never been convinced that I could have been followed to Warm Springs, yet within a day of my arrival they'd burned down Jay's house, broken into my motel room and stolen my photos of Luce's paintings. I'd told Charlie where I was going and why; no one else had known. And I was very much afraid that I now knew how the demons had found out what was in my shoulder bag that morning after our trip to Scotland. They didn't have to follow us; Charlie simply told someone. He told them where to go and they set a fire; he told them what I was carrying and I was mugged. I'd thought it odd that, having slogged our way through awful terrain to find the place, Charlie hadn't been more excited about seeing Luce's work. All he'd wanted was confirmation that it *was* Luce's work. Perhaps he hadn't dared to look closely for fear the art would enter his corrupted soul and reveal it.

The crucial thing I'd learned was that whatever Charlie knew, the Bigs knew, too. Thank God there was so much I'd never told him out of ordinary caution of his prolixity. He'd known nothing about Karen Cooper, Waldo and Miriam, Giorgio Servadio or

Luce's family and friends in Paris and Switzerland. He did know about Greyling, though; I'd told both him and Ambrose about what I'd seen Greyling do at Golden Square. And now I'd unwittingly led him straight to Greyling myself. Had Charlie insisted on driving us to Devon just for the fun of it, as I'd thought? Or was he, on instruction, sticking close to me in case I led him to Luce? It was hard to believe that I was seen as so important, but I couldn't rule it out. In a perverse way, if the Bigs believed I'd find Luce, it validated my own belief in the strength of my connection to her.

That night Charlie's condition deteriorated; they discovered a blood clot on his brain and had to saw open his skull to remove it. No one was able to say how much brain damage might have occurred. In the days that followed, as I sat by his bed reading to him, playing tapes of his favourite music, talking to him and gazing miserably down upon that wrecked body, one of the things I wondered was whether he would want me to finish him off, and whether, if he did, it would be the right thing to do. And if it was, would I be able?

The man and his body – or what was left of it – became quite separate in my mind. The man was a creature of memory and imagination: my dear friend and constant companion. His body, also my constant companion, was a fragile yet stubborn thing, a mass of badly functioning matter that I hated as much as I loved. Poor Charlie, trapped in that ruin.

Was it cruel to keep him hanging on, if what he'd really wanted was to die? But I clung to the Charlie I had known, and to my belief that, if he survived, he could be that person again. Like thousands of people sitting by beds in hospital rooms, I realised how much I loved him, and how terribly I'd miss him if he was gone.

Considering the crowds of 'friends' who'd populated Charlie's house night and day, eating his food and drinking his booze, smoking, dropping, snorting and shooting his drugs, it was notable how few turned out to visit him in hospital. Perhaps I'm being too harsh. The word would have got around that he was not the most scintillating company. Lady K, also, seemed to find it both draining and futile to linger at his bedside and confined her visits to ten minutes in the morning and ten in the evening.

I heard nothing from Fergus or anyone else. Lucifergus Lights had been booked for a number of shows, but the organisers of each told me they'd cancelled. Pymander Productions had gone to ground and I felt, with no justification, that they'd abandoned me. I tried to phone Greyling, but his number was ex-directory.

Having met Fergus and the others, I'd thought I was on the verge of getting much closer to Luce. After following her like a shadow for all these months, it had seemed that noonday was approaching and I'd unite with her at last. My hopes, desires and fantasies knew no bounds: I was the true companion she'd been waiting for all her life; we'd fall in love but it would be no ordinary love, rather a complete joining of two beings destined to be together. Et cetera. And then it was like the door slammed shut, the connection was severed and we were further apart than ever.

Why, I wondered, if she was so powerful, couldn't she help Charlie? Or at least send someone to say hello. One of her famous postcards would be nice. Surely she knew he wasn't truly evil but was being manipulated. And what about me? Was I just a pawn to be used and discarded . . . like Charlie? Greyling's great war of good and evil loomed over us like a black thundercloud, but who gave a fuck? All I wanted was for Charlie to live and have a chance to be happy again. If my pursuit of Luce had led the demons not only into my life but into Charlie's, was it time to quit?

As soon as he got out of hospital I'd head down to Devon to see Greyling and get some answers to the many questions that bedevilled my mind as my body endured its forced stillness at Charlie's bedside. Maybe some time I could take Charlie there, too. He needed to get away from the city, from all the temptations. I pictured myself pushing him around in his wheelchair, like Luce had pushed Fergus. And he'd learn to walk again. Somehow. I stopped short of fantasising that his amputated leg would regrow, but I was sure that my being there would help him. And Greyling was a shrink – Charlie could talk to him and maybe that would help.

I was uncertain what interest the Bigs might continue to take in Charlie. Would they back off, or would they try to kill him? I guarded him as well as I could, perfectly prepared to shoot any demon-simulacrum who approached, but I was limited to visiting hours. Perhaps they were waiting to see if he would die on his own. Or perhaps – my mind had grown very suspicious indeed – that blood clot on his brain *was* their attempt to finish him off. Could Ambrose have done it while we sat in silence by the bed?

I saw no more of Ambrose, thank God, but I felt that I was being watched and frequently caught glimpses of people with demons' typical plastic appearance, though I could never be sure. I also frequently felt surges of fear and dread, but I had plenty of reasons for these that did not involve the actual presence of a demon.

I continued to play my role as an obedient agent of the NOHRM, though I had an uneasy feeling that my cover, as it were, had been blown. The Bigs obviously knew I'd attended the masquerade ball, and that Luce was there. What they didn't know, apparently, was whether she'd been shot or killed. After long consideration, and in the absence of any word from Fergus or the Pymander Productions gang, I decided that it might serve her best if they believed she had died there, so I started a rumour that Luce had been killed that night at Conway Hall by an unknown assailant and his body spirited away to be buried in secret. Fuelled by absolute denials on the part of the authorities, this story took hold and to this day most people believe that Luce died on that night.

The various sites contending to be his final resting place are well known. The two most popular are Silbury Hill in Wiltshire and the Castlerigg stone circle in Cumbria. This was in the days before omnipresent tourists and constant surveillance, and it was not implausible that a dedicated group of people could have interred someone undetected even in a public site such as these.

Every year at the winter solstice Lucians from all over the world congregate in these and other, less famous, places, usually part of a tour that includes the sites of the secret gigs in London. The mystery of who killed Luce, and why, still fires the imaginations of conspiracy theorists, as evidenced by the always lively discussion threads dedicated to the topic on various Luce groups and forums. None, I need hardly add, has guessed the truth.

❧

Charlie, against all the odds, began to recover. Agonisingly slowly, and with setbacks – infections, bed sores, blocked tubes. The first snowdrops – he recognised me. Buds swelling on the chestnuts – he spoke! A few days later Clement brought the Meissen tea set from the house and we had a tea party in the hospital room, with all the doctors and nurses. Charlie actually smiled.

He remembered nothing about the crash or the events preceding it – no Fergus, no drive to Devon, no masquerade ball. Wiped from his memory – the doctors said it was common for recent memories to be lost; they might or might not return. In the hope of deterring the Bigs from any attempt to silence him, I put it about that Charlie's amnesia covered the entire previous year, was total and permanent.

He developed quite a nostalgic streak and liked to dwell on older memories, from the beginning of our friendship. Every day when I arrived he'd have a new old memory to share, and I think it helped him to revisit the innocent days of his youth. He remembered in great detail a sailing boat we used to have, and a summer spent on the Isle of Wight, and Maisie, a dog who'd died ten years earlier. He cried about that like it had just happened. He was good on our university days, and the early days in London. Recent history was spotty. When I probed for memories of the man who'd been 'running his life', he claimed to have no recollection of any such person, though a look of distress passed across his broken face.

Charlie's thinking was slow and tentative. Sometimes he struggled to remember a word or a name, which embarrassed him and made him angry. He'd begun physiotherapy, which made him weep with pain and frustration. Since mercurial exuberance and joyful recklessness had been two of his most dominant characteristics, it was no wonder he seemed the merest shadow of himself.

Although the police report on the crash concluded that it had been deliberate, Lady K chose to ignore this minor detail. She, like many women of her age and class, was extremely skilled at the comprehensive blanking out of anything unpleasant, such as her son's flamboyant suicide attempt in the very centre of London. If the matter had to be mentioned at all, she referred to 'The Accident' and made disparaging remarks about the Aston Martin, as though it was all the car's fault. A Bentley would never have done such a thing.

But I knew, and I could not ignore it, and one day I asked Charlie why he'd wanted to kill himself.

'Oh, did I? Maybe it seemed like the thing to do at the time,'

358

he drawled, through his lopsided mouth. His attempt at the old insouciance was painful to see.

'Did anybody tell you to, or suggest it?'

'Don't remember a thing,' he said gaily. 'All lost in the mists of oblivion.'

I'd begun to wonder whether Charlie's death had been part of the Bigs' plan from the beginning: he was to kill Luce (witnessed by Ambrose) and then kill himself before he could be arrested and tried. His last decision, his last surge of pride and courage, had been to take Mr Big with him. This scenario, in any case, convinced me, though unless Charlie regained his memory and chose to share it, I would never know for certain. Nevertheless, I added it to the growing list of crimes committed by the Bigs.

My fury at what they had done to Charlie was a fire all but drowned in a lake of sadness and remorse; it burned alone, silently feeding a desire for revenge. Charlie had managed, if not to kill, at least to obliterate Mr Big; I longed to dispatch a demon, too. I was aware that this was not a rational desire. I urged myself to be cautious, to maintain the pretence of obedience, but I found myself regularly fingering the gun in my pocket, wondering if I'd dare to use it, and what would happen if I did.

In the absence of a trustworthy adviser, I turned to books and spent the time between visiting hours in the Reading Room at the British Library. Quite a lot had, even then, been written on the subject of the astral plane; enough, after a couple of weeks of research, to convince me of the reality of the place. It is defined as a dimension intermediate between the incorporeal realm of pure mind and the fully corporeal world of matter and is described in near-identical terms in the literature of every major and indeed minor religion or philosophy. Ambrose was right: there were worlds upon worlds in there, and without a guide, the unwary were well advised to keep out.

Most of the books tended to be very high-minded; none was in the least helpful on the subject of how to kill an astral entity that had the power and the temerity to appear physical. My demonic simulacra seemed to be highly unusual in their ability to manifest and act on the material plane. The only phenomenon that offered, if not explanation, at least terminology, was that of 'bilocation', in which someone is able to appear in two places at once.

> The prevailing theory suggests that [bilocation] is a projection of a double. The double may be perceived by others as a solid physical form, or may appear ghostly. Typically, the double acts strangely or mechanically . . . Bilocation is an uncommon but ancient phenomenon. It is said to be experienced, and even practised by will, by mystics, ecstatics, saints, monks and holy persons, and magical adepts.*

From the study of philosophical texts about the astral and the numerous other planes of existence I moved on to explore the topic of demonology, which promised a more practical slant. Here I came across any number of unpleasant astral entities, such as dybbuks, golems, black beasts and so on, as well as ghosts, ghouls, dhouls, faeries, phantasms, spectres and wights of every stripe, but the advice on how to deal with them was abstruse and presumed that one either had or was able to purchase extensive magical expertise: spells and talismans, charms and incantations.

European occultists of the late nineteenth and early twentieth century, liberated from religious dogma and inspired by contact with alternative traditions such as Qabala and Vedanta, with their long history of scientific enquiry into the nature of reality, had

---

* R. E. Guiley, *Harper's Encyclopedia of Mystical and Paranormal Experience* (Harper: San Francisco, 1991), p. 57.

applied rigorous methods to the study of the astral plane. They had developed useful theoretical models but tips for dealing with astral entities, should one encounter them unwillingly, took the form of meditations, purifications and rituals. Effective, no doubt, in dealing with so-called 'psychic attack', but I didn't think a demon pointing a gun at me was likely to wait around while I performed them.

There was always prayer, but it's known to be only as reliable as the strength of one's belief and the purity of one's soul. I lacked belief and had doubts about my soul. The only thing I believed in was Luce, and if prayers to Luce worked, I thought, they'd have worked by now. I had no reason to suppose she'd wish to help Charlie who, I was fairly sure, had tried to kill her. She might have helped him for *your* sake, a niggling voice whispered in my ear, seeing as *you're* so close to her, but I tried to ignore it.

I was at the Library one afternoon, reading Dion Fortune's *Psychic Self-Defence*, when a feeling of dread came over me. Suspecting the presence of a demon, I looked around but there was no one other than my fellow researchers bent over their books, browsing the open shelves or clustered at the main desk. And then I saw him, making his way across the vast room. My own Mr Big. So Charlie's car crash hadn't killed him after all – or it had, but he'd returned. He seemed to glide in a shroud of cold air, his dead eyes fixed on me. The book was of no use at all, unless I threw it at him. I willed my hand to move to my pocket, to grasp my gun, to point it, to shoot . . . but I was frozen. Partly it was the paralysing miasma of fear, but also it was the sheer impossibility of doing such a hideously noisy thing in the Reading Room.

He placed a white envelope of the sort that usually contained Mrs Big's directives on the desk in front of me, turned and walked away without speaking. The awful feeling receded, and

I gazed at the envelope. What was Mrs Big saying by using him to deliver this routine item? The message I got was that he was as alive as ever, and they knew exactly where I was and what I was doing at all times.

I opened the envelope and read the instructions. Mrs Big requested that I investigate . . . John Greyling. Nice one, I thought, and prevaricated by providing a lengthy treatise telling them all they already knew in the fullest detail, adding the usual array of obfuscating fictive embellishments at which I'd become so skilled, adding that he was my personal psychoanalyst.

I knew that my days as a double agent were numbered and I would soon have to extricate myself from Mrs Big's long-tentacled grasp, but as to how . . . I had no idea. I added it to the list of topics on which I would seek Greyling's advice.

Now.

It's one a.m. I'm trying to write, but I can't concentrate. I give up, take a bath and go to bed, but I can't sleep. Now the bathroom door won't stay shut, and there seems to be another crack developing down one side of the door frame. I can't help imagining one of those mysterious YouTube cracks happening right now, under this very building. No point in complaining to the management; they know I'm crazy. But I can't get that image out of my mind. I'd better investigate myself.

I dress and step out into the corridor. Someone's snoring, someone's singing tunelessly, someone's flushing their loo. Someone's crying. I go downstairs. The door labelled Basement is locked. I try the other doors, but they're locked, too. All but the one at the end, which says Fire Exit. I push it cautiously; no alarm sounds.

It opens onto the back of the building, which I've never seen before. The cloudy sky reflects the dull urban light, revealing a flat, weedy expanse bounded by a sagging chain link fence. I smell buddleia and dog shit. Beyond are trees, scrub, rows of shipping containers. Larger structures hulk in the distance - warehouses, perhaps, or the hangars of a disused airfield.

I turn to find that the door has closed behind me; from this side, it's locked. I don't mind. It's a warm night and - I pat my pockets - I've got my cigarettes and lighter and phone. I use the light on the phone to examine the wall of the building for cracks. As I work my way along I nearly fall down a set of shallow steps. They lead to a door that must give onto the basement. I try the handle. To my great surprise, the door opens. Someone must have forgotten to lock it.

'Do come in,' says a voice. It would have given me the most awful fright but for the tone, which is very soft and gentle.

I step into a small, low-ceilinged room. A lamp sheds a cone of light onto a workbench; the speaker is an old man with a screwdriver in one hand and a pair of needle-nose pliers in the other. A piece of mechanical apparatus, in bits, is spread before him.

'I beg your pardon,' I say. 'I had no idea anyone was here.'

'Can't sleep?'

I shake my head.

'Nor me. Age, I suppose.'

'I suppose so.'

We introduce ourselves. His name is Isidore Berger; it turns out he's a sort of occasional caretaker and handyman. I realise I've seen him before, in the corridor or on the stairs.

'But there's nothing to do at night,' he says. 'I pass the time fixing old clocks. What do you do?'

'Write. Fret. Rewrite.'

'Fancy a cup of tea?'

'Yes, please.'

He fills a kettle, assembles mugs, milk and sugar and accepts the offer of a Gitanes. 'Friend of mine used to smoke these,' he says, giving an appreciative sniff.

I sit on an ancient, springless sofa and leaf through a tool catalogue. Isidore seems perfectly content to carry on with his clock repair and I begin to feel, in a very pleasant way, like a comfortable piece of old furniture.

'Have you noticed any cracks?' I ask after a while. 'That's what I was looking for.' I tell him about the cracks I've seen on YouTube.

He shakes his head. 'I'll have a look round in the morning.'

'I reported my concerns, of course.'

'Oh? No one told me.'

'They think I'm crazy.'

We have a good laugh about that.

After a second cup of tea I decide maybe I should go and am about to ask how to get back into the building when I hear a low whistle and - though I immediately dismiss it as a mishearing - the whicker of a horse.

Isidore's face breaks into a smile. 'Come and meet my nephew,' he says. My mind, still snagged on the incongruity of the horse, immediately pictures a young centaur.

Outside, the sky has begun to pale and in the ambiguous light I think, for a moment, that it is indeed a centaur. A horse and rider approach, leading a second horse. We walk down to the chain link fence and pass through a gap into the waste ground. The rider is a young lad of perhaps eighteen or nineteen with a tangle of dark curls and laughing eyes.

'Look who I have,' he says, sliding off the horse he was riding, a gleaming bay with four prancing white feet. He and Isidore walk around the beast, whose name is Ducati, making appreciative comments.

'I didn't know you had a friend with you,' the lad says, 'or I'd have brought another horse. Do you ride?' he asks me.

'Haven't in years.'

'You never forget. Come on, Beauregard can take us both, and Uncle Izzy can ride Ducati. If he thinks he can manage. We'll just amble along easy.'

Isidore has already vaulted quite nimbly onto Ducati's ever-shifting back. The lad – Rider, he's called, though I don't know if that's name, nickname or job title – assists my rather less nimble ascent to the broad and placid back of Beauregard and scrambles up behind me. We make our way along a well-worn path through the waste land, past the abandoned shells of warehouses, across a dank green stream, through an underpass beneath a rumbling road, past row upon row of polytunnels, then suddenly we're in the country-side.

I'd forgotten how intense nature is, the smells, the colours, the sounds. The sun rises, bathing everything in blinding brightness. We come to a farm-yard where a woman, who I gather is Rider's mother, cooks breakfast on an open fire while children of various ages frolic among ducks, chickens and puppies. There's a cowshed, a pig sty, henhouses, paddocks and stables with the friendly faces of twenty or so horses poking over their doors. I sit on a crate. A tribe of orange cats watches from windowsills, the bonnet of a tractor, a woodpile. People come and go; two old women, a teenage girl with a baby on her hip, a grizzled man of middle years who shoos aside the cats and drives off on the tractor. I'm given a bacon butty and a cup of instant coffee. One of the children falls, scraping his knee. I dust him off and comfort him, and receive an appreciative glance from Rider's mother. Isidore plays with the children, gossips with the old women, then we mount up again and ride back to town. I feel more secure on the horse; we do a bit of trotting and a brief canter.

Isidore shows me how to get into the house and tells me to stop by any time. I tell him I certainly will. The Jungian in me is quite delighted to have found him in the basement of the house in which I dwell. And maybe, it occurs to me, the cracks are a good thing. Neither literally nor metaphorically am I enamoured of this edifice. If it falls down, fine with me, though I do hope I'm not at home when it happens.

22

Death Road

&

*Charlie Comes Home. Greyling in the Garden.
Bilocation. The Insurance Policy. A Singularly Ill-
equipped Soldier. The Persuasive Colleague. I Devise
a Plan. Everything That Charlie Was Not. The End
of Youth. Escape by Insanity.*

London and Devon, March 1968

Although Lady Kelmont was devastated by the catastrophe
that her son had become, there was without doubt a part
of her not altogether displeased at the chance to take over
Charlie's life on a wholesale basis. She'd scarcely known a tenth
of what he'd got up to, but the little she did know had alarmed
her considerably. Now the days of feeble remonstrances from
the distant sidelines were over. Her son was once again as helpless as a baby; she was determined that this opportunity would
not be wasted.

When the worst was over, she turned her formidable management skills to arranging Charlie's future. At her request, I helped
Clement adapt a set of ground-floor rooms for Charlie, with all
the same kit he had in hospital. The doctors were nearby, a nurse

was to live in the next room and a physiotherapist to come every morning and afternoon. A special cook was hired to cater for Charlie's radically revised digestive system.

In early March he came home. As soon he was comfortably settled I had a little conversation with Clement, reminded him not to let Mr Big or anyone like him into the house, and offered him my gun. He replied with a smile that told me he was, as usual, one step ahead and touched his pocket, where a distinct bulge marred the line of his suit.

I hired a car and drove to Devon. The Bigs knew of Greyling's existence and they knew where he lived, but nevertheless I preferred that they did not know I was going there now, so I took all the usual precautions – roundabout routes, much stopping and starting and ducking in and out of alleys and side streets.

I arrived in the late afternoon. The air was mild and fragrant, green with new shoots and unfurling leaves. When I turned off the engine and got out, the silence closed about me like wings. Greyling came around the side of the house. Evidently he'd been gardening; the knees of his old corduroy trousers were muddy and he was carrying a pair of loppers. He greeted me with warmth but no surprise. I watched as he finished pruning an overgrown fuchsia and helped him drag the branches to a smouldering bonfire. The thought crossed my mind that I could just stay here for a while, maybe for ever, helping in the garden and absorbing the intoxicatingly fresh smells and the utter peace.

In the warm kitchen, with a cup of tea before me, I asked what had happened to Luce after the Conway Hall gig, but he said he had no idea. And his dear nephew Fergus? Ditto. No one can lie with a straighter face than a shrink, though I took the baldness of the lie as a compliment: he didn't mind my knowing that he did indeed know perfectly well.

He'd heard, of course, about the car crash, which had made national headlines for several days. He'd known that something was amiss with Charlie from the start, he told me. I thought he'd picked up on the drugs; he had, but it wasn't that. While Fergus and I washed up after lunch, Greyling had gone upstairs for a nap but, finding himself unaccountably restless, had come back down for a book. From the landing and through the half-open sitting-room door he'd glimpsed Charlie searching the drawers of his desk. Out of curiosity he'd allowed him to continue uninterrupted until it was apparent he'd found nothing of interest, had closed the drawers and moved away. Greyling then came noisily down the rest of the stairs. When he entered the room Charlie was sitting in a chair, reading a newspaper.

I wondered, later, whether Greyling's whole 'upstairs for a nap' routine had been a charade whose sole purpose was to give Charlie – or me – the opportunity to reveal ourselves and our agendas.

If I was to have any hope of useful assistance, Greyling had to know the whole story, so I poured it out: Mr Big's corruption of Charlie (Greyling shook his head sadly, and winced at the mention of heroin); Ambrose's Secret Masters ('Such an old con. You wouldn't believe how many people think they've been contacted by the Secret Masters'); Mrs Big ('I've rarely encountered her. She generally uses others to do the practical work, but she's the one in charge, the most skilful and dangerous of the lot. That innocuous, motherly appearance of hers is utterly deceptive'); my employment as an agent of the NOHRM, their pursuit of Luce and my attempts to mislead them (a grunt of grudging respect) and their recent request for me to investigate Greyling himself. When I described the obfuscations I'd contrived, he laughed out loud, but when I set out the painful evidence that Charlie had shot at Luce, he was silent.

His implicit confirmation shook me more than I'd expected; some part of me had longed to be proved wrong and another scenario revealed or at least suggested. So it was true: Charlie had tried to kill Luce. In his brief moment of lucidity, the night after the crash, that was what he'd wanted to know. He'd been hoping, I believe, to have failed, yet I'd inadvertently told him he'd succeeded. I had to allow him to continue in that belief, torment him though it might. Was this a suitable punishment for him? Was it a suitable punishment for me, who'd arranged the meeting between assassin and victim? From whom should I seek forgiveness?

Greyling and I went for a walk by the river. Lambs bleated, a crow cawed, birds chirped and sang like mad in the dusk. The high western sky was pale, with small, rosy-tinted clouds that mirrored the sheep here below. London, with its hospital beds and car crashes, seemed another planet. In this idyllic place, I longed to forget about demons, and evil, and all that snared and corrupted the soul. Nature, I felt, could save me all by herself . . . if I had time. But I didn't have time. If I was to have any hope of getting free of the Bigs, I had to know what I was dealing with, and only Greyling could help. I needed practical advice of the sort that books had failed to provide.

The astral entities I'd read about were insubstantial and encounters with them brief, hazy and of obscure purpose. They tended to be single-minded and dim-witted. If they were able to affect the material plane at all, it was in a haphazard and crude fashion – poltergeists, for instance, flinging chairs across a room, or house-ghosts causing mirrors to drop off walls. How was it, I asked Greyling, that the three we'd encountered at Golden Square were able to appear so real?

'Haven't you figured it out? They look like humans and act like humans – more or less – because somewhere a human is lying in a trance and sending their astral body out. There's great advantages, as you can imagine.'

'But we all go about in our astral bodies during sleep, or so I understand, though we confine our perambulations to the astral plane. We don't suddenly appear on the physical plane, do we? We flit around and don't remember when we wake, or only as a vague dream.'

'With practice,' Greyling said, 'one can improve on that.'

'Do you mean bilocation? I've read about saints and lamas who were able to project a simulacrum of themselves miles away from their physical body, but it's supposed to be extremely difficult and rare.'

'It *is* extremely difficult. It takes a phenomenal amount of concentration and energy. I can't do it, and I know . . . hardly anyone who can. It used to be quite rare, though lately it's become more common.'

'Lately?'

'In the last twenty years or so.'

The penny dropped and my mind flashed back to V's story, and to Waldo and Miriam in their cosy Taos kitchen. Miriam had been drugged and sent out in her astral body under another's control. I thought of Lance, with his capacity for violence, his ability to kill. Had that been used, too?

'It's as though especially talented people were being collected,' I said.

'Yes.'

'And trained, and assisted by drugs.'

'Yes.'

'And bred.'

'I won't ask how you know this, but yes. There's something you should see. I suspect it's what your friend Charlie was looking for.'

We walked in silence back up to the house. In the sitting room Greyling went to the bookcase, unlocked a wall safe that had been hidden behind books (the Jung, appropriately), removed a thick manila folder and handed it to me.

'This is my insurance policy, so to speak. It's why they haven't simply killed me by now. Or, I should say, arranged a convenient accident. These are copies – the originals are in my lawyer's safe. Mrs Big, as you call her, knows that if I die under suspicious circumstances – and all circumstances are suspicious in my case – these documents will be made public.'

'Does Fergus know about this insurance policy?'

'He knows that when I die he's to contact my lawyer.'

I looked though the papers. Dated from the late 1940s to the early 1960s, they were the records of a series of experiments at a place identified as Lab 12. There was no clue as to the location, though the spelling was British. The experiments were designed to measure and control psychic skills: telepathy (TP), telekinesis (TK), clairvoyance (CV), also called remote viewing (RV),* precognition (PC) and astral projection (AP). The subjects, identified by name/number codes and ranging in age from three to sixty-eight, had also been tested for resistance to various diseases and for tolerance of sleep deprivation, starvation, stress, cold, heat and pain, as well as electric shocks (voltage levels detailed) and a long list of drugs and poisons. The experiments included ones that caused the subjects' hearts to be stopped for increasing lengths of time. Most files ended with a stamp: a black letter D with a date written in.

'How did you get these?'

'I . . . came upon them.'

'In a secret laboratory?'

'I thought they might be useful.'

'You just happened to be visiting this place.'

'And without an invitation. Very rude of me.'

'I see how this explains the simulacra,' I said, 'but people are

* The US government's remote-viewing programme, as reported by Jon Ronson in his 2004 book, *The Men Who Stare at Goats*, is widely believed to have been a front, intended to fail in order to divert attention from the real programmes, which remained (and, no doubt, still remain) secret.

being used against their will – at least, some of them are. There are humans running these places. This isn't research, it's torture and coercion.'

Greyling looked grim. 'There is not now nor has there ever been any shortage of humans willing to do evil. Some crave it for its own sake and seek it out, some are all too willing to obey evil orders. Some believe they are doing good. There are men and women who choose to enlist but, yes, some operate under coercion. It's hard to be sure because it's difficult to trace the astral double back to its physical base if it doesn't want to be followed – but we're getting better at it. If we can find out where the person's physical body is, we can . . . act.'

'Act?'

'I told you. I'm a soldier. And so, perhaps, are you.'

'If I am,' I said, 'I'm a singularly ill-equipped one. You shut those two into a fire they'd obligingly provided, but I can't do that. Anyway, how can you justify killing them if they might be innocent victims acting against their will?'

'I don't kill them. All I do is disable them temporarily. In my experience – and it's happened to me more than once – being killed in one's astral body, while definitely unpleasant emotionally and a considerable shock to the system, probably won't kill you physically. There will be illness of some sort, anything from a head cold, a rash or a fever to a stroke or heart attack. Actual death of the physical body is rare, though not unheard of. Personally, I don't have the power, and I know . . . hardly anyone who does. One doesn't like to kill a human being. No matter how corrupted by evil they've become, one wants to believe they can be redeemed. The two I trapped in the fire will have shot back to their physical bodies in some distress, but they didn't die. Their precipitous exit forced them to leave a trail. A colleague of mine followed and persuaded them to . . . mend their ways.'

'A colleague – you mean Luce?'

Greyling said nothing, which confirmed it.

'Persuaded?'

'My colleague is very persuasive.'

I'll bet she is, I thought, and by now adept at keeping one step ahead of the pursuit, even turning it to her advantage. I realised that Luce – and 'colleagues' – might have been raiding these secret labs for years, rescuing the inmates and destroying the buildings. No wonder the demons were out to get her.

We ate dinner at the kitchen table: a shepherd's pie that Mrs Yates, the daily, had left in the Aga. After dinner we settled in the sitting room with cups of coffee to which Greyling added a generous shot of brandy. I took up the issue that was most urgent for me: how to extricate myself from the NOHRM, my escalating campaign of inanities and inaccuracies not having deterred them.

Although I now knew the simulacra I'd encountered were simply people in souped-up astral bodies, I found that I continued to think of them as demons on account of the profound fear and revulsion they provoked and the evil they did – and for lack of a convenient alternative term. Their ability to appear on the physical plane, Greyling told me, made them temporarily vulnerable to physical means: if I shot one, the simulacrum would die ('destabilise') and disappear ('lose integrity') within a minute.

Greyling thought that the single most important fact was that I'd always given away my fee; their hold could be broken. He meant, I suppose, their astral hold. This gave me hope, although his suggestion, that I simply cease to obey, I knew I didn't dare take up. The box of white powder hemmed me in on that side.

His next idea, that I leave town and hide away in some cheap foreign country for at least a year in the hope that they'd forget me, I'd already considered and dismissed. I couldn't abandon Charlie to the Bigs or the scarcely more tender mercies of his mother.

But sitting there, talking with a psychoanalyst, gave me an

idea. Inanity having failed to discourage them, I would try insanity. I'd already planted the notion that I was in psychiatric care . . . now all I had to do was fall spectacularly over the edge into downright madness. If I could not lose myself physically, I would lose my mind and cease to be the person they'd employed. My reports would become confabulations of hallucinogenic magnificence; I would let my imagination rip. Enthusiasm redoubled, my devotion to the NOHRM fired by paranoia on an epic scale, I would tell them all about UFOs and alien invasions, cosmic plots to rule the world, armies of spectral warriors ravaging the cities. I would pelt them with daily reports, hourly reports. I would dedicate myself wholly to saving the world on behalf of the NOHRM. And I'd have fun doing it.

This strategy was warmly endorsed by Greyling, who offered free psychoanalysis that he was sure would cure me of my sad condition, though not too soon. I was sufficiently cheered by this decision of strategic brilliance to join him in a game of chess, which he won, though not easily.

❦

When I woke it was dark, that total dark you only get deep in the countryside. I didn't know where I was. I heard the gentle burbling of a river, my fingers encountered the chenille of the bedspread and I remembered. Greyling's house. I gazed out of the uncurtained window at the fading stars, dozed and dreamed. In my dream I was with Charlie in the DB6, driving along a smooth, deserted road through purple and yellow hills – Scotland somewhere, I think. We were young, eighteen maybe. Charlie was swigging from a vodka bottle and making the car weave all over the road. We were laughing and singing. I woke with the song echoing in my mind – it was Luce and the Photons' 'Death Road'.

I dressed quietly, tiptoed downstairs and let myself out. I'd planned to go for a walk by the river, but the intensity of the stillness, the beauty of the approaching dawn overwhelmed me and I just stood in the middle of the dew-bedecked lawn as the sky paled to silver, then to the palest clear blue.

Greyling joined me, bearing two mugs of tea. We sipped and watched the sun break through the trees and I asked if I could bring Charlie out some time, when he was a bit better. Greyling said that would be all right. After a while we went inside for some breakfast; all this country air was giving me an appetite. While Greyling made toast and eggs, I phoned Clement to say I was about to head back. He told me that Charlie had died in the night.

The news struck me like a blow, although how can I say I was surprised? I had desperately wanted him to survive, to live, to return from wherever demons and drugs had taken him, to be my friend again. I'd clung to that dream, but it was a delusion. It was never going to happen. It was too late long ago. I left for London without breakfast and arrived at Belgrave Square around noon, just as Charlie's body was being removed by the undertakers.

His mother said he'd died of heart failure; it was something the doctors had told her might happen at any time. Clement told me the truth. It had not been, as I'd feared, an attack by a demon – or maybe it was. Charlie had stashes all over the place; we'd cleaned out the ones we knew about, but junkies are canny. Charlie fixed himself up the first chance he got. Was he befuddled? Was it an accident that the heroin he used was pure? He'd died before the syringe was half empty. Clement had found him, tidied him and got rid of the evidence. When the situation was explained to the doctor, he'd agreed to put heart failure as the cause of death, so as to avoid further scandal and embarrassment for the family.

A week later I was with Lady Kelmont in the Bentley, following

377

the hearse bearing Charlie's body home to Warwickshire. She wanted me to ride with her, she explained apologetically, because she would rather not be alone. This was, for her, an extraordinary display of emotion. She'd aged ten years since the crash; her eyes were red and her hands shook. 'You knew him best,' she said. I wish I had, I thought.

It was raining lightly when we arrived at the little church where generations of Charlie's family have been welcomed into and waved from this world. The funeral service, with its archaic, formulaic pronouncements, was hard to bear. Intended, I suppose, to give comfort, it made me want to scream. For his mother's sake I sat still and bit my tongue. Charlie had never hated his family, his role, his place in society; he'd merely disregarded them when it suited him. When necessary, he'd not chafed at playing his part – always punctual and correctly dressed for weddings, christenings, funerals. In recent years, his father increasingly out of it, he'd even opened the village fête at his mother's side. In time, I knew, he'd have settled into the traditions without demur, put the wild days of youth behind him. He'd have taken his seat in the Lords; he'd have married an extremely appropriate person, had children, grandchildren. Would we have remained friends?

The coffin seemed awfully big, a monstrous thing. It was polished to a hard sheen and had shiny brass handles. It was everything Charlie was not: square-edged, tight-lidded, heavy, opaque, unmoving, impermeable. I pictured Charlie dancing. He'd rather his body was just laid in the earth, I thought – or perhaps burned. Yes, Charlie would have liked to be burned, to ascend as a dancing wisp of flame towards the sun. I imagined the funeral I'd have given him: music all night (I made a mental playlist), free drugs, vintage champagne, an orgy and dancing until dawn, then the lighting of the pyre.

By the time we emerged from the church the sun was breaking

through the clouds. Steam rose from the granite slabs in the graveyard as though the ancient spirits were still in the process of departing. I really did not want to watch Charlie being lowered into the dark, muddy hole, but Lady Kelmont kept me by her. 'You knew him best,' she said again.

That didn't stop the rest of the assembled company from making snide remarks. They had always regarded me as precisely the sort of bad influence who was sure, one day, to lead Charlie to his doom. Which now I had. They hated seeing me at Lady K's side, but they loved it that I'd proved to be as vile as they'd always thought. The only one who was decent to me turned out to be the Australian cousin who would now inherit both the title and the vast, if entailed, estate when Lord Kelmont died – surely not long now. When everyone went up to the house for tea (drinks), I slipped away and caught a train back to London.

Charlie's death seemed to have killed my own youth. In our teens and early twenties, as the sixties dawned like a miraculous technicolour revelation out of the grim monochrome of the fifties, we children of the war framed our world with touchingly naive assumptions: we were special, the golden children of a golden age of art and music, beauty and pleasure. The world was done with strife and was ready for a new Eden, all flowers and light and peace. Of *course* everything would turn out right for us, for *all* of us. No one would fuck up their life. No one would make irredeemable mistakes, suffer or die in misery and failure; everyone would succeed at everything, everyone would be happy all the time. It would last for ever, we'd always be sailing into our gorgeous future, a calm sea before us and a warm breeze filling our sails. Whoever was on the tiller surely knew what they were doing . . . didn't they? But now I saw there was no one on the tiller and no way to avoid the storms and catastrophes of the ungovernable sea.

379

I'd had the idea to hold a wake for Charlie at Belgrave Square, a party to end all parties, but I was too sad. I walked through the rooms for the last time; the family was selling the house, after two hundred years. The murals had been painted over; Sotheby's was taking everything away for auction. Clement, given a generous bonus, was planning to retire to Jamaica and open a bar in Negril with his brother-in-law. We shared a last joint and wished each other well.

&

Now that I had no reason to stay in England, I was determined to drop off the Bigs' radar altogether. The insanity plan was good, but it needed a second layer of subterfuge. Through the same friend of a friend from whom I'd acquired my little gun, I got in touch with a forger and negotiated for a new identity. I opted for an American passport – only a few quid more than a British one and far more useful, I was informed. I set up a Swiss bank account so I could access my royalties and congratulated myself on having had the good sense always to write under a *nom de plume*. I could continue to be Chimera Obscura whoever and wherever I was.

Thus equipped, I set about losing it as conspicuously as possible. It was not difficult to present myself as deranged by grief at Charlie's death, driven mad by despair. I bombarded Mrs Big with increasingly bizarre reports: talking pigeons in the park, men in strange hats pursuing me (from whom, in a nice twist, I pleaded with her to rescue me), trips on alien spacecraft, coded messages on the BBC news, a Maoist conspiracy to put ice-nine in the Thames.

It helped with the verisimilitude that I'd started seeing demons everywhere. Once, I almost shot a particularly plastic-looking girl who'd followed me to an alley behind a bar where I'd been drinking and raving. It was only the smudged mascara that saved her; it turned out she was looking to score some drugs.

Rant as I might, my gibberish was ignored; my stipend arrived on schedule, with a request to investigate an ayahuasca cult in Cornwall. I'd have loved to check it out as I'd been wanting to try ayahuasca for years . . . but I was too busy acting crazy.

Was anybody reading my reports? Had my exquisitely crafted decline even been noticed? I'd hoped my spectacular blow-out would provoke a visit from Mr Big or perhaps even Mrs Big; if it had, my plan was to pretend to mistake them for aliens and patriotically shoot them on the spot. I thought I might manage to give their physical body at least a bad headache. Some of the demon-simulacra might be operating against their will, but I was certain that excuse did not apply to Mr or Mrs Big. They were evil humans, using their psychic skills for evil ends and I'd kill them if I could; failing that, I'd do my best to hurt them.

But when after two weeks of the most ridiculous delirium no one had paid any heed, I began to wonder whether all the business of assignments and reports and stipends was merely a way to keep me on a tether, tied to them by my own fear. Nevertheless, I'd set in motion the script of my descent into madness; I would act it out.

I spent my last day in London writing a series of unhinged missives to agent and editor, family and friends, telling them I'd had enough of it all and was taking myself off to a detox clinic in Maine/a yoga ashram in Rishikesh/a private sanatorium in Oslo/a salt-bath cure in the Yucatán/a Buddhist monastery in Ceylon/the Peace Corps in Mali and a few others I can't remember.

I would take with me only my most precious possessions – those related to Luce. I packed up all the rest of my stuff and took it to my parents' house – or, I should say, my brother's.

He'd turfed dear old Mum and Dad out of the Redington Road house; they'd retired to a cottage in Hampshire. I chose a time when he'd be at work and Cindy home alone with their ghastly baby. I told her it was Neil's idea that I should use the attic to store my things.

My plan was to travel on my own passport at random for some weeks, making every effort to elude any followers without appearing to do so. When I was sure I'd evaded pursuit I would vanish, re-emerge under my new identity and head straight for New York, where I knew it would be easy to lose myself and stay lost.

I'd already begun to picture all the ways in which the new me would be an improvement on the one I was leaving behind. To get away from the demons of the NOHRM was also, in my mind, to get away from death and disillusionment, guilt and remorse. Without such grim impediments, I imagined my new life stood a good chance of being a better and a happier one. I was still young enough to think these things can be shed like an ill-fitting overcoat.

I set out on this adventure on a bright morning only to find the green van waiting at the kerb. Mr Big emerged, envelope in hand. I felt for my gun, but I'd got rid of it – airports had begun to install metal detectors. Now that I understood what he was, the usual sensation of fear, though distinctive as ever, had less of a hold on me. I studied him with curiosity, wondering whether his astral form resembled his physical.

'Do you really look like that?' I asked.

He gave me his dead-fish stare.

'Like a dead fish, I mean.'

He proffered the envelope; I took it. 'Now run back to Mummy,' I said, and made a shooing motion. He got into the green van and it drove off. If one can't shoot somebody, it's gratifying at least to be extremely rude.

I opened the envelope. It contained fifty pounds and a typed note. The note said: 'Take some time off.' Although it was somewhat deflating to be ordered to do what I was about to do anyway, I proceeded with my plan, stopping only at Ahmet's café in Goodge Street to stuff the money into the Palestinians' box.

Now.

I'm in Piccadilly Arcade buying patchouli eau de cologne. I thought I'd be one of the few succumbing to nostalgia for that fragrance, but the assistant at this charming Florentine chemist tells me it's quite popular with the young, though also with people of a certain age. Next door I buy a fringed paisley silk scarf that reminds me of one I had in 1965. More and more I find that I'm attracted to things purely because they remind me of things I once had.

As I leave the shop I'm nearly knocked over by a tall, stooped old man in a baggy tweed suit, thick and heavy and altogether unsuited to summer in town. Grouse-shooting on a wintry moor, more like. He's hurrying along, sweating profusely, muttering to himself, intent on an apparently fruitless search through his numerous pockets.

'Eh?' he says. 'Eh? Oh, it's you, is it? Just who I wanted to see.' He seizes my arm with a veiny old hand and drags me along. Good God, it's Ambrose. The same round specs balance on the same thin nose, though his hair is now sparse and greasy grey. Its meagre locks dribble over his shoulders like limp noodles but his grip is very firm indeed.

'Come and have lunch at my club,' he says. 'I'll tell you all about it there.'

'All about what?' I ask, but he's not listening. He talks non-stop throughout the short walk to St James's Square and seems to be under the impression that we're continuing a conversation we left off only yesterday. It occurs to me that he thinks I'm someone else but no, he calls me by name several times. He rambles on about repairs to his palace, the difficulty of getting a certain brand of socks he likes. It sounds almost normal, but . . . not quite. His eyes are too bright and a white crust is accruing in the corners of his mouth. His articulation is a bit odd and I suspect that the continuous side-to-side workings of his jaw indicate ill-fitting dentures.

I note, as we enter, that the club steward gives us a curious look, but he escorts us to the grand dining room with perfect courtesy. Pausing in his monologue only long enough to order roast duck and a bottle of Malvern water (I second the duck, but request Pinot Noir), Ambrose takes off on the subject of the forgeries that are surreptitiously being substituted for his Titians and Rembrandts with the connivance of someone I'm guessing is his butler or valet, a loathsome creature called Malingruber or Malingerer or something like that, who seems perversely bent upon thwarting the wishes of his lord at every opportunity.

'But,' Ambrose's voice drops to a whisper and he leans across the table, 'I have spoken to the Secret Masters about him and they have given me every reason to believe that . . . steps will be taken to correct the situation. He is an aberration in the divine unfolding of the plan. And aberrations must be . . .' he glares about him '. . . squashed.' He brings his fist down upon the table so hard that the cutlery jumps and everyone looks our way.

The steward, a man of monumental dignity, approaches from the doorway behind Ambrose. 'There is a telephone call for you, my lord. If you would care to follow me?'

'You can't fool me with that old trick,' Ambrose says, spitting a little. He sits up straight and attempts a basilisk stare, though the effect is somewhat marred by the unceasing activity of his jaws.

The steward makes a small bow, giving me the briefest of glances that nevertheless manages to combine appraisal, sympathy and warning. I reply with my most affable smile. He withdraws to the doorway where he has a whispered conversation with two men. The younger one, with an audible sigh, shrugs off the older one's restraining hand and strides briskly up to our table. A curt nod to me indicates that I'm of no importance in this matter.

'Father,' he says to Ambrose, 'I must ask you to come home with me.'

'Bugger off, you putrid little dickhead,' says Ambrose, very loudly. 'You're no son of mine. Your syphilitic whore of a mother fucked a blue-based baboon and you came out. Nothing to do with me.' The entire room winces as one, except for me. I can't resist a grin. Hadn't I just been longing for a serious nutter?

'Now, now, Father.' The son laughs ingratiatingly.

'What an amusing old dear you are. You know you're not well.' Then he makes the mistake of taking Ambrose's arm and trying to lift him from his chair.

Ambrose resists with surprising vigour for a man of his age. His son beckons helplessly to the older chap, who'd remained at the door. 'See, Father, here comes Dr Malgrowski. We'll let him help us, won't we?'

Dr Malgrowski approaches Ambrose from behind. His right hand slides into his pocket and he withdraws a syringe, flips off the cap and makes a quick lunge, aiming for the shoulder. With a howl of rage, Ambrose fends him off and struggles to his feet, overturning the chair.

'To me! To me!' he cries. 'Masters, send forth the legions!' His voice rises to a piercing shriek; everyone clasps their ears and recoils. Ambrose seems to grow in stature. When he points his right hand at his son in a powerful gesture of condemnation I can almost imagine a bolt of lightning flying from his fingertips. 'Adonai!' he shouts. 'Agla!' He really has quite a voice on him. 'Raphael, Gabriel, Michael, Auriel, mighty archangels, protect me!'

He turns and makes a dash for the high windows overlooking St James's Square, clearly believing he's going to leap through and escape in a shower of glass and glory. Unfortunately, the window is triple-glazed. He bounces off, knocking himself out, and is carried away.

Peace and decorum return. The diners resume their lunch; the noise of conversation, slightly elevated for a few minutes, soon recedes to its usual dim murmur. I finish my roast duck and the Pinot Noir but decline the steward's offer of a post-prandial brandy with my *café filtre*.

23

The Thread

§&.

Dream Turned Nightmare. A Writer in New York.
Aleatory Rambles. Eleven Broome Street. The Waiting
Room. Three Chambers. A Proper Head-fuck. The
Police Raid. Escape on Foot. A Cause Célèbre.
Who Is the Artist? The Demon on the Train.

New York, May 1972

In the dream I'm following the thread, eternally traversing a
dark place between memory and hope . . . and then I lose the
thread, or it breaks – that varies from night to night. But the
fear and despair that overwhelm me are the same every time,
and the sense of terrible aloneness. My companions have disappeared and I'm afraid. I'm afraid that my friends have all been
killed, I'm afraid I'm about to stumble into a bottomless pit, I'm
even afraid of the dark I used to love so much. I hear footsteps
behind me, off to the left. No, the right. Maybe there's more
than one. I fumble for my gun, but I'm shaking so much I drop
it. I kneel down and grope for it desperately. My terror grows
into a silent scream that fills my mind, but I'm too paralysed
with fear to let it out. I huddle on the stony floor and make

myself as small as possible. They're getting closer, they're near, they're here . . .

I woke in a cold sweat, as usual. Ever since I'd fled England, the Dream of the Cavern had taken this new, disturbing form. I'd tried alcohol, Valium, Librium, even on occasion heroin, but they didn't help. I might have left Mr and Mrs Big behind in London, but I had the awful feeling that they were following me in the astral land of dream. Nor was my waking life immune from the suspicion that I was being watched, though the demons I saw almost always turned out to be just plastic-looking people. I say almost, because I'm fairly sure that on several occasions someone whom I'd identified as a potential simulacrum inexplicably vanished as I approached.

Scalding hot shower, black coffee with a shot of brandy, a line of coke and a joint: my morning routine served to shut the nightmare up in a box for the day. I kept it there by the self-denying yet also nobly self-asserting act of pounding the typewriter. I was still the Scribe, damn it. For my bread and butter, I wrote *Night Eye* books, reviews, essays and criticism. For my soul, I wrote short stories, novels and plays. The thread to Luce had slipped from my fingers, but the relentless rat-a-tat of words across the page kept me sane.

I'd been based in New York for four years and had the anonymous life down to a fine art. I corresponded via post-office boxes and lived in furnished sublets. I paid the rent up front, in cash, staying at each place for only a few months, then decamping with no forwarding address. New York was the kind of town in which you could do that. My current abode, of which I was rather fond, was a top-floor railroad flat on 5th Street in the East Village above a shop that sold antique kimonos, which it had become my habit to wear around the house. Because of what follows, it's worthwhile mentioning that the shop had in its window a painting of a misty Japanese mountain-scape; the owner, a tiny, round lady named Mitsuko, said it depicted an area close to where she had been born, near a town called Koya. The scene had a peculiar fascination for me (it was why I'd taken the flat); several times I tried to buy it from her, raising my offer each time, but she wouldn't sell.

Next door to Mitsuko was an excellent Indian restaurant which supplied my meals via a bucket and pulley arrangement to my fire escape. Drugs were delivered by Angel, my friendly neighbourhood dealer. I'd acquired a sweet little gun (a Vest Pocket Colt) and another US passport in a different false name for ease of exit, should exit be required at short notice. I was determined that the demons would never again catch me unprepared.

If sometimes I felt like a bad actor, my casually constructed life the most unconvincing of scripts . . . well, who doesn't?

When I'd first come to the city I'd passed the nights in bars and clubs, but these days I just wandered the dense, intense, fervently seething work of art that is New York: north, south, east and west, streets and avenues, tunnels, bridges and back alleys, Manhattan, Brooklyn, Queens, up to the Bronx and out on the ferry to Staten Island. The city was a vast, self-generating treasure hunt that spread and spread, coiled back on itself, concealed and revealed itself in layers of stone and steel, brick and glass, glitter and trash. Willingly seduced, I followed wherever it beckoned; this approach led me to some very interesting places.

Around dawn I'd make my way home and fall into bed. Then, if I was lucky, a few hours of oblivion before being awakened by the nightmare. I spent the day writing about the previous night's adventures – fact and fiction – then sallied forth again in search of more.

It was on one of these aleatory rambles, on a warm night in May 1972, that I came upon a queue of people outside an unmarked doorway at eleven Broome Street, near the East River.

390

It was an area of warehouses and small factories, abandoned tenements and empty lots – chronically ill lit, potholed, all but deserted in daytime and at night positively sepulchral. Lately I'd found myself strangely drawn to this remote fringe of Manhattan, which seemed to me so liminal as to border on another world. I liked to stroll the tarry old piers under the Williamsburg Bridge, whose tall pillars and soot-crusted iron girders loomed like a cathedral built by a race of giant machines. The traffic flowed overhead, a purring, pulsing rhythm that merged with the liquid rushing of the river. The dark water slipped by, drawing the myriad lights into swirling star-wheels; it had a mesmeric effect that was – if I was in the right mood – better than any drug.

I asked a man what he was queuing for. He wasn't sure if it was a bar or a club or a happening, an art exhibit or a multi-media performance piece, but he'd heard it was amazing. I joined the queue and learned that the venue had opened only the previous night; some people were back for a second visit. The ones who'd been before refused to describe it; they just smiled and said, 'You'll see.'

No one knew what the place was called. That was not so unusual; idiosyncratic little places were springing up all over. Flagrantly secret, nameless and ephemeral, private yet open to anyone who could find them, they cultivated their esoteric themes and acquired their devoted clientele. Eventually they'd have to have a nickname, which became a name, and then everyone came, and the ultra-cool moved on to the next, nameless place.

People were going in and coming out at a steady rate. Most of those leaving seemed bemused, perhaps a trifle stunned. Many were smiling. A few were so consumed with laughter they could barely walk; some were quietly weeping. Several immediately took places at the end of the queue.

After about half an hour I reached the door. I entered a plain, white-walled space with three further doors, each apparently leading to a different room. The casual chatter of the queue gave way to nervous giggles and whispers. The room held no clue as to what lay ahead. Unfurnished and unadorned, it was a blank canvas of a space, a stage set designed to induce a sense of ambiguity, uncertainty, expectation – a surrealist's *Let's Make A Deal*, perhaps, where you never learn what's behind the doors, or the front parlour of a Dadaist brothel. A pleasant-looking middle-aged couple served juice and cookies, conducted people to one or another room as it became free and helped some who seemed reluctant to leave.

A chap who'd been a few places ahead of me in the queue emerged from one of the rooms looking bewildered. 'You told me it would only take ten minutes,' he said to the man who'd shown him in.

'It did.'

'But you left me in there for hours.'

'No, we didn't. You entered at ten forty-five and it is now . . . ten fifty-eight.'

The fellow glanced at his watch, frowned and lifted it to his ear, shrugged, said, 'Wow,' laughed and left.

That was the moment I realised I'd found the thread again. The surge of excitement and desire made my knees go weak and I had to tell myself to breathe calmly. Luce was near, or at least a new work of her art. I readied myself joyfully for a proper head-fuck.

When my turn came I was shown into a small, black-painted space, empty but for a comfortable chair facing a large TV screen set into the wall. A pair of headphones on the chair bore a sign saying 'Put Me On'. Next to the chair was a switch marked 'Start'. I sat, donned headphones and flicked the switch.

The memory of what happened fragmented and faded almost at once, maybe because it was so rudely interrupted. This is what remains, written in haste and confusion when I returned home that night, bruised and bloody.

Colours seem to travel forwards and back. Dots and splashes of green float on a red ground, then reverse, become red marks on a green ground. After-images dance with their twin-opposites. A swirl of petals or snow, hovering shapes that fly out at me, then recede. Snatches of melody, vaguely familiar. Rhythms that shift and flow on the border of hearing.

A feeling of being pulled two ways at once. The effort of trying to figure out what's going on makes me queasy so I give up, and immediately get a peculiar though not unpleasant sucking sensation, like being stretched out into a long, slender tube, then whoosh! Falling – or rising? Hard to tell – like Alice down or up the rabbit hole. Geometric shapes, kaleidoscope stars, melting rainbows. It's a painting of Luce's become a living world. Sounds cascading, a crystal waterfall. Images of people, too fast to see. Karen, Fergus, Greyling and many more, fluttering by like lantern slides. Is this Luce's life, or mine? I emerge into an open space with nothing but light all around me. A melting, burning sensation . . . I can only describe it as love, but it's like no human love I ever knew. And yet it's so familiar. I've known this feeling, I've known this Luce, somewhere beyond the marrow of my bones.

The light begins to resolve into sensory realities: the fragrance of roses, a flash of peacock iridescence, a writhe of sinuous motion like a snake in water. A doorway to a garden, hot sun, bright flowers. I step towards it and it changes. It's a lake of black water below a house with glowing windows; it's a church with hundreds of candles burning; it's a vista of high, snow-covered mountains; it's a desert at midnight. Gravity tugs at my body, colours and sounds coalesce: the cool night air, the diamond sky, the smell of the desert. Luce is there, waiting for me. She reaches out her hand, she smiles, she says . . .

❀

393

The interruption was sudden and violent; it felt like the universe had exploded. My mind was brutally wrenched from wherever it had been; my body, abruptly reinhabited, was thrown against the wall. Steel-toed boots kicked me, truncheons battered my head and arms. The room was full of police.

I was hauled out to the waiting room and herded together with the occupants of the other rooms, the people who'd been in the queue, the middle-aged couple. We were being frisked, read our rights and then pushed towards the door, through which I glimpsed a police van, rear doors open, waiting at the kerb. Although not functioning at my absolute best, I knew that submitting to this programme would not be a good idea. I was in the country on a false passport and carried an unlicensed gun. There were drugs in my flat. Animal mind took over, did a quick assessment of numbers, proximities and distances, retrieved a map of the neighbourhood from my memory, chose its moment, released adrenalin like a bolt of electricity. I kicked one cop in the balls, another in the knee and ran like fuck. I ducked into an alley, flung myself over a fence into the next street, sprinted down another alley, skidded around the corner and dived into the shadows under the bridge. My lungs were on fire and my blood was pounding so hard I thought I was going to have a heart attack. I rested there until I was sure no one had followed me, then made my way home.

The next day, in hat, wig and sunglasses, I got a taxi and directed the cabbie to drive past the place. The street was cordoned off; several buildings, including the one I'd been in, had burned in the night.

The event as reported in the press bore little resemblance to what I'd witnessed. The authorities said that the fire had started first. When the emergency services arrived, they'd discovered a drug den/brothel/gang headquarters. People were injured as they attempted to escape the fire, but all were rescued and several had been booked for petty offences, such as drug possession and resisting arrest. The middle-aged couple, identified as Doug and Elaine Portman, had been arrested on charges of racketeering. It was hinted that they were major figures in the criminal underworld, who'd been under surveillance for some time.

But they had picked on the wrong people. The Portmans became a *cause célèbre*. Civil liberties had been egregiously violated and lawyers queued to take on the case. Three weeks after their arrest the Portmans, who'd been released on a very high bail, held a news conference. A rumour circulated that the police were preparing a new story – the criminal enterprise had actually been in an adjacent building, the fracas having regrettably spilled over into the Portmans' perfectly respectable premises in the confusion of the fire. It did not matter; I knew they'd achieved their objective: the destruction of Luce's art. I wondered how they'd found it, but they must have numerous channels of information – agents, watchers and followers on the physical plane but perhaps also on the astral. Word of the extraordinary doings at eleven Broome Street had spread fast among the night-trippers of Manhattan; I imagined that something with such a powerful effect on people's minds would blaze on the astral plane like a beacon.

The Portmans, looking decidedly unbowed, sat flanked by lawyers and patiently took questions about the arrest, their treatment by the police, the plans for their defence.

I finally got my turn. 'Who is the artist?'

Their lawyers replied that Mr and Mrs Portman were under no obligation to disclose that information. Their manner suggested that the question had arisen before.

The press conference ended without interesting revelations. I was across the street, buying a pretzel, when I saw the Portmans slip out of the service entrance of the building. I didn't want to harass them but longed for a chance to ask some questions in private, so I followed. If they stop somewhere for a coffee, I thought, I'll say hello and try my luck.

I soon became aware that I was not the only one following them. The pavements were thronged, but the same trim, blonde woman, wearing a dark blue topcoat and grey trousers, was always behind them as they walked along 48th Street, turned down Madison Avenue, west on 44th Street, south on Fifth Avenue, west on 40th, south on Sixth, west on 35th. As I kept pace with them, I became aware of waves of evil washing off that well-groomed, neatly dressed figure. From time to time I caught a glimpse of an expressionless face with blank, staring eyes. One time, a light changed in front of me and I was forced to stand for several seconds exactly where she had stood. It made my skin crawl. Why was she following the Portmans? Was she going to kill them? Did she believe they would lead to Luce? My hand felt instinctively for the warm, reassuring solidity of the little gun in my pocket.

Our straggling procession entered Penn Station and followed the Portmans onto a train on the Long Island Line. I knew this journey well, having spent many summer weekends with friends in the Hamptons. The train was moderately full and I took a seat some distance behind the demon, who sat nine or ten rows behind the Portmans. I would wait, and watch, and if the opportunity presented itself, I was determined to shoot her. When the conductor came around I bought a ticket to Montauk, the furthest station on the line.

For three hours we rolled along. The other passengers gradually left the train, and by the time we passed East Hampton we four were the only people in the carriage. Night had fallen and we rattled through darkness illuminated only by our own distorted reflections in the grimy windows.

I needed a pee, and knew from previous experience that there was a toilet at the far end of the carriage behind us, the last one.

When the train left Amagansett, the station before Montauk, I slipped out of my seat and made my way there. The last carriage was entirely deserted.

I was washing my hands when the fear came. The demon must have followed me, and I doubted she needed to use the toilet. The only possible reason was to kill me, to get me out of the way.

I didn't think a great deal about what I was going to do; in fact, it felt like I was observing the scene from a distance while an actor in my body played the part that had been written. I had that sense one gets when watching a film – one doesn't know exactly what's going to happen, but it's certain that something will. And when it does, it will seem inevitable.

My gun was in my hand as I slid the bolt. I opened the door fast, took one look at that blank face, pointed the gun at her chest and pulled the trigger. She collapsed to the floor. The report of the gun had sounded awfully loud to me, and I could only hope it had been masked by the clank and clatter of the train. I discovered that I was shaking and sank into a seat, keeping my eye on the body. Within a minute (though it seemed like an hour, during which the most horrible feeling came over me that I'd been mistaken all along and had murdered an innocent bystander) the simulacrum faded away, becoming oddly granu-lated in appearance before vanishing altogether.

I recovered my bullet from the floor and smoked a cigarette to calm my nerves. I seemed to have become a soldier in Greyling's war – I hoped he'd be proud of me. The thought of Greyling reminded me of tea. What I longed for, even more at that moment than I longed for Luce, was a cup of tea, but there was no tea to be had.

The train pulled into Montauk station. I hurried after the Portmans and caught up with them in the parking lot. 'Excuse me . . .' I called.

They turned back. 'I recognise you,' Mr Portman said. 'From the press conference. Have you been following us?'

'Er, yes, I have.'

'Why?'

To protect you from evil, I thought. 'To ask for an interview,' I said, introducing myself. 'I'm writing a book about the artist who created the videos at eleven Broome Street – and many other works of art in various media. I've been making a record of . . . this artist's life and work for many years.'

'You're English,' Mrs Portman said.

'Yes.'

'Are you the one he calls the Scribe?'

'Yes, I am.'

'He said we might hear from you.'

The most exquisite shiver ran through me. Had Luce known I would find the show at eleven Broome Street, and that I'd track down the Portmans . . . had he anticipated this very moment? Could he sense it now, that cosmic click when imagined future becomes realised present? I felt a gentle tug on the thread that linked us as it made a stitch in folded spacetime. *Hello*, I whispered silently, and . . . *thank you.*

'You were at the gallery when the police came,' Mrs Portman said. 'You'd just gone in.'

'Yes.'

'You were the one who kicked the policeman and got away.'

'That was me.'

'We should have done that, honey.'

Mr Portman laughed. 'Next time we will.'

'Come and see us tomorrow,' Mrs Portman said. 'Tonight we're too tired to talk.'

They gave me directions to their house, then got into their car and drove off with a friendly wave. I found a room at a B&B.

24

Resurrection

&

Doug and Elaine Portman's Story. Tragedy on the
Mountainside. Carrying a Corpse. He Touched Her.
Belief Is Bullshit. Cause and Effect.
Have You Ever Wondered?

Montauk, May 1972

The next morning, following the Portmans' directions, I walked
east on the wide, empty beach, enjoying the sunshine, the
tang of sea air, the refreshing absence of humanity. The house
was about half a mile east of the village. Tucked among the high,
sheltering dunes, it was modest in size, a traditional cottage of
weathered shingles, with a small modern extension and a deck
that looked out to sea.

Mr and Mrs Portman greeted me warmly and invited me in.
Elaine ('Oh, you English. Why don't you drop all that Mr and
Mrs stuff?') made a pot of coffee and we sat at the long kitchen
table. The house was a comfortable blend of old and new, with
whitewashed beams and sliding glass doors framing the mutable
vista of sand, sea and sky. A convoluted piece of driftwood hung
on the wall above the stone fireplace and a line of grey pebbles

399

wandered along the mantel, whose only other ornament was a black-and-white photograph of a dark-haired girl with pale eyes. She looked vaguely familiar and I felt at once that I liked her, but I couldn't recall where I might have met her.

As Doug polished his horn-rimmed glasses, I could sense the ordering of his thoughts: careful and methodical, he wanted to present things accurately. I guessed – correctly, as it turned out – that he was a lawyer. He wore that uniform of the American upper-middle-class at leisure: cashmere V-neck sweater over button-down shirt, chinos, deck shoes. About sixty, his face was lined, his hair mostly grey, but there was a lightness in his eyes and a youthful timbre to his voice.

Elaine sat at his side. A wedge of bright sun fell across her hands as she took an orange from a blue ceramic bowl and peeled it expertly, the skin coiling away in a single thick ribbon. She divided the fruit into segments and handed them around. Perhaps ten years younger than her husband, she looked rather chic, topping her chinos with a silk blouse and the ubiquitous cashmere, in her case a cardigan. Their presence in that run-down district on the Lower East Side seemed more and more incongruous.

When I asked how they had come to be involved, Doug explained that they'd met Luce (whom they knew as Peter Lucian) in Japan the previous year. 'It was February, around the time of our daughter Rachel's twenty-fourth birthday.' His eyes flicked to the photograph on the mantel. 'She was doing a PhD in Japanese literature at Tokyo University and had just begun her dissertation. We'd come to Japan to visit her.'

'We were hiking in the mountains near Koya,' Elaine said.

Koya? Was Luce the source of my inexplicable affinity for the landscape in Mitsuko's shop window? The thread twitched again, as a current of silent laughter passed along it.

'It's beautiful country,' Doug was saying, 'quite wild, and at that time of year there were few tourists about. It was late in the day and we were high up on a steep trail when we were caught in a sudden downpour. Rachel started having an asthma attack. Of course she had her inhaler . . .'

'It was in her backpack, so we got it off her and opened it . . .'

'I couldn't find the damn thing, and . . .'

'I started looking in my pack, thinking maybe I'd put it in there.'

'But I was sure it was in Rachel's, so I emptied it out to see . . .'

'Right onto the path, which was so slippery and uneven . . .'

'Rachel was coughing and wheezing, her eyes were bugging out – I was desperate.'

'You dumped it out . . .'

'It fell out . . .'

'It fell out and down the cliff and disappeared into the ravine.' Elaine looked at her husband fondly. 'You always were such a klutz.'

'I nearly killed myself going after it. It was terrifying.'

'He's afraid of heights,' Elaine said. 'He was so brave.'

'Thank you, darling. But I never, never want to go through anything like that again.'

'Me neither.'

There was a pause. 'When I came back,' Doug said at last, 'having almost broken my neck and not found the damn thing, Rachel was dead.'

'I'd been doing mouth-to-mouth, CPR, everything.'

'We didn't know what to do.'

'I just wanted to hold her,' Elaine said. 'As though I could freeze time, reverse it. And I was praying. Silently, because *he*,' she gave her husband a gentle poke in the ribs, 'pooh-poohed that stuff. But I was remembering prayers I'd not heard since childhood, my Russian grandfather muttering in Hebrew – all jumbled up, I'm sure. But sincere. So, so sincere.'

401

Doug cleared his throat. 'We called for help; no one heard. We thought surely someone would come by, but no one did. Eventually we decided we had to get down the mountain somehow.'

'You decided. I would have stayed there all night. I'd still be there now.' Elaine gathered up the long curl of orange peel and remade it into a sphere, which she cradled in her hands.

'The track was steep and wet and dark. Rachel's body was very heavy. After a while I knew I couldn't carry her much further. Elaine heard the wind chimes first. Then we saw a gate and a path. It led to a little cabin by a waterfall, with windows glowing in the dark. The place looked so rustic, I didn't think they'd have a phone, but maybe they'd know where the nearest one was. A man in a kimono answered the door and greeted us with the usual deep bow. Everything about him was so Japanese that at first I assumed – because of his almost-white hair – that he was an old Japanese man. But when the light fell on his face I saw he was young, Caucasian . . .'

'That's beside the point. We showed up at his door – desperate and bedraggled, bearing a corpse.'

'So the point is that he was completely unfazed. He spoke to us in English – with an English accent like yours – and told me to lay Rachel on the floor.'

'I started to cry and I couldn't stop,' Elaine said. 'The sight of her body, lying there . . .'

'I was trying to explain what had happened. Then I turned away to comfort you, and when I looked up again he was sitting by Rachel. He just touched her once. On her forehead.'

'Oh God, it still makes me . . . I can't put it in words. Excuse me.' Elaine got up and left the room. The orange peel, abandoned on the table, briefly retained its shape, then collapsed gently.

Doug rearranged his cup and spoon. 'Rachel had been dead for hours. She was stone cold, her lips were blue, her face was grey. Rigor mortis was beginning. I should know – I carried her. She was not asleep, not unconscious – she was dead. And then she wasn't. She sat up, the colour rushed into her face, she gasped a couple of times, looked at him and started laughing. We couldn't believe what we were seeing. The feeling was indescribable. It still is.' He stood abruptly. 'Would you like to go for a walk?'

We set off along the beach. There was not another soul in sight and only an occasional house among the dunes. The sun shone strongly, sparkling on the cold blue water of the Atlantic. Flecks of spindrift blew from the white-caps and tumbled across the sand.

'As you can imagine,' Doug said, 'we don't often speak of what happened. Besides the fact that it's upsetting, who would believe it? We did try telling one or two people but to put it politely – and they did – they thought we were suffering from delusions. No matter what we said, they remained convinced that panic had made us incapable of reliable observation, either about Rachel's true condition or the amount of time that passed.'

'So you believe Peter Lucian brought Rachel back to life?'

'We took her to a doctor the next day. She was in perfect health. He found no trace of asthma; an X-ray revealed no lung damage. Not only did she come back to life, but a lifelong ailment vanished. So, do I believe? Let me tell you, belief is bullshit. Belief is what people have when they can't bear not knowing. I don't have belief. I have a rational mind, and it tells me that Rachel was dead and then, later, she was alive. That is not the usual order of events. We live in a world of cause and effect: cause, by definition, must precede effect. What caused the change from death to life? Peter Lucian, that's what. Beyond that, I don't know. Do you know? Do you understand him? I mean, who are you, anyway? No offence meant.'

403

'None taken. I'm just a writer. But no, I wouldn't exactly say I understand him. I hope to, eventually.'

He laughed. 'Good luck. All my life I hated not knowing what was going on. I built a brilliant career in the law by being the one who understood things better than anyone else. I made things make sense. *Made* them. Forced them to, by will and intelligence and most of all by the application of reason. Implacable, indomitable reason. And now I find that at the centre of my life,' he tapped his chest, 'there's an impenetrable mystery. So I chucked it all in. End of brilliant career. When we got back to New York I simply couldn't do it any more. All those mergers and acquisitions, all the things that had seemed both real and important suddenly were neither. These days I haven't got a clue about anything, and I've never been happier.'

We walked in silence for some time, a silence pervaded by Doug's quiet, bemused happiness. Seagulls swerved through the air, their cries floating over the wash and suck of the surf. In the distance a sailboat danced across the waves, bright red spinnaker swollen with wind.

The cabin Doug and Elaine had come to was, they'd learned, one of a number of guesthouses in an artists' and writers' colony on the estate of a wealthy and reclusive old man. Rachel had refused to return to Tokyo, insisting that she wanted to stay in the mountains with Peter Lucian.

'From the first she treated him as an old friend and acted as though the entire purpose of our trip to Koya had been to bring her there. We couldn't argue with that, could we? We were still in a state of shock. Peter didn't seem to mind, so arrangements were made for Rachel to stay in another cabin on the estate while she wrote her dissertation.'

Doug, finding his life happily shattered, had taken early retirement from his law firm and now worked pro bono for a charity. Elaine was training to become a psychotherapist. They divided their time between their city flat on Riverside Drive and the Montauk house. Three months ago Rachel and Peter had come to New York, rented the Broome Street place and set about creating the videos. Doug had been pleased to put his DIY skills to use building the little viewing rooms.

So Luce had been at Broome Street for the last three months! Now I knew why I'd been drawn time and time again to that remote district by the East River.

'The place was meant to run itself,' Doug said, 'but we liked meeting the people so much we spent a lot of time there.'

'Why do you think the police raided the place and arrested you?'

'They made a mistake, that's all. I'm sure they'll drop the charges.'

'Why wouldn't you reveal who the artist was?'

'He asked us not to. He wanted to remain anonymous. I must say, the police were curious as well, but it was none of their business.'

'Especially since they were at the wrong place.'

'Well, yes. Exactly.'

'So what's he like, Peter Lucian?' I asked.

Doug gave me a curious glance. 'I thought you knew him.'

'I do and I don't. I've found that everybody knows him differently.'

'Well, I'm sure you know he's a very private person. We didn't see that much of him. I don't think he ever went out. We asked them to dinner many times, but only Rachel came. Peter just worked. Every time we were there he was working on the videos. He'd pop down from his studio, have a cup of tea with us – special tea that he had sent from England, PG Tips it was called – then make his excuses and disappear. Elaine wanted to go up there, see what he was doing – she's congenitally nosy – but Rachel told us it was off-limits. She was very

405

protective of Peter, said he needed seclusion in order to do his work.

'I did try to ask him, one time, about what he'd done to . . . make Rachel not dead. I got him alone, cornered him, I guess. It makes me cringe when I remember. Me being all man-to-man, what-have-you-done-to-my-daughter-sir. Except the words never got out of my mouth. I'd manoeuvred him into position, trapped him in the hallway, had my question framed and ready – the language clear and well thought out, so that his answer would have to be unequivocal, legally binding. What an arsehole I was. He just looked at me. He knew exactly what I'd been planning. I think maybe my mouth opened, but no words emerged. I remember noticing that he was taller than I'd realised – you know how slight and slender he appears, but he was eye to eye with me, and I'm nearly six feet. He gave me the sweetest smile and continued up the stairs to his studio.

'Look, I have to ask, have you ever wondered . . . whether Peter Lucian is actually a woman? Elaine thinks the whole idea is absolutely nuts and won't even consider allowing me to raise the subject with Rachel. I mean, obviously at first I was sure he was a man, but there in the hallway – maybe it was a trick of the light. And for an instant I felt . . . well, a feeling, let's say, that I only have for women. Never mind. For Christ's sake don't tell Elaine I said that. It doesn't matter, anyway. After what he did he could be a Martian for all I care. Who knows? Maybe he is.'

Away down the beach an old man stood gazing out to sea while his dog, a big black poodle, gambolled in the surf. As we approached he and Doug greeted each other with a cheery wave.

'Hey, Shep, how's Mephistopheles?' Doug asked.

'All better now, as you see.'

'Mephistopheles hurt his paw a couple of weeks ago, a piece of broken glass,' Doug explained to me.

The dog trotted up; we petted it, then it scampered back into the water.

We strolled on. 'I only saw part of one of the videos,' I said, 'but it was very intense. What do you think the effect was meant to be? What did you and Elaine make of them?'

'What the effect was meant to be? Gosh, I don't know. Just beauty, I think. Is beauty *meant* to have an effect? We loved them. Each piece was different, but they were all beautiful. Like this.' He gestured to sea and sky. 'They were real. They had life. Colour, light, movement, the sense of things always changing, time unfolding . . .' He laughed. 'I don't know where that came from. Sometimes when I think about Peter's work I find words popping into my head.'

'Maybe you should write them down.'

'Oh, I'll leave that to you.'

Conversations with the punters who'd passed through the gallery had led Doug to conclude that people experienced the videos in many different ways. 'Some said it was like an especially vivid, dramatic dream, with characters, settings, a story. Neither Elaine nor I got anything like that . . . or we didn't think we did. For us, as for most people, they were mesmerising, entrancing, but pretty abstract. Images came and went in glimmers and flashes. You never knew what you were seeing, or you'd decide it was something, then it would change, or maybe its background changed so it looked different. Geometric shapes, squiggles, wavy lines, things moving, expanding and contracting, patterns meshing, separating – all to that strange music, which was, for sure, hypnotic. There were suggestions of landscapes, natural forms like trees and flowers, spirals, stars, shapes that suggested people or animals. Nothing definite, or so I thought. But lately I've been getting flashes of memory – at least, they feel like memories – that don't link up with anything I can recall happening in my life. It's like remembering a fragment of dream. Elaine

407

gets this, too. We've concluded that the memories must have their source in Peter's videos.'

My own experience of Luce's art has led me to conclude that the stories, images and sensations it evokes are not to be found in the material artefact – which functions, like LSD, merely as a gateway – but are created by the perceiver's interaction with the art. They do not have objective existence but are no less potent for that: their intense subjectivity is what makes them so powerful. I asked Doug if he'd ever had any unusual feelings or sensations watching the videos.

'Oh, yeah. I sure did. It was a very emotional experience. I don't know how, but even the abstract images – with the music, of course – aroused strong emotions, complex feelings. Happy emotions and sad ones and everything in between. They made me realise that *everything* means so much more than we think it does. A lot of people came out of the rooms really wrung out emotionally. But that's not all. There was another sort of feeling, not an emotion, that was unique to the videos. They gave me a sort of vertigo – not quite dizziness, that would be unpleasant. Tingling, weightlessness, the sense of floating. A little disconcerting at first, but I got to like it quite a lot. Definitely an unusual sensation. Maybe that's what it feels like to take drugs? I wouldn't know, I never have. But I was so struck by the experience that I asked Peter how he'd achieved the effect.'

'What did he say?'

'Do you know, I can't really remember. Which is odd, because I'm usually excellent at recalling exactly what people have said. It was the first time I saw one of the videos. Peter noticed that it had affected me. It pleased him. Come to think of it, I may have been a guinea pig for him – I think I was the first person, other than himself and, I suppose, Rachel, to see it. He was watching for my reaction, and even before I spoke, he knew that it had had the desired effect. So when I gathered my wits, I asked him how he'd done it, how sound and light – because that's all it was – induced, well, whatever they induced. He answered me readily, but I can't remember what he said. I know it seemed a satisfying explanation at the time.' Doug frowned and rubbed his forehead. 'There was something about helical scans, parabolic harmonies, symbiotic frequencies, wave function parameters. Does it mean anything to you? No? Well, it all made sense to me at the time. I was gratified that he'd taken the trouble to be so forthcoming and flattered that he thought I'd understand. But I don't. I don't get it. None of it. But it doesn't matter. You know what? I discovered I can get that floating feeling back any time, just by remembering the images, picturing them in my mind.'

We turned and walked back in silence. A few families had come down to the beach; children played in the surf, their shrieks echoing the gulls' high calls. A tall-masted yacht, sails snapping, was tacking up the coast. I liked Doug Portman's world; it seemed he'd acquired some kind of serenity that enabled him to navigate unperturbed through these seas whose storms and uncertainty brought me so much unease.

I asked if he knew where Peter and Rachel were now. Peter, I learned, had left as soon as the exhibit was up and running. Doug had no idea where he'd gone; he'd simply disappeared. Rachel said he did that all the time, and made nothing of it. She herself had stayed in Montauk for a couple of weeks, then gone back to Japan.

I told Doug my plan was to go to Koya next, to see Rachel. He gave me directions to the artists' colony and we parted on the beach below his house with a warm handshake and a half-hug appropriate to my Englishness and his lawyerliness.

I made my way back to the city. The very strangeness of the Portmans' story was peculiarly comforting to me. Things were returning to reality after a lengthy detour on the unreal plains of normality. Life without Luce, or the quest for Luce – though I cannot say it was exactly dull in most people's sense of that word – had lacked dimension. And I'd felt abandoned – if not by her, then by fate, which I'd imagined had been drawing us together. But now my old life was beckoning. Peter Lucian's video, incomplete though it was, had reached into me like a key, turned a rusty lock. A door was cracking open, showing me the way to go.

As the train trundled through the flat fields of Long Island, I thought about what Doug had said. His view of beauty notwithstanding, I was convinced that Luce's art, in all its forms, was – and still is – intended to have an effect. Although, of course, beauty in any form has an effect – it can soothe the troubled soul, bring peace to the unquiet mind, et cetera, and very grateful I am, too. I've availed myself of those benefices on many occasions. No, I mean that she intended it to affect *certain* people in *certain* ways, and she was fishing for us with her subtle and varied nets. I believe that while some of those who experienced her art got only the beauty: the infusion of wonder, the stimulation of exquisite emotions, the elevation of spirit, the tickling of their finer aesthetic sensibilities, there were and are others whose psychic make-up renders them susceptible to more specific influences.

Luce's art, at Broome Street as in other instances, was designed to induce – if the perceiver was ready – an altered state of consciousness, a trip to other dimensions of self and reality. Doug's description of the floating sensation that he'd experienced had sounded familiar to me. I'd had the same kind of feeling during the video, and it echoed the accounts I'd read of astral or out-of-body experiences. I'd felt distinctly and unpleasantly separate from my body when the police had burst in and kicked it; the complete video, I felt sure, would have returned me gracefully to my physical self.

410

In the space of twenty-four hours I dismantled my gimcrack little New York life, tossed the Colt, regretfully but with heartfelt thanks, into the East River and burned my first forged passport. That identity had come to seem at least as real to me as my former, supposedly real one, though writing fiction had – among other things – undermined any sense I might once have had of identity as an absolute. I felt a certain sadness at the thought of leaving behind for ever the name, the self, the life it represented; I resolved to use it as a character in a story, so as not to extinguish it entirely.

It was at the airport that I sensed, once again, the presence of a demon. I had to assume they knew I'd shot one of their number, though I had no idea how long the effects of that would last. Had I given it a heart attack or only heartburn? Perhaps this was the same one, fully recovered and pissed off. I couldn't spot it among the crowds and had to rely on the increase or decrease of the sensation of evil to tell me of its proximity.

Without a gun I felt hideously vulnerable, but now I knew I was not abandoned; Luce was with me, guiding me. The thread of our connection was alive and humming once again.

I abandoned the flight to Tokyo I'd booked and instead charted a random zigzag of planes, buses and trains that took me, over the course of the next two weeks, from New York to Seattle, Des Moines, Philadelphia, Miami, Tulsa, Minneapolis, Houston and Los Angeles. When I'd gone three days without feeling a demon, I got a flight to Tokyo via Honolulu.

25

Shiro-Kuro

🐌

Rachel Portman's Story. His Wanders. She Has Become a Doorway. The Shrine of Kannon. The Gift of Stones. A Harmonic Plaiting of Brain Waves. Remembering and Forgetting. A Sun, a Son.

Japan, May–June 1972

In the hills above Koya it looked as though little had changed for hundreds of years: the mists, the ancient forests, the tiny villages and quaint dwellings clinging to the slopes. I checked into the same simple, rustic inn where the Portmans had stayed.

The first morning dawned cool and cloudy, but the sun soon broke through. Following Doug's directions, I took the path north into the pinewoods. After spending all day clambering about, I realised I'd taken the wrong turning down at the bottom. I tried to retrace my steps, but ended up on the opposite side of the mountain. It was dusk before I found my way back to the inn.

That night I couldn't sleep. I sat by the window and watched as, some time after midnight, the clouds blew away and the moon was revealed, round and smiling, its watery radiance spreading over the hills. All I'd meant to do was step outside for a while, but something drew me into the pines, where the moonlight swam among the shadows like silver eels. Turning left, right, left, I found the path that led up the ravine. There came a time after the moon set when it was too dark to proceed and I waited, perched on a step cut into the rock, with the sound of a torrent rushing far below. At first light I heard the bamboo wind chimes.

The sky faded to grey; the dense greens of the forest emerged from night lush and dripping with dew. The track rose and turned, cleaving to the side of the mountain. I spotted the narrow gate; entering, I climbed a long, rising arc of shallow steps beside a sibilant brown-black brook.

As I walked up the path, everything I saw I seemed to remember and I knew what each turn would reveal. It was Luce's familiarity that I was feeling; this was a place where she had spent much time. I had the sense of coming home, and with it the assurance of absolute safety. Here I could let down my guard. My heart felt lighter than it had in years, and I found that I was smiling. On the rounded top of a particularly beautiful boulder, all pitted stone and mosses, a small bare spot called to my finger-tips and I touched it lightly as I passed, as if I'd done it a thousand times before. An old man in a patched kimono was sweeping the path. He smiled and bowed. I bowed and smiled back. An arched wooden bridge crossed the stream; the little cabin sat in a glade by a waterfall, bamboo wind chimes at the door.

A woman stood on the veranda; I recognised Rachel from her parents' photograph. She wore a blue kimono, her dark hair fell over her shoulders, and her eyes, which in the photo had been merely pale, were the clearest celadon. My heart gave a little lurch – but was it my own feeling, or Luce's? She welcomed me with a smile, taking my cold hands in her warm ones and drawing me in. I introduced myself and explained how I'd met her parents, et cetera, but from the very first our connection through Luce rendered us so familiar to each other, so at ease, that such formalities were superfluous.

I took off my shoes and we sat on the *tatami*. The room was exactly as I'd pictured it from Doug and Elaine's description: perfectly proportioned, spare and unadorned. I realised that I was sitting where the dead Rachel had been laid by her father.

The living Rachel served tea – proper English tea. And amaretti biscuits.

'Peter's favourites,' she said.

'Is he here?'

She shook her head. 'He's off on a wander.'

I drank tea and ate biscuits. That sip and crunch, those flavours and textures were so incongruous in the bare Japanese room that I started laughing. Rachel joined in at once, as if laughter had been bubbling all along under her skin and now, merrily, came out to play.

I don't think she ever invited me to stay; it was just assumed that I would. A nearby cabin was available, one of thirty scattered about the woods. It was hard to estimate the number of residents since many were reclusive. There were Europeans, Americans and a few Australians as well as Japanese. Some were here to get away from the world or to recover from disasters domestic, artistic or cosmic; others were writers or painters, sculptors, weavers, potters, here to get some serious work done. Quite a little tribe of calligraphers, rather cliquish, determined to maintain ancient skills. No one paid, no one asked permission, no one kept track of anyone. Some had lived here for decades; others stayed a few days, weeks or months. People came and went as they pleased; if you *wanted* to stay, it was right for you to do so. There would be a place for you. If it ceased to be right, you would no longer wish to remain. The place somehow engendered a congruence of desire and what, for want of a better English word, one might call appropriateness.

Conditions were Spartan. There was neither electricity nor indoor plumbing; the cabin was unheated except for a tiny wood-burning stove. Once a day food was delivered in stacked bamboo dishes: rice and vegetables, steamed or raw. I made tea on the wood-burner, bitter green *sencha* from a black iron teapot served in a roughly made cup. An austere pleasure, suited to that austere yet deeply pleasurable place. My notion of a day's visit stretched into two days, a week, two weeks.

The bed was a thin, pillowless futon that at first I'd contemplated with dismay, but I was sleeping better than I had in years. Ever since I'd killed that demon on the train something had shifted in me; the Dream had changed again. I was still alone and still afraid but I no longer cowered on the floor, frozen in panic. I moved through the caverns as stealthily as my pursuers, drawn on by a sense of purpose transmitted, like a pulse, along the slender thread that guided me.

After a couple of days I decided I ought to introduce myself to the owner of the estate, to thank him for his hospitality. I assumed he must live in some grand house, a distance apart from the guesthouses. My early perambulations revealed no such place, so I asked Rachel where to find our patron.

She laughed. 'You see him every day.'

'I do?'

'The old man. He sweeps the paths and tends the grounds in the mornings, then he prepares the food and delivers it. In the afternoons he gathers firewood. His name is Bokumin.'

The next time I saw Bokumin I made an especially deep bow, and thanked him in my awful Japanese. He smiled and bowed exactly as before, so I don't know if he understood me.

The estate included an ancient shrine dedicated to the demi-god Kannon, the Japanese name for the Bodhisattva known as Kuan-Yin in Chinese and Avalokiteshvara in Sanskrit, whose form is at various times male or female, androgynous or neuter.

415

Pilgrims came, wending their way up a narrow track towards the spot, high on the mountainside, where s/he was reputed to have sat for forty days and nights in meditation, causing the sun and moon to stand still.

The shrine was tended by a tiny nun, toothless and infinitely wrinkled, either mute or observing a permanent vow of silence. Several times a day she would pass as I sat by the waterfall, always bringing me a small stone which I saw her pick up from the path. I would give polite thanks and mime appreciation of the stone's wonderful qualities. I was lying; none was discernible. She would watch, expression unreadable, as I pretended to study the stone carefully. I concluded she was dotty, but nonetheless, once I'd accepted the thing and it was in my hands, I found myself compelled to search out the meaning. Did it reside in the particular stone, or was it stones in general to which she wished to draw my attention? Perhaps they represented the Stone of the Philosophers. There was, I knew, an esoteric tradition of Buddhist alchemy – did they have the concept of the Stone that transmutes lead to gold, human to god? Or maybe the stones were meant to represent earth, the corporeal form. Or, since they came from the path, did they represent the soul's path towards enlightenment? Perhaps they were a divination technique, intended to give me insight about my true nature, my destiny, or whether today would be a good or bad day. Then again, maybe they didn't mean anything at all. Maybe each one was a thing in itself, a Kantian *ding an sich*. I tried to look at them that way, but the more closely I looked, the more my mind began to invent meaning – or to imagine it was discovering a pre-existing one. I compared, assessed, made fine discriminations among the stones; I assigned value to colour, shape and individual markings. Before I knew it I'd generated a whole system with its own logic, symbolism, sets of fixed terms and variables.

One morning was different. A single stone wasn't enough; the old nun brought me stones, rocks and pebbles, large ones and small ones, smooth ones and rough ones. No sooner had I accepted one (smile, bow) than she fetched another. A pile grew at my feet, a sense of absurdity grew in my mind. I had the feeling this could go on for ever. At last I said, in my halting Japanese and with firm gestures, that I did not want any more of these stones. She slapped her knees and hooted with laughter. After that I got no more stones from her, just the occasional cackle as she passed.

Pilgrims of a different sort – young, trendy and chatty – came to worship at the (metaphorical) shrine of Hikaru Ishi, a novelist with a maniacally dedicated cult following. Only the Japanese can be truly fanatical about a writer. Hikaru Ishi had, some time in the past (my understanding of Japanese verb tenses was very shaky, and for a long time I had the firm notion that the era was the 1950s), written three short novels, the *Shiro-Kuro* (White-Black) trilogy, while staying at the colony. They'd been published by Bokumin's private press.

How long did it take me to realise that Hikaru Ishi was Peter Lucian? Quite a while, since no one ever told me. Rachel assumed I knew. It was only when I picked up a bit more Japanese that it dawned on me. Hikaru Ishi means light (or shining) stone.

I spent some time with the young fans who found their way to the place where their sacred texts had been written, and tried to understand why they loved the books so much. Given the limitations of language – most had some English, few were anywhere near fluent – I gathered that it wasn't just the story or the characters, it wasn't just that they embodied so perfectly the spirit of the age, the fears and hopes of their generation.

I got an inkling of the nature of their passion when I heard many of them speak of the books as though they were food, or a drug. They read them over and over, sucking juice out of the words, imbibing a reality that – they tried to tell me – was more than words, was an *experience*. What sort of experience? I would ask. Very strange, disorienting, like falling-up-into-the-sky, not-know-if-you-be-here-or-there, turns-your-head-inside-out type of experience. After which, they all said, one never looked at the world in the same way again. In other words, they were typical Lucian head-fucking art.

One of the young fans had not been content merely to suck up his experience like the rest. He was doing a degree in neuro-science and he decided to investigate. Taking encephalograms of people while they were reading the books, he observed unusual brain wave patterns. As near as I could understand him, people were awake and asleep at the same time – some sort of harmonic plaiting of alpha, beta, theta and gamma waves. It sounded a bit like tripping to me. He'd like to research LSD, he said, but unfortunately it was illegal. I told him that had never stopped me, nor should it stop any true scientist.

❧

There was something profoundly and beautifully strange about Rachel Portman. Even if I hadn't known what had happened to her, I would have been drawn to that quality of strangeness. I was reminded of what Giorgio Servadio had described as Lukas's transparency: the perception that through him something else was visible, apprehensible, even approachable. Rachel had been to another land; she had returned and now she was a door, a door that might at any moment open to reveal a distant vista. And through that door I seemed, sometimes, to catch a glimpse of Luce laughing and waving hello.

Rachel, for obvious reasons, was aware of Peter's special abil-ities – at least, some of them. She took them for granted and assumed that I did, too. The impenetrable mystery that had

418

entered the heart of her father's life was, for her, as natural as the air she breathed – though that was, in itself, a miracle.

Since she was the only person I'd ever known or was likely to know who'd come back from the dead, I had to ask her about it, though I didn't want to make her feel that she was some kind of freak who was obliged to exhibit herself. But she wanted very much to tell the story in her own words.

'That asthma attack was the most terrifying experience of my life. I couldn't breathe, my parents were panicking – it was my worst nightmare come true. When my inhaler was lost I knew I was going to die. The agony was so intense.' Her hands made clawing movements at her chest and throat. 'And the fear made it worse, building and building on itself. It was like being sucked into an abyss lined with gnashing teeth, ripping me apart. When I remember it now, it's like remembering a horrible dream.' She shook her head, as though astonished that it could have felt so real at the time.

'But the nightmare suddenly ended. There was a way out, a way I'd never seen.' She made a gesture like a snake slipping through long grass. 'I discovered I could . . . step away. I saw my body lying on the ground. I couldn't understand why my mother was so concerned with it, why she couldn't see that I wasn't in it any more. Sometimes she would look up and I thought she saw me, but she'd always turn back to that vacant corpse and ignore me. She was deaf and blind.

'Then something drew me away, into the forest. It was like I'd never seen a forest before. Everything was alive – trees, stones, the air itself. Sort of pulsing with light, not ordinary light, the kind you see, but a different light that I could smell and taste and hear and touch.

'I came upon a path, or more like a scent trail, you know, like animals follow. A sweet, clear scent like roses. As I followed it I began to hear someone calling me, with so much love in his voice. Then I saw him. He reached out his hand and when I woke up, there he was. I'd never seen him before, but it was like I'd always known him.' She laughed. 'He teases me about my flair for dramatic entrances.'

According to Rachel, Peter Lucian had lived in Japan for most of his life, although he travelled almost constantly: his 'wanders'. For months at a time he simply walked wherever the spirit led him, with no fixed destination in mind. She thought he'd probably covered most of the globe, which chimed with what Wingbow had told me. He would tell her stories about places he'd been and people he'd known, or make up songs about them.

Peter's parents, both now dead, had been English – his father a doctor, his mother an authority on Japanese art. They'd been close friends of Bokumin and when the Second World War broke out they had taken refuge, along with other members of the intellectual and artistic expatriate community, on Bokumin's estate. Peter had been born here. This place, he'd told her, was 'protected'; one of only two – the other was in England.

He spoke several languages fluently but he was most comfortable in Japanese, so it was natural that he should write his three novels in that language. I wondered – still wonder – whether its ideographic qualities enable his meaning to be carried more directly into readers' minds than is possible with a purely alphabetic language. Although they're now available in a dozen languages, the peculiar effects apparently do not survive translation.*

'Every time I read the books in Japanese,' Rachel told me, 'they flip something in my head and I feel like I did after I died, when I woke up out of my body and wandered in the forest.

---

* Takasu Aiko and Linda K. Caraday, 'The Mystery of *Shiro-Kuro*: Neurological Implications of Psychomimetic Literature', *British Journal of Neuroscience*, 58 (1987), p. 304.

They take me right back into that world. When I translate them into English, as I'm trying to do, it doesn't work. I think probably they can't be translated.'

Between wanders, Peter had written a novel a year for three years. When Rachel arrived he'd been working on the last volume of the trilogy. It was published about the time they left for New York. I noted with interest that Luce and I had been writing novels at the same time; perhaps that accounted for the sense I always had that when I was writing fiction, I was as close to Luce as I'd ever been. Well, almost.

I asked about his writing habits – writers always want to know that sort of thing about each other. Rachel said he wrote with a ballpoint pen, in black ink on unlined paper; slowly but without pauses, sipping his English tea and nibbling the occasional amaretti biscuit. He'd write for a few hours, go for a long walk, return and write some more. He sat not at a desk but cross-legged with a board over his knees; he never edited. I found that impossible to believe, but she assured me the pages went straight into a box and he never looked at them.

The *Shiro-Kuro* books tell the story of a pair of twins called Shiro ('White') and Kuro ('Black'). Due to certain attributes of the Japanese language the gender of a character need not be apparent; throughout the novels, one never knows whether Shiro and Kuro are male or female.

They're born in Hiroshima as the bomb falls, killing their mother and father. I'd already encountered this mythic moment in Luce's story, though from the other side, as it were. The persona known as Lou Peterson had been born that same day (in Bethlehem, Pennsylvania) to an American air-force officer involved in the making and deploying of the bomb. Both are tales of birth out of death, but not just any death, and certainly not just any birth. The dividing of the atom (the word means 'indivisible') and the dawning of *L'Age Atomique* represent a physical-world event of such archetypal power that it cuts right through the dimensions. What better occasion for the birth of the avatar of a new aeon?

In the chaotic aftermath of destruction the twins are separated and adopted by different families, far from one another. This was so reminiscent of my childhood fantasy of a lost twin that it gave me a jolt of recognition: the first of many. Although separated in the material world, the twins meet in the land called Ikai. This Shinto term refers to the Otherworld, a dimension inhabited by spirits of all sorts, i.e. the astral plane. For Kuro, however, these encounters are lost in the darkness of night, of dream, of forgetting. Sometimes Kuro is called 'Forgetting', *Wasure*; while Shiro is named 'Remembering', *Omoide*.

It was obvious to me that Shiro's story was based on Luce's life, full of incidents about which I'd heard from diverse sources. There's a character like Greyling, a canny old warrior, and others in whom I recognised Francis, René, Fergus, Karen, Waldo, Wingbow, Thobo Rinpoche and even little Gauri from Kathmandu. The beings that I called demons figure prominently in the narrative, where they're known as Akuryo ('evil spirits'). Evil humans are also not scarce. On the whole, it's a hellish world the twins are born into and through which they must try to find their way.

I recalled the solarised photo on the cover of *L'Age Atomique*, the dark twin and the light one back to back, mirror images of each other. If Shiro was Luce, who was Kuro? It's often read as a parable, Rachel told me, in which Kuro is all of us dim and forgetful humans, almost all of the time. But the queerest feeling came over me as I listened to the story, for it seemed to me that I recognised myself in the person of Kuro. The name echoed my own Obscura, and events in Kuro's life bore an uncanny resemblance to certain events in my own. Like me, Kuro is adopted by an unsympathetic family with a cruel brother. Like me, Kuro follows an eccentric life driven by a passion for a distant figure, is captured by the Akuryo, recruited to work for them and ends up as a double agent. Like me, Kuro becomes a warrior and vanquishes demons.

I asked Rachel if Shiro and Kuro ever meet in the physical world.

'The final book ends ambiguously. Peter says it's up to Kuro to write the last chapter. I think – no, I *know* – love will win in the end. Love must win.'

❧

'I want to tell you about something,' Rachel said to me one afternoon, as we sat in the sun by the waterfall. 'I know you're leaving soon.'

I hadn't told her, but the thought had recently come to me that it was time to return to the world. It wouldn't have surprised me to find, when I did go back out there, that time had passed differently: my two weeks had been two hundred years, or two hours. I'd been trying to recall what fairy tale featured that situation; I knew I'd read it as a child. I'd thought it was a true story, and spent a lot of time looking for doorways to that other world – to any other world.

'I read a lot of fairy tales when I was a kid,' said Rachel, not for the first time linking to my thoughts. I don't think she did it deliberately or even knew she was doing it. I'd grown accustomed to it, and indeed had begun to wonder if it wasn't a more common phenomenon than I'd realised. 'I used to think they were true stories.'

'Me, too.'

'There was one, I can't remember what it was called. It was about a girl who marries a wonderful prince, but never sees him. She has no reason to be unhappy, but her evil step-sisters plant seeds of doubt in her mind and she begins to fear that he's really a monster. So she decides to spy on him.* It wasn't exactly like that, but that's the general idea.

'When I first came here Peter seemed so utterly serene and self-contained, like a still pool that reflected nothing but light and pure air. I imagined that I would just live near that pool for ever. But nothing remains the same and gradually I started to feel that I was here for a purpose. I began to suspect that he knew it, too, but some sort of reticence kept him from simply telling me. Later I understood. He knows his power, and wished me to choose freely.'

She'd been holding a sheaf of paper and now handed this to me. 'Something I wrote . . . about something that happened. Take it, read it, copy it if you like. For the record. And know . . . it's my soul I'm showing you.'

This is what she wrote:

I have to write this down because if I don't I'll think it was a dream. I'm still not sure what I saw. I've suspected for a while that Peter never sleeps. I tried to stay up with him, but never managed. So I began my great deception. I ceased trying to stay up late. I retired early to my cabin, slept for a few hours, then crept back and hid behind a rock, watching his window. I watched every night for a week and though I never saw him go to bed or sleep, he did nothing other than the ordinary things he did every day. He wrote, or played his *koto*, or played with the cat, or just sat.

---

* The story Rachel means goes by various names; in its oldest form, it's the Greek myth of Eros and Psyche ('Love' and 'Soul'), about a god who falls in love with and marries a human girl. He is too beautiful for human eyes to behold, so to protect her, he only meets her in total darkness. Fear and doubt lead her to spy on him with a candle while he sleeps, and she is blinded by his beauty.

He began to notice that I looked tired. Did he know? I have to wonder. How on earth did I ever think I could deceive him?

Then last night – or this morning as it must have been – he came out of his cabin and went up the path towards the shrine. I followed, terrified of making noise. Peter always walks so softly, but I felt like an elephant. Fog rolled up the valley, making everything look like a ghost. I started getting so spooked, I nearly turned back. I should have turned back. Why am I courageous about all the wrong things?

I carried on as long as I could see any kind of a path in front of me, no longer sure if I was still following him or wandering aimlessly. I lost track of time. I began to wonder whether I'd fallen asleep behind my rock and was dreaming all this.

Did he know that I was following? Suddenly it seems impossible that he didn't. Did he know that I was watching? And so what I saw, I didn't see by accident but because he let me see? Because he wanted me to see? Did he lead me there in order to show me? I wish I understood.

It was so quiet, like the whole forest was holding its breath. The mist thinned, the moon shone through and I caught a glimpse of water. It was a small hot spring, hidden in the forest, that I'd never known was there. The pool spread out below me, steam rising.

Peter was standing at the edge. He started to untie his obi and I realised he was going to bathe. I'd never seen him naked. That's when I should have turned away, but I didn't. The steam drifted across and I lost sight of him, then I saw a slender, white-skinned woman wading into the pool. The jealousy I felt shocked me with its intensity. It truly felt like a knife to my heart. And then the steam cleared and the whole area of the pool was revealed and I saw there was only one person there and it was Peter and he was the woman, too, he was both and his beauty – her beauty – hit me like a bolt of lightning and I think I must have cried out. I'd blundered into some great mystery that I had no right to see.

He – she – looked up. Our eyes met and I was filled with shame and remorse for the miserable smallness of my being. I turned and ran.

Later.

He's sleeping now, actually sleeping. Her eyes are closed, his breath rises and falls so softly. I stroke her hair and he doesn't notice. I'll get used to this, somehow. I will have to go on calling her Peter.

He came to me. I asked why he'd brought me back from the dead, which seemed a lot of trouble to go through for someone as useless as me. I was trying to be cold and mature, but it came out as childish and mean. You only did it to see if you could, I said.

Ra-hel, he said. He always says it that way.

I started crying. I don't even know what I was crying about, it wasn't any longer a personal thing of me and him. I was crying for the gaping chasm between us, between everybody. I was crying for my poor human heart, abandoned here in the land of death. I was crying for everyone who longs for something real but finds that again and again, they've pushed it away. I was crying for every poor stupid human being who stumbles blind and deaf through life.

And then he showed me. It's not something I can put into words. He held me, and wiped my tears, then he kissed me and *showed* me. Straight into my mind – images, meaning, feelings, the whole story, all the stories. It lasted only a minute or two but it's still unfolding. I understand, but I can't describe what it is that I understand. It's so wonderful it makes me laugh. And that's the best thing. I'm laughing with him – with her. Right now. All the time.

I made a copy and returned the papers to Rachel; she was sitting where I'd left her, and seemed to be dozing in the sun.

We sat together in silence for a while. There was no need to comment on what she'd shown me; the state of trust between us said everything we needed to say.

Bokumin appeared, smiling, and handed Rachel a postcard. It was of the Eiffel Tower and on the back was a drawing of a radiant, starry sun.

'That's from Peter, isn't it?' I asked. 'What does it mean, the sun?'

'I think it's a pun. He means *son*.' She placed her hand on her abdomen.

'Oh, son. Son? You're pregnant?'

'Yes.'

I'd known it was time to leave Koya and now I had a destination: Paris, where Luce had been about a week ago. I spent the final night in my cabin not sleeping, wanting to soak up every possible moment of being there. Somehow I was sure I'd never return.

In the morning I went to Rachel. She knew what I was about to say. She laid her hand – her kind hand – across my lips.

'It's not me you love,' she said. 'It's Peter in me. And Peter in you.'

I have often wondered where, of all the places she went in her wanders, Luce was happiest. But perhaps that's not a relevant question where Luce is concerned. No, the question is for me and the answer is, with Rachel in Japan. I knew it even then . . . so why did I leave? How did I know that I had to leave?

The place sucked me in, rolled me around, and gently spat me out.

Now.

Christ. Neil has appeared, with Cindy. Here, in my
flat. Thank God, or I should say, thank Luce, ever
since his last visit I've kept all evidence of her
tidied well away, and always close my laptop before
opening the door.

Neil says he'd told me they'd stop by tonight, but
I have no recollection of it. Yes, it's true that my
memory has flaws, and I don't always recall, for
instance, whether I've locked the door, and have to
get up once or twice to check. That sort of thing
happens to everybody. But I'm sure I would have remembered if he'd said they were coming, because I would
have tried to talk him out of it and we'd have had an
argument, a memorable argument.

Oh, I get it. He told Cindy he'd arranged this with
me – perhaps implying that I'd requested the visit.
And didn't tell me in order to avoid the argument.

I can't believe what I'm hearing. He seems to be
suggesting that I come and live with them in Redington
Road.

'Not *with* us, of course,' he says. His tone is unctuous, placatory. 'You'd have your own entrance, your own kitchen, TV, all that.'

'It was the au pair's flat,' Cindy adds, in a similar tone. 'Completely independent. Completely. Of course there's a door through to the house, in case you needed us.'

'I've asked them, you know, the authorities, and they say you could,' Neil says.

This is the most appalling thing I've ever heard. Obviously, after Neil's last visit and what he saw, he's decided he needs to keep an eye on me. My face evidently betrays my feelings, because they engage in a little delicate back-pedalling.

'Oh, just think about it, OK? Only an idea. Whenever you're ready.'

Is it possible they're both demons after all? I don't offer tea and they go away.

When they're gone I look around my three hundred and sixty-six square feet with renewed appreciation. I certainly can't say I *like* the place - in fact, I hate it - and it can never be other than ghastly in most ways. It's a thoroughly depressing place to have ended up but it's *my* depressing place. I've even grown fond of the woodchips who inhabit the Flatland behind the wallpaper, and the pattern of the linoleum has come to seem as soothing as the sea. I don't want to live in somebody else's house. In the *au pair's* flat. The horror, the horror.

26

The Last Bridge

*René Laverre's Story, Part 2. A Magnificent Drunk.
His Human Hands. She Made Everything Explode.
The Inside and the Outside. A Lost Aria. Night
Wanders in Paris. A Roadside Shrine. Saving
Monsieur Mouse. She Forgives Him.*

Paris, June 1972

The City of Light was a shock to the system. In Koya I'd been steeped in silence, wrapped in nature like a silk kimono, cocooned in other-worldly peace. I looked back at it as though it was a distant, mythical land that someone had once told me about. Right in my face was . . . the real world. Christ, what an awful place. The tightly packed buildings shut out the light, the streets were jammed with cars, buses and lorries, whose foul emanations congealed in the air. How did anybody breathe this stuff?

The courtyard in Montparnasse had a forlorn air and I knew right away that its resident genius had departed. Atelier Asher, I learned, was still in use as a photo studio, but Monsieur Asher had retired to England. I was told to enquire at his London gallery. I stopped by Stephen Aubrey's apartment building where the concierge said he'd moved away; she had no forwarding address. At Le Poulet d'Or they told me Madame Boucher had died the previous year; the restaurant was now owned by her niece, 'la belle Madeleine', who'd married the Algerian chef.

It seemed there was no one left. I walked down to the river; my favourite little hotel was just the other side of the Pont Neuf, and I was longing for a shower and a good dinner. Evening was approaching and rain began falling, giving all the streetlights fuzzy golden halos. Most people were hurrying along, head down, but one lonely figure leaned against a lamppost at the mid-point of the bridge, watching the passers-by. As I approached I recognised Lucie's friend René Laverre. It took him a moment to recognise me, but when he did he clasped my hand in a fervent grip. 'Have you seen her?' he asked.

He could only mean one person. He had a mad gleam in his eyes and the odour of whisky on his breath. 'You must know where she's gone. Please tell me. I promise I won't . . . I won't . . .'

'Won't what?' I asked, but he only shook his head sadly. 'When was the last time you saw her?'

'Last Tuesday night,' he said. His look was miserable.

I wondered what could have happened. 'You want to talk about it? Let's go somewhere for a drink, get out of the rain.'

He insisted we go to a particular bar on the Left Bank, with a first-floor room overlooking the bridge. He was obviously well known; other patrons shifted without protest to give us one of the tiny window tables. We squeezed in, the chairs so close our knees touched.

It was really pissing down now, the outside of the glass a watery blur changing colour with the traffic lights: green, amber, red. The whoosh of passing cars, faint strains of mellow jazz from the hi-fi behind the bar, the clink of glasses and the murmur of many muted conversations enclosed us in a densely woven mesh

431

of sound. René lit a thin, dark cheroot, sending clouds of pungent smoke to join the yellowish haze hovering below the ceiling. He took a deep pull of the double whisky which the waiter had placed before him as soon as we sat down.

'It is not,' he said, 'a *carnal* desire. Truly it is not. No, it is a desire of my soul. Of my *soul*, do you understand?'

'Absolutely.'

He propped his cheroot in the ashtray and placed his hands flat on the table. 'So why . . . why did I . . . ? It was my hands, they are beasts. Look at them.'

I looked. They were rather elegant hands, with long fingers, clean, well-shaped nails, a scattering of black hairs. Not particularly bestial, in my opinion, and I told him so.

'You think so? You think so? Well, maybe. I don't know what made me . . . what made them . . . do what they did.' He winced, as though he was wearing an uncomfortable yet necessary garment – a hair shirt, perhaps. 'Can you read palms?' he asked.

'Of course.'

He turned his hands palm up and showed them to me. 'Tell me what you see.'

I took his hands in mine, angled them towards the light, studied them closely. A friend of mine had put herself through university by doing this at parties, and I thought I could probably put together a convincing reading.

'You are a man of hidden depths,' I said.

René nodded.

'The course of your life has not always run smoothly.'

He nodded again.

'You loved someone once, and you love her still. You felt you were destined for great things together.'

He took his left hand back to wipe a tear from his eye. When he returned it to me there was a wet streak on his fingertip. I had the desire to taste it.

'You've spent a long time wandering,' I said. 'It hasn't always been easy to remain true to yourself. Sometimes you thought you were lost. But you have always found a path to follow.'

'That's so true. You really are good at this, you know.'

'Thanks,' I said, though by now I realised I was speaking of myself. 'But the story isn't over. See here? Your life line and your heart line connect again.' I indicated the spot where a minor line bridged the two major ones.

He peered down at his hand. 'It's her, isn't it? I'll see her again.'

'Of course you will. You were right all along. It's your destiny.'

This digression reassured him of my capacity to understand; more whisky steadied him and he returned to his subject with renewed purpose, elbows on table, picking up where he'd left off. 'Not a carnal desire, you see. You see? But I am a man with a body. And where my body stops and my soul begins I don't know.'

I shook my head sympathetically. 'Neither do I.'

'But what *is* the soul? you ask.'

I tried to tell him I hadn't asked that at all, but he didn't hear me. This was clearly a matter to which he'd given some thought and he wanted to share his conclusions.

'The first point to remember is that since the soul itself creates time, when we speak of the soul we must speak of something outside time, do you understand? Do you understand? Yes?' He had a habit of repeating a question as if to avoid hearing the answer. 'Outside time, you see. You see? Which means that it could have happened tomorrow or maybe it will happen last year.'

'What could happen . . . have happened?' I struggled with his mingled verb tenses.

'The great . . .' His hands gathered an invisible cloud into a sphere and offered it to me.

I was reminded of the old nun with her incessant gifts of stones. I mimed taking it, holding it, examining it, admiring it. 'What is it?' I asked.

'It is the greatest treasure, and it's nothing at all.' He laughed, a childlike, delighted laugh, as though he'd opened an unprepossessing box to reveal an astonishing surprise. 'You see? You see?'

'Ah yes, I see. I think I do. And you saw Lucie . . .' I prompted him.

'I couldn't believe my eyes. Because I'd been deluded before. For years I'd been seeing her everywhere, and it would always turn out to be someone else. You know? You know how that happens? You see someone and it's not who you thought it was, but you keep seeing her everywhere.' He sat back heavily and stared at the floor.

'So when you saw her . . .'

He drained his whisky, raised his eyes and looked at me. I watched the alcohol penetrate their depths and spread, soaking into his brain cells. 'I . . . saw . . . her,' he repeated solemnly, as though it was a gospel in which I was instructing him.

He was a magnificent drunk, perhaps the greatest I have ever known. He maintained that crazy high-wire act, almost but not quite losing it, reeling from peak to peak by gravity-defying leaps of idiosyncratic logic and metaphors improbable yet singularly true. And all with such touching sincerity.

'When I saw her, and I knew it was really her and not just another mirage, she made an explosion in my head. Yes, an explosion, like an atom bomb! but all inside my head. It made me go *phwwwt*!' He gestured so wildly he sent his empty whisky glass skidding sideways into the lap of the person at the next table, who returned it with a smile.

Unlike most drunks, whose intoxication mires them in baser emotions – anger, sentimentality, self-pity – René was elevated, each sip of whisky taking him higher. His troubles no longer mundane, his miseries no longer personal or petty, his errors no longer mere mortal sins, he brought his drama to an Olympian arena and made myths of his inner conflicts. I could see why he loved to drink – it gave him the intellectual energy and the spiritual daring to transcend his human woes. Many people – most, I would say – grow uglier the drunker they get. Not René. He had the rare gift of becoming more beautiful the closer he veered to the edge of madness.

'Tell me about the explosion in your head,' I said.

'Ah, the explosion. That was something.' He drew a circle on the table with his finger. 'Look here.' He tapped his finger inside the circle. 'What was here, became *there*.' Finger tap outside circle. 'Here . . . there. And what was *there*, ah, you wouldn't believe it, but it became *here*.' Finger tap inside circle. 'Inside. You ever feel something like that? Yes, I think so. So you see? You see?'

Of course I did. It was the head-fucking, turn-you-inside-out Luce-effect, and she could do it, when she chose, in person as well as through her art in all its forms.

'After the explosion,' René said, 'everything was different. The street, the cars, the rain, the air. I didn't know if it was then or now. I had the thought that all the years had been a dream, or not a dream, they really had happened, but they'd collapsed into themselves like a telescope and were here, somewhere, in my pocket or lying by the side of the road or floating through the air like a speck of dust or a drop of rain, one of many, hundreds, millions . . . or maybe it was I who had expanded, zoomed out; I was immense, I was huge. I could see the "years floating by like flowers on the river".'

'"Like stars, like suns, like you and I."' I finished the quotation from Luce's song 'Sweeternity'.

'That's it, that's it. It's time, you see? Time that is the great lie. And we all believe, we believe the lie. And why? Desire. Desire, that is why.'

I was following him pretty well through the dreams and telescopes, the flowers and rivers, but with time and desire he lost me.

Reading confusion in my face, he spoke slowly, as though to a clever child who really should have understood this by now but for some reason is being uncharacteristically obtuse. He pointed again to the imaginary circle on the table. 'You see? Inside, outside. If you think you are inside,' tap tap, 'you think there is an outside.' Tap tap. 'And so of course you desire it. See?'

'Ah, I see. Of course you do.'

'But isn't desire a form of love? you ask. René, you say, tell me about love.' He raised his glass to his lips, found it empty, glared at it as though it had offended him deeply and craned around to signal the waiter, who was already approaching with another double. René seized it and drank half of it down with a grimace. Evidently he didn't much care for the taste of the stuff, but had learned to endure the unpleasant experience of drinking it for the sake of its effects.

He caught hold of the waiter's hand and pressed it to his cheek. 'This is my dearest friend Ferdinand,' he said to me. 'He has saved me once again. Isn't he magnificent?'

I agreed that Ferdinand, an impish septuagenarian with a purple-veined Jimmy Durante nose, was indeed magnificent.

'My name is Jean-Louis,' said Ferdinand.

'Pleased to meet you,' I said.

'No it's not,' said René.

'Whatever you say, sir,' said the waiter, withdrawing with a bow.

'Tell me about love,' I said to René.

'Ah, love.' He sighed. 'It was raining. Like tonight.' He gestured to the rain-streaked window. 'I was crossing the bridge. The *bridge*, you see? You see? It's not just stones, metal, *concrete*

436

things. No, it's a *bridge*. You see? A *bridge*. I'd crossed it and crossed it a thousand thousand times and never knew. Until she showed me. Pont Neuf, you see? Most people think it's the "New" Bridge, but there's a secret meaning. It's the *ninth* bridge. The last bridge, because the next – there is no next, because it would be the tenth, which is the first one all over again. In a higher dimension.' He took a deep pull on his cheroot, exhaled slowly through his nostrils. 'I worked that part out myself.'

'Ah, yes. Very clever of you. So you were on the bridge and it was raining . . .'

'But she didn't get wet! No! Not a drop touched her. They hit her force field, yes, her force field, you know?' He stared fiercely out into the night, as though by an effort of will he could recreate the moment. The beams of passing cars moved over his face, casting trickling shadows refracted by the rain. The traffic lights were green and he looked like he was under water. Then they changed to red and he looked like he was on fire.

René tore himself away from his vision, sighed again and poured the rest of the whisky down his throat. He leaned back, gazed at the ceiling, gave a brief shudder.

I couldn't begin to imagine what it was like to absorb that much alcohol; I've always been an extremely moderate drinker, and was still sipping my first whisky and soda. René inhaled and exhaled with great care, as if calibrating the precise amount of oxygen to add to the potent mix in his bloodstream. When he'd got it right he lowered his eyes to mine. He gazed down at me from a vast distance above, a personal firmament beyond the reach of sober minds. I could see the celestial heights unfurling within him like Tiepolo clouds. Rarefied vistas were being revealed to him, grand harmonies emerging out of chaos and discord. Everything was falling into place.

'She was standing at the centre of the ninth bridge.' His voice took on an incantatory tone. 'The river flowed beneath her feet,' he gestured in the direction of the Seine's flow, 'the cars went this way and that.' He indicated the crossing line of the road. 'The rain was falling down.' A vertical line intersected the other two. 'But maybe it never happened at all. Or maybe it hasn't happened yet.' René frowned; his eyes were struggling to focus on a point in the middle distance. 'Sometimes I'm not sure. Maybe I only dreamed it. Could that be possible? Could it?' He had the look of a man who's suddenly realised that the boat he thought he was in doesn't exist and he's in fact drowning.

'No, I'm sure it really happened,' I said. Boat back in place, relief all around. 'Tell me more. Did you speak to her?'

'I said her name and something a little stupid, like Is it really you? What are you doing here? and that's when I knew she'd been waiting for me, she'd been expecting me. And it all went backwards from there and I remembered.'

He made a gesture like flinging aside a curtain, flicking a chunk of ash from the cheroot onto the next table, whose occupants were engaged in a passionate kiss and didn't notice.

'What did you remember?'

'I remembered that she'd told me she would meet me on this day, at this hour, on the bridge. But I'd forgotten. And yet I'd come, I was there. And so I'm thinking, This is crazy. You see? You see why I wonder if I'm crazy? But she was there, and I was there, and it came back to me, how we'd walked together all those years ago, after the fire at Disques Cybellines, back to her flat in Montparnasse. We'd crossed the bridge together; it had been raining. That was when she showed me the secret, but I forgot. It seems impossible that I could have forgotten the most important thing in the world, but I did. Maybe that's *why* I forgot – it was too big, too important for my mind to hold. And she sent me reminders – the postcards.' He took out the leather wallet and showed me the cards with their drawing of a bridge – now very worn indeed and augmented by newer ones.

438

'But now I know that she hadn't left me with nothing after all. It was I who'd lost it. I'd lost everything she gave me.'

'What did she give you?'

His eyes filled with a strange light and he smiled. 'I wish I could tell you. I wish I could show you but I can't, it's not possible.'

'Try, please.'

He stubbed out his cheroot. 'Why do you want to know?'

'So I can remember, too,' I said, thinking of poor, forgetful Kuro.

'I'm sorry,' he said. 'I'm sorry. I can't help you.'

The waiter approached and spoke briefly in René's ear. René shrugged, stood and made his way towards the bar. His gait was remarkably steady, though he reached out with both hands as he went, almost but not quite touching chairs or shoulders as he edged among the tables. I had the feeling he wasn't entirely certain where the floor was, but trusted to guesswork and luck. He staggered a bit for the last couple of yards, reaching for the bar with both hands. He made it, anchored himself, then turned and leaned against it. By now everyone was clapping and calling his name.

A hush fell over the room. René closed his eyes and tilted his head as if listening; he took a long, slow breath and sang. *'L'âme se rapprochant de son créateur est la cause du temps et de la lumière.'* (The soul drawing near her maker is the cause of time and light.)*

The words were very apt in the context of our conversation, and the melody, though unfamiliar, had a certain quality I recognised. Could this be from Luce's opera, *Le Seul*? As far as I

* Unknown to me at the time (and only just revealed when I googled the phrase in the hope of finding that someone, some time, had possessed a copy of the libretto and uploaded it – no luck), this line is not original Luce but a translation into French of a quotation from *The Divine Pymander*.

439

knew no recordings had ever been made, no score existed. A shiver ran down my spine. I was hearing the echo of a lost work.

René's voice, roughened by drink and smoke, still had some of the sinuous power that must have made him a spectacularly good singer in his youth. It floated above the drone of the city, winding its way through the tangled thoughts of a roomful of mundane minds. All were momentarily transfixed by beauty. I could see it happening in their faces – masks slipped, misery and banality washed away, some kind of light rekindled in their benighted souls. They drank it in like nectar.

> *Quand j'aurai attendu assez longtemps,*
> *Tu viendras.*
> *Quand mon cœur sera pur,*
> *Quand mes pas me ramèneront,*
> *Tu viendras.*
> *Je t'ai vu, il y a longtemps,*
> *Dans l'embrasure de la porte, sous l'arbre,*
> *Entre cette année et un autre jour.*
> *Tu viendras, tu viendras.*
> *Dans tous les yeux de mes miroirs,*
> *Entre ces mains blanches et noires,*
> *Ici dans mon cœur de feu*
> *Je t'attendrai.*

(When I have waited long enough, you will come. When my heart is pure, when my steps lead me back, you will come. I saw you, long ago, in the doorway, under the tree, between this year and another day. You will come, you will come. In all the eyes of my mirrors, between these hands white and black, here in my heart of fire, I will wait for you.)

When the song ended there was a long moment of silence. People were fumbling for handkerchiefs, wiping their eyes. Amid the applause that followed, René wandered erratically towards the exit and would have walked out into the street, but Ferdinand/ Jean-Louis stopped him gently and beckoned to me. I grabbed René's jacket from the back of his chair, left some money on the table and joined them at the door.

'You take our friend home, yes?'

'Yes, of course. Where does he live?'

I was told an address off the rue des Écoles. The old waiter helped René on with his jacket. Reaching into the pocket, he extracted a set of keys and handed them to me. 'This, the street door. These two, his flat. It's on the third floor, at the front. Good night.'

The rain had ceased, though the earlier downpour had cleared the streets, deserted now but for an occasional lady of the night sheltering in a doorway. We walked along the river under the trees, whose rustling green canopy dripped onto our heads. Lights glowed in windows, casting golden rays. A streetlamp blinked and went out as we passed.

'You see?' René spoke softly. 'You see how time . . .' He sighed and shook his head. 'It's not what one thinks it is.'

'No, I suppose not.' I didn't know precisely what he meant, but I'd found that few things were.

He fumbled in an inner pocket and brought out a silver flask. Courteously offering it to me first – I had the tiniest sip, just to be polite – he took a deep swallow. We strolled on. 'So what happened with Lucie?' I asked, on the off chance that he could be guided back to the subject.

'Look there.' René stopped and pointed to an archway where a dark man and a blonde woman embraced, their faces hidden from view.

For an instant I thought that he'd opened a crack in time in order to show me what had happened. There was a watery, sepia quality to the light, like an old movie; the silent, constrained writhings of the lovers' bodies oddly two-dimensional, as though on a screen. We watched them for several minutes until an adjustment of their position – for ease of ingress, one supposed – caused them to catch sight of us. The woman made a rude gesture and drew her companion deeper into the shadows.

I was beginning to wonder if I'd ever find out what had happened when René had last seen Lucie. He was capable of endless detours – no, more than that, of ignoring entirely what I took to be the road we were on. Although maybe we were on a different road than I imagined. As we approached the end of his street he resisted my attempts to guide him onto it.

'We must walk a little longer,' he said. 'There's always a chance . . .'

'A chance of what?'

'A chance of meeting Lucie, of course. Isn't it obvious? I forgot our appointment before, and yet I was there, so maybe it will happen again. It's like a secret code in the computer.' He tapped his head. 'Who can say what's in there, tucked away? And then it springs open at the right time and you remember.'

His words gave me the eerie sensation that just such a lost memory was at that very moment on the verge of unfolding in my consciousness. I waited for it but, like an almost-sneeze, it never came.

'I go to the bridge, naturally,' said René, setting out his *modus operandi*. 'Every night. But . . .' he raised his finger and gave me a canny look '. . . since I had not known it was that sort of a place until she showed me, there might be other places, perhaps where we are right now, who knows?' He gazed intently about.

I, too, began to gaze about us, looking for anything of significance. Of course, as soon as you do that, everything appears fraught with potential significance. Then again, maybe that's because it is. Just because it seems significant (if only to a slightly deranged mind) doesn't mean it's not. There comes a time when even the most devout sceptic must discover that he's biting his own tail.

My attention was rewarded almost at once as we approached a Japanese laundry. In the window, a mannequin in a Noh-theatre mask carried a striped laundry bag. Wearing a slim white suit and a broad-brimmed fedora above the mask, it was an uncanny evocation of Luce. The window display – curious that a laundry would take such trouble – was framed by green silk curtains like a stage set or the roadside shrine of a local deity. No doubt these were all items that had been left for cleaning and never claimed by their owners.

The uncertain light of the streetlamp cast the painted face into shadow and made the figure seem almost alive. For an astonished instant I thought it moved, but it was only its clothes moving in a small current of air within the shop. Perhaps a back window had been left open a crack and was causing a draught.

On the floor by the mannequin's feet stood two items. One was a toy dog, about a foot high – a black poodle. I was reminded of the dog Mephistopheles on the beach at Montauk, which reminded me of Luce and the Photons' song 'O Mephistopheles', but could discern no further significance.

The other item, a vase of silk roses, was more promising. Roses, of course, I have always associated with Luce. The vase, a kitschy item in black and gold, depicted a typical Japanese landscape – mountains, trees, clouds – with the addition of a dragon writhing through the air. There was some writing around the base of the vase; I bent closer to look. It said, 'Bienvenu à Koya'.

Well! I'd scarcely expected my attention to signifiers to be so promptly rewarded. But what did it signify? Maybe it was just Luce saying hello, in that way she has of peeking through any crack in the surface of things. That was how I decided to take it, in any case.

The mannequin was evidently an old friend to René, who

443

saluted it respectfully and was about to turn away when he stopped and looked again. He'd spotted a mousetrap in the furthest corner of the window display, nearly hidden behind the drapery. I saw to my horror that a mouse was caught, but only by its foot. Its struggles to free itself were heart-breaking. I swear it looked at us with imploring eyes. The next thing I knew, René had grabbed a rubbish bin and, using it as a battering ram, smashed the glass. Reaching in, he picked up the terrified mouse, trap and all. We ran away, ducked round a corner and then proceeded with consummate nonchalance. René freed the mouse from the trap. Its foot was probably broken, so we decided it was best not to release it straight away, but to keep it safe and allow it to recover from its ordeal. René tucked it gently into his pocket where it seemed to settle contentedly enough. I had a Hershey's-with-almonds bar in my bag; I picked out a couple of the nuts and René dropped them into his pocket. Small sounds indicated that the mouse was eating.

'That was for Lucie,' René said. 'She could never stand to see an animal suffer.'

The act of smashing the window had wearied him at last, and we walked to his apartment building in silence. As we climbed the stairs he leaned heavily on my arm, apologising for the always-about-to-be-repaired lift. With every step he looked older. The rapture faded from his eyes and he was just another tired man with only a hangover to look forward to. Until he could get drunk again, and remember.

I got him out of his jacket – Monsieur Mouse safe in the pocket – hung it on a hook by the door and guided René to his bed. I pulled off his shoes and loosened his tie, propped a pillow under his head and pulled a blanket over him.

He sighed and thanked me.

'What happened, René?' I asked, in one final attempt to get the story.

All his rhapsodic peregrinations exhausted, he answered me at last. 'I wanted her so much, you see. And yet I had her, I knew I had her, I'd found her true mind, her true heart, and she'd found mine. We'd sung together, shown each other everything, everything. But there was her body, and there were my hands. Before I reached for her, I had her. As soon as I reached for her, I lost her. By my very act. Because, you see – you must see this – if having her, and knowing her, had been real for me, I would never have needed to . . .'

'But you did reach for her. You touched her.'

René nodded, searching my face as though I held the clues to his deepest and most personal mystery. As perhaps I did. I had a feeling I knew what had happened, and although it had clearly had a devastating effect on René, I have to admit I was amused. Here, it seemed, was yet another Lucian head-fuck for the unwary. 'She was also he, wasn't she?'

René exhaled with a groan, as though he'd released a great burden, his eyes closed and he fell asleep.

In the kitchen I found an appropriate box for Monsieur Mouse, which I equipped with torn toilet roll for bedding, a tiny dish of water, some cheese, a bit of bread and another nut from my chocolate bar (he'd eaten the ones in the pocket). He seemed OK, and his little foot, though badly bruised and bloody, didn't look terribly out of alignment. Perhaps it would heal. All the while I did these things I had the sensation that Luce was looking over my shoulder; if I failed in any detail of Monsieur Mouse's care, she'd know about it.

Throughout the evening, I'd been uncertain of what my own feelings were for René. Luce was so vivid an icon in his mind that of course I saw her as he saw her, felt for her as he did. But I also had feelings for him, and it was more than being moved by his story and drawn to his artistry; more even than the recognition of aspects of myself in him. Luce's feelings were

445

being transmitted, as so often before, through the thread that linked us. They flowed with my blood, pulsed with my heart, coloured my perceptions. There was love and pity, and a sort of affectionate, poignant nostalgia. Digging deeper, I came to sadness and regret, a feeling that I'd abandoned him long ago, knowingly consigned him to a half-life of loss and yearning, and now wished only to give him some salve for his aching soul.

I wondered, not for the first or last time, what Luce wanted. It was easy to understand what René wanted. If Luce stood before me now, would I not reach out to touch? And yet, as René had said, it was not a carnal desire, or not merely a carnal desire. It was a longing to meet, to unite, to know: a desire of the soul. If one has a soul, and the soul has a body, then surely the desires of the one are the desires of the other, though they may pass through many refractions and distortions.

Did Luce intend to affect others as she did, or were the mind-blowing experiences that she provoked mere by-products of her going about her own concerns? Perhaps, early on, she had noted her inadvertent effects and learned to use her powers intention-ally. After all, isn't that what all children do as they learn to communicate and manoeuvre, to advance their interests and protect their weaknesses in the insane adult world?

And then there were the times when she radically altered the course of another person's life: Fergus un-paralysed, Rachel brought back from death, Gauri given sight, the miracles at Warm Springs, the numerous healings, physical and moral, that Wingbow said Lucha left in the wake of her travels. Surely she had reasons for these actions, other than simple compassion. But maybe compassion isn't so simple. If one really could affect people, for good or for ill, how would one choose what to do, and to whom?

I fell asleep on the sofa and woke to the smell of coffee. René, moving gently so as not to hurt his head, brought me a cup.

446

Sober, he was another man. Less dramatic, perhaps, more ordinary, but sweet and kind and interested in other people. Most drunks are such narcissists. Sunlight flowed through the window, bringing cheerful sounds from the street below. I peeled an orange and we shared it, not neglecting Monsieur Mouse, who seemed quite chipper.

Later, we headed out to get some breakfast. As we passed her door his concierge handed him his post and he flicked through the letters as we walked. Suddenly he stopped, staring at a postcard in his hand. On the front was a picture of Big Ben. I looked over his shoulder. On the back was a drawing of a bridge.

'She forgives . . . he forgives me,' he said, and tears came to his eyes. 'See? The bridge, that's all that matters.' The look of joy and relief on his face was so radiant I felt its warmth like a small sun. I, too, was immensely happy – a happiness experienced from, as it were, both sides: René's and Luce's. Through the thread that linked us, I fed back to her the knowledge that this card, her gift, had done what she'd intended. It had salved his troubled soul.

After breakfast, we stopped by the Japanese laundry to commiserate about their smashed window. Juvenile hoodlums, no doubt. While I distracted the elderly proprietor, René slipped a hundred francs into the till. In the evening I caught a flight to London.

Now.

It's hard to tell what's going on in my groups and forums. They've all started buzzing like bees about to swarm. My innocent - all right, my deliberately provocative - posts seem to have had a sort of alchemical effect, as though I've added a drop of just the right magical elixir that each one needed to wake it up. An extraordinary number of posts are of sightings of Luce, and several report encounters involving conversations . . . and more intimate contact.

I've received an email from a strange address that proves to be invalid when replied to. It invites me to a Tor chat. Intrigued, I log on.

myself: Hello?

ev38821fh897sp76 (after a pause): Hello, thanks for joining me.

myself: No problem, what's up?

ev38821fh897sp76: You've said some interesting things.

What could they mean? Are they referring to my internet postings? Which ones? Is this someone from alt.fan.human, or the *L'Age Atomique* group? And how did they get my email address, anyway? Best to reply ambiguously.

> **myself:** I'll take that as a compliment.
>
> **ev38821fh897sp76:** I'm guessing you know Luce pretty well. I'd love to get together some time, swap stories. I know Luce pretty well, too. Maybe I could tell you something. I know a lot of secrets.

Who the fuck is this? Could it be a member of the Pymander Productions gang? What's the significance of the present tense?

> **myself:** Who are you?
>
> **ev38821fh897sp76:** I'll tell you when I see you. Let's get together soon. Where are you?
>
> **myself:** Same place as you: hidden in the aether behind an alphanumeric code.
>
> **ev38821fh897sp76:** Ha ha. Keep it that way. I wanted to warn you that the internet is not private or discreet. It's being watched. You're being watched. Not everyone is who or what they seem.

ev38821fh897sp76 vanishes from the screen and I'm left with a vague unease. Very likely it's just a fantasist, wanting to play. Conspiracy theories have swirled around Luce from the beginning, most no more outlandish than the truth . . . which *The Book of Luce* will soon reveal to all. It's possible that ev38821fh897sp76 really does know something, is perhaps part of some underground network of Lucians. Maybe he - or she - is genuinely on my side, on Luce's side, and the warning is sincere and well meant. But it's equally possible that ev38821fh897sp76 is a demon, or a front for demons, who, pretending to be on my side, is attempting - rather crudely, I must say - to get me to reveal who I am. I may not be as clever as I used to be, but I'm not as dumb as that.

27

To Be Kept Until Dead

*Fergus Meakin's Story, Part 2. Wingbow and Obelisk.
The Demons' Revenge. Greyling's Fate. Escape by
Smallness. Footsteps on the Gravel. Escape by
Forest. Nature Helps. Lost. Devon Sunshine.
The Shepherd and the Sheep.*

England, June 1972

I returned to London cautiously. Were the Bigs still aware of me? Were they interested? Did they know it was I who'd shot that demon on the train? Too many uncertainties for comfort. Having learned never to enter a situation without an exit strategy, I rented a bedsit in Brewer Street (under a false name, paying cash, in a building with a back exit, from a landlord who asked no questions) and set about acquiring one. I was pleased to discover that most of my criminal connections were still in business, including my old forger, from whom I acquired yet another American passport in yet another new name. Nor was it difficult to obtain a small gun, though this time I decided I had to have a silencer – the loudness of the shot I'd fired on the train had appalled me, and I couldn't

451

count on always being lucky enough to have so much covering racket.

Inevitably, I ran into old friends and acquaintances. To anyone who recollected the bizarre way I had last exited the stage, I explained that the sanatorium/yoga retreat/Peace Corps had done its job and I was quite well again, thank you. Some of my friends had gone mad in their turn; most had barely noticed I'd been gone.

At Paul Asher's gallery in Dover Street – glassy, glossy and so exclusive I was surprised they let me in – I was informed by a glacial blonde that Mr Asher didn't do interviews. Nevertheless I made her write down my name and promise to pass it on to him.

Greyling was next on my list. I hired a car and drove to Devon. It was a warm, murky day and, though only late afternoon when I arrived, evening came early in the deep valleys. As I turned down the long driveway I pictured the cosy kitchen, a friendly cup of tea. The steering wheel jerked and twisted in my hands; the drive was more rutted than I remembered. Brambles and nettles pushed in from the sides and the low branches of a hazel brushed past my open window. There was an ominous air of neglect.

Weeds grew through the gravel of the parking area and the paths; the lawn was a ragged jungle. I shut off the engine and got out. It was silent but for the rustle of leaves in the old apple tree above. No one was at home, nor had been for some time.

How foolish it had been to assume he'd be here, just as I'd left him. He'd been an old man then, and four years had passed. Had he died? It came as a wrench to think I'd never see him again; I hadn't realised how much I'd counted on it. Maybe he'd gone into a home somewhere, in which case I'd surely be able to find him. But why was this place abandoned?

I peered in at a window but couldn't make anything out. The

front door proved to be unlocked; I pushed it open with a hideous creak. The hall was littered with debris, the staircase was a charred skeleton and the sky was visible through a gap in the roof.

As I stepped forward there was a sudden rush of air, a blur of movement and something hit me very hard on the head. The next thing I remembered was intense pain and a voice repeating, 'Shit, shit, shit.' Someone was shaking me, which was the source of most of the pain.

'Ow, stop that,' I said.

He stopped, which permitted me to sit up and hold my head in my hands. It needed to be kept still. I opened my eyes. 'Hi, Fergus.'

'Hey, all right?' he said, as though we'd just run into each other at the pub.

'Great, thanks. Yourself?'

'Not too bad. Sorry about, you know.'

'It's OK. Not concussion, I don't think.' I fingered the growing lump on the top of my head.

'Stupid log was rotten.' He pointed to a broken chunk of wood. 'Lucky for you, though.'

'Yeah, I'm so lucky. Why the fuck did you hit me?'

'Didn't know it was you.'

'So anybody else you'd whack, no questions asked?'

'Safe than sorry. You know how it is.'

'No, I don't. How is it?' I took a good look at him for the first time. Unkempt beard, badly cut hair, some kind of scabby skin condition.

'Got a fag?' he said.

I offered him the packet and he grabbed five or six with a dirty hand and fumbled for a match, scratching at himself in a manner that suggested lice. I edged away.

'Tea?' he said.

'That would be lovely, thanks.'

'You can get some at the chip shop.'

'What?'

'You can't park your car here. If you leave it in the village you can pick up some tea on the way back. And maybe some chips, too?'

'Why can't I park here?'

'Someone might see it.'

Perhaps the blow to my head had slowed my mental processes, but Fergus wasn't making much sense. 'Why shouldn't anyone see it?'

'They'd think someone was here.'

'Who would, and why is that a problem? And what happened here, anyway? Where's your uncle?'

Fergus made a small, irritated noise. 'Look, move the damn car. If you decide to come back, come on foot. Wait till dark. Make sure no one follows you. Bring tea and food. And some baccy.' He got up, stepped through a broken window and disappeared.

I drove into the village and parked by the pub, where I had a sandwich and a beer. They kindly provided, as well, some aspirin for my headache. As it got dark I procured fish and chips, tea and tobacco and, thus laden, began the hike – about two miles, I reckoned – back to Greyling's.

There was no place to hide on the narrow, single-lane roads, trapped between high hedgerows as in a tunnel. When a car came along I had to lean into the hedge to let it pass. I got some odd looks, pedestrians being rare in these parts. Someone stopped to ask if I needed a lift. Just friendly neighbours, I supposed, but Fergus's suspicions had infected me. I looked closely at the occupants, greenly illuminated by the lights of their dash, while fingering the gun in my pocket and keeping my own face in the dark. An ordinary middle-aged couple. Too ordinary? Was there something too smooth about their faces, too blank about their eyes? A shiver passed over my skin. Was it a genuine reaction to the presence of demons, or just an indication of my own susceptibility to paranoia? I prattled on about how nice it was to walk on summer nights. It was a relief when their tail-lights vanished around a bend and the concealing darkness enveloped me once more.

The night was moonless and overcast, my path lit only by the pale froth of cow parsley fringing the lane. Even without seeing it, I could have been guided by the fragrant, invisible river of its scent. There's something deliciously weightless and timeless about walking in the dark, and for a while I forgot where I was going in the sheer delight of it.

In my oblivion I walked right past Greyling's driveway; when I realised, and turned to retrace my steps, I heard – or imagined I heard – a noise in the adjacent woods, which suggested that someone else had also stopped and turned. The situation bore an uncanny resemblance to the Dream of the Cavern at its nightmarish worst. All pleasure vanished and that awful, para-lysing fear spread like a toxin from my fingertips to my toes.

In the darkness, without sight, other senses awakened. My skin seemed to have sprouted a million antennae, all quivering with tension. If my heart hadn't been terrified of making a noise it would have been thumping like a bass drum; instead it fluttered in tiny, panicked beats like a trapped bird. And yet I'd seen nothing, heard nothing that couldn't be attributed to the normal activity of nocturnal animals. It was only a badger, I told myself firmly and, with an effort, unglued my feet and dragged them back along the road.

Greyling's drive, when I found it, was a blacker blackness that dropped away beneath me. I was hurrying now, praying not to stumble. Fate was not in a kind mood that night; I hit a pothole, twisted my ankle and fell headlong into a clump of nettles. Trying to save the tea, I pirouetted sideways into the adjacent long-armed bramble.

It proved impossible to extricate myself. My hands and face seething with nettle-sting, I'd manage to pull one thorny branch aside, only to have it snap devotedly back when I went after another. Annoyance was doing a good job of counterbalancing fear; I wouldn't have minded meeting Mrs Big herself if she'd had a pair of secateurs I could borrow. Finally I tore myself loose, shredding fabric and flesh. I groped in the dark to retrieve my carrier bags. I'd landed on the fish and chips, but who cared? One tea had spilled, the other miraculously not. I limped down the drive, cursing silently.

The way things were going, there was every likelihood that Fergus would bash me over the head again as soon as I got within range. We should have agreed a signal. I approached on tiptoe and paused by the front door.

'Fergus?' I said softly.

His reply came so close to my ear that I jumped.

'What have you brought?' he whispered.

'Huh? Oh, right, so you know it's me. Though I don't think there are a lot of other idiots wandering around the countryside in the middle of the night. I brought tea, fish and chips, or mash actually, Golden Virginia and blue Rizlas.'

'Come around to the back.'

I found my way to the broken window through which Fergus had exited before. His hand emerged from within and helped me over the sill. He'd made a sort of nest for himself in a corner of the sitting room where the light of a single candle flickered dimly over the burned-out bookcases, the charred mounds of sofa and chairs. He devoured all the food and drank all the tea. When he'd finished he rolled a cigarette and lit it, inhaling deeply. 'I don't suppose you have any hash?'

'No, sorry.'

'Shit. I was hoping you did. Haven't had any since, oh, Christ, since years. Look, d'you think you could lend me a few quid? Just to help me get by, you know?'

I gave him most of what I had, about twenty pounds.

He tucked it carefully away. 'Thanks. Thanks a lot. 'Preciate it. You're all right, you are. I looked for you, you know, but you'd gone away. Your upstairs neighbour said you'd had a nervous breakdown.'

'Yeah, something like that. I had to get out of town for a while.'

'Smart move. I should have done that, too.'

'What happened? I last saw you at Conway Hall, not long before the shooting. What happened to the Holy Ghost? Is he all right?'

'No, not particularly. He died.'

Although I'd long suspected this, the sense of loss struck me hard, reawakening my own mourning for Charlie. All this time, I realised, I'd been hoping that Francis had survived. I'd heard stories about him from so many people that he'd come to seem as real to me as someone I actually knew. Had he made the strange journey from 'invisible friend' to solid, corporeal man only to stop that bullet? From what I'd heard of his devotion to Luce, that might have seemed to him worthwhile.

'How's Jukebox?' I asked. 'Did she have the baby?'

'I don't know.'

'What about the others? Wingbow and Obelisk? And your uncle John? Fergus, will you please tell me what happened?' It was increasingly obvious that some catastrophe had occurred, and the tension was killing me.

The candlelight wavered over Fergus's tired face. He stared into the flame and rubbed his eyes with the back of his hand. 'It was about three months after that Conway Hall fiasco. Maiya – Wingbow – was staying with me. Luce had sent word to everyone to lie low. She said to keep away from each other, but

457

I suppose Maiya and I didn't think that applied to us. That day I went to my studio as usual. We weren't doing any gigs, but there's always some tinkering to do with the equipment. Maiya had gone to visit friends in Islington.

'When I got home she wasn't back yet, so I made some dinner for us. By nine she still wasn't back . . . and then there was a knock at the door. It was the police. They arrested me and handcuffed me and took me to the station, where they questioned me for hours without telling me what it was all about. They asked me where I'd been all day, and lots about my personal life, like was I in love with Maiya, what were our plans, all that sort of thing. Eventually they told me . . .' Fergus took a deep, ragged breath '. . . that Maiya was dead. She and Bobby – you know, Obelisk – died in a fire at my studio and I was being charged with arson and murder. I couldn't believe it. I was sure they were lying, but why? Bobby, I'd thought, was staying with a friend in North Wales. When I'd last seen Maiya she was on her way to Islington. Why had they gone to the studio? It made no sense. It was like an awful nightmare, and I kept telling myself to wake up, but . . . it went on and on.'

Tears were running down his grimy cheeks. I patted him on the shoulder, too shocked to speak. All this must have happened, I realised, not long after I left London. So pleased with my own cleverness at escaping from the Bigs, I'd flitted away, ducked out of sight, saved my own skin.

Fergus blew his nose and wiped his fingers on his trousers. 'They told me I could call a lawyer. I didn't have a lawyer, but I remembered that Uncle John had one. He'd made me memorise the guy's name because I was to call him if – when – Uncle John died. Marcus Drayton. I thought he was probably some sort of estate lawyer who'd sort out Uncle John's will and all that, but he was the only lawyer I knew, so I called him. And he came right away. He was just what I'd expected: old and posh. But pretty sharp. The police, he said, had a theory that I'd caught Maiya and Bobby together, locked them in the studio and set it on fire. But I wasn't to worry, it would all be sorted out, he'd get me bail that afternoon or the next day. I asked him to tell Uncle John, and he said he most certainly would.'

The murders of Wingbow and Obelisk were hideously like what Greyling had done to the demons at Golden Square – was this their reprisal? I thought of Wingbow, and that walk we took together, and the wonder and beauty of the web of light she'd shown me. And loyal, taciturn Obelisk . . . and maybe others, too. Had the demons gone after the whole Pymander Productions gang? Grief and rage rose up in me, and with them the longing for revenge. With a sense of foreboding, I asked what had happened to Uncle John.

'Mr Drayton came back that evening and told me bail was for the moment out of the question, as I was to be charged with another arson and murder. I'd thought things couldn't get any worse. Ha ha. He'd tried to telephone Uncle John, got no answer, learned the line was out of order. So he drove here straight away. Pretty dedicated, I'd say. He found the place burned down and police tape across the door. At the police station he learned that Uncle John had died in the fire, which had happened two days earlier – my alibi for that time was only Maiya. They'd just put out a warrant for my arrest and he'd had to inform them that I was already in custody in London. He told me he had one more errand to do "on Dr Greyling's behalf", as he put it, and after that he would return with an associate who specialised in criminal law, and they'd work out my defence. That was the last I saw of him. The next day a much younger fellow turned up and introduced himself as Mr Drayton's associate who would now take over my case. Drayton was in hospital. He'd been seriously injured in a mugging the night before and was unlikely to survive.'

The horror of Fergus's story rendered me speechless. After

459

what had happened to Charlie, perhaps I should not have been so shocked. Had I not known this was a war? Had I not realised there would be consequences? I'd left the war to others while I hid in another country, behind another name. Had I truly escaped . . . or had they let me get away for reasons of their own? Had they been using me all along to lead them to the others?

Taking the candle, I made my way across the room towards the burned and tumbled bookshelves that had concealed the wall safe. On the way I stubbed my toe on something, which turned out to be the safe itself. It was lying on its back, door open, and there was nothing within. Holding the candle closer, I noticed a hole drilled through the lock.

So much for the 'insurance policy'. I hoped Greyling had managed to overcome his scruples about killing and take at least one of them with him when he went. He had not, I was sure, gone down without a fight. Perhaps he was even now a vengeful ghost, a soldier still, fighting the war on the astral plane. I stared into the tumbled ruin of his library and pictured his sharp blue eyes, his crisp indomitability. He relished the battle, I was sure. I gave him a mental salute, as crisp as I could manage.

Fergus was trying to roll another cigarette with shaking hands. I took it from him and finished the job, thinking I'd have to look after him somehow, take him home with me, clean him up, get him a set of false ID, get him out of the country. I let him smoke for a minute in peace, then asked what had happened next.

'I fell apart. I lost my mind, I lost the power of speech. They told me I had fits of screaming and crying, but I don't remember those. I felt like I was shut in a hollow, dark place, an empty place. All kind of noises echoed about, but nothing I could understand. I was like that for months. I was declared unfit to plead and the judge ordered that I be detained indefinitely for psychiatric treatment. When they really want to fuck you over,

460

that's how they do it, you know. Any ordinary criminal does his time and then he's out. But if they say you're crazy, you're crazy until they say you're not. Which could be any length of time at all. Could be your whole life. And of course, once they get you, they can make you as crazy as they need you to be. Oh, man, those drugs. Pills, shots. You never know what's real. You wake up, they shoot you up with one thing. If you fall asleep, they shoot you up with another. Shit to make you shit, shit to make you stop shitting. Shit to make you dream weird dreams, shit to wipe out any dreams you ever had. Shit to make you forget who you are, shit to make you want to die.' He was rocking back and forth as he spoke, eyes fixed on the darkness beyond the dim sphere of candlelight. Somewhere inside he was pacing a cage, still caught in a nightmare trap.

I patted him on the shoulder again and he pulled himself back to the present with an effort, as though climbing out of a hole. He took a long drag of his cigarette.

'Uncle John used to talk about good and evil, how evil thrived on ignorance and fear. I was seeing it for real. The police, the judges, the doctors and nurses who were really just jailers. Oh, not evil like mass murderers – I've met some of those, and at least, if I may say, you know where you stand with them. You know what they are. No, I mean the ones who don't come with labels saying they're evil motherfuckers – just ordinary petty people who fall into evil out of sheer stupidity, then cling to it out of terror at change. Obey orders. Heil fucking Hitler.'

'But they finally let you go?'

He snorted. 'They were never going to let me go. They have a code, you know. A little code in your file that means Never To Be Released. It says, To Be Kept Until Dead. I saw it. They're not supposed to let you see your file. But they are stupid, so stupid. In some ways that makes it worse, because they do such horrible, stupid things to you, and you can't, you absolutely can't

461

reason with them, or expect them to behave rationally, but if you can keep your wits about you, which is in no way easy, but not impossible, you can play them like a fucking light show, blink them on and off, twitch them this way and that. Patient, that's what you have to be. You have to get them to think it's all their own idea. Stupid fucking brutes. You have to get them to think you're OK, but you can't just act sane. They'll think you're faking. No, I discovered the great secret of it. You have to convince them you don't give a fuck. Then they lose interest. You're boring, like a dead mouse. You have to play dead, like a very, very smart mouse. Then the cat will look away and bam! you're out of there.'

'You escaped? How?'

'I'd begun having these strange dreams. They cut right through the drugs. There was an old man in them, always the same guy, a scruffy old geezer. Sometimes he had – this is funny – a sheep with him. I've always liked sheep. When I tried to follow him I'd come up against a high wall. Then one night I noticed a door in the wall, a tiny, low door like in Alice in Wonderland. Through it I saw a garden, and sun, and flowers, and blue sky . . . and I knew that if I made myself small enough to get through that little door, I'd be free. The next week I learned that there was to be a new programme. Certain trustworthy and relatively stable inmates would be selected to work in the warden's garden and learn horticulture. I didn't dare show too much interest, but by careful manoeuvring, and making myself really, really small and insignificant, I got chosen. It was a big old garden, Victorian, with acres of vegetables and trees and shrubs and flowers. It had its own walls, of course, that separated it from the warden's house and the road, but it was outside the main wall. I stuck it out for nearly a year, making myself smaller and smaller. Four months ago I saw a chance and I took it. Probably if I'd planned it I'd have screwed up, but I happened to be passing with a wheel-barrow of manure when the warden himself came into the garden from his house and failed to pull the gate fully closed. He didn't notice, but I did. I just . . . walked out. It had been raining, so we were wearing waxed coats over our uniforms, with yellow stripes on the sleeves to set us apart. I covered those with mud. Soon as I could, I stole some clothes from a washing line. I never stay anywhere. I move about at night and hide during the day. People throw out a lot of food, you know. I didn't mean to come here but a couple of days ago I found myself near, and remembered how happy I'd been here. I had no idea what had become of the place . . . Shh, what's that?' Fergus blew out the candle.

'I don't hear . . .' I whispered, but then I did. Was that the crunch of gravel from the front of the house, the soft pad of a footfall? I heard a liquid sound from very near and smelled the sharp tang of urine. Fergus had pissed himself. I wasn't far from it myself. A tiny little voice in the back of my mind said Badger? Deer? Fox? Kids? Burglars? but was drowned out by a wave of terror. There were demons near, I was sure. The flavour of that fear was unmistakable.

It was my nightmare in awful reality, but I had the thread to guide me and my gun in my hand, which proved surprisingly steady. I took hold of Fergus's sleeve and drew him to the gaping window where I paused, listening with my whole body. The air was mild and still; here at the back of the house, nothing was moving. Overgrown laurel bushes pushed up against the wall; we dropped down among them and crept towards the woods at the end of the garden. Halfway there lay the rotting bulk of a shed; we hid behind it for a moment to listen again. There were definitely sounds of movement from the house and my last hope of badgers died when, peering around the corner, I caught a glimpse of a man-shaped shadow, then another, as they stepped out of the window. They seemed to sniff the air as though questing for our scent. Should I try to shoot them? In this darkness I was unlikely to hit either one, let alone both, and there might be

463

more, perhaps coming around the side of the house. Stealth was the only option.

Fergus was silent at my back, though I could feel his violent trembling. I gripped him firmly and, keeping low, we scuttled into the woods. Out of nowhere a strong breeze started up and the rustling of the leaves in the trees covered the sounds we made. Once or twice I thought I glimpsed a figure behind us, but branches always shifted to block the view. It felt like nature was helping us. We pushed on, trying to move fast but quietly, climbing out of Greyling's little valley. The hillside was steep, littered with huge boulders into which we stumbled blindly, and slippery slopes of leaf litter that had to be negotiated on hands and knees. Fergus stuck to me like a burr, his breath coming in short, sharp gasps.

I tried to recall what I knew of the terrain around there. Wooded valleys interspersed with pastureland that edged into moor. Few roads, and roads were in any case too risky. My plan was to make for my car by a roundabout route, then take Fergus to London and get him out of the country. Instead, we got lost.

We'd climbed out of the valley but the land was still densely wooded, not open farmland as I'd expected. Without the angle of the slope to guide us in the dark, I feared we were prone to wander in circles. At first light a drenching fog rolled in faster than I'd have thought possible, great sideways gusts of it obscuring everything.

'Devon sunshine,' muttered Fergus, his first words since we'd fled the house.

The woods thinned. We came to a field path and turned left: a fifty-fifty chance of being the correct direction. The fog began to drift off in cloudy tatters, revealing an astonishing patch of blue sky straight overhead. A sheep appeared on the path, then another. They saw us and stopped, uncertain whether to bolt. Others approached; they milled around. We stood still. Fergus was smiling; I recalled he'd said he liked sheep. Some decided to turn back the way they'd come, others to carry on past us. Urgent bleating ensued, as ewes and their lambs tried to stick together. Then the whole mass shifted and began to move in our direction, and I made out the swift black-and-white of a sheepdog trotting up the path, and behind him an old man with a crook, evidently the shepherd.

'You two look like you could use a cup of tea,' he said, when he came up to us. Fergus was still smiling; he nodded our assent.

The sheep were guided into a nearby field and we followed the old man to a little thatched cottage at the edge of the woods. It was one of those places that had scarcely changed since medieval times: a well-weeded vegetable patch in front, pecked by hens, then thick stone walls, low beamed ceiling, ancient iron wood-burning range. No electricity; a single cold-water tap at a stone sink. An outhouse, quite lovely, with tiny ferns growing in its walls and a view of distant moor.

We had tea and thick slices of bread and butter with jam. From the first I felt like the odd one out. Neither Fergus nor the old man said much, but they'd apparently arrived at some sort of understanding, for when I rose to go, Fergus stayed.

The morning was so bright, sweet-scented and clean that the terror of the night before seemed like a bad dream. I found my car where I'd left it and drove to London without incident. My bruises, scratches and muddy clothes testified that I had, indeed, spent the night scrambling around the woods, but I was no longer quite so certain of the cause. What had I heard? Mysterious noises. What had I seen? Shadows. Had those demons been real, or figments of Fergus's perfectly reasonable paranoia, transmitted to me? That I was susceptible to psychic influence I could not doubt. Had the demons generated the fear, as I'd thought, or had fear generated the demons?

Now.

Is nostalgia getting the better of me at last? I have such a strong desire to revisit these old places. What the hell, why not? I succumb. I pack a bag, get an overnight pass, sign out, hire a car and drive to Devon.

Like the last time, it's a cloudy summer afternoon; it's quiet and peaceful and slightly damp. The single-lane roads are the same, high-hedged and crowded with weeds. I'm a bit surprised at how unerringly I find my way; I thought I'd get lost at least once. At the top of Greyling's driveway a sign says 'B & B'. Well, at least I won't be intruding on a private family. If it looks nice I'll take a room.

It looks nice, and bigger than before. It must have been largely demolished, then rebuilt; I can discern the part of the old frontage that escaped the worst of the fire. A wing has been added to either side, in a vaguely Edwardian style.

A couple of other cars are parked in front. The apple tree, ancient fifty years ago, is no more, its place taken by a trio of birches. I ring the doorbell and am promptly greeted by a young woman with a frisky Jack Russell at her heels.

'Don't mind Jacko,' she says. 'He doesn't bite. If he gets too friendly just say, "Bugger off, Jacko" very firmly and he'll desist.'

I'm shown to a pretty room overlooking the meadow and the river below, and told that tea is now being served in the garden. I make my way there and join half a dozen guests for a classic Devon cream tea.

When the young woman comes to clear the tea things I ask her about the history of the house.

'The front part is quite old,' she tells me. 'Mid-fifteenth century. There was a big fire in the 1960s and the place lay derelict for a long time. My parents bought it in '82. They restored what could be restored and added on. Oh, here's my dad now. He loves to talk about the house. You can ask him.'

An old man approaches across the lawn. The sun is in my eyes and his face is in shadow; for a moment he looks like Greyling, then I see he's just an old man, about Greyling's height and with something of his upright demeanour, wearing similar clothes in which he's evidently been gardening, for the knees of his trousers are muddy.

The young woman goes off to fetch him some tea and I ask how he came to buy the house.

'Bought it from the government,' he says. 'Crown property. There was a horrible murder here in 1968 – a chap killed his father by locking him in and setting the place on fire. But don't worry, that part burned to the ground. You're not sleeping in a room where a murder occurred – we're not haunted, not in the least, though we could probably charge more if we were.'

It's obvious that he relishes this macabre tale and I refrain from correcting him.

'The young fellow was declared insane and got put away, but he escaped and was never recaptured. He'd been the only heir and of course couldn't inherit. No other relations turned up, so it went to the Crown, and they put it up for auction. It was an enormous mess but the setting is so good we couldn't resist. Soaked up a huge amount of money, you know, but we had to do things right.'

He goes on to tell me about the trials of the renovation, the ancient masons' marks found on the foundation stones, the Iron Age scraps found at the bottom of an old well, the idiosyncrasies of lime mortar.

In the long evening I go for a stroll by the river, recalling how Greyling and I had walked here. I feel his presence beside me so intensely that I look around, half expecting to see him or at least an apparition of some sort, but there's only a cloud of midges zooming around in a spiral – though, oddly, the entire cloud is keeping pace with me as I walk and stopping when I stop. *Greyling*, I say to it, *I hope you're well and happy in Heaven, or Valhalla, or in a new life, or wherever you are. I'm still down here, trying to elucidate. Wish me luck?*

The cloud of midges approaches, swirls around my head, then drifts erratically towards a clump of hazel on the riverbank.

I have dinner at the old pub in the village, a gastro-pub now, with pretensions that the food does

468

not live up to. Back at the B & B I go to bed early. I don't sleep particularly well at the best of times, and I'm still trying to wean myself off the Seroxat. But mainly it's memories, and they're not soothing ones.

At first light I set off to try to retrace the escape route I took with Fergus. Of course I get lost almost at once. The initially clear morning turns misty, then rainy. I'm not dressed for this. Eventually I find my way to a road where I ask directions from a passing motorist. He sees my face fall when I learn that it's at least two miles by road to the village – and two miles further to the B & B. He offers me a lift. He's fat and grotty, can't possibly be a demon, so I accept gratefully.

At the B & B I have a hearty breakfast and pay my bill, then set out for the drive back to London. Before long I come upon a queue of cars stuck in the narrow lane. Soon the cause is revealed: a great many sheep are coming the other way. Everybody edges over to give them room to pass; some locals call out greetings to the shepherd, who's puttering slowly behind the flock on a mud-spattered quad bike with a collie on the back. He waves his thanks politely as he squeezes past each car.

He's a thin, wiry old man with weathered, sun-toughened skin, wild white hair and a beard that still shows a trace of ginger. The watery blue eyes, the pointed nose, both now wreathed in many wrinkles but . . . unmistakably Fergus. He doesn't recognise me. I wonder if I should stop him, say hello, but he's already passed, the queue of cars is starting to move. I let it go.

469

28

Where It All Began

❦

*Sleight of Hand. A House Called Farundell. The
Alchemist. Harpsichord and Theremin. Lord Francis
Damory. A Russet-haired Child. Jukebox. The Island.
Crashing the Party. The Sugar Cube. The Trip.
A Transfusion of Green Blood. The Obsidian Pool.
The Cavern. The Human.*

England, June 1972

Back in London, the cool blonde at Paul Asher's gallery was icier than ever and pretended not to remember that I'd called before. I was, it must be admitted, not the prettiest sight, with a great bramble gash across my face. As we chatted, I noticed that on the desk by her elbow was an out-tray with several envelopes waiting to be taken to the letterbox. The third one down was addressed to Mr P. A-something, the rest of the name and the address obscured by the ones on top of it.

On a shelf behind her, in binders labelled with their names, were the catalogues describing the pieces available from each of the gallery's artists. A plan presented itself.

'Could I look at Mr Asher's catalogue? I'd like to buy a print.'

470

'Mr Asher's prints start at one hundred and twenty guineas,' she said.

'That's very reasonable.'

She rose and turned towards the shelf; I nudged the top two envelopes aside; she returned and dropped the catalogue in front of me with a thud and a sweet smile. 'Let me know which ones you want.'

She was so sure I was taking the piss that I almost bought one just to spite her. The one I liked most showed an island in a mist-streaked lake, whose pellucid surface reflected a sky of clustering, back-lit clouds. One remained from an edition of six huge prints made by the photographer himself, four feet by six, signed, numbered and dated. Four hundred guineas. I handed back the catalogue with a disdainful expression. 'These are not his best work,' I said. 'Please let me know if you get anything good.'

I walked out with the pleasant buzz that comes from petty personal triumphs. The name on the envelope had indeed been Mr P. Asher; the address was *Farundell, Exley, Oxon.* Farundell was obviously the name of a house. Exley I knew: it was a few miles up the River Isis from Oxford, with, as I recalled, a good pub where I'd gone in my student days.

I stopped at the library to see if I could learn anything about Farundell. Grade I listed, it was mentioned in several guide books; Pevsner calls it one of the finest Tudor country houses in Oxfordshire. Since 1187 the site of a Carmelite nunnery, after the Dissolution it had come to Sir, later Lord, Roger Damory. The family had prospered with wool and mining, and by 1800 owned some twenty-five thousand acres. The house was extended in the mid-eighteenth century and remodelled in the late-nineteenth. The estate, still owned by the Damorys, was now reduced to a more manageable nine hundred acres. The house and gardens were, for a fee, open to the public on Saturday and Sunday afternoons in June, July and August.

I wondered what connection Paul Asher had to this place. Perhaps he was staying there as a houseguest, or maybe – I recalled that he was half English – this was the English side of his family. The next day was Saturday; I'd go as an ordinary visitor. If I didn't spot Paul Asher somewhere about, I'd ask for him. At worst they'd turn me away and all I'd have would be a nice trip to the country.

Saturday was a perfect summer's day. I hired a car and headed for Oxfordshire, reaching Exley around twelve and stopping for lunch at the pub. It seemed unchanged; I recalled long arguments about Empedocles and quantum mechanics over beers in the garden, and romantic interludes among the rowing boats moored under the bridge.

I got directions to Farundell: it was across the river and a mile or two further into the hills. As soon as I left the main road I entered one of those ancient landscapes that England does so well: winding lanes, old stone walls, trees grown so massive that the road has, over the centuries, bent itself obligingly around them. Green rolling hills, white sheep and brown cows, a red kite circling above. I'd heard that this part of Oxfordshire was home to one of the last surviving colonies of that bird.

As I crested the hill, stone walls gave way to a pair of tall iron gates. This must be Farundell. A lad of about fourteen in a Blue Öyster Cult T-shirt manned a booth. I bought one ticket for parking, another for the gardens, and a third for a guided tour of the house.

The long driveway was bordered by thick woodland on one side; on the other, horses grazed the gently sloping meadows. A pretty grey foal cantered along the fence beside me. There was no one in sight except for an old man cutting the tall grass in an orchard, swinging his scythe with easy grace.

I parked among several other cars in a wide, gravelled court-yard. A sign indicated that the stable block and tea room were to the left, the gardens straight ahead. The house itself spread away to the right, golden-grey Cotswold stone, draped in ivy and white roses. Elegantly proportioned despite its hybrid nature, whoever had designed its additions over the years had treated the past with respect. I could make out the remains of the medieval wing, neatly subsumed within a sprawling Tudor manor, itself in due course exalted into a stately Georgian mansion. The Victorian alterations must have been mainly internal, or perhaps on the other side of the house. For all the imposing bays and mullions on this, its northern side, I had a sense that the house really faced the other way, southwards towards the Isis, if my sense of direction hadn't deserted me.

A rope hung across the entrance to the porch; the massive iron-hinged door was shut. A card said that the house tour would begin at two o'clock: in about twenty minutes. I strolled across the courtyard and into a verdant walled garden where several other visitors were moving among the flowerbeds or sitting in arbours. At the far end, a spring emerged from a rock and flowed, tinkling brightly, into a marble basin. I realised how thirsty I was. A tin cup stood beneath a printed notice that said *NOT DRINKING WATER*. Someone had augmented that stern, official admonition with hand-written addenda so that it read, *They have made us say that this is NOT DRINKING WATER but we've been drinking it for centuries and it's fine*. It was delicious.

When I returned to the house at two, I found the door open and a group gathering within. The stone-floored hall was flanked by doors, all closed. A carved oak stair rose to a stained-glass window, parted and rose again.

Against one dark-panelled wall stood a board, evidently erected on open days, with a display of photographs. The earliest, from the 1860s, was a group portrait of family and servants arranged in the courtyard. An ancient *grande dame* of immense dignity and girth, identified as Lady Evangeline Damory, was enthroned among the serried ranks of her relations, ranging from an old man with walrus moustaches to an infant in yards of lace. Phalanxes of footmen, housemaids, cooks and kitchen-maids on one side and rows of keepers, under-keepers, gardeners, under-gardeners, grooms and stable hands on the other outnumbered the family by about five to one.

Next came garden parties, with ladies in lace and parasols, men in beards and linen suits. This was the arty aristocracy at play: the captions identified Bertrand Russell, Maynard Keynes, David and Frieda Lawrence, Roger Fry, Vanessa Bell, Ottoline Morrell and Augustus John, with his arm slung over the shoulders of his great friend and rival Jarlath Quinn. Maggie Quinn, née Damory, the sensation of the Edwardian stage, cut a glamorous figure in ropes of pearls, bracelets to her elbows and a cigarette in a long holder.

The photographs taken after the First World War had an altogether more casual feel. Most were just family snaps, but there was one, dated 1924, formally posed in perhaps conscious imitation of the first. It showed a much reduced household – five or six house servants, nearly all female. Three or four gardeners were old men or young boys. Lord Perceval Damory sat in the centre, surrounded by his family. The caption listed Maggie and Jarlath Quinn and several others, but my eye was caught at once by the names Stephen Aubrey and Paul Asher. I recognised them both, though they were very young. Stephen Aubrey, described as a tutor, sat between two children. Paul Asher was identified as Lord Damory's secretary. He stood behind his employer and a little to one side. He seemed to be sharing a joke with a teenage girl on his other side; his head was tilted towards her and he was smiling. She was making a face at the camera, which distorted her features considerably, but there was something familiar about her. The caption identified her as Alice Damory Quinn.

The same Miss Quinn appeared in a newspaper clipping from 1928, standing beside a huge stone sarcophagus. The article went on to say that the family was donating to the British Museum the contents of a Roman-era temple of Isis discovered at Farundell. Miss Quinn, described as a student at Somerville College, Oxford, was unmistakably the person I knew as Inès Asher.

A trim woman of middle years in a blue blazer and no-nonsense shoes appeared and introduced herself as Mrs Coleman, senior volunteer tour guide. I was busy ruminating on the revelation of Inès Asher's true identity and didn't pay much attention as she launched into a well-rehearsed lecture on the early history of the house, with numerous erudite asides about Tudor politics. She pointed out the stair and the linen-fold panelling and other features of the hall before taking us through a pair of double doors into a long room that spanned the house from front to back. This was the 'famous Damory Library, containing the largest collection in England of sixteenth-, seventeenth- and eighteenth-century alchemical and Rosicrucian texts'.

Mrs Coleman drew our attention to the Aubusson carpets, a Grinling Gibbons overmantel, a pair of Riesener commodes and a Hepplewhite desk. It was obvious that the room was in daily use: there were piles of books by every chair, and the sun, slanting through the windows, revealed a patina of cat-hair on a worn damask sofa. Tall glass-fronted bookcases lined the walls, alternating with paintings in gilded frames.

Mrs Coleman led the way to a striking portrait of a lean-faced, scholarly man in austere black robes and skullcap, with a cool, analytical gaze and a quill in his hand. Shelves behind him held mathematical instruments and chemical apparatus, piles of books and manuscripts with hieroglyphic writing. A stuffed crocodile hung from the dim ceiling; a human skull glowered from a niche. Mrs Coleman identified the sitter as Tobias Damory, 1538–1620, a renowned Elizabethan scholar and the founder of the Library. The painting bore a plaque identifying it as *The Alchemist* by George Gower.

'He's an immortal,' said an American voice behind me, and I turned to behold a chubby young woman dressed all in black, laden with jangly silver jewellery depicting moons and pentagrams, brandishing a guide book with the triply redundant title *The Hidden Secrets of Occult England*. 'It says he discovered the secret of eternal life, faked his death to avoid persecution and now lives as a hermit in the Himalayas.'

Mrs Coleman smiled indulgently. It was evident she'd heard it all before. 'Of course, here at Farundell we're very proud of all our hidden, secret, occult . . . secrets, but if it's true, all I can say is, poor chap. It doesn't sound like an amusing place to spend eternity, does it? I'm sure the family would make him very welcome if he cared to come home.'

The American girl ignored her and, pushing to the front of the group, began what appeared to be a magical ritual before the portrait, Mrs Coleman intervening just in time to prevent her lighting a joss stick. 'Fire regulations, dear.'

The rest of the visitors drifted away to examine the bookcases and the other paintings and I turned to Mrs Coleman. 'But Tobias Damory *was* an alchemist?'

'That simply means he was a scientist, an enquirer into nature. He was extremely well respected in his day, though there was,' she conceded, 'a fine line between legitimate, Church-sanctioned science and black magic. As for his immortality, well, several men of that era were reputed to have achieved the Great Work, as it's called: the transmutation of lead into gold. And themselves into . . . something more than human. Both are perhaps metaphors for arriving at a higher level of understanding. But Tobias here,' she gestured affectionately towards the portrait, 'is safely buried in the family graveyard.'

'Just 'cause there's a grave doesn't mean it contains anyone, or that they're who it says on the tombstone,' said the American girl, completing her ritual with an elaborate genuflection.

Mrs Coleman moved off to gather the group around another painting at the far end of the room but I remained, staring up at Tobias Damory. Though hundreds of years separated him from his descendant Alice Damory Quinn, alias Inès Asher, the resemblance was definitely there in the line of nose and jaw, but most of all in the penetrating gaze.

I returned the look. *You're not dead, are you, Tobias?* I asked him, and for a moment glimpsed the faintest shadow of a smile flitting across his thin lips. *You really are living in the Himalayas, aren't you?* The shelves behind him seemed to melt away, revealing a vista of high mountains. I knew then who he was: Thobo Rinpoche, the ageless holy lama of Lo Manthang, the person whose assistance Luce, powerful Luce, had sought when her own efforts to help Francis had failed. Thobo Rinpoche, on whom Professor Inès Asher and her strange daughter Lucha had previously paid a call. Just a family visit.

I didn't yet see the full picture, but I had the most acute sensation of pieces shifting, realigning, dropping into place. Glimmers of connection began to appear between things that I'd thought utterly disparate. Slightly unnerved and deeply intrigued, I made my own inner obeisance towards Tobias/Thobo and followed the tour across the hall.

The Music Room was large and bright, with sheet music piled atop a grand piano by the French doors, a cello case in a corner, a violin case and other instruments on a shelf; the Damorys, it seemed, were a musical lot. This, surely, was Luce's real family, and Alice/Inès, as I'd always suspected, her real mother. The identity of her father – like that of many avatars – remained obscure.

Mrs Coleman led the group to an ornately painted double

harpsichord that had belonged, she told us, to the great castrato Celestino and had been played by George Frideric Handel himself. Apparently the family's association with music was at least as famous as its bibliophilia; Mrs Coleman had a lot to say on the subject. My attention was caught by a portrait showing a handsome, frock-coated man seated at a harpsichord – the same one, and in this very room. Auburn curls cascaded over his shoulders and yards of creamy lace draped his throat and wrists. His hands, poised over the keyboard, wore many rings. He gazed out at the viewer, smiling a distinctly sardonic smile, clear hazel eyes seductive and amused. A plaque identified the artist as Allan Ramsay and the sitter as Lord Francis Damory.

Like someone from the court of the Sun King, I remembered René saying. Rings on every finger, according to Madame Boucher, and silver buckles on his shoes. Yes, there were the silver buckles. Another piece of the puzzle slipped into place with a smooth click. I'd never seen him without a mask, but this had to be Francis, Lucie's imaginary friend who, through LSD, became Frankie, the Holy Ghost, Chico, Dermot and Franz: her keyboard player and constant companion through all her personae. This was the man for whom she had risked life and liberty to rescue from the hell of the prison lab, the man who had died to save her at Conway Hall. Fergus had said she called him Grandpapa, and took it for a joke. In reality he had to be – I made a quick calculation – at least her five- or six-times great-grandfather. His gorgeous, baroque affectations of dress were not affectations at all, merely his accustomed garb. And the tall tales he'd told – at least some of them – had been the simple but unbelievable truth.

'He's a famous ghost.' The American girl appeared at my elbow. '"Lord Francis Damory, the legendary ghost of Farundell, appears on nights of the full moon and plays the harpsichord until dawn,"' she recited.

Mrs Coleman joined us. 'Your information is a trifle out of date, my dear,' she said. 'I regret to say that Lord Francis no longer haunts Farundell.'

The American girl pouted. 'It says here that he does not appear to *everyone*. Just because *you* don't see him doesn't mean he's not around.'

Mrs Coleman's smile tightened. 'I'm afraid that no one has seen him for years.'

'Humph,' said the American girl, and stomped off.

'How many years?' I asked. 'Just out of curiosity.'

Mrs Coleman considered. 'Do you know, I'm not really sure. Twelve? Thirteen? Before my time here. It is true that only some people could see him, indeed saw him often, while he remained invisible to most. Contrary to the young lady's guide book, he abided by no known schedule, so his absence was not immediately apparent.'

'Perhaps at last he rests in peace,' I said, not facetiously, though I think that's how she took it.

I lingered in the Music Room as the tour proceeded upstairs, basking in the deeply pleasurable sensation of penetrating long-abiding mysteries. Thobo Rinpoche was Tobias Damory the immortal, Frankie the Holy Ghost was Francis Damory, who'd stopped haunting Farundell when he achieved corporeality. As questions morphed into answers, new enigmas were generated. And then I noticed the theremin in the corner.

There was the sound of hurrying steps and a russet-haired little girl of about four ran in from the hall. She saw me, stopped, and was about to run back out when footsteps sounded and a woman's voice called, 'Francie? Where are you?'

The girl gave me a cheeky grin, pressed her finger to her lips and dived out of the French doors. In that instant I knew who she must be: the child of Francis and Jukebox, born after Francis died at Conway Hall. And that theremin must be Jukebox's. I recalled that Fergus had described her as a cousin of Luce's, though I hadn't assumed that was the literal truth. Perhaps it was, after all. The pieces were whizzing into place so fast that I had to sit down on the piano stool to get my breath.

A slim woman in jeans and a T-shirt came in, a look of amused annoyance on her face. Her dark hair was pulled back in a pony-tail; her eyes were framed by laughter-lines; the strong nose and wide mouth were pure Damory. 'Oh, sorry,' she said, when she saw me. 'I think the tour has gone upstairs. Have you seen a little girl?'

'Out of the door,' I said. 'And I know the tour has moved on. I lingered to pay my respects to Francis, the Holy Ghost.' I gestured to the portrait. 'And to you. Jukebox, I presume.' I rose and made her a deep bow. 'I'm Chimera Obscura, the Scribe.'

'Oh,' she said. 'Oh, my God,' and sat down abruptly on a chair. She looked from me to the portrait on the wall and burst into tears. 'Sorry,' she said, fumbling for a handkerchief. 'Sorry. It was just so sudden. I haven't seen or heard from anyone from those days in so long. Not since Conway Hall. Were you there? I remember Fergus said he invited you.'

'Yes, I was there.'

'Do you know what happened? I've never been able to figure it out. I'd turned away to fiddle with my amp and the next thing I knew there was fire and smoke with everybody running around like madmen and falling over each other in the dry-ice fog. Apparently someone shot at the stage and Francis . . .' she gazed at the portrait for a long moment, '. . . Francis jumped in front of Luce. When I got to them Luce was trying to make the blood stop . . . but it wouldn't. We were going to take him to hospital but he refused. Just bring me home to Farundell, he said.'

'I didn't see much myself, but I do know what happened.' And then I had to tell her about Charlie: what he'd done, and why, and how he'd died, and the part I'd played. If she wasn't in touch with anyone from Pymander Productions, she wouldn't know what had happened to Wingbow and Obelisk, Fergus and Greyling, so I had to tell her all that, too. Never have I had so much painful news to relate at one time to one person. I couldn't bear to look at her while I spoke; when I did, I saw that tears were running down her cheeks, too.

Being English, we dealt with our emotion by moving respectfully apart. I crossed to the other side of the room, wiped my eyes and lit a cigarette. She rose and stood for several long minutes at the French doors. Past her shoulder I could see the small figure of her daughter, running and tumbling across a wide lawn with an ebullient spaniel. Even wars have survivors.

From the hall came the sound of the tour group leaving. The American girl appeared to be repeating questions she'd asked earlier – something to do, no doubt, with the secret, hidden, occult history of the house.

'Look,' I heard Mrs Coleman say, her voice ever so slightly raised in exasperation. 'If I knew any hidden secrets you'd be absolutely the first person I'd tell. But I'm afraid all we can offer you is tea and cake, rather good cake, if I may say, so if you'd like to have a little stroll over to the tea room, yes, right over there . . . Thank you *so* much for coming.' There was the sound of a door closing and a bolt being vigorously thrown. Mrs Coleman breathed an audible sigh of relief and it seemed the house did, too, as it reverted once again to a family home.

Jukebox turned back to me. Her eyes rested briefly on Francis's portrait, love tinged with such delicate sadness that it pierced my heart, then she gave herself a shake and set aside her grief like a well-worn shroud. 'I'm forgetting my manners,' she said. 'Would you like a cup of tea?'

'Very much,' I said, and followed her along several passages to a vast Victorian kitchen. She put on the kettle and set out mugs; we introduced ourselves. Her name was Gwen and she was the daughter of the present Lord Damory (Alice/Inès's uncle), which made her Luce's first cousin once removed. I noticed that when we spoke about Luce Gwen hesitated before using a personal pronoun, as though waiting to see whether I myself regarded Luce as male or female. I opted for the feminine, Luce having been identified as female by Fergus and Wingbow. Gwen flowed right along with this choice, but I suspected she knew the truth.

We took our tea, with a glass of milk for Francie and a box of amaretti biscuits (what else?) outside to the lawn where girl and dog, temporarily worn out, lay in the shade of a huge old oak. The sun shone, the sky was cloudless blue, grasshoppers rasped, pigeons cooed and clattered in the branches. Below us a broad meadow sloped down to a lake with a rocky island that I recognised from Paul Asher's photograph. The scene was idyllic, yet shaded with tragedy by memories of the ones who'd died: Francis, Wingbow, Obelisk, Greyling, Charlie . . . and how many more? Gwen would later give me the names of three other members of the Pymander Productions gang whose real identities she knew and ask me to find out what had happened to them. I never had the chance to complete these enquiries.

The lad in the Blue Öyster Cult T-shirt, gatekeeping duties done for the day, came round the side of the house, was introduced as a cousin of some sort, tickled Francie until she shrieked, grabbed a handful of biscuits and sloped off.

Gwen laughed when I described the sleight of hand at Paul Asher's gallery that had led me to Farundell. Paul, she told me, had a flat in the old stable block but was at the moment travelling; she didn't know where. It scarcely mattered: following his trail had led me nearer to the heart of Luce than I could ever have imagined.

'And where's Luce?' I asked, for I'd begun to feel that I was quite close.

'I don't know. No one ever knows. She comes and goes.' Luce, Gwen told me, had over the years been a frequent though irregular visitor to Farundell, always turning up unannounced and never staying long. Farundell, I realised, must be the other 'protected' place that Rachel had mentioned.

Gwen had known Francis as a 'ghost' all her life; it had been he who'd inspired her love of music and had given her her first piano lessons, aged five. She told me his story. Like Tobias his great-great-grandfather, Francis had become an alchemist and eventually achieved the Great Work: the elixir of immortality. The perfection of the human race was his passion, and through all the centuries he'd remained certain that it was not only possible but inevitable. Mindful of Tobias's example, he had kept his alchemical success a secret, faking his own death many times until 'a small miscalculation' had led to the loss of his physical body, though not his actual death. He'd been compelled to abide on the material plane, yet not as a material man – until he found LSD, the miraculous chemical that would restore him to corporeality. V had read him right: he was an in-between being, perhaps the only one of his kind. It was no wonder, I thought, that the government scientists had been so pleased to catch him. When Francis died, Gwen told me, his body had immediately begun to grow lighter and had evaporated within a few hours.

'I know he believed that it was his destiny to take care of Luce. It was worth everything to him, everything, to protect her. He realised that this was why he'd remade his body: so that it could stop the bullet meant for Luce. I understood; I'd have done the same thing. The love we had for each other was always part of our love for Luce.'

'Did he know you were pregnant?'

'Yes. I told him . . . just before he died. It made him laugh, but laughing wasn't very good for him. He died laughing. Literally.'

She laughed too, a light, fond laugh. I pictured the charismatic, debonair figure I'd never met, a man who knew how to swagger through life . . . and how to make a dramatic exit. 'And he no longer haunts Farundell?'

'Oh, he's around. I feel him from time to time. But he doesn't *haunt*. He's leaving me to get on with it.' Her eyes rested on the drowsy face of their daughter, lying with her head cushioned on the silky flank of the spaniel.

I wondered if Gwen knew about Rachel. If she did, she wasn't telling me, so I didn't feel it was my place to tell her. Luce lived her life – her lives – in sealed compartments for her own sufficient reasons. If these separate lives were destined to connect, fate would see to it and needed no clumsy intervention from me.

Two old men were walking slowly up towards the house, arm in arm. They paused to greet us; Gwen introduced her father, Daniel, and his friend Arlen. Young Francie, calling him Uncle Arlen, reminded him it was almost time for her music lesson, which he was to provide. She raced ahead to prepare and the two men followed at a more leisured pace.

As they vanished into the house Gwen looked at me and suddenly snapped her fingers. '*Now* I know where I've seen you,' she said. 'I've been trying and trying to remember. You looked so familiar, but I couldn't quite place it.' She was grinning, as though she'd uncovered a great surprise. 'You don't remember, do you? You don't recognise me.'

I shook my head.

'It was a long time ago. And we were awfully young.'

I racked my brains, then shrugged helplessly. 'Can I have a clue?'

'A party on the island, a big party.' She gestured across the lake. 'Let's see, it was 1958, June, I think . . . I was eighteen. Do you know, I believe you crashed the party, because I asked around after and no one knew who you were.'

484

'That was *here*? I remember that party, it was my first acid trip . . . the most amazing experience. I recall an island, but it didn't look like that. There was a meadow running right down to the lake.'

'The party was on the other side of the island,' Gwen said. 'You must have come up from the river and never seen it from this side.'

'Oh, the *other* side,' I repeated, laughing. 'You're right, I did crash your party. I'd been out on the Isis with some friends – we'd hired a couple of rowing boats at the pub in Exley. It was a very hot afternoon, wasn't it? We heard music drifting across the fields so we tied up on the bank and walked over to investigate. People were being ferried across to the island and we . . . joined them.' I gazed at Gwen – the mischievous eyes, the quirky smile. 'I remember you now. You were the pixie in the tree. With the flute and the sugar cube. You changed my life.'

'It was Luce who changed your life. She prepared a few cubes and told me to offer them to people. When I asked how I should choose, she said they'll choose themselves. They'll come to you. Make sure they know what it is and ask them if they're ready.'

'Luce was *there*? On the island, at the party?'

Gwen nodded. 'At least some of the time. I didn't see her after that, but it's a pretty big island. You seemed very ready indeed, if I may say.'

'I was. Oh, I definitely was. How many sugar cubes did you give out?'

'Well, as it happens, just that one. After I left you I went down to the lake and . . . I fell in. The others melted in my pocket.'

The past came rushing forward, bursting through the present. Luce . . . it had been Luce even then, reaching into my life and fucking with my head. She'd set an acid-baited destiny-trap and I'd fallen in. Somewhere on that island, deep in the heart of that first trip, something had happened – something so profound that it couldn't be retained like an ordinary memory but had buried itself deeply in my consciousness. It had been sleeping but now it was awakening, tickling the back of my mind. This, *this* was the real beginning of the thread that linked me to Luce.

I tried to explain things to Gwen, but I'm not sure I made much sense. I knew one thing: I had to return to that island, retrace the trip, find my way back to that hidden beginning. Gwen agreed to take me; I waited while she went up to the house to tell someone where she was going. In a few minutes she returned and we walked down to the lake. A little blue boat was tethered to a ramshackle dock. I sat in the stern as Gwen untied the rope, pushed off and began rowing towards the island, about half a mile away.

The clear greenish water slid beneath us, slippery as time. I had ceased to follow the thread; it was pulling me now, reeling me in. I was carried along by the rhythmic strokes of the oars, their small splashing noises, the shifting reflections of sun on water. As we came around the island's western, rocky side things began to look familiar: the fields and water meadows that led down to the Isis, the broad pasture at the lake's far edge.

'There was a barge, and a boatman dressed like Charon,' I said, remembering. He'd worn a tunic of hessian sacks, sandals and a false beard made of sheep's wool. To be on the safe side, and to ensure I was able to return, I'd tipped him generously.

'That was Mr Pym with the sheep barge. I can't imagine how we ever persuaded him to dress up like that. He's the head gardener. The only gardener, these days.'

Gwen ran the boat up on a pebbled beach and we climbed out. The meadow rose in a gentle slope towards the wooded crest of the island. Now populated only by a small flock of Jacob sheep, then it had been thronged with party-goers in varying stages of tipsiness and every imaginable attire, from Bermuda

shorts to blazers and regimental ties, beatnik-black stovepipes
to proper afternoon dresses and vintage twenties beaded frocks.
Children paddled in the shallow water; others dived from a high
rock. Wet dogs were causing havoc among the better-dressed.
It had been one of those parties that immediately split into two
parties as, like curdling milk, the hip and the square separated,
forming homogenous coteries that regarded each other, if at all,
with amusement, scorn or suspicion.

'Do you still have parties here?' I asked Gwen.

'Not on that scale. No one has the time to organise things
like that any more. We have the occasional full moon party in
the summer, weather permitting, of course, very informal, just
whoever's around.'

An exceptionally good jazz quintet had been playing under a
marquee near the shore, mellow riffs wafting by on a breeze
laden with the scent of new-mown hay. The memory of that
smell immediately summoned back the secret gig in Camden,
when that fragrance, or the illusion of it, had triggered my recollection of the party on the island. At the time, there had seemed
no reason why that particular memory should just then have
resurfaced. Now, I understood perfectly. This was a loop in the
thread. I waited, and, sure enough, the scent appeared again,
carried on a gust of wind from a field on the far side of the lake,
where a tractor was cutting the grass.

'I should have brought a picnic,' said Gwen. 'Or at least a
bottle of wine.'

'Or champagne. I remember maids with champagne and
lobster canapés on trays.'

'Lobster canapés! I remember those, too. These days it's strictly
BYOB, and you'd be lucky to get a sandwich.'

My friends and I had colonised a spot near the top of the
slope, under a magisterial elm. The tree was still there; Gwen
and I strolled up the meadow and stood in its thick, warm shade.

The scene from the past, in tentative shimmers, superimposed itself over the present.

I'd lit up a hash pipe and someone began playing guitar, picking out a counterpoint to a languorous duet of trumpet and violin drifting up from the jazz band. The champagne and the hash, the light wavering through the leaves, the flux of sounds near and far had induced a pleasantly dreamy state. I'd left my friends and wandered off, heard the flute, met the pixie in the tree . . . and nothing was ever the same again.

'It was that way, wasn't it?' I asked Gwen. 'Where I found you.'

'Just up there.'

Beneath the trees it was cool and dim, the forest floor springy with layers of fallen leaves. A squirrel chattered on a branch; a deer, unseen until it moved, leapt away through the undergrowth. I thought I glimpsed my doppelgänger walking ahead, refracted through the suddenly malleable matrix of time. *You've no idea*, I said to that young, innocent, adventurous self, *what's about to happen to you.*

I remembered how it began. I'd been so busy checking my watch and wondering when I'd start to feel the effects that at first I didn't notice that the colour of the sky had changed from blue to a deep, vibrant mauve. As I stared at it, tiny pinpricks of gold appeared, burst and dissolved. Then the trees acquired pink halos, each fluttering leaf limned in gently pulsing light. I looked at my clothes: they were shifting through all shades of green, merging with the meadow, the grasses, the trees. A transfusion of green blood was flowing into me from . . . well, from everything.

I must have wandered for hours, becoming ever more porous. Not going anywhere, not looking for anything, I was just a poem unfurling into the deepening day. I'd found the perfect drug and I remember thinking I wanted to be like that all the time; everyone should be like that all the time. Breathing, simply breathing, was the most sublime bliss. I moved like a sylph, insubstantial, slipping between sunbeams. I walked on tiptoe; I walked without touching the ground at all. The sheer delight of it was making me laugh, a silent, inner laugh that chimed like bells. I was filled with a wild, effervescent joy. An ultraviolet fountain bubbled in my heart and streamed out through my eyes and my fingertips, through the pores of my skin. All my senses were wide, wide open.

Gwen walked beside me in silence, letting me feel my way into the past. She understood that I was questing the most elusive prey: a wisp of memory. I glimpsed a brief smile; perhaps she had her own memories to pursue. She stopped by a rocky outcrop that narrowed the path and turned to me, the mischievous look in her eyes.

'Do you happen to remember? We met, right here. You were coming down the hill, I was going up. It was the first I'd seen of you since I gave you the acid. It must have been close to midnight – the moon was very bright. Your eyes were so wide, you looked like you were made of moonlight and shadows. You told me about a bird with phosphorescent plumage that flies at night and lights its own way through the jungle. You said you'd seen it yourself, though it was very rare. Then you told me I was beautiful and you kissed me. You disappeared and I never saw you again.'

'Was that you? I remember a beautiful face glowing in the darkness. You were the first person I encountered after . . . after whatever it was that happened. I was coming down the hill, you say? I wonder where I'd been all that time. There was a sort of glade, with tall marble columns – but maybe I hallucinated that.'

'Oh, no, you didn't. It's at the top of the hill. The columns came from Cyprus, a temple of Aphrodite. Francis put them there, in fact. He was into landscape gardening on a fairly grand scale.'

We continued up the path through the sun-dappled shadows of the leaves, plain green now, though the memory of their pink halos hovered at the edge of vision. I recognised the place, though the space I recalled as broad and open, carpeted with iridescent green moss and tiny, winking star-flowers, was now thronged with nettles, hemmed in by holly and brambles. The columns were deep in ivy.

Gwen sighed. 'We can't get a tractor up here so it has to be scythed by hand. Can you believe hardly anyone knows how to do that any more? All they can do is turn on motors and ride great big machines up and down in straight lines. The only one who can scythe is Mr Pym himself and he's got all the orchards to do. But I'll ask him to come out here when he can.' She picked up a fallen branch and began whacking at the nettles, making a path to the centre. 'Is this the place you remember?'

'More or less. It looked different. Everything had become transparent at that point, I think. I could see the veins in the trunks of the trees and the earth was hollow.'

'Well, it is, actually. There's a cave under here.'

'A cave?' Memory flashed: I was moving in utter darkness, deep into the heart of the earth. There was warmth, and a sweet fragrance . . .

'There used to be a stair,' Gwen said, 'but everything's so overgrown, I'm not sure we can get down there.' She whacked her way to the opposite side of the glade, where a giant oak had fallen. Its massive roots, long washed bare of earth, clawed the sky. It had stood at the top of a steep cliff; the remains of stone-cut steps could be seen disappearing under its weathered trunk and skewed branches.

'I remember those steps,' I said.

Gwen and I clambered over the fallen tree and fought through the brambles, branches and ubiquitous nettles. Before we reached the bottom of the steps I knew what we'd find: a pool of water, its still surface reflecting the far-off disc of sky, the forest close-circling it and shutting out all but a narrow shaft of light. I looked around, almost expecting to see the pile of my clothes on the rock where I'd left them. They had seemed an obscenity, a grating, choking suffocation. I'd stepped out of them with a writhe and a shudder, like a snake shedding its skin, and slid into the cool, obsidian-black water.

'I went swimming in there,' I said to Gwen.

'Brrr. Wasn't it icy?'

'Oh, no, it was . . . indescribably delicious.'

'Is that the thing you wanted to remember?'

'No. There's more.' The trickle of memory turned into a flood; the past glowed vivid, tangible, becoming more real than the present. I saw myself emerging from the pool, glittering; I'd turned into a liquid, living rainbow. That was when I heard the melody, a sweet, high air that was also the scent of roses. It stroked my mind with silky fingers and seemed to draw me on.

'Where's the cave?' I asked, and Gwen led me around the edge of the pool, through a thicket of laurel and a hanging curtain of ivy into a silent, dim cavern. Just enough light penetrated to reveal that it was about eight feet high and forty feet deep; the walls, ceiling and floor shaped into a smooth oval.

'This cave was inhabited since the Stone Age,' Gwen said, sounding like a tour guide. 'Tools have been found, flints, that sort of thing. Francis made it into a grotto. Over a hundred thousand shells went into the decorations. It's rather splendid. But you can't see any of them, can you, because it's dark. I should have brought a torch.'

Memory tugged at me, pulling me deeper. 'There's more, isn't there? It went down from here.'

'There's an underground chamber. It used to have statues and wall-paintings from a Roman temple. The family donated them to the British Museum in lieu of death duties when my grand-father died. It's been empty for ages.'

I followed Gwen as she groped her way to the back of the cave. As my eyes adjusted to the gloom I made out a set of worn stone steps descending into even deeper blackness.

'Yes,' I whispered. 'Down here. I went down here.' I moved forward, my hand on the wall beside me. The stone felt warm and alive. The stair turned, turned again. I closed my eyes; I didn't need them. The thread was tugging me gently on. I stepped into the darkness and let the memory rise at last.

Later, Gwen told me I'd been in there for only a few minutes, though it had felt much longer. She waited on the steps; she heard me breathing, and a few times I sighed or softly exclaimed. And then I emerged looking, she said, much as I'd looked that night fourteen years ago: wide-eyed, radiant.

It had been, I suppose, a classic enlightenment experience. I'd encountered truth, or reality or gnosis or god – whatever you want to call it, and it had blasted open my mind. It was everything and it obliterated everything; it had killed me and resurrected me. I was transformed, turned inside out and reborn. If it was something that was possible to put into words it would not have been so impossible to remember in the first place, and the memory of it, rekindled there that day, proved scarcely more enduring. But I knew one thing: I had not been alone. The truth, the reality, the god had been a person. Luce and I had met, and the experience had so over-whelmed my human consciousness that I, like poor forgetful Kuro, could not retain it – except as the strange, lambent image of a self-luminous, night-flying bird and the fading glow of ecstasy.

In silence, Gwen and I made our way out of the cavern, past the pool, up the stair, over the fallen oak and out into the bright afternoon. With each step the past receded and I spiralled back into the present. When we reached the meadow we sat for a while in the shade of the old elm.

'I think I know what happened,' Gwen said. 'I can see it in you. I could see it in you then. That light. And that kiss, which was, you know, really quite intense. Luce was in there, wasn't . . . she?'

I nodded, then thought, Does she mean in the cavern, or in me? and understood that it didn't matter. 'It "made me what I am,"' I sang softly, quoting Luce's song, 'Human'.

'Oh!' Gwen looked at me with wonder dawning in her face. 'The rest of that line, how does it go? "I found you or you found me in this beautiful darkness, beloved human, dark heart of life, you made me what I am." Don't you realise?'

'Realise what?'

'It's *you*. You're the human. "Beloved human, dark heart of life." The song's about *you*. When we were recording that song, I asked Luce about it, because it's the only one on the album that's clearly about an actual person, a real person she'd known. She said something that seemed enigmatic at the time, but now I understand. She told me she'd met someone just once, but the experience had transformed her; it made her realise who she was and what she had to do. She's never stopped, not for a day since then. Before that, I think she was trying to lead an ordinary life, enjoy herself, play music, paint. I'd never glimpsed who she really was, what she could do. But after that, it was like someone had flipped a switch in her, turned her on, set her alight.'

I was stunned into silence. At first I couldn't believe it, then I didn't want to, then I wanted to but didn't dare . . . but in the end I had to. Gwen rowed us back to the house; we went up to her room where she put on the *Human* album and played the song for me three times before I was convinced. It's one of the songs whose lyrics have given the most trouble to would-be interpreters, not least because the vocals are double- or triple-tracked and in several languages. T. K. Quelling provides the following translation (slashes separate text sung simultaneously):

I found you or you found me
In this beautiful darkness,
Beloved human, dark heart of life,
You made me what I am.
And now I know/and now I am
What I am because of you,
Beloved human, dark heart of life.
Inside you/inside me,
Enfolding/incarnating, broken/born
Reality – that's you/that's me, my love.
Sweet apple of earth/
Sweet fruit of the tree,
Beloved human, dark heart of life.
Loving/killing,
Knowing you/knowing me.*

Gwen invited me to stay for a drink, then dinner with Lord Damory, Uncle Arlen and assorted other family whose names I don't remember. All that went by in a bit of a blur, and I can recall nothing about the meal or the conversation. The words of 'Human' echoed in my mind.

By the time dinner was over it was nearly eleven, and when I announced my intention to get a room at the pub in Exley, Gwen wouldn't hear of it. 'We have masses of room,' she said.

I did not get much rest that night. Damorys surrounded me, generation piled on generation. How many had slept in this room where I lay beneath an ornate Jacobean ceiling, listening to the whispers of the walls? Luce herself, perhaps. Her cherished great-great-something-grandfather, Francis. If he no longer haunted the place as a ghost or displaced astral entity or whatever he had been, his presence certainly lingered.

* T. K. Quelling, *op. cit.*, p. 29.

The connection between me and Luce had turned out to be not only deeper and older than I'd thought, but possessed of an entire other dimension. Something about that encounter in the underground chamber had been important to Luce, had affected her, shaped the course of her life as it had mine. Did she know what would happen when she sent Gwen out with the sugar cubes? Was it pure chance that I got the only one, that my aimless meanders through the woods led me to Luce? She must have known I was coming, even if she didn't know who I was . . . other than a human, ready to wake up, ready to love.

Around dawn I fell into an uneasy sleep in which the Dream of the Cavern merged with yesterday's visit to the island cave. The thread of memory coiled behind me, the thread of destiny pulled me on. The sense that I was moving inexorably towards that longed-for finding of Luce was still there, but now twinned with its mirror image: that I was falling further and further from a place I had once been, a paradise I had touched, tasted and lost.

I woke about ten, dressed and went downstairs to the kitchen, where I made myself a cup of tea. The household was busy dealing with another open day; when I finally found Gwen there was no chance for more than thanks and a hug.

I was about to get into my car when another car pulled up. Two people got out and began unloading suitcases from the boot. They were Paul and Inès/Alice Asher. We greeted each other with mutual bemusement. I didn't even attempt an explanation.

'So nice to see you both,' I said cheerily, and drove away. As I passed the orchards the old man – Mr Pym, I supposed – was at work with his scythe. He looked up and waved to me, and I waved back.

Now.

I've researched public records for the names Gwen gave me all those years ago. Death certificates reveal that all three died during the spring and summer of 1968: one in Cardiff, one in Truro and one in Southall, London.

I don't have the contacts I used to, and anyway this is so long ago, I'm not sure how one would go about delving further into the circumstances of their deaths. Google searches are useless: the names are not uncommon. So last week I decided to put the matter into the hands of a private investigative agency. I chose an outfit with a Mayfair address and rang them up, speaking to a Ms Bannerjee whose carefully modulated tones suggested the utmost discretion, though I detected the tiniest note of surprise when I described the information I wanted – cheating business partners and unfaithful spouses being their usual fare. She took down the three names and dates, plus my bank card details for a five-hundred-pound retainer.

Now they've telephoned and invited me to come to

the office to receive the report. I ask if it can't be emailed to me but, no, it needs to be presented in person. Intrigued, I make my way to Brook Street.

I'm shown into a conference room with several chairs around a table and told that Ms Bannerjee will be with me shortly. The large mirror dominating one wall strikes a discordant note and sends a warning tingle down my spine. My most innocuous face locks into place, my mildest manner coats me in a protective gel. I'd quite like to get up and leave, but that would certainly arouse suspicion. I wait in silence.

Ms Bannerjee enters and sits across from me. She's an efficient-looking young woman in a staid navy-blue trouser suit, with scraped-back hair, bad acne and a serious expression.

'I'm sorry to have to tell you that we're unable to undertake the investigations you requested.' She hands me a cheque. 'We are returning your retainer in full.'

'Do you mean you couldn't find out anything at all?'

'We are unable to proceed. That's all I can say.'

I consider offering more money, but I get the impression that Ms Bannerjee and her firm wouldn't touch this job for any amount. Mutely I accept the cheque and leave. In the waiting room there's a man, an exceptionally ordinary man in a beige suit, with neat hair and colourless eyes that fix on me as I cross the room.

My skin crawls and I know at once what he is. I note the queasy rise of fear and dread in my gut, the weird, numbing effect. I keep my face as expressionless as his, make my legs carry me across the room, out of the door, down the corridor and the stairs and into the street. I walk away as fast as I can, checking

497

from time to time to see if I'm being followed, but that's silly, they have no need to follow me - they know who I am, they know where I live.

My recent suspicions are justified, after all. The only problem is that I haven't been suspicious enough. I'm not being paranoid; demons are definitely around, and keeping an eye me. For how long? Since my return to the UK? Is this the NOHRM, still at it after all these years? And was the encounter in the waiting room staged just to let me know they're watching? Or perhaps to make sure I'm who they think I am. Hard to believe they consider me worthy of interest. Surely they can't think I'll lead them to Luce. Do they suspect that she's still alive, or alive again? They can't imagine I myself pose any danger . . . can they? No one knows I'm writing *The Book of Luce* . . . or do they? Neil knows, or at least suspects.

I learned long ago that the astral entities with whom I've contended over the years aren't the only demons. A demon can be an indwelling spirit, driving a person to evil. A demon can be a mind-set, a network of controls operating within the ordinary human and like a virus corroding the goodness, warping the igno- rance, replacing the genuine self with a robot - and then manipulating the robot through fear and greed. Where the human soul flees to during such an occupa- tion I don't know; nor do I know how responsible it should be held for what's done in its absence.

Back at World's End, I can't sleep. The amorphous anxiety of Seroxat withdrawal morphs into the very concrete fear that I'll be unable to finish my work, complete *The Book of Luce* and release it to the world. I check that my door is locked, and check again.

All at once I realise what the problem is – I don't have an exit strategy. No wonder I feel trapped and helpless. I've played the harmless, gormless nutter for so long that sometimes I forget how crafty and clever I really am. I feel better already. Now all I have to do is devise a strategy and execute it.

This new-found resolve, or perhaps I should call it bravura, tarnishes a bit in the morning sun. How on earth am I to proceed? Fifty years ago Chimera Obscura knew everyone, was owed favours right and left, had fingers in many pies and connections all over the world. Chimera Obscura knew how to obtain false documents and guns. I don't.

Nonsense, I tell myself. The briefest glance at the tabloid press reveals that false papers are practically *de rigueur* in some quarters, and troves of illegal guns are always being discovered. In my day, you could buy one from the back door of the police station, metaphorically speaking. But you had to know someone. Well then, I will simply have to find someone. Surely, in this best of all possible worlds, anyone with discretion, determination and cash can buy whatever they want. I stop at the bank and withdraw a thousand pounds, then sally boldly forth, guided by the vague idea that the East End is more or less the place to look.

I'll need a dedicated phone for any criminal connections I manage to make, so on the way I stop at Tottenham Court Road. I'm very much encouraged when the second shop I enter agrees to sell me a pay-as-you-go phone, accepting cash as well as my story (delivered with panache and a French accent) that I'm a tourist who's been robbed of phone, credit cards and ID, and must buy a new phone in order to report the losses. Naturally I provide a false (French) name and address. Next, I find a photo booth and obtain a strip of passport photos. I rather admire the cocky angle of my head, the steady gaze.

My old forger operated his false documents service behind the front of a perfectly legal and successful printer's shop in Whitechapel. In order to maintain my momentum I make my way there, telling myself that even if the firm's no longer in business, or in *that* business, the next step will present itself to me. All I have to do is take the first one, take it confidently and whole-heartedly, with faith in my destiny.

The firm is still in business, though considerably tarted up, along with the rest of the neighbourhood. Fortified with a small shot of vodka from the nearest pub, I enter.

A high counter separates the customer area, furnished with a row of plastic chairs, a water cooler and a tea machine, from the large open office beyond, where people are hunched over their computers. To one side is a drawing table, an archaic vestige in the age of digital-everything, where an old man sits, apparently drawing on actual paper with a real pencil, though a laptop is open at his side.

A young man comes to the counter and greets me.

I clear my throat. 'I'd like to order some business cards.'

He reaches languidly for an order form, clicks his ballpoint pen. 'Name on card?'

'Hieronymous Hegarty Holdings,' I say, spelling it out with an utterly straight face.

The young man begins to write it down. The old man

at the drawing table has looked up; now he approaches the counter.

'I'll handle this customer,' he says. 'Hieronymous Hegarty Holdings is an old client.'

My forger, I recall, had a son whom he was training up in the business - both businesses. This must be that man. He raises the counter and gestures to me to precede him into a small, untidy office. He says little, merely asking what name, place and date of birth should appear. I'm not offered any choice of nationality. We negotiate a price of five thousand pounds; he accepts my one thousand as a deposit, takes the strip of photos and tells me to come to the back door at precisely ten twenty-five p.m., two nights hence.

Feeling a bit like a character in a comic strip (Kim Darke?), I suggest we synchronise watches. He doesn't have a watch, but we check to see that our phones display the same time. He shows me to the door and I head back to World's End in triumph. Destiny must truly be on my side. I'd never dared hope things would be so easy. Tomorrow I'll find a gun.

I sleep better than I have in a long time, wake and head into town with another pocketful of cash and the confident certainty that a gun will fall into my hands as easily as a false passport. I used to meet the contact from whom I bought my guns in a workers' café in Brixton. Dishearteningly, the place isn't there any longer. Nothing in the least resembles how I remember it - everything seems to be a housing estate. I wander helplessly for a time, then find my way to a small, grubby area - I really can't call it a park - with a few sorry-looking trees poking through cracked concrete, a patch of dead grass and a rubbish bin next to a half-broken bench. I sit on the unbroken end of the bench and light a Gitanes. Bravura has worn off; I feel old and futile, and what's worse, I feel stupid. Had I really thought someone would just come up and offer to sell me a gun? No one's even offered to sell me any weed, and I know it's around; I can smell it. I guess I don't look like a prospective customer for anything dodgy; all my years of perfecting a bland ordinariness have resulted in this: no one notices me at all.

Fate, I say, *or Luce, or anyone . . . if I'm meant to succeed, help me now.*

Almost immediately, a young man with lovely dreadlocks appears. He looks clean and trustworthy; when he glances at me in passing, I smile and raise my eyebrows. He heads my way! I prepare a greeting, but it turns out he only wants to drop something into the rubbish bin. I'm deeply disappointed, then I notice that he places the object (a crumpled though not empty manila envelope) carefully at the edge of the bin, rather than dropping it in any old way.

He's turning away – I must speak at once. 'Excuse me,' I say, 'but do you know where I can buy some weed?'

That stops him. He turns and looks at me incredulously, then comes to sit at my side. Due to the broken nature of the bench he has to sit rather close. He smells pleasantly of patchouli . . . and top-quality pot. Surely Luce has sent him to help me.

'Don't give me that incredulous look,' I say. 'I've done more drugs than you could ever hope to do.'

'Sorry, sorry,' he says. 'No offence. It's good to

see the old folks living up to their reputation. It's just that you look so straight.'

'Thank you. It's what's known as protective colouration.'

This amiable exchange having broken the ice, we negotiate for a quarter ounce of the most outrageous-smelling skunk I've ever encountered. He warns me, unnecessarily, not to smoke too much at once; I'm getting high just smelling it through its little plastic bag.

'By the way,' I say, when this transaction is discreetly concluded, 'have you any idea where I could obtain a small handgun? Purely for personal protection.'

'Whoa.' He gets up and backs away. 'Whoa there. You some kind of cop? Protective colouration, yeah. Answer is no. I don't know anything about guns. You got the wrong man.'

He hurries off. I sigh. It had all been going so well. I'm sure he'd know where to get a gun. I've blown it somehow. I'll have to start again. Ah no, he's back. I knew it. He was only testing me.

'Come with me,' he says, and we set out together. My heart is pounding a bit. This is exactly what I wanted, but nevertheless . . .

'Where d'you live?' he asks.

'Enfield. World's End, to be exact. Why do you want to know?'

'Because that's where you're going.'

We've come to the tube station; he takes my arm and firmly escorts me down the stairs. 'Got a travel card? Come on.'

He guides me all the way to the platform and waits

with me until a train arrives. 'You know the way? That's good. Off you go. And keep out of trouble, you silly old fool.' He practically pushes me into the carriage. As the doors close he gives me a friendly grin and wags an admonitory finger.

No one tells you that the worst indignity of age is being treated like a child by well-meaning people a third your age.

I'd like to say I pick myself up and try again – after all, I've made real criminal contacts and *nearly* succeeded in buying a gun – but I've seen myself through my young friend's eyes, and I'm ludicrous. No one will sell me a gun.

Back at home, I find a very realistic-looking BB-pistol on Amazon. It's called 'The Terminator'. Dealing with demons is mostly about intention, imagination and will – as Ambrose demonstrated so effectively all those years ago. I request express delivery and am really quite comforted to know that it'll be here tomorrow.

29

Mr and Mrs Big

§

*A Meal Interrupted. Subterfuge and Action. The Gig
Is Up. A Curiously Unsatisfying Killing. The
Unidentified Assailant. Luce's Box. Ahmet Talks.*

London, June 1972

During the week following my visit to Farundell I prowled London, the thread humming in my hand. I was sure that Luce was near, and expected at any moment to come upon her presence in an art exhibition, a concert, a happening. I went around in a haze of nervous anticipation. From time to time I thought I glimpsed a demon following me or watching from a shadowed doorway. I would walk right up to him or her – my gun, with silencer attached and safety off, firmly grasped within my pocket. But they always turned out to be just an ordinary person. The surge of fear I felt when approaching them I put down to any soldier's fear of confrontation, heightened by my generally edgy state. That I would kill the next one I saw I had no doubt; the thought of what they'd done to Charlie and Francis, Fergus, Greyling and the others fed the small, sour flame in my gut where the longing for revenge burned and seethed.

Late one night I stopped into Ahmet's café in Goodge Street. I was tired and hungry; the warm lights and exotic posters offered a soothing respite. It was nearly closing time and I was the only customer, but he greeted me with his usual silent smile, providing a plate of hummus, salad and bread, then retiring to the kitchen where I could hear him pottering about.

I had just picked up my fork when Mrs Big walked in. The jolt of fear was so abrupt that I dropped the fork and it fell to the floor with a clatter. She sat down at the next table, her manner calm and casual, as though we had arranged this appointment. Her smile sent waves of queasy dread through my mind.

Initially thrown into a panic, I soon reassembled myself into two parts: subterfuge and action, or appearance and reality. Subterfuge greeted her with perfect civility, even managing to suggest that I was pleased to see her and eager to resume my work for the NOHRM. Action, under cover of retrieving my dropped fork, guided my right hand to my pocket, extracted my gun beneath the table, angled it towards her heart and shot her. The pop was satisfyingly small; the clatter from the kitchen continued uninterrupted. She slumped to the floor. I left a couple of quid on the table for Ahmet, and didn't stay to watch the body vanish.

The gig was up. I knew it was time to leave London and commended myself for having the forethought to have an exit prepared. All I had to do was grab my new false passport (hidden in my bedsit) and pack a few things. Taking extreme care that I was not followed, I returned to my room by a circuitous route, entering the building through the back door.

I need not have gone to so much trouble; Mr Big was waiting for me. I saw no point in wasting time on conversation: I shot him on the spot and he fell to the floor. I put on the radio for a bit of noise and shot him again several times in the head and heart, in the hope that his physical body, wherever it was, would endure considerable suffering even if I could not kill it.

Feeling that shooting a demon was a curiously unsatisfying experience, I watched as his body began to fade, becoming fainter and then disappearing altogether. As a final gesture, I composed a hasty report to the NOHRM, addressed to the old post-office box address, saying that I had encountered a pair of aliens pretending to be my beloved NOHRM contacts, assassinated them on behalf of Our Government and would await further instructions.

I gathered a few things to take with me. As ever, all I had that mattered were the notes and records of my search for Luce, which, with my new passport, I retrieved from beneath a floor-board.

The news came on the radio. I paid little attention until I heard the words 'murder in Goodge Street'. With increasing horror I learned that a middle-aged woman had been shot in a café by an unknown assailant. There was no time to think; I had to get out fast. Throwing everything into a satchel, I scarpered. I didn't dare hail a taxi, the tube and buses had stopped running for the night, so I walked. I headed south, aiming first for the river, where I got rid of my gun, then in the general direction of Dover and a ferry to France (the airports, I'd decided, would certainly be watched). It was hours and miles before I managed to have a coherent thought and construct a plan. My main concern was the Luce-related documents I carried. It was imperative that they did not fall into the hands of the demons or the police. But where could I hide them?

By eight o'clock I had reached Dartford. A post office was opening as I passed and that gave me an idea. I went in and purchased a packing box into which I put all the Luce material. They provided some tape and green twine, which left green streaks on my hands. I addressed the box to myself, care of my brother at the Redington Road house and consigned it to Her Majesty's postal service. Half sick with fear and exhaustion, and looking over my shoulder constantly, I made my way among rush-hour crowds by bus and train to Dover.

At Dover I had an hour to wait for the next ferry to Calais. Not wanting to hang about the brightly lit waiting area, I ducked into a dim, smoky bar and ordered a Bloody Mary: food and drink in one. The television was showing the BBC news and I listened in trepidation, skulking deep in the shadows, as the announcer presented an update on the Goodge Street murder. The victim was named as Mrs Margaret Jones, aged fifty-two, a civil servant.

It was then that it truly sank in: I'd killed another human being. To me, Mrs Big had been just a paradigm of evil. I'd given her a ludicrous name, but she was a person with a name of her own: Mrs Jones, Margaret Jones . . . Margo, Meg, Maggie Jones? Someone's wife, daughter, sister . . . mother? Good God, did she have children? Did she love anyone? Did anyone love her? For all I'd carried a lethal weapon, for all I'd longed to take revenge for the murders of my friends, it was still a huge shock to realise what I'd done. Was I sorry? She was a soldier and so was I, apparently. She would have killed me – or had me killed – the minute I ceased to be more useful alive. After all she'd done, I could not feel sorry that she was dead, though I certainly regretted having killed her, if only for the hassle it was already causing me.

The assailant was still unidentified, said the TV. Then Ahmet's face appeared and I had a pang of regret for involving him in the affair. An enterprising reporter was questioning him about the incident in his café and I listened in wonder as he replied that both victim and murderer had been unknown to him. He went on to give a detailed description of the assailant: a fat man of fifty or fifty-five, with a greasy, pock-marked face and shifty eyes, wearing a blue suit. In his opinion – Ahmet was being unusually loquacious – the man was an Israeli agent.

Now.

I got to know Mrs Big - Margaret - quite well during
the early months of my incarceration, when my disor-
dered state allowed her unlimited access to my poor,
defenceless mind. Disencumbered of her physical form,
she haunted me with a vengeance. She took every opportunity to remind me that it was she who'd seen most
clearly the thread that linked me to Luce, she who
had believed in the reality of our connection. For
this reason I valued her company, though I cannot say
I enjoyed it.

Ever the devious one, she pretended to be my friend,
my only true friend. Luce, she told me, was the real
evil, the deceiver, the dangerous illusion: the
psychosis. Since a similar line was taken by the
doctors, it's no wonder I lost my way for a time in
the dark nights of doubt. It was Greyling who vanquished
her - I don't know how. He appeared one morning after
an awful, tear-filled night in which drugs and fear
and guilt and remorse had again wrecked the fragile
eidolon of myself that I'd spent the daylight hours

constructing. He told me that Margaret wouldn't be visiting me any more.

'She's seen the light at last,' he said. 'A colleague of mine had a little word with her and our Margaret has . . . undergone a change of heart.' That was the last I ever saw of him - not counting the cloud of midges.

This skunk is turning out to be just the thing for Seroxat withdrawal. I should have thought of that before, but Seroxat makes one stupid and accepting, too stupid and accepting to see how stupid it is to be so accepting.

Tonight I will collect my new passport and a back door will once again be open to me. I'm too excited to get any work done, and pace my flat until it's time to set out for Whitechapel.

The street is deserted. I'm nervous. I haven't done anything like this in years. I finger the gun in my pocket and although I know it's only a toy the shape is comforting to my hand. Could a demon tell the difference between a toy gun and a real one? Perhaps that depends on how strongly I believe in the gun myself.

I'm a few minutes early, so walk up and down. Nonchalantly. One or two cars pass. At precisely ten twenty-four I turn into the narrow side alley where I was told I'd find the building's back door, identified by a Hazchem sticker - for the printing chemicals, I suppose. I make myself breathe calmly. At the door I knock twice, wait, then knock again five times. Nothing seems to be stirring within and I wonder if I should repeat the signal.

A man comes around the corner. I stroll away from

the door and pretend to consult my phone, looking up and giving him a brief, casual nod as he approaches. In such a narrow road, naturally he will pass quite near . . . but he seems to be making straight for me. I glance behind, and see another man approaching from the other end of the alley. Oh shit. Shit, shit, shit. Are these demons? Fear washes over me, my legs feel like they're turning to jelly. The men's faces are visible now: they're rough-looking, unshaven, ugly. Not demons, just muggers. The printer set me up. God knows where I get the courage but I stand straight, put my back to the wall and take out my gun.

'Come any closer and I'll shoot,' I say, impressed with the firmness of my own voice.

'Oh, no,' cries one, in a high voice, and for a moment I think I've got him properly terrified.

'Please don't shoot!' the other says, mimicking the falsetto, then guffaws. 'Is that a Terminator? I got my nephew one of those last Christmas.'

The first one clucks disapprovingly and plucks the gun from my hand. 'Aren't you too old to be playing with toys?' And then he hits me very hard in the stomach. I collapse in a heap of pain and shock, in which position I'm perfectly placed to receive a number of robust kicks.

When I come to, the alley is once more deserted. My phone and gun have disappeared. I stagger to my feet and check my pockets. The envelope containing the four thousand pounds is gone, though they've left me my wallet with twenty quid. How kind.

I make my way to the main road and flag down a cab. Back home at World's End I take some paracetamol, rub arnica over my entire person, make a Scotch and soda, light a joint and lie on the bed until daybreak. What an idiot I am.

I must finish *The Book of Luce* before anything worse happens to me.

30

The Meeting

❦

The Citadel of Precise Probability. On the Road to
Emmaus. In the Desert. I Leap to Join Her.

Nevada, September 1974

After my flight from England I lived a wary, vagabond existence for over a year, staying in no lodgings for longer than
a week or two. By the end of 1973 I'd settled, more or less, in
Los Angeles, where, under a different *nom de plume*, A. N.
Tilogy (nobody got it), I worked as a script doctor, making serious
money for the first time in my life; an original screenplay of
mine had just been optioned by a major studio.* LA was a city
of self-invented characters; no one looked more than skin-deep
into anyone's identity, lest their own suffer from a similar scrutiny.
It was also a city in which false ID and unlicensed guns were
ridiculously easy to obtain.

* The film was made a couple of years later. It's called *Diary of a Painter*,
and it's about an artist who comes to believe that his self-portraits have
acquired a life of their own and committed a variety of transgressions. It stars
Keir Dullea and Sissy Spacek, with a wonderful cameo from Bette Davis.
You can get it on DVD. It's not bad.

513

Having entrusted my most valuable possessions (the Luce material) to Neil, I dared not lose touch with him, nor did I dare ask him simply to send the box to me, for that would be to reveal its supreme value. I had too many memories of him destroying anything for which I betrayed the least fondness. What he did to my teddy bear is still too painful to speak of. So I began a correspondence with him, an innocuous, mundane correspondence, for which I provided a series of post-office box addresses. After initial stiffness, we settled into a routine of Christmas and birthday cards, postcards from holidays and updates on the progress of his children.

In June 1974 he wrote to say that our mother had died; two months later our father followed. In the rush of sentimentality this provoked, he decided we had to get together and I allowed myself to be persuaded. We agreed to meet in September in Las Vegas, of all places. Neil, the newly elected vice-president of the British Actuarial Society, was to give a speech at an international conference of actuaries held in that citadel of precise probabilities. He and Cindy would stay on for a week's holiday; I'd join them for a day or two.

Having always kept the most scrupulous lookout for demons, and having seen none since I'd shot Mr Big, I had believed myself free of them – at least in the material world. The demon-esque beings I encountered in LA invariably turned out to be people who'd overdone the face lifts, make-up and hairspray. I continued to suspect, however, that the Bigs or others like them were tracking me on the astral in case I led them to Luce, of whom I'd also – to my sorrow but also to my relief – found no trace. No great new art had come to light, no transcendent happenings. Luce was, no doubt, on her wanders: free, anonymous and ephemeral, passing through place after place, touching life after life and moving on.

I was therefore very worried when, during the week before

514

the Las Vegas trip, I saw the same bland-faced man on three occasions: in the window of the coffee shop across from my current sublet, in the doctor's office when I went to renew my prescription for sleeping pills and in the post office when I checked my box.

There was only one way that they could know who I was, and that was through the PO box. They'd staked it out and I'd walked right into the trap. But how did they know the box was mine? Neil was the only one whose letters were addressed to my real name. Suspicion would, over the years of my incarceration, grow into the conviction – hard to shed – that he was a demon.

I had a flight booked to Las Vegas but I didn't feel safe without my gun and I couldn't take it on a plane. So I drove to the airport and parked my car in the long-term lot, then led my followers, if I had followers, around the airport for an hour or so, in and out of all those crowded shops with more entrances and exits than walls. When I was reasonably sure I wasn't being watched I ducked into a toilet, changed my clothes, donned a wig and a hat and took a circuitous route to the Avis counter in Arrivals where I hired a car.

I arrived in Las Vegas at about eight. The sun was setting but the air was still hot as an oven and dry as sand. Neil and Cindy had booked me a room in their hotel, the Hilton: immense and ghastly. I began having regrets even before I'd checked in. On the bedside table I found a basket of fruit and a cheery message from Cindy. I rang through to their room and we arranged to meet in the bar.

I tried, I really tried. I got all the way to the entrance of that glassy temple of senseless inebriation. Was it the soul-destroying Muzak? The mesmerising glitter? The smell of cheap money? The smoothness of people's faces? Or was it dread at the sheer enormity of the pile of meaningless chat I was going to have to wade through, perhaps even contribute to? Neil and Cindy,

engaged in animated conversation with, I supposed, other actuaries and their spouses (if I went over there, my God, I'd have
to *meet* those people), had not seen me. They looked like they
were enjoying themselves. They would not, I was sure, enjoy me
any more than I would enjoy them. They would long to return
to their actuarial friends and I would long to leave, just leave
and be anywhere else.

Telling myself that I'd face all this far better tomorrow, I
backed away. Karen Cooper, on the other hand, I'd really enjoy;
a visit with her would fortify me for Neil and Cindy. We'd kept
in touch; a couple of years ago she'd moved back to the house
in Warm Springs that her brother had rebuilt. Before I left LA
we spoke on the phone and I told her I'd drop by as I would
be in the neighbourhood, more or less. At the hotel's front desk
I left a message for Neil and Cindy, saying I would join them in
a day or two.

I drove north into the desert, window open to the hot night
air, hurtling along the tunnel of my headlights with only the
rhythmic whip-whip-whip-whip of the telephone poles giving
evidence of the passage of time. Then, when I turned onto the
road heading north, not even that, and time passed only as the
steady, slower thrump . . . thrump . . . thrump of the road itself,
felt more than heard as I passed over its regular concrete sections.

About eleven, in the middle of nowhere, about fifty miles from
Warm Springs, I got a flat tyre. I pulled over to change it, and
as I lifted the spare out of the boot and set up the jack I began
to feel curiously happy. Why, I wondered, should having to change
a tyre in the middle of the night make me so happy?

And that's when I heard it, that silvery hum, and smelled the
scent of roses. I laughed aloud; *this* was why I'd come to Nevada
– not to see Karen and certainly not to see Neil. I'd come for
Luce, only Luce. Her wanders had led her here.

The feeling that drew me out into the desert – how to describe it? It was a yearning of almost unbearable intensity – yet, unlike most yearnings, which are desperate and hopeful and unlikely to be fulfilled, it was accompanied by a vivid and certain knowledge of finding, of complete consummation.

I moved as if in a dream, my whole body tingling in anticipation, my feet finding their way across the rocky terrain. It was like the journey to the cave on the island at Farundell: so easy, so inevitable. It was like falling into myself.

A few hundred yards from the road the desert ended in a curve of low cliff. The moon rising over the escarpment revealed a slender figure approaching from the east. Near, nearer, a few yards, a few feet. A foot away. *Oh Luce*, I thought, or said – it didn't matter. I was laughing; maybe I was crying, too.

We touched hands, so lightly, right to left like twins meeting in a mirror. *Hello, you; hello, you.* Her eyes . . . what colour were they? Silver-grey-green, and hair silver-white, quite short. *You must cut it every day*, I thought, and she laughed. Did we kiss? I'm still not sure whether it happened on the physical plane at all.

'Thank you,' Luce said. 'Thank you for everything.'

And then I heard footsteps and felt the first flash of fear. Moving shadows were approaching from all directions. I had a terrible sense of destiny closing in, a tunnel narrowing to a single point, a moment, this moment. Were they demons or police, military, FBI? Whoever they were, I knew it was me they'd followed and I'd led them, as they'd always thought I would, to Luce.

I took out my gun and stepped in front of her, but she side-stepped me. 'Put away the gun,' she said. 'Don't kill, don't be afraid. Death is an open door.'

I could see them then, eight or ten faceless figures in dark clothes and balaclavas, the moonlight glinting on the metal of their guns. Large guns, and all pointed at us. Again I tried to step in front of Luce; again she sidestepped me. I heard a quick *phut*, *phut*, felt a sharp prick and saw the tail of a barb sticking into my thigh. I fell onto my side, eyes open, gazing along the length of my right arm, past my hand, past the gun, to Luce. A barb quivered in her shoulder and she collapsed to the ground a few feet away, eyes still open, still full of love. She kissed my mind, a final benediction. I was floating: no pain, no fear. A hand appeared, black-gloved, wrapped my floppy, numb fingers around my gun, pointed it at Luce and pulled the trigger three times. Blood spurted from wounds to heart and throat and head. There was a sudden burst of luminosity, then she rose from her corpse like a bird escaping from a cage – a gay, laughing leap of delight.

The gloved hand turned the gun and bent my arm so that the barrel was pressed to my temple. As he pulled the trigger I leapt to join Luce.

❧

Obviously I didn't make it. I regained consciousness nineteen days later, but it was weeks before I could speak and far longer before I began to remember and understand what had happened.

The first face I saw, when I opened my eye in that hospital bed, was Karen Cooper's. It had been she who'd found me – found us – in the desert. On her way to Tonopah in the early morning she'd noticed my hire car on the side of the road, stopped to offer assistance, saw vultures circling not far off, and went to investigate.

Neither of us was recognisable. Luce was clearly dead, but Karen saw that I was alive, just. The shot had shattered my right eye, temple and the bridge of my nose, though it only nicked my brain. The doctors told me how lucky I was that my gun had been a mere .22 calibre, and they didn't mean it ironically.

The legal complications were prodigious, not least the confusions caused by my false ID. When I didn't return to Las Vegas for several days, Neil and Cindy made a half-hearted report to the police, and it was only then that the authorities were able to connect me with the car abandoned at the roadside (rented in the false name) and the two bodies in the desert. A further wrinkle developed when, my real name revealed, they contrived to link me with the murder of Mrs Margaret Jones in London.

The ID found – planted – on Luce's body was that of a petty drug dealer from Las Vegas named Sylvester Piggen, similar to Luce in build and colouring. (What happened to the real Sylvester Piggen one can only imagine.) A bag in my pocket contained an ounce of heroin, and had both his and my fingerprints on it. The prosecution's case was straightforward: I'd shot him and then myself. Since it was perfectly obvious that this is exactly what had happened, they had no need to explain why I might do such a thing. Lurid scenarios (lovers' tiff, drug deal gone wrong) were constructed by the tabloids and, not surprisingly, believed by Neil, Cindy, my state-appointed lawyer and everyone else, except Karen.

Unable, when I recovered a portion of my wits, to grasp the full magnitude of the trap into which I'd fallen, at first I tried to explain that it had been Luce I'd shot, and that it hadn't been me who shot her but men in black with tranquilliser darts, a black-gloved hand using my own to pull the trigger of my gun. This, my lawyer argued (to save me from the death penalty; he believed he was doing me a favour), was proof of the severe mental illness that had caused me to murder the young drug dealer in the first place. Fergus had said it true: when they really want to screw you over, they declare you insane. Although it was as fiendish a trap as one could imagine, I don't believe they intended me to live and endure the pain of having survived. Like poor old Charlie, I was meant to shoot Luce and then, neatly, do away with myself.

After the trial, Karen enquired what had happened to

'Sylvester Piggen's' body, supposing it to have been buried in some municipal cemetery. Knowing it was Luce, she wanted to honour it and also, she confessed to me many years later, to steal it and reinter it by the house in Warm Springs, at the spot where Lou used to sit and gaze out over the desert. But they told her that, as no family had come forward to claim it, it had been donated for medical research. So the government got it and perhaps are studying it still, trying to figure out who Luce was, what Luce was. I could tell them the answer's not in the body, not in brain or blood or DNA. It's in the mind, and the mind of Luce is not dead.

Now.

During the early years of my 'rehabilitation', I got into, or pretended to get into, Christianity. I'd noticed that people who professed a belief in that particular version of God were more kindly treated. The chaplain was a real sweetie, with his secret vodka flask. And, in a rather self-flagellatory way, I found much to identify with in the story of Judas Iscariot, the disciple who, possessed by a demon, betrayed Jesus to his enemies. Between sips, the chaplain told me that God forgives even Judas, and the thought warmed me almost as much as the spirits he shared.

The fact that I had intended no betrayal, the fact that Luce had welcomed me and death with equal love, did not assuage my guilt. I would far, far rather have died. If they hadn't drugged me I could have shot myself and made a better job of it. Yet suicide, now, was not an option. I was condemned to live; I allowed myself no easy way out.

It was only when the *Gospel of Judas* was discovered and an English translation published in *National*

521

Geographic in 2006 that a new understanding dawned. In that gospel, Judas is the best-beloved disciple, the one who truly sees what Jesus is: an emissary from a higher dimension. And the one who knows the beauty of death, its release. 'And as for you,' Jesus says to him, prophesying, 'you will surpass them all, for you will sacrifice the human who clothes me.' Like JC, like all avatars, Luce knew that the Human carries the seed of death.

It's midnight in World's End. The moon, a few days from the full, casts a slab of silver over my computer. *The Book of Luce* is finished. I've fulfilled my task, I've told the story, and if I haven't finally elucidated everything, I've done the best I can. I've emptied myself out and all that remains is a husk, an echo. I feel hollow, but not in an unpleasant way, rather like a glass emptied of wine. And it was a good wine, a sublime vintage.

Now what? Get the book out there. My old agent is still alive - at least, her name is on her company's masthead. I email them the manuscript. My old publishers have been swallowed by a larger firm, which was in turn swallowed by one still larger. I send a copy to them, too. Nothing left to do but wait and imagine what it'll be like to be a famous writer again. That'll show Neil, when my little hobby becomes a best-seller, wins all the prizes . . .

I'm making myself a celebratory cup of tea when I hear a noise from my sitting room. I watch in horror as a blank white envelope slides slowly under my door, exuding the unmistakable, malign ordinariness of a communication from the NOHRM. Just seeing it sends a shudder of dread down my spine.

I look out of the window. A woman in a beige suit leaves the building, crosses to a car, gets in, but doesn't drive off. I step back and draw the curtains.

I feel sick, and trapped. I have no false ID, I have no solid, reassuring gun. My life as Chimera Obscura is long over; it's only in my imagination, these last few months, that I've been smart and brave and agile once again. It's only memories, and I've come to the end of them.

But nothing must stop *The Book of Luce*. I can't wait for agents and publishers; I'll have to forgo the glittering prizes. I take my laptop into the kitchen so I don't have to see the baleful white envelope, and in a couple of hours I've published *The Book of Luce* on Amazon. 99p, who could resist? I log on to all my groups and forums, post a link to the book and send a press release to the news outlets and bloggers. That's it, it's out there, I've outfoxed the demons. Now it doesn't matter what they do to me.

Actually, it does. They can kill me, but I bloody well refuse to be pinned down like a mouse in a trap. I peer out of a crack in the curtains; the demon is still there in her car, watching my building.

And then the plan arrives, fully formed, on shining, inevitable wings. What to take? One small satchel will suffice. Toothbrush, a change of clothes. My cigarettes, the skunk. Memory stick with *The Book of Luce*. The box of rose petals, which seem to have grown even more fragrant. I tuck it into my pocket and am surrounded by a cloud of scent. And, of course, the hat. I rummage in the boxes for the fedora with the peacock feather. Cash, only about two hundred pounds. A cheque will have to do. I pack all the Luce-related material into a box, together with my laptop, and address it to Karen in Warm Springs. She will be the keeper of the archive. I sling my bag over my shoulder, adjust the hat to a jaunty angle, tuck the box under my arm. I'm ready. I take a last look around and bid farewell to these three hundred and sixty-six square feet, to the friendly woodchips, the serene linoleum. At the door I step over the envelope, then pause, turn and spit on it. A childish gesture, but satisfying. I tiptoe downstairs and slip out of the back door.

Isidore's light is on. We've become friends these last few weeks, in our mutually taciturn way - cups of tea, visits to the farm, hacking around the fields. I stick my head through the door.

'Nice hat,' he says.

'Thanks. I just wanted to say goodbye.'

'You're leaving?'

'Yes.'

'Do they know?' He means the authorities.

'No. I need to go via the farm, if that's all right.'

'Wow, daring escape, eh? I'll walk you to the farm.'

Through the chain link fence, across the waste ground, past the remnants of industry, out into the countryside. The air is fresh and my heart is light. It's summer, I'm free, I'm dancing at dawn once again. Well, walking, anyway. Plodding. But on the move. I laugh aloud and Isidore laughs with me. The sun's coming up when we arrive; Rider is in the stableyard, grooming Ducati.

I've finally understood why that image of me in my peacock-feathered hat riding a horse by a lake has been stuck in my head. So simple, really. It felt like a memory, but it wasn't one . . . yet. A memory-to-be, resonating from the future like the peal of a distant bell.

'I want to buy Beauregard,' I say, taking out my chequebook.

They look at me as though I'm mad.

'Seriously. I need a horse. I have plenty of money, you know. I used to be a famous writer. Royalties piled up over the years while I've lived so . . . frugally.'

'Why do you need a horse?' Rider asks.

'Because I can't go by train, or car, or bus.'

'Why not?'

'They're watching me.'

'Who is?'

'Long story.'

Isidore and Rider exchange glances.

'Where are you going?' Isidore asks.

'Oxfordshire.'

'You're crazy,' Rider says.

'We know that. So, can I buy Beauregard? Or another horse? Not Ducati or anybody like him, obviously.'

There's some discussion. They don't seem to think I'm fit to undertake such a journey on my own.

It's nearly seven when we finally set out: me on Beauregard, Rider on Ducati, Isidore on a horse called Jim. We have saddlebags stuffed with bacon butties, flasks of tea and horse-food. They tell me to put my money away, but Rider's mother, who's agreed to send my parcel to Karen, accepts fifty pounds for postage.

Before I left I looked up the route on Google Maps and printed it out. If I stick to back roads, green lanes and bridle paths, there's no way anyone will be able to find me. Rider says he knows every track, lane and byway between here and Wales and I can forget about Google Maps.

The thought that I will simply have vanished gives me the most enormous pleasure. Neil and Cindy, after initial consternation and resentment of the administrative hassles that I've once again imposed upon them by my irresponsible behaviour, will be profoundly relieved to be rid of me. I picture Neil's plump, doughy face and I know that in some sad, tiny, tucked-away part of himself, he longs to shake loose his wings, step out of the open door of the cage and, like me, fly off. And perhaps he will, some day. Who can say? He is, after all, my baby brother. The least I can do is set an example.

I think, as we ride, about death. After I complete this final task I believe I'll allow myself to claim that reward. But no way am I going to hang myself like that other Judas. Yuck. Too gruesome. In fact I feel a great distaste for violent death of any sort. After I've delivered *The Book of Luce* to the place where it all began I'll leave Beauregard with Isidore and Rider and just walk, carrying on into the west I suppose – isn't that the direction the soul always goes when it turns, at last, for home? Sooner or later I'll grow tired, I'll lie down somewhere and . . . that will be that.

The thought crosses my mind that I might be dead already, my corpse abandoned in my bed in World's End, and what I'm experiencing now *is* my soul's journey into the west . . . but no. My body is definitely still with me. I know this because, after three hours in the saddle, it aches.

We stop to eat and rest the horses. The dim but constant noise of traffic has gradually been left behind; all of a sudden I realise I can't hear it any more. There's a moment of pure silence, broken by a blackbird's call.

We ride on. It's too hot to go fast; we walk, or trot for a bit. Sometimes an hour or more goes by with not a glimpse of houses, roads or people. We encounter the occasional dog-walker, one or two other riders, an old man with a butterfly net, a young family in a brightly painted gypsy caravan, farmers working their fields or tending their animals. This is a different world. I suppose it's always been here, but to me it feels new and strange. It's like when you're a child, exploring, with no idea of what could possibly be around the next corner. You've not yet learned that really, it's all the same shit, no matter where you go.

The hours pass, lulled by the steady pace of the horses. We're in the Chilterns now: broad hay meadows, low wooded slopes, cool valleys with rushing streams. We pause to drink, munch our last bacon butties (humans) and oats (horses). As evening approaches Rider phones some friends who have a farm near Little Chalfont; we arrive at dusk, riding down out of the hills towards the welcoming lights of their yard.

They give us dinner and a place to kip in the stable, with horse blankets and straw pillows. I sleep amazingly well and have no dreams. Perhaps I'm *in* the dream now. We're up at first light; Rider's friends provide breakfast, sandwiches and oats for the journey. It's drizzling; they give us bin bags to wear. I offer money; they smile and shake their heads. This really is a different world.

The next two days go by in the same placid way. Walk, trot, rest, eat, walk. A bit of drizzle, then sun. Clouds come and go. We sing old songs: Raggle Taggle Gypsy-O, Greensleeves, Barbara Allen, Green Grow the Rushes.

The sun is low but still strong as we ford the Isis below Exley. We go via field paths, approaching Farundell from the river, by the water meadows, beside the lake. There comes a moment when the slanting rays cast the shadows just so, and Beauregard's ears prick forward . . . and I know, this is it: this is the moment, a shimmering doorway suspended in the bright air. I pass through it with an almost audible pop and . . . I'm into the unknown future again. What now?

It occurs to me for the first time that dropping in like this might be presumptuous. I know the place is still in the Damory family - I looked it up. And I know it's still open to the public on summer weekends - but is Gwen still alive? Is she here? Would she remember me? If Gwen's no longer around I'll ask for her daughter Francie - she'd be in her late-forties now. I'll give her the Book and leave. If neither Gwen nor Francie is around I'll . . .

'Hey, look,' Isidore says. 'I think they're having a party.'

He points ahead to where a small group of festively clad people have gathered at the lakeside. Several are carrying bottles of wine; a few have picnic baskets. They wave and call Hello. It seems that once again I'm crashing a party.

And here comes the sheep barge, with an old man poling it to the shore. I have a moment when I truly believe I've gone back in time, but when he gets

528

closer I see he's not dressed as Charon, though he looks very similar to the other old man, the head gardener, what was his name? Mr Pym. This fellow might be his son.

A woman separates herself from the group at the shore and approaches as we dismount. Could it be? Hair quite grey, but I recognise that quirky smile. It's Gwen.

'Hello,' I say. 'I didn't know you were having a party. I seem always to be crashing.'

She laughs and kisses me, and says, 'Oh no, you're not crashing. *They* said you were coming. It was *their* idea to have a party on the island tonight.'

Before I have a chance to ask who *they* are and how *they* knew I was coming, Isidore appears at my shoulder. 'Aren't you going to introduce us?'

'Of course, sorry. Gwen, may I present Isidore Berger, and Rider. Guys, this is Gwen Damory, a very dear old friend.'

Isidore, displaying a courtly streak that I didn't know he possessed, bows and kisses Gwen's hand. She looks surprised, and rather pleased. Rider, after a moment's hesitation, follows suit, but she pulls her hand away with a laugh.

I explain to Gwen why I've come, and offer the memory stick.

'Ah, they said you were bringing something wonderful. Bring it to the island. You can give it to them your-self. But you're staying, aren't you? They said you would stay.'

'Who is this *they* you keep talking about?'

'You'll see.'

We turn out the horses into an adjacent paddock and

529

stow the tack in a shed, then stroll back to the lake-shore. The barge, having taken one lot over to the island, is returning for another, mainly children and dogs.

We pile on. 'This should be the last load, Mr Pym,' Gwen says to the old man.

He makes a sceptical sound, somewhere between an aye and a nay. As I thought, the son. He truly is the spitting image of his father.

The journey across the lake is raucous, Gwen's chatting to everybody and trying to keep an eye on the children and I have no chance to speak with her. As we near the island, half the children and all of the dogs jump off the barge with a tremendous splash and race to the shore.

We disembark. Gwen is swept away on a tide of wet children and dogs. The meadow, still lit by the rays of the setting sun, is dotted with picnic blankets. Someone's strumming a guitar, someone's practising a juggling routine, someone's tossing a frisbee to a dog. Children zoom about like pinballs and there's a low burble of conversation and laughter.

Isidore, Rider and I have plastic cups of very decent wine thrust into our hands. 'Nice hat,' someone says to me. It's all a little surreal, but it's just a party and I know how to do parties. Isidore and Rider seem perfectly at ease - Isidore is deep in conversation with Mr Pym and Rider's joined a group of teenagers by a campfire.

Gwen reappears. 'Come and meet Francie - you remember Francie, don't you? - and David.'

Could Francie and David - whoever he is - be *them*? Gwen leads me to a group of people sitting under a tree. A woman I know must be Francie gets up as we approach, taking the hand of a man standing nearby and drawing him along.

Gwen introduces me. Yes, this is Francie, and the man is her husband David. If this is *Them* I'm perplexed. They're very friendly and welcoming but they don't display any sign of knowing who I am or why I've come. We chat a little about how I'd met Francie when she was a child, et cetera. Then another woman joins us, an old woman with long white hair and celadon eyes.

'This is my mother,' says David.

'Oh,' I say, 'oh, Rachel,' and I realise that David is Peter Lucian's son and suddenly it's all a bit too much, I'm in tears but whether it's for joy or sorrow or love I don't know. Rachel hugs me and takes me to sit by her on a blanket beneath the tree.

'Rachel,' I say, as soon as I can speak, and because it's the one thing that must be said, 'Rachel, I killed him. I led the killers straight to him.'

'Hush,' she says, and puts her hand, her kind hand, across my lips. 'I know what happened.'

'How? How do you know?'

'He told me. He showed me so I'd be ready, so I'd understand. He knew it would happen, but he's not gone, you know.' Her eyes are laughing. 'Don't you feel him? He's so near. They see him every day.'

'*They*? Who's this *they*?'

'You'll see. They're around somewhere.'

On a sudden impulse I take the box of rose petals from my pocket and give it to her. 'He gave me this, and now . . . I want you to have it. They remain fresh, the petals. They don't die. I've found it more comforting than I can say.'

She accepts it with a smile, and gives me a kiss.

David refills my wine glass, Francie offers me a cheese sandwich. After the mythic aura with which I've invested the Damorys for the last forty-odd years, this is all so normal I wonder whether I'm dreaming. Lord Francis Damory's daughter, holding hands with Luce's son. Wine, and cheese sandwiches. What next, amaretti biscuits?

Rachel rummages in a picnic basket, brings out a tin of them and offers it around.

'Midges bothering you?' David says, as I wipe at my eyes. 'Try some citronella. Darling, pass the citron-ella,' he says to Francie, and a little bottle of oil comes my way. 'Just dab it on your temples.'

I do, and return the bottle with thanks.

It's dusk. Someone's going around hanging coloured lanterns in the trees. Isidore has joined us and is laughing at something Gwen has said. He leans forward and whispers in her ear; she laughs too. I do believe they're flirting.

From somewhere in the woods comes the sound of a bamboo flute – no, two flutes, intertwining. The music is sweet and poignant and seems familiar, though it's not any melody I recognise. It's getting closer . . . then I glimpse two pale figures moving through the trees, coming down the hill. A boy and girl of perhaps fifteen or sixteen emerge from the shadows, finishing their duet.

'Ah, here they are,' says Francie. 'Our twins,' she adds, to me. 'Lucy and Peter.'

One dark, one fair. Shining eyes, slender coltish limbs, open smiles. Lovely, ordinary children in jeans and T-shirts . . . but so much more.

532

They come straight up to me, greet me by name, kiss me quite solemnly. Gwen and Isidore, Rachel, David and Francie all watch, lending the moment a faintly ceremonial air as I give them the memory stick. There's no need to say what it is; they know.

Lucy puts it in her pocket. 'Thank you,' she says, and 'Thank you so much,' says Peter.

And now they're just kids, they don't want to hang out with their parents, they're off to join the other teenagers around their campfire. Lucy squeezes in next to Rider and starts talking to him. He seems captivated. The firelight flickers over their beautiful young faces.

I'm both here and not here. A part of me has stepped back, watching the scene from a place just outside. It's so lovely, so human. It's flowers in the river, it's life going on.

I rise to join that self outside. I think no one has noticed my departure but at the edge of the woods I look back and meet Rachel's eyes. She blows me a kiss; I catch it and send one back to her, then turn and move slowly up the path.

The moon is rising behind me. Watery light slants through the trees, colouring everything black and silver. The scents of the forest rise rich and warm, mingling with the fragrance of roses. I take off my shoes and socks so I can feel the earth beneath my feet. The thread is humming in my hand but I no longer need it. I know the way. Luce is waiting.

Appendix: Lucian Chronology

§&

1946–59:. . . . . Lucienne, adopted child of Paul and Inès Asher

June 1958: . . . . encounter with the Human

August 1958: . . . . heals Fergus

October 1958–May 1959:. . . . at the Conservatoire Rameau, Paris

May 1959: . . . . opera *Le Seul*

June 1959: . . . . Pierre Lumière; album *L'Age Atomique*

1960?–62:. . . . . Piers Lightfoot, with Timothy Leary and others in upstate New York

March 1962–May 1964: . . . . . Petra Lumis, the wandering troubadour

May 1964–September 1964: . Lou Peterson and Awarehouse, San Francisco

16 September–
7 October 1964: . . . . with Karen Cooper at Warm Springs

7 October 1964: . . . . Las Vegas

9–16 October 1964: . . . . Petra Lumis, with Waldo Seton Smith in Taos

October–December 1964: . . . Lukas Steiner, with Giorgio

Servadio and Gauri; India and
Nepal

December 1964–June 1965: . Lucha, in Nepal with Thobo
Rinpoche

June–December 1965: . . . . . . travels from Nepal to England
with Wingbow

December 1965: . . . . Luce forms Pymander Productions

December 1966: . . . . *Human* album released

20 January 1967: . . . . first secret gig, Nine Elms

17 February 1967: . . . . second secret gig, Brompton

29 March 1967: . . . . third secret gig, North Kensington

31 March 1967: . . . . mystery appearance at the Astoria

8 April 1967: . . . . mystery appearance at the Saville

23 April 1967: . . . . fourth secret gig, Camden

Summer 1967: . . . . peripatetic wall painting in
Scotland

22 December 1967: . . . . final Luce and the Photons gig, as
Metatrix at Conway Hall

1968–72: . . . . as Peter Lucian and Hikaru Ishi in
Koya, Japan; the *Shiro-Kuro* novels

May 1972: . . . . with Rachel; the Broome Street
videos

Gaps in this chronology may be assumed to have been occupied
with global wanders, though it's quite possible that Luce created
other personae and other works of art than these. I leave it to
future scholars of Lucianity to augment this Book.

Selected Bibliography

Abercrombie, Arthur, 'The Uncanny Arts of Luce and the Photons: Still Inscrutable After All These Years', *NME, Luce and the Photons 30th Anniversary Special Edition*, December 1996

Barritt, Brian, *The Road of Excess: A Psychedelic Biography*, London, Psi Publishing, 1998

Burleigh, Nina, *A Very Private Woman: The Life and Unsolved Murder of Presidential Mistress Mary Meyer*, New York, Bantam Books, 1998

Churton, Tobias, *Gnostic Philosophy from Ancient Persia to Modern Times*, Rochester, Vermont, Inner Traditions, 2005

Crayston, Fielden and Schmidt, eds., *Encyclopedia of American Artists*, Princeton, Princeton University Press, 2002

Dellida, Jean, 'The Eternal Present: Gnosis Then and Now', *Trends in Consciousness*, 7, 2000

Freke, Timothy, and Gandy, Peter, *The Jesus Mysteries*, London, Thorsons, 2000

Gaussère, Bernard de, *The Meaning of Action*, Chicago, Reiland Jacobson, 1949

Greyling, John, *The Reality of Myth: Evolution and the Avatar*, London, Hutchinson Granger, 1955

Guiley, R. E., *Harper's Encyclopedia of Mystical and Paranormal Experience*, Harper, San Francisco, 1991

Henderson, Patrick M., 'Luce and the Photons in Perspective', *Journal of Musicology*, 46, July 1986

Higgs, John, *I Have America Surrounded: The Life of Timothy Leary*, London, Friday Books, 2006

Hutter, M. L., *Language, Thought and the Rise of Civilization*, New York, Harper and Row, 1978

Kranstein, L. J., *The History of Optical Art*, London, Routledge & Kegan Paul, 2003

Lacarrière, Jacques, *The Gnostics*, San Francisco, City Lights Books, 1989

Lambert, Henry P., *Great British Artists: Turner to Powell*, London, Thames Press, 2010

Leary, Timothy, *The Psychedelic Experience*, http://www.leary.ru, pdf., n.d. accessed 23 February 2016

_____, *Flashbacks*, London, Heinemann, 1983

Lee, Martin A., and Shlain, Bruce, *Acid Dreams: The Complete Social History of LSD: The CIA, the Sixties and Beyond*, New York, Grove Press, 1985

Nathan, Curtis B., and Delahaye, Henry P., *Traditions of Initiation*, Cambridge, Cambridge University Press, 1983

Quelling, T. K., *The Light of Many Tongues*, New York, Corinthian Press, 1970

Roberts, Andy, *Albion Dreaming: A Popular History of LSD in Britain*, Singapore, Marshall Cavendish, 2012

Rosenfeld, Simon, *A History of Secret Orders*, Oxford, Oxford University Press, 1962

Smith, Waldo Seton, *Petra Lumis: An Eschatological Fable*, Santa Fe, Coyote Howl Press, 1964

Takasu, Aiko, and Caraday, Linda K., 'The Mystery of *Shiro-Kuro*: Neurological Implications of Psychomimetic Literature', *British Journal of Neuroscience*, 58, 1987

V, *Daily Life in the House of Ghosts*, Chicago, Freedom and Fortitude, 1966

Acknowledgements

Without the understanding, patience and support of my agent, Judith Murray, and my editors, Kate Parkin and Anne Perry, I doubt I would have had the strength to finish this book. Their unwavering belief in me and in Luce means more than I can say. I am grateful to Sienna Latham, Nick de Somogyi and Jason Shulin for their extremely useful comments on an early draft, and to Dany Seignabou for help with the French. I must also thank the eternal spirit of David Bowie, whose genius at art and life has been the most profound inspiration to me in my art and life. Special thanks to my friend Vince Baldassano. And last but not least, Balin.

The Book of Luce, though complete in itself,
is the third in L. R. Fredericks's loosely linked
and non-sequential *Time and Light* series of novels.

The others, *Farundell* (2010) and *Fate* (2012)
are published by Hodder/John Murray.